Praise for Chloe Neill and the

'Debut author

wonderfully compelling

world building, I was drawn page one, and

kept reading far into the night. can't wait for the next

book in this fabulous new series'

Julie Kenner, *USA Today* bestselling author

'There's a new talent in town, and if this debut is any indication, she's here to stay! Not only does Neill introduce an indomitable and funny heroine; her secondary characters are enormously intriguing . . . truly excellent!'

Romantic Times

Friday Night Bites

'Proving that her debut was no fluke, Neill continues to build a world where newly revealed vampires and humans have an uneasy truce. Exploring this world through feisty and funny newbie vampire Merit's eyes, she reveals a mix of the funny, the treacherous and the dangerous. This qualifies as first-rate fun!'

Romantic Times

'Ms Neill has created an urban fantasy world that's easily believed and a pleasure to visit. *Friday Night Bites* is wonderfully entertaining, and impossible to set down. There's plenty of supernatural action to entice fans of the paranormal, while the suspense and romance open this series up to fans in a variety of other genres. I'd happily recommend the Chicagoland Vampires series as a delicious escape to get hooked on'

Darque Reviews

Twice Bitten

'Neill continues to hit the sweet spot with her blend of high-stakes drama, romantic entanglements, and a touch of humour . . . Certain to whet readers' appetites for more in this entertaining series!'

Romantic Times

'Refreshing urban fantasy'

Publishers Weekly

Also by Chloe Neill from Gollancz

ChicagoLand Vampires series

Some Girls Bite

Friday Night Bites

Twice Bitten

Dark Elite series

Firespell

Hexbound

A ChicagoLand Vampires Novel

HARD BITTEN

CHLOE NEILL

The right of Chloe Neill to be identified as the author of this work
has been asserted by her in accordance with the
Copyright, Designs and Patents Act 1988.

First published in Great Britain in 2011 by
Gollancz
An imprint of the Orion Publishing Group
Orion House, 5 Upper St Martin's Lane, London WC2H 9EA
An Hachette UK Company

1 3 5 7 9 10 8 6 4 2

A CIP catalogue record for this book is available
from the British Library

ISBN 978 0 575 10018 3

Printed in Great Britain by
Clays Ltd, plc

The Orion Publishing Group's policy is to use papers that are
natural, renewable and recyclable products and made from wood
grown in sustainable forests. The logging and manufacturing
processes are expected to conform to the environmental regulations
of the country of origin.

www.chloeneill.com
www.orionbooks.co.uk

To Jeremy, Baxter, and Scout, my three favorite boys,
with much thanks to Sara, the mistress
of Meritverse conformity.

By the pricking of my thumbs,
Something wicked this way comes.

William Shakespeare

CHAPTER ONE

⊷ ⊶

MAGIC IS AS MAGIC DOES

Late August
Chicago, Illinois

We worked beneath the shine of floodlights that punched holes in the darkness of Hyde Park—nearly one hundred vampires airing rugs, painting cabinet doors, and sanding trim.

A handful of severe-looking men in black—extra mercenary fairies we'd hired for protection—stood outside the fence that formed a barrier between the blocks-wide grounds of Cadogan House and the rest of the city.

In part, they were protecting us from a second attack by shapeshifters. That seemed unlikely, but so had the first onslaught, led by the youngest brother of the leader of the North American Central Pack. Unfortunately, that hadn't stopped Adam Keene.

They were also protecting us from a new threat.

Humans.

I glanced up from the elegant curve of wooden trim I was swabbing with stain. It was nearly midnight, but the golden glow of the protesters' candles was visible through the gap in the fence. Their flames flickered in the sticky summer breeze, three or four dozen humans making known their quiet objections to the vampires in their city.

Popularity was a fickle thing.

Chicagoans had rioted when we'd come out of the closet nearly a year ago. Fear had eventually given way to awe, complete with paparazzi and glossy magazine spreads, but the violence of the attack on the House—and the fact that we'd fought back and in doing so had thrown shifters out into the open—had turned the tides again. Humans hadn't been thrilled to learn we'd existed, and if werewolves were out there, too, what else lurked in the shadows? For the past couple of months we'd seen raw, ugly prejudice from humans who didn't want us in their neighborhood and camped outside the House to make sure we were aware of it.

My cell phone vibrated in my pocket; I flipped it open and answered, "Merit's House of Carpentry."

Mallory Carmichael, my best friend in the world and a sorceress in her own right, snorted from the other end. "Kind of dangerous, isn't it, being a vampire around all those would-be aspen stakes?"

I looked over the trim on the sawhorse in front of me. "I'm not sure any of this is actually aspen, but I take your point."

"I assume from the intro that carpentry's on your agenda again this evening?"

"You would be correct. Since you asked, I'm applying stain to some lovely woodwork, after which I'll probably apply a little sealant—"

"Oh, my God, *yawn*," she interrupted. "Please spare me your hardware stories. I'd offer to come entertain you, but I'm heading to Schaumburg. Magic is as magic does, and all that."

That explained the rumbling of the car in the background on her end. "Actually, Mal, even if you could make it, we're a human-free abode right now."

"No shit," she said. "When did Darth Sullivan issue that dictate?"

"When Mayor Tate asked him to."

Mallory let out a low whistle, and her voice was equally concerned. "Seriously? Catcher didn't even say anything about that."

Catcher was Mallory's current live-in boyfriend, the sorcerer who'd replaced me when I made the move to Cadogan House a few months ago. He also worked in the office of the city's supernatural Ombudsman—my grandfather—and was supposed to be in the know about all things supernatural. The Ombudsman's office was a kind of paranormal help desk.

"The Houses are keeping it on the down-low," I admitted. "Word gets out that Tate closed the Houses, and people panic."

"Because they think vampires pose a real threat to humans?"

"Exactly. And speaking of real threats, what are you learning tonight in Schaumburg?"

"Har-har, my little vampire friend. You will love and fear me in due time."

"I already do. Are you still doing potions?"

"Actually, no. We're doing some different stuff this week. How's the head honcho?"

The quick change of subject was a little weird. Mallory usually loved an interested audience when it came to the paranormal and her magic apprenticeship. Maybe the stuff she was learning now was actually as dull as carpentry, although that was hard to imagine.

"Ethan Sullivan is still Ethan Sullivan," I finally concluded.

She snorted in agreement. "And I assume he always will be, being immortal and all. But some things do change. Speaking of— and how's that for a segue?—guess who's now got a big ol' pair of spectacles perched on the end of his perfect little nose?"

"Joss Whedon?" Although it had taken her a little while to get used to the idea of having magic, Mal had always had a thing for the supernatural, fiction or otherwise. Buffy and Spike were particular objects of affection.

"Gad, no. Although wouldn't that totally give me an excuse to pop into the Whedonverse and, like, magically correct his eyesight or something? Anywho, no. Catcher."

I grinned. "Catcher got glasses? Mr. I'm-so-suave-I-shaved-my-head-even-though-I-wasn't-balding got *glasses*? Maybe this is going to be a good night after all."

"I know, right? To be fair, they actually look pretty good on him. I did offer to work a little abracadabra and hook him up with twenty-twenty, but he declined."

"Because?"

She deepened her voice into a pretty good imitation. "'Because that would be a selfish use of magic—expending the will of the universe on my retinas.'"

"That does sound like something he'd say."

"Yep. So glasses it is. And I'll tell you, they are little miracle workers. We have definitely turned a corner in the bedroom. It's like he's a new person. I mean, his sexual energy level is just off the—"

"Mallory. Enough. My ears are beginning to bleed."

"Prude." A piercing *honk* rang through the phone, followed by Mallory's voice. "Learn to merge, people! Come on! Okay, I've got Wisconsin drivers in front of me, and I have to get off the phone. I'll talk to you tomorrow."

"Night, Mal. Good luck with the drivers and the magic."

"Smooches," she said, and the line went dead. I tucked the phone back into my pocket. Thank God for besties.

Ten minutes later, I had a chance to test my "Ethan is still Ethan" theory.

I didn't even need to glance back to know that he'd stepped behind me. The rising chill along my spine was indication enough. Ethan Sullivan, Master of Cadogan House, the vampire who'd added me to its ranks.

After two months of wooing, Ethan and I had spent a pretty glorious night together. But "together" hadn't lasted; he'd reversed course after he'd decided dating me was an emotional risk he couldn't afford to take. He'd regretted that decision, too, and he'd spent the past two months attempting, or so he said, to make amends.

Ethan was tall, blond, and almost obscenely handsome, from the long, narrow nose to the sculpted cheekbones and emerald green eyes. He was also smart and dedicated to his vampires . . . and he'd broken my heart. Two months later, I could accept that he'd feared our relationship would put his House at risk. It would have been a lie to say I didn't feel the attraction, but that didn't make me any less eager for a rematch, so I was warily standing my ground.

"Sentinel," he said, using the title he'd given me. A House guard, of sorts. "They're surprisingly quiet tonight."

"They are," I agreed. We'd had a few days of loud chants, picket signs, and bongo drums until protesters realized we weren't aware of the noises they made during the day, and the denizens of Hyde Park would tolerate noise after nightfall for only so long.

Score one for Hyde Park.

"Makes for a nice change. How are things out here?"

"We're moving along," I said, wiping away an errant drip of stain. "But I'll be glad when we're done. I don't think construction is my bag."

"I'll keep that in mind for future projects." I could hear the amusement in his voice. After taking a second to check my willpower, I looked over at him. Tonight Ethan wore jeans and a paint-smeared T-shirt, and his shoulder-length golden hair was pulled back at the nape of his neck. His dress might have been casual, but there was no mistaking the air of power and unfailing confidence that marked this prince among vampires.

Hands on his hips, he surveyed his crew. Men and women worked at tables and sawhorses across the front lawn. His emerald gaze tracked from worker to worker as he gauged their progress, but his shoulders were tense, as if he was ever aware that danger lurked just outside the gate.

Ethan was no less handsome in jeans and running shoes while taking stock of his vampiric kin.

"How are things inside?" I asked.

"Moving along, albeit slowly. Things would go faster if we were allowed to bring in human construction workers."

"Not bringing them in does save us the risk of human sabotage," I pointed out.

"And the risk that a drywall contractor becomes a snack," he mused. But when he looked back at me again, a line of worry appeared between his eyes.

"What is it?" I prompted.

Ethan offered up his signature move—a single arched eyebrow.

"Well, obviously other than the protesters and constant threat of attack," I said.

"Tate called. He asked for a meeting with the two of us."

This time, I was the one who raised my eyebrows. Seth Tate, Chicago's second-term mayor, generally avoided mingling with the city's three Master vampires.

"What does he want to meet about?"

"This, I assume," he said, gesturing toward the protesters.

"Do you think he wants to meet with me because he and my father are friends, or because my grandfather works for him?"

"That, or because the mayor may, in fact, be smitten with you."

I rolled my eyes, but couldn't stop the warm blush that rose on my cheeks. "He isn't smitten with me. He just likes being reelected."

"He's smitten, not that I can't understand the emotion. And he hasn't even seen you fight yet." Ethan's voice was sweet. Hopeful.

Hard to ignore.

For weeks he'd been this attentive, this flattering.

That was not to say he didn't have his moments of snark. He was still Ethan, after all, still a Master vampire with a Houseful of Novitiates who didn't always please him, and to add insult to injury, he was nearing the end of a months-long rehab of that House. Construction didn't always go quickly in Chicago, and it moved even more slowly when the subject of the construction was a three-story den of vampires. An architectural gem of a den, sure, but still a den of night-walking bloodsuckers, blah blah blah. Our human suppliers were often reticent to help, and that didn't exactly thrill Ethan.

The construction notwithstanding, Ethan was doing all the right things, making all the right moves. Problem was, he'd shaken my trust. I hoped to find my own happily ever after, but I wasn't yet prepared to trust that this particular Prince Charming was ready to ride off into the sunset. Two months later, the hurt—and humiliation—was still too real, the wound too raw.

I wasn't naïve enough to deny what was between me and Ethan, or the possibility that fate would bring us together again. After all, Gabriel Keene, the head of the North American Central Pack, had somehow shared with me a vision about a pair of green eyes that looked like Ethan's . . . but weren't. (I know. "What the hell?" had been my reaction, too.)

I wanted to believe him. Just like every other girl in America,

I'd read the books and seen the movies in which the boy realizes he made a horrible decision . . . and comes back again. I wanted to believe that Ethan mourned the loss of me, that his regret was real, and that his promises were earnest. But this wasn't a game. And as Mallory had pointed out, wouldn't it have been better if he'd wanted me from the beginning?

In the meantime, while I weighed the new Ethan against the old Ethan, I played the dutiful Sentinel. Keeping things professional gave me the space and boundaries I needed . . . and it had the added benefit of irritating him. Immature? Sure. But who didn't take the opportunity to tweak their boss when they had the chance?

Besides, most vampires were members of one House or another, and I was immortal. I couldn't exactly sidestep working with Ethan without damning myself to an eternity spent as an outcast. That meant I had to make the best of the situation.

Avoiding the intimacy in his voice, I smiled politely at him. "Hopefully he won't need to see me fight. If I'm brawling in front of the mayor, things have definitely gone south. When do we leave?"

Ethan was quiet long enough that I looked over at him, saw the earnestness in his expression. It plucked my heartstrings to see him look so decided about me. But whatever fate might have in store for us down the road, I wasn't taking that exit today.

"Sentinel."

There was gentle reprobation in his voice, but I was sticking to my plan. "Yes, Liege?"

"Be stubborn if you wish to, if you *need* to, but we know how this will end."

I kept my face blank. "It will end as it always does—with your being Master and my being Sentinel."

The reminder of our positions must have done it. As abruptly as he'd turned on the charm, Ethan turned it off again. "Be downstairs in twenty minutes. Wear your suit." And then he was gone, striding purposefully up the stairs and back into Cadogan House.

I swore quietly. That boy was going to be the death of me.

CHAPTER TWO

A FISTFUL OF VAMPIRES

Leaving Cadogan House used to be a bit of a trick, mostly involving avoiding the irritation of the paparazzi on the corner who were waiting to snap our pictures. Now it was actually dangerous.

We were both in black suits (official Cadogan wear) and in Ethan's black Mercedes convertible, a slick roadster he parked in the basement beneath the House. We drove up the ramp that led to the ground level, then waited while one of the fairies stationed at the gate pushed it open. A second stood in front of the ramp, his wary gaze on the protesters who were beginning to move in our direction.

We pulled onto the street. The fairy at the gate closed it again, then joined his partner at the side of the car. We moved at a crawl as humans began to gather around us, candles in hand. They moved without sound, their expressions blank, like zombie believers. Their silence was completely unnerving. That was worse, I think, than if they'd been shouting anti-vampire epithets or obscenities.

"Apparently they've seen us," Ethan muttered, left hand on the steering wheel, right on the gearshift.

"Yes, they have. Do you want me to get out?"

"As much as I appreciate the offer, let's let the fairies handle it."

As if on cue, the fairies took point, one at each door. "We pay them, right? For the security?"

"We do," Ethan said. "Although, as they detest humans even more than they detest us, it's probably a task they'd have taken on for free."

So fairies hated vampires, but hated humans more. Some humans hated vampires and, if they had known what the fairies were, probably would have hated them, too.

And vampires? Well, vampires were like politicians. We wanted to be friends with everyone. We wanted to be liked. We wanted political capital we could trade later for political benefits. But we were still vampires, and however political and social we might have been, we were still different.

Well, most of us, anyway. Ethan often remarked that I was more human than most, probably because I'd been a vampire for only a few months. But looking out at the protesters, I felt a little more vampire than usual.

The protesters stared into the windows, holding their candles toward the car as if nearness to the flame was enough to make us disappear. Luckily, fire was no more hazardous to us than it was to humans.

Ethan kept both hands on the wheel now as he carefully maneuvered the Mercedes through the crowd. We crawled forward one foot at a time, the humans swarming in a cloud so thick we couldn't see the road ahead. The fairies walked alongside, one hand on the roof of the petite roadster like members of the Secret Service in a presidential motorcade. We moved slowly, but we moved.

And as we moved, we passed two teenagers who stood on my side of the car, arms linked together—a boy and girl. They were so young, and they were dressed in shorts and tank tops like they'd spent the day at the beach. But their expressions told a different story. There was hatred in their eyes, hatred too intense for sixteen-year-olds. The girl had smeared mascara beneath her eyes as if she'd been crying. The boy watched the girl, his hatred for me maybe prompted by his infatuation with her.

With jarring suddenness, they began to chant together, "No more vampires! No more vampires! No more vampires!" Over and over again they cried out the mantra, zealotry in their voices, like angels ready to smite.

"They're so young to be so angry," I quietly said.

"Anger isn't merely for the old," Ethan pointed out. "Even the young can face misery, tragedy, and twist sadness into hatred."

The rest of the crowd seemed to find the teenagers inspiring. One person at a time, they echoed the chant until the entire crowd had joined in, a chorus of hatred.

"Get out of our neighborhood!" shouted a human close to the car, a thin woman of fifty or sixty with long gray hair, who wore a white T-shirt and khaki pants. "Go back to where you came from!"

I faced forward again. "I'm from Chicago," I murmured. "Born and bred."

"I believe they had a more supernatural dominion in mind," Ethan said. "Hell, perhaps, or some parallel dimension inhabited solely by vampires and werewolves and, in any event, far from humans."

"Or they want us in Gary instead of Chicago."

"Or that," he allowed.

I forced myself to face forward, blocking out the sight of their faces at the window, wishing I could will myself invisible, or somehow merge into the leather upholstery and avoid the discomfort of listening to humans scream about how much they hated me. It hurt, more than I would have thought possible, to be surrounded by people who didn't know me but who would have been more than happy to hear I was gone and no longer polluting their neighborhood.

"It gets easier," Ethan said.

"I don't want it to get easier. I want to be accepted for who I am."

"Unfortunately, not everyone appreciates your finer qualities. But there are those of us who do."

We passed a family—father, mother, and two young sons—holding a hand-painted sign that read HYDE PARK HATES VAMPS.

"Now, that," Ethan grumbled, "I have little patience for. Until the children are old enough to reach their own conclusions about vampires, they should be immune from the discussion. They certainly should not have to bear the weight of their parents' prejudices."

I nodded and crossed my arms over my chest, tucking into myself.

After a hundred feet, the protesters thinned out, the urge to berate us apparently diminishing as we moved farther from the House. My spirit deflated, we headed northeast toward Creeley Creek, which sat in Chicago's historic Prairie Avenue neighborhood.

I glanced over at Ethan. "Have we thought about a campaign or something to address the hatred? Public service announcements or get-to-know-you forums? Anything to help them realize we aren't the enemy?"

He smirked. "Our social chair at work again?"

As punishment for challenging Ethan to a fight—although I'd been suffering from a bit of a split vampire personality at the time—Ethan had named me House social chair. He thought it a fitting punishment for a girl who spent more time in her room than getting to know her fellow vampires. I'll admit I was a bookworm—I'd been an English-lit grad student before I was changed—but I'd been making inroads. Of course, the shifter attack had put a damper on my plans for a barbecue social mixer.

"I'm just a Novitiate vampire trying to make it through the night with a little less hatred. Seriously—it might be something to consider."

"Julia's on it."

"Julia?"

"House director of marketing and public relations."

Huh. I hadn't even known we had one of those.

"Maybe we could hold a lottery for one of the Initiate spots next year," I suggested. "Get humans interested in being a Cadogan vampire?"

"*I've got a golden ticket,*" Ethan began to sing, then chuckled.

"Something like that. Of course, if you open a spot up to the public, you probably increase the odds of adding a saboteur to the House."

"And I think we're rather full in the saboteur department lately."

Thinking of the two traitorous vamps the House had lost since I joined, I nodded. "Wholeheartedly agreed."

I should have knocked on wood, offered up a little protection against the jinx I'd caused by talking about sabotage . . . because it suddenly looked like the protesters had called ahead.

Our headlights bounced off two SUVs that were parked diagonally in the middle of the street, six hefty men in front of them, all wearing black T-shirts and cargo pants.

"Hold on," Ethan yelled out, pulling the steering wheel with a screech of burning rubber. The roadster banked to the right, spinning clockwise until we sat perpendicular to the SUVs.

I looked up. Three of the men jogged around us, guns at their waists, surrounding the car before Ethan could pull away from the roadblock.

"I am not crazy about this situation," I muttered.

"Me, either," Ethan said, pulling out his cell phone and tapping keys. I assumed he was requesting backup, which was fine by me.

"Military?" I asked Ethan, my heart beating wildly.

"It's unlikely official military would approach us this way. Not when there are significantly easier means with less potential collateral damage."

"Whatever else they are, I assume they're anti-vamp."

Two of the three men in front of the car unholstered their weapons, approached us, and pulled open the doors.

"Out," they said in unison. I took mental inventory—I had my dagger, but not my sword. I hoped I wouldn't need it.

"Anti-vamp, indeed," Ethan muttered, then slowly lifted his hands into the air. I did the same.

Steady, Sentinel, he telepathically told me. *Say nothing aloud unless it's absolutely necessary.*

You're the boss, I replied.

All evidence to the contrary. The words were silent, but the snark was obvious.

We stepped outside onto the dark Chicago street. The vibration in the air—the buzz of steel I could feel after my katana had been tempered with blood—was intense. These guys, whoever they were, were well armed. Our hands in the air, their weapons trained on our hearts, we were escorted in front of the Mercedes. As vampires, we healed quickly enough that bullets wouldn't generally do us in. An aspen stake to the heart, however, would do the trick without question.

Now that I thought about it, their guns didn't exactly look off-the-rack; they looked like custom units, with muzzles a little wider than those in the House's arsenal.

Is it possible to modify a gun to shoot aspen stakes? I asked Ethan.

I'd prefer not to find out, he replied.

My stomach churned with nerves. I'd become used to the fact that my job called for violence, usually perpetrated by crazy paranormals against me and mine. But these weren't paranormals. These were gun-wielding humans who apparently believed they were beyond the reach of the law, who believed they had the authority to stop us and hold us at gunpoint within the bounds of our own city.

The third man in front of us—big and bulky, with acne-marked skin and a military haircut—stepped forward.

Watch him, echoed Ethan's voice in my head.

Hard to miss a human tank heading right for me.

"You think we don't know what you're doing to our city?" Tank asked. "You're killing us. Sneaking around in the night, pulling us from our beds. Enticing us, then drinking us down until there's nothing left."

My chest tightened at his words. I certainly hadn't done any of those things, nor did I know of any other vampires who had, at least not since Celina Desaulniers, Chicago's vampire bad girl, had disappeared from the scene. But Tank seemed very convinced he was telling the truth.

"I've done nothing to you," I told him. "I've never met you, and you don't know anything about me except that I'm a vampire."

"Bitch," he muttered, but he snapped his head back when the rear door opened on the left-hand SUV. Two booted feet hit the pavement, followed by another man in the same black uniform.

Unlike the others, this one was handsome, with long, wide eyes and high, pert cheekbones, his dark hair perfectly parted. His hands behind his back, he walked toward us while Tank closed the SUV's door.

I guessed New Guy was the one in charge.

"Mr. Sullivan. Ms. Merit," he said.

"And you are?" Ethan asked.

New Guy smiled grandly. "You can call me . . . McKetrick." The pause made it sound like he'd only just decided on the name. "These are some of my friends. Fellow believers, if you will."

"Your manners leave something to be desired." Ethan's tone was flat, but angry magic peppered the air.

McKetrick crossed his arms over his chest. "I find that insult rather comical, Mr. Sullivan, coming from an interloper in our city."

"An interloper?"

"We're humans. You're vampires. But for the result of a genetic mutation, you'd be like us. And that makes you aberrations in our town, uninvited guests. Guests that need to mind their manners and take their leave." His tone was matter-of-fact, as if he hadn't just suggested we were genetic aberrations that needed to hightail it out of the city.

"I beg your pardon," Ethan said, but McKetrick held up a hand.

"Come, now," he said. "I know you understand me. You seem to be an intelligent man, as does your colleague here. At least from what we know of her parents."

My parents—the Merits—were new-money Chicago. My father was a real estate investor mentioned in the papers on a daily basis. Smart, but ruthless. We weren't close, which made me that much less excited to learn I was being judged on the basis of his narcissistic press coverage.

Don't let him faze you, Ethan silently said. *You know who you are.*

"Your prejudices," he said aloud, "are not our problem. We suggest you put down the weapons and continue on your way."

"Continue on our way? That's truly rich. As if your kind are merely going to continue on your way without bringing this city into all-out supernatural war?" He shook his head. "No, thank you, Mr. Sullivan. You and yours need to pack, leave, and be done with it."

"I'm from Chicago," I said, drawing his attention to me. "Born and raised."

He lifted a finger. "Born and raised human until you switched sides."

I almost corrected him, told him that Ethan had saved me from a killer hired by Celina, brought me back to life after I'd been attacked. I could also have told him that no matter the challenges I faced as a vampire, Ethan was the reason I still drew breath. But I didn't think McKetrick would be thrilled to learn that I'd been nearly killed by one vampire—and changed without consent by another.

"No response?" McKetrick asked. "Not surprising. Given the havoc your 'House' has already wreaked in Chicago, I'm not sure I'd object, either."

"We did not precipitate the strike on our House," I told him. "We were attacked."

McKetrick tilted his head at us, a confused smile on his face. "But you must recognize that you prompted it. Without you, there would have been no violence."

"All we want is to go about our business."

McKetrick smiled magnanimously. He wasn't an unattractive man, but that smile—so calm and self-assured—was terrifying in its confidence. "That fits me fine. Simply take your business elsewhere. As should be clear now, Chicago doesn't want you."

Ethan steeled his features. "You haven't been elected. You haven't been appointed. You have no right to speak on behalf of the city."

"A city that had fallen under your spell? A city finally waking up to your deviance? Sometimes, Mr. Sullivan, the world needs a prophet. A man who can look beyond the now, see the future, and understand what's necessary."

"What do you want?"

He chuckled. "We want our city back, of course. We want the departure of all vampires in Chicago. We don't care where you go—we just don't want you here. I hope that's understood?"

"Fuck you," Ethan said. "Fuck you, and your prejudice."

McKetrick looked disappointed, as if he truly expected Ethan to see the error of his ways.

He opened his mouth to retort, but before he could answer, I heard it: cutting through the night like roaring thunder, the sound of rumbling exhaust. I glanced behind me and saw the headlights— a dozen in all—moving like an arrow toward us.

Motorcycles.

I began to grin, now knowing whom Ethan had contacted on his cell phone. These weren't just motorcycles; they were shifters. The cavalry had arrived.

The troops looked back to their leader, not sure of the next step.

They cut through the darkness like sharks on chrome. Twelve giant, gleaming, low-riding bikes, one shifter on each—brawny and leather-clad, ready for battle. And I could attest to the battle part. I'd seen them fight, I knew they were capable, and the tingle that lifted the hair at the back of my neck proved they were well armed.

Correction—eleven of them were brawny and leather-clad.

The twelfth was a petite brunette with a mass of long, curly hair, currently pulled back beneath a Cardinals ball cap. Fallon Keene, the only sister among six Keene brothers, named alphabetically from Gabriel down to Adam, who'd been removed from the NAC and sent into the loving arms of a rival Pack after he took out their leader. No one had heard from Adam since that exchange had taken place. Given his crime, I assumed that wasn't a good sign.

I nodded at Fallon, and when she offered back a quick salute, I decided I could live with her poor choice of baseball allegiances.

Gabriel Keene, Pack Apex, rode the bike in front, his sun-kissed brown hair pulled into a queue at the nape of his neck, his amber eyes scanning the scene with what looked like malicious intent. But I knew better. Gabriel eschewed violence unless absolutely necessary. He wasn't afraid of it, but he didn't seek it out.

Gabriel revved his bike with a flick of his wrist, and like magic, McKetrick's men stepped back toward their SUVs.

Gabe turned his gaze on me. "Problems, Kitten?"

I looked over at McKetrick, who was scanning the bikes and their riders with a nervous expression. I guess his anti-vamp bravado didn't extend to shifters. After a moment he seemed to regain his composure and made eye contact with us again.

"I look forward to continuing this conversation at a more appropriate time," McKetrick said. "We'll be in touch. In the meantime, stay out of trouble." With that, he slipped back into the SUV, and the rest of his troops followed him.

I bit back disappointment. I'd almost wished they'd been naïve enough to make a move, just so I could enjoy watching the Keenes pummel them into oblivion.

With a roar from custom mufflers, the SUVs squealed into action and drove away. Pity it wasn't forever. I checked the license plates, but they were blank. Either they were driving around without registrations or they'd taken off the plates for their little introductory chat.

Gabe glanced at Ethan. "Who's G.I. Joe?"

"He said his name was McKetrick. He imagines himself to be an anti-vampire vigilante. He wants all vamps out of the city."

Gabe clucked his tongue. "He's probably not the only one," he said, glancing at me. "Trouble does seem to find you, Kitten."

"As Ethan can verify, I had nothing to do with it. We were driving toward Creeley Creek when we hit the roadblock. They popped out with guns."

Gabe rolled his eyes. "Only vampires would find that a limitation instead of a challenge. You are immortal, after all."

"And we prefer to keep it that way," Ethan said. "The weapons looked custom."

"Anti-vamp rounds?" Gabriel asked.

"It wouldn't surprise me. McKetrick seemed like the type."

"And my sword is at the House," I pointed out to Gabe. "You give me thirty-two inches of folded steel, and I'll take on anyone you want."

He rolled his eyes, then revved his bike and glanced over at Ethan. "You're headed to Creeley Creek?"

"We are."

"Then we're your escorts. Hop in the car and we'll get you there."

"We owe you one."

Gabriel shook his head. "Consider it one more notch off the tab I owe Merit."

He'd mentioned that debt before. I still had no idea what he thought he owed me, but I nodded anyway and jogged back to the Mercedes.

I slid inside the car. "You said the fairies detested humans.

Right now, I feel like 'detest' is hardly a strong enough word. And it looks like we can add one more problem to the punch list."

"That would appear to be the case," he said, turning on the engine.

"At least we're still friends with the shifters," I said as we zoomed through the stop sign ahead of us, the shifters making a shieldlike V of bikes around the car.

"And officially enemies with humans again. Some of them, anyway."

As we moved down the street and finally began to gain speed, our escort of shape-shifters beside us, I turned back to the road and sighed.

"Let the good times roll."

CHAPTER THREE

SCIENCE FRICTION

Creeley Creek was a Prairie-style building—low and horizontal, with lots of long windows, overhanging eaves, and bare, honeyed wood. It was bigger than the average Prairie-style home, built at the turn of the twentieth century by an architect with a renowned ego. When the original owner died, his estate donated the house to the city of Chicago, which deemed it the official residence of the mayor. It was to Chicago what Gracie Mansion was to New York City.

Currently living there was the politician Chicago had always wanted. Handsome. Popular. A master orator with friends on both sides of the aisle. Whether or not you liked the slant of his politics, he was very, very good at his job.

The gate opened when we arrived, the guard who stood inside the glass box at the edge of the street waving us onto the grounds. Ethan circled the Mercedes around the drive and pulled into a small parking area beside the house.

"From a House of vampires to a house of politicians," he muttered as we walked to the front door.

"Said the most political of vampires," I reminded him, and got a growl in response. But I stood my ground. He was the one who'd traded a relationship with me for political considerations.

"I look forward," he said as we walked across the tidy brick driveway, "to your turn at the helm."

I assumed he meant the day I'd become a Master vampire. It wasn't exactly something I looked forward to, but it would get me out of Cadogan House.

"You look forward to it because we'll be equally matched? Politically, I mean?"

He slid me a dry glance. "Because I'll enjoy watching you squirm under the pressure."

"Charming," I muttered.

A woman in a snug navy blue suit stood in front of the double front doors beneath a low overhanging stone eave. Her hair was pulled into a tight bun, and she wore thick, horn-rimmed glasses. They were quite a contrast to the patent platform heels.

Was she going for sexy librarian, maybe?

"Mr. Sullivan. Merit. I'm Tabitha Bentley, the mayor's assistant. The mayor is ready to see you, but I understand there are some preliminaries we need to address?" She lifted her gaze to the threshold above us.

The old wives' tale was that vampires couldn't enter a house if they hadn't been invited in. But like lots of other fang-related myths, that was less about magic and more about rules. Vampires *loved* rules—what to drink, where to stand, how to address higher-ranking vampires, and so on.

"We would appreciate the mayor's official invitation into his house," Ethan said, without detailing the reasons for the request.

She nodded primly. "I have been authorized to extend an invitation to you and Merit to Creeley Creek."

Ethan smiled politely. "We thank you for your hospitality and accept your invitation."

The deal struck, Ms. Bentley opened the doors and waited while we walked into the hallway.

It wasn't my first time in the mansion. My father (being well moneyed) and Tate (being well connected) were acquaintances, and my father had occasionally dragged me to Creeley Creek for some fund-raiser or other. I looked around and concluded it hadn't changed much since the last time I'd visited. The floors were gleaming stone, the walls horizontal planks of dark wood. The house was cool and dark, the hallway illuminated with golden light cast down from wall-mounted sconces.

The smell of vanilla cookies permeated the air. That smell—of bright lemons and sugar—reminded me of Tate. It was the same scent I'd caught the last time I'd seen him. Maybe he had a favorite snack, and the Creeley Creek staff obliged.

But the man in the hallway wasn't one I'd expected to see. My father, dapper in a sharp black suit, walked toward us. He didn't offer a handshake; the arrogance was typical Joshua Merit.

"Ethan, Merit."

"Joshua," Ethan said with a nod. "Meeting with the mayor this evening?"

"I was," my father said. "You're both well?"

Sadly, I was surprised that he cared. "We're fine," I told him. "What brings you here?"

"Business council issues," my father said. He was a member of the Chicago Growth Council, a group geared toward bringing new businesses to the city.

"I also put in a good word about your House," he added, "about the strides you've taken with the city's supernatural populations. Your grandfather keeps me apprised."

"That was . . . very magnanimous of you," Ethan said, his confusion matching my own.

My father smiled pleasantly, then glanced from us to Tabitha. "I see that you're heading in. Don't let me keep you. Good to see you both."

Tabitha stepped in front of us, heels clacking on the floor as she marched deeper into the mansion. "Follow me," she called back.

Ethan and I exchanged a glance.

"What just happened?" I asked.

"For some unknown reason, your father has suddenly become friendly?"

There was undoubtedly a business-related reason for that, which I assumed we'd find out soon enough. In the meantime, we did as we were told, and followed Tabitha down the hallway.

Seth Tate had the look of a playboy who'd never quite reformed. Tousled, coal black hair, blue eyes under long, dark brows. He had a face women swooned over and, as a second-term mayor, the political chops to back up the looks. That explained why he'd been named one of Chicago's most eligible bachelors, and one of the country's sexiest politicians.

He met us in his office, a long, low room that was paneled floor to ceiling in wood. A gigantic desk sat at one end of the room in front of a tufted, red leather chair that could have doubled as a throne.

Both the desk and throne stood beneath an ominous five-foot-wide painting. Most of the canvas was dark, but the outlines of a group of suspicious-looking men were visible. They stood around a man positioned near the center of the painting, his arms above his head, cowering as they pointed down at him. It looked like they were condemning him for something. It wasn't exactly an inspiring painting.

Tate, who stood in the middle of the room, reached out a hand toward Ethan, no hesitation in the movement. "Ethan."

"Mr. Mayor." They shared a manly handshake.

"How are things at the House?"

"I'd say the mood is . . . anticipatory. With protesters at the gate, one tends to wait for the other shoe to drop."

After they'd shared a knowing look, Tate turned to me, a smile blossoming. "Merit," he said, voice softer. He took both my hands and leaned toward me, pressing a soft kiss to my cheek, the scent of sugared lemon floating around him. "I just met with your father."

"We saw him on the way out."

He released me and smiled, but as he looked me over, the smile faded. "Are you all right?"

I must have looked shaken; being held at gunpoint could do that to a girl. But before I could speak, Ethan sent a warning.

Don't mention McKetrick, he said. *Not until we know more about his alliances.*

"There was a protest outside the House," I obediently told Tate. "It was unnerving. A lot of prejudice was thrown around."

Tate offered an apologetic look. "Unfortunately, we can't deny the protesters their permits for First Amendment reasons, but we can always step in if matters escalate."

"We had things well in hand," I assured him.

"Gabriel Keene's announcement that shape-shifters exist hasn't done much for your popularity."

"No, it hasn't," Ethan admitted. "But he came to the fight at the House when our backs were against the wall. Going public— getting his side of the story out there—was the best of a bad set of options for protecting his people."

"I don't necessarily disagree," Tate said. "He doesn't make the announcement, and we end up having to arrest every shifter there for assault and disturbing the peace. We couldn't just let them off without some justification. The announcement gave us that reason, helped the public understand why they'd joined the fight and why we weren't arresting them on sight."

"I'm sure they appreciate your understanding."

Tate offered a sardonic look. "I doubt that kind of thing interests them. Shifters don't strike me as the most political types."

"They aren't," Ethan agreed. "But Gabriel is savvy enough to understand when a favor's been done, and when a favor needs to be returned. He wasn't happy about making the announcement, and he has even less interest in his people getting pulled into the public's fear of vampires. He's working on that now, keeping his people out of the public's notice."

"That's actually the reason I've asked you to meet with me," Tate said. "I realize it's an unusual request, and I appreciate your coming on such short notice."

He sat down in the throne behind his desk, the onlookers in the portrait now pointing down at him. Tate gestured toward two smaller chairs that sat in front of his desk. "Please, have a seat."

Ethan took a chair. I took point behind him, Sentinel at the ready.

Mayor Tate's eyes widened at the gesture, but his expression turned back to business fast enough. He flipped open a folder and uncapped an expensive-looking fountain pen.

Ethan crossed one leg over the other. The signal: he was moving into political-chat position. "What can we do for you?" he asked, his voice oh-so-casual.

"You said the mood at the House was anticipatory. That's the concern I have about the city more broadly. The attack on Cadogan has reactivated the city's fear of the supernatural, of the *other*.

We had four days of riots the first time around, Ethan. I'm sure you'll understand the tricky position that puts me in—keeping the citizenry calm while trying to be understanding toward your challenges, including Adam Keene's attack."

"Of course," Ethan graciously said.

"But humans are nervous. Increasingly so. And that nervousness is leading to an uptick in crime. In the last two weeks, we've seen marked increases in assaults, in batteries, in arson, in the use of firearms. I've worked hard to get those numbers down since my first election, and I think the city's better for it. I'd hate to see us slide backward."

"I think we'd all agree with that," Ethan said aloud, but that was just the precursor to the silent conversation between us as Ethan activated our telepathic link. *What's he building toward?*

Your guess is as good as mine, I answered.

Tate frowned and glanced down at the folder on his desk. He scanned whatever information he found there, then lifted a document from it and extended it toward Ethan. "Humans, it seems, are not the only increasingly violent folk in our city."

Ethan took the document, staring silently down at it until his shoulders tensed into a flat line.

Ethan? What is it? I asked. Without bothering to answer, Ethan handed the paper over his shoulder. I took it from him. It looked like part of a police transcript.

Q: *Tell me what you saw, Mr. Jackson.*

A: There were dozens of them. Vampires, you know? Fangs and that ability to get inside your mind. And they was blood-crazy. All of them. Everywhere you looked—vampire, vampire, vampire. Bam! Vampire. And they were all over us. No escape.

Q: *Who couldn't escape?*

A: Humans. Not when the vampires wanted you. Not when they wanted to take you down and pull that blood right out of you. All of 'em were on you and the music was so loud and it was pounding like a hammer against your heart. They were crazed with it. Crazy with it.

Q: *With what?*

A: With the blood. With the lust for it. The hunger. You could see it in their crazy eyes. They were silver, just like the eyes of the devil. You get only one look at those eyes before the devil himself pulls you down into the abyss.

Q: *And then what happened, Mr. Jackson?*

A: [*Shaking his head.*] The hunger, the lust, it got them. Drove them. They killed three girls. Three of them. They drank until there was no life left.

The page stopped there. My fingers shaking around the paper, I skipped the chain of command and glanced up at Tate. "Where did you get this?"

Tate met my gaze. "Cook County Jail. This was from an interview with a man who'd been arrested for possession of a controlled substance. The detective wasn't sure if he was drunk or disturbed . . . or if he'd actually seen something that required our attention. Fortunately, she took the transcript to her supervisor, who brought it to my chief of staff. We've yet to find the victims of whom Mr. Jackson spoke—no missing persons match his descriptions—although we are actively investigating the accusation."

"Where did this occur?" Ethan quietly asked.

Tate's gaze dropped down to Ethan and narrowed. "He said West Town, and he hasn't been more specific than offering up the neighborhood. Since we haven't identified a crime scene or the victims, it's possible he exaggerated the violence. On the other hand, as you can see from the transcript, he's quite convinced the vampires of our fair city were involved in a bloodlust-driven attack on humans. An attack that left three innocents dead."

After a moment of silence, Tate sat back, crossed his hands behind his head, and rocked back in the chair. "I'm not thrilled this is going on in my city. I'm not happy about the attack on your House and whatever animosity lies between you and the Packs, and I'm not happy that my citizens are scared enough of vampires that they've lined up outside your home to protest your existence."

Tate sat forward again, fury in his expression. "But you know what really pisses me off? The fact that you don't look surprised about Mr. Jackson's report. The fact that I've learned you're well aware of the existence of drinking parties you call 'raves.'"

My stomach clenched with nerves. Tate was normally poised, politic, careful with words, and invariably optimistic about the city. This voice was the kind you'd expect to hear in a smoky back room or a dark restaurant booth. The kind of tone you'd have heard in Al Capone's Chicago.

This was the Seth Tate that destroyed his enemies. And we were now his targets.

"We've heard rumors," Ethan finally said, a master of understatement.

"Rumors of blood orgies?"

"Of raves," Ethan admitted. "Small gatherings where vampires drink communally from humans."

Raves were usually organized by Rogue vampires—the ones that weren't tied to a House and tended not to follow traditional

House rules. For most Houses, those rules meant not snacking on humans, consenting or not. Cadogan allowed drinking, but still required consent, and I didn't know of any House that would condone outright murder.

We'd come close to having raves pop into the public eye a few months ago, but with a little investigation on our part, we'd managed to keep them in the closet. I guess that blissful ignorance was behind us.

"We've been keeping our ears to the ground," Ethan continued, "to identify the organizers of the raves, their methods, the manners in which they attract humans."

That was Malik's job—Ethan's second-in-command, the runner-up for the crown. After a blackmailing incident, he'd been put in charge of investigating the raves.

"And what have you found?" Tate asked.

Ethan cleared his throat. Ah, the sound of stalling.

"We're aware of three raves in the last two months," he said. "Three raves involving, at most, half a dozen vampires. These were small, intimate affairs. While bloodletting does occur, we have not heard of the, shall we say, frenetic violence of which Mr. Jackson speaks, nor would we condone such things. There has certainly never been an allegation that any participant was . . . drained. And if we had heard of it, we'd have contacted the Ombudsman, or put a stop to it ourselves."

The mayor linked his fingers together on the desktop. "Ethan, I believe that part and parcel of keeping this city safe is integrating vampires into the human population. Division will solve nothing—it will only lead to more division. On the other hand, according to Mr. Jackson, vampires are engaging in violent, large-scale, and hardly consensual acts. That is unacceptable to me."

"As it is to me and mine," Ethan said.

"I've heard talk about a recall election," Tate said. "I will not go down in flames because of supernatural hysteria. This city does not need a referendum on vampires or shape-shifters.

"But most important," he continued, gaze burrowing into Ethan, "you do not want a bevy of aldermen showing up at your front door, demanding that you close down your House. You do not want the city council legislating you out of existence."

I felt a burst of magic from Ethan. His angst—and anger—were rising, and I was glad Tate was human and couldn't sense the uncomfortable prickle of it.

"And you do not want me as an enemy," Tate concluded. "You do not want me requesting a grand jury to consider the crimes of you and yours." He flipped through the folder on his desk, then slid out a single sheet and held it up. "You do not want me executing this warrant for your arrest on the basis that you've aided and abetted the murder of humans in this city."

Ethan's voice was diamond-cold, but the magical tingle was seismic in magnitude. "I have done no such thing."

"Oh?" Tate placed the paper on his desk again. "I have it on good authority that you changed a human into a vampire without her consent." He lifted his gaze to me, and I felt the blood rush to my cheeks. "I also have it on good authority that while you and your vampire council promised to keep Celina Desaulniers contained in Europe, she's been in Chicago. Are those actions such a far stretch from murder?"

"Who suggested Celina was in Chicago?" Ethan asked. The question was carefully put. We knew full well that Celina—the former head of Navarre House and my would-have-been killer—had been released by the Greenwich Presidium, the organizing body for European and North American vampires. We also knew that once the GP let her go, she'd made her way to Chicago. But we hadn't thought she was still here. The last few months had been too drama free for that. Or so they'd seemed.

Tate arched his eyebrows. "I notice you don't deny it. As for the information, I have my sources, just as I'm sure you do."

"Sources or not, I don't take kindly to blackmail."

With shocking speed, Tate switched back from Capone to front-page orator, smiling magnanimously at us. "'Blackmail' is such a harsh word, Ethan."

"Then what, precisely, do you want?"

"I want for you, for us, to do the right thing for the city of Chicago. I want for you and yours to have the chance to take control within your own community." Tate linked his hands on the desk and looked us over. "I want this problem solved. I want an end to these gatherings, these raves, and a personal guarantee that you have this problem under control. If it's not done, the warrant for your arrest will be executed. I assume we understand each other?"

There was silence until Ethan finally bit out, "Yes, Mr. Mayor."

Like a practiced politico, Tate instantly softened his expression. "Excellent. If you have anything to report, or if you need access to any of the city's resources, you need only contact me."

"Of course."

With a final nod, Tate turned back to his papers, just as Ethan might have done if I'd been called into his office for a friendly chat.

But this time, it was Ethan who'd been called out, and it was Ethan who rose and walked back to the door. I followed, ever the dutiful Sentinel.

Ethan kept the fear or concern or vitriol or whatever emotion was driving him to himself even as we reached the Mercedes.

And I meant "driving" literally. He expressed that pent-up

frustration with eighty thousand dollars of German engineering and a 300-horsepower engine. He managed not to clip the gate as he pulled out of the drive, but he treated the stop signs between Creeley Creek and Lake Shore Drive like meek suggestions. Ethan floored the Mercedes, zooming in and around traffic like the silver-eyed devil was on our tail.

Problem was, we were the silver-eyed devils.

We were both immortal, and Ethan probably had a century of driving experience under his belt, but that didn't make the turns any less harrowing. He raced through a light and onto Lake Shore Drive, turned south, and gunned it. . . . And he kept driving until the city skyline glowed behind us.

I was almost afraid to ask where he was taking us—did I really want to know where predatory vampires blew off political steam?—but he saved me the trouble when we reached Washington Park. He pulled off Lake Shore Drive, and a few squealing turns later we were coasting onto Promontory Point, a small peninsula that jutted into the lake. Ethan drove around the tower-topped building and stopped the car in front of the rock ledge that separated grass from lake.

Without a word, he climbed out of the car and slammed it shut again. When he hopped the rock ledge that ringed the peninsula and disappeared from sight, I unfastened my seat belt. It was time to go to work.

CHAPTER FOUR

THE SAVAGE BEAST

The air was thick and damp, the sharp smell of ozone signaling rain. The lake looked like it was already in the middle of a squall: whitecaps rolled across the water like jagged teeth, and waves pounded the rocky shoreline.

I glanced up at the sky. The anvil-shaped marker of a gigantic thunderstorm was swelling in the southwestern sky, visible each time lightning flashed across it.

Without warning, a *crack* split the air.

I jumped and looked back at the building, thinking it had been struck by an early bolt of lightning. But the building was quiet and still, and when another *crack* shattered the silence, I realized the sound had come from a stand of trees on the other side of the building.

I walked around to investigate and found Ethan standing at the base of a pine tree like a fighter facing down a forty-foot-tall opponent. His fists were up, his body bladed.

"Every time!" he yelled. "Every time I manage to bring things under control, we become enmeshed in bullshit *again*!"

And then he pivoted and thrust out—and punched the tree.

Crack.

The tree wobbled like it had been rammed by a truck, needles *whoosh*ing as limbs moved. The smell of pine resin—and blood—lifted in the breeze. And those weren't the only things in the air. Magic rippled off Ethan's body in waves, leaving its telltale tingle around us.

And that, I thought, explained why he'd driven here instead of the House. With that much anger banked, there was no way Ethan could have gone home. Cadogan's vampires—even those who weren't as sensitive to magic as I was—would have known something was wrong, and that certainly wasn't going to ease the anticipatory mood. It was an obvious downside of being a Master vampire—to be all riled up with nowhere to go.

"Do you have any idea how long—how *hard*—I've worked to make this House successful? And this human—this temporary blip in the chronology of the world—threatens to take it all away."

Ethan reared back for a second strike, but he'd already split his knuckles and the poor tree probably wasn't faring much better. I understood the urge to rail out when you were being held account-able for another's evils, but hurting himself wasn't going to solve the problem. It was time to intervene.

I was standing on the lawn between the building and the lake; I figured that was a perfect place to work off a little tension. "Why don't you pick on someone your own size?" I called out.

He looked over, one eyebrow defiantly arched. "Don't tempt me, Sentinel."

I peeled off my suit jacket and dropped it onto the ground, then put my hands on my hips and, hopefully for the last time tonight, pulled out my vampire bravado. "Are you afraid you can't handle me?"

His expression was priceless—equal parts tempted and irritated—the masculinity warring with the urge to tamp down the challenge to his authority. "Watch your mouth."

"It was a legitimate question," I countered. Ethan was already walking closer, the smell of his blood growing stronger.

I won't deny it—my hunger was perked. I'd bitten Ethan twice before, and both times had been memorable. Sensual, in ways I wasn't entirely comfortable admitting. The scent of his blood triggered those memories again, and I knew my own eyes had silvered, even if I wasn't thrilled about bring tempted.

"It was a childish question," he growled out, taking another step forward.

"I disagree. If you want to fight, try a vampire."

"Your attempts at being clever aren't serving you, Sentinel."

He moved within striking range, blood dripping from his right knuckles, which were split nearly to the bone. They'd heal, and quickly, but they must have hurt.

"And yet," I said, squeezing my own hands into fists, "here you are."

His eyes flashed silver. "Remember your position."

"Does putting me in my place make you feel better?"

"I am your *Master*."

"Yes, you are. In Hyde Park and in Creeley Creek, and wherever else vampires are gathered, you're my Master. But out here, it's just you and me and the chip Tate put on your shoulder. You can't go back to the House like this. You're pouring magic, and that's going to worry everyone even more than they already are."

There was a tic above his eyebrow, but Ethan held his tongue.

"Out here," I quietly said, "it's just you and me."

"Then don't say I didn't warn you." With no more warning, he offered up his favorite move, a roundhouse kick that he swiveled toward my head. But I dropped my arm and shoulder and blocked it.

That move thwarted, Ethan bounced back into position. "Don't get cocky, Sentinel. You've only taken me down once."

I tried a roundhouse of my own, but he dodged it, ducking and spinning around the kick, before popping up again. "Maybe so," I said. "But how many Novitiates have beaten you before?"

He scowled and offered a jab combination that I easily rebuffed. For all the vampiric power we could put behind our shots, this wasn't a real battle. This was play-fighting. The release of tension.

"Never fear," he said. "You may have gotten me down, but I've been above you before, and I'm sure I'll manage it again."

He was being arrogant, letting the gentle, insistent veneer he'd been wearing lately slip. But I'd managed to transmute his anger into romantic steam, which softened his punches.

I swatted away a halfhearted jab. "Don't get your hopes up. I'm not that kind of hungry."

"My hopes, as you call them, are perpetually up when you're in the vicinity."

"Then I'll try to stay farther away," I sweetly responded.

"That won't exactly be conducive to your standing Sentinel."

"Neither will your being arrested," I said, bringing him back to the point.

Ethan ran his hands through his blond locks, then linked his fingers together atop his head. "I am doing everything I can to keep the city together. And it's only getting harder. And now, within a few hours, we see the ugly side of freedom of speech, we learn Chicago has a militia, and we discover Tate's out for blood. *My* blood."

My heart clenched in sympathy, but I resisted the urge to reach out to him. We were colleagues, I reminded myself. Nothing more.

"I know it's frustrating," I said, "and I know Tate was out of line with the warrant. But what can we do but try to solve the problem?"

Frowning, Ethan turned back to the lake, then walked toward it. The edge of the peninsula was terraced into stone rings that formed giant steps into the water. He shed his suit jacket, placing it gingerly on the stone ledge before sitting down beside it.

Was it wrong that I was a wee bit disappointed he didn't just shed the shirt altogether?

When I joined him, he picked up a pebble and pitched it. Even with the chop, it flew like a bullet across the water.

"This doesn't sound like a rave," I said. "What Mr. Jackson described, I mean, at least not like how you've described them before. This didn't sound like it was about seduction or glamour. This isn't some underground hobby." As I waited for him to answer, I pushed the bangs from my face. The wind was picking up.

Ethan wound up and threw another pebble, the rock zinging as it skipped ahead. "Continue," he said, and I incrementally relaxed. We were back to politics and strategy. That was a good sign.

"I've experienced First Hunger, and First Hunger Part Deux. There was a sensual component to both, sure, but at base they were about the blood—the thirst. Not about conquering humans or killing them."

"We are vampires," he dryly pointed out.

"Yes, because we drink blood, not because we're psychopaths. I'm not saying there aren't psychopathic vampires, or vampires who wouldn't kill for blood if they were starving for it, but it doesn't sound like that's what happened here. It sounds like violence, pure and simple."

Ethan was quiet for a moment. "The hunger for blood is antithetical to violence. If anything, it's about seduction, about drawing the human closer. That is the quintessential purpose of vampire glamour."

Glamour was old-school vampire mojo—the ability of vampires to entrance others, either by manipulating their targets or by adjusting their own appearances to make themselves more attractive to their victims. I couldn't glamour worth a damn, but I seemed to have some immunity toward it.

"This is the second time raves have gotten us in trouble," I pointed out. "We've avoided them until now, and it's time we shut them down. But we can't go in assuming this is some run-of-the-mill party that got out of hand. This just sounds . . . different. And if you want a silver lining, at least Tate's giving you a chance to resolve the problem."

"Giving me a chance? That's putting it mildly. He's doing precisely what Nick Breckenridge attempted to do—blackmailing us into taking action."

"Or he's giving us an opportunity we didn't have before."

"How do you figure that?"

"He's forcing our hands," I said. "Which means that instead of tiptoeing around the GP and worrying what this House or that might think of us, we're forced to get out there and do something about it. We get to spend some of that political capital you're always harping about."

Ethan arched an eyebrow imperiously.

"Talking about. Talking about in well-reasoned and measured tones."

This time, he rolled his eyes.

"Look," I continued. "The last time we worked on the raves, you made me focus on the media risk. Tonight, we've proven that worrying someone might find out about the problem doesn't actually *solve* the problem. We need to get in front of the issue. We need to close them down."

"You want to tell vampires they can no longer engage in human blood orgies?"

"Well, I wasn't going to use those words, exactly. And I did plan to take my sword."

He smiled a little. "You are quite a thing to behold when you've got steel in your hands."

"Yes," I agreed. I touched a hand to my stomach. "And now that we're looking on the bright side, let's find some grub. I am starving."

"Are you ever not starving?"

"Har-har." I nudged his arm. "Come on. Let's get an Italian beef."

He glanced over at me. "I assume that has some meaning important within Chicago culinary circles?"

I just stood there, both saddened that he hadn't experienced the joy of a good Italian beef sandwich—and irritated that he'd lived in Chicago for so long and had so completely sequestered himself from the stuff that made it Chicago.

"As important as red hots and deep dish. Let's go, Liege. It's your turn to get schooled."

He growled, but relented.

We drove to University Village, parked along the street, and took our places in line with the third-shifters on lunch breaks and the UIC students needing late-night snacks. Eventually we placed our orders and moved to a counter, where I taught Ethan to stand the way God intended Chicagoans to stand—feet apart, elbows on the table, sandwiches in hand.

Ethan hadn't spoken since his own eight-inch Italian beef sandwich had been delivered, still dripping from its dip in gravy.

When his first bite left a trail of juice on the floor in front of his feet—and not on his expensive Italian shoes—he smiled grandly at me.

"Well done, Sentinel."

I nodded through my bite of bread, beef, and peppers, happy that Ethan was in a better mood. Say what you might about my obsession with all things meat and carbohydrate, but never underestimate the ability of a stack of thin-sliced beef on a bun to make a man happy—vampire or human.

And speaking of happiness, I wondered what else Ethan had been missing out on. "Have you ever been to a Cubs game?"

Ethan dabbed his mouth with a paper napkin, and I got a glimpse of his knuckles—already healed from the blows. "No, I have not. As you know, I'm not much of a baseball fan."

He wasn't much of a fan, but he'd still tracked down a signed Cubs baseball to replace one I'd lost. That was the kind of move that threw me off balance, but I managed to keep things lighthearted.

"Just stake me now," I said. "Seriously—you've been in Chicago how long and you've never been to Wrigley? That's a shame. You need to get out there. I mean, for a night game, obviously."

"Obviously."

A couple of large men with mustaches and Bears T-shirts moved toward the high bar where we stood, sandwiches in hand. They took a spot beside Ethan, spread their feet, unwrapped their own Italian beefs, and dug in.

It wasn't until bite number two that they glanced over and noticed two vampires were standing beside them.

The one closest to Ethan ran a napkin across his dripping mustache, his gaze shifting from me to Ethan. "You two look familiar. I know you?"

Since my photo had been smeared across the front page of the paper a couple of months ago, and Ethan had made the local news more than once since the attack on Cadogan, we probably did look familiar.

"I'm a vampire from Cadogan House," Ethan said.

Our area of the restaurant, not full but still dotted with late-night munchers, went silent.

This time, the man looked suspiciously at the sandwich. "You like that?"

"It's great," Ethan said, then gestured toward me. "This is Merit. She's from Chicago. She decided I had to try one."

The man and his companion leaned forward to look at me. "That so?"

"It is."

He was quiet for a moment. "You had deep dish yet? Or a red hot?"

My heart warmed. We might have been vampires, but at least these guys recognized that we were first and foremost Chicagoans. We knew Wrigley Field and Navy Pier, Daley and rush hour traffic, Soldier Field in December and Oak Street Beach in July. We knew freak snowstorms and freakier heat waves.

But most of all, we knew food: taquerias, red hots, deep dish, great beer. We baked it, fried it, sautéed it, and grilled it, and in our quest to enjoy the sunshine and warmth while we could, we shared that food together.

"Both," I said. "I got him pizza from Saul's."

The man's bushy eyebrows popped up. "You know about Saul's?"

I smiled slyly. "Cream cheese and double bacon."

"Oooh," the man said, grinning ear to ear. He dropped his napkin and threw his hands into the air. "Cream cheese and double bacon. Our fanged friend here knows about Saul's Best!" He raised his giant paper cup of soda in a toast. "To you, my friend. Good eats and whatnot."

"And to you," Ethan said, raising his sandwich and taking a bite.

Hot beef in the name of peace. I liked it.

"I'm surprised you told him we were vampires," I told Ethan on the way back to the car. "That you admitted to it, I mean, given what we saw earlier tonight."

"Sometimes the only way to counter prejudice is to remind them how similar we are. To challenge their perceptions of what it means to be vampire ... or human. Besides, he wouldn't have asked who we were if he hadn't at least suspected, and lying probably would have irritated him further."

"Quite possibly."

He smiled magnanimously. "Besides, you clearly wooed them with your cream cheese and double-bacon talk."

"Who wouldn't be wooed by cream cheese and double-bacon talk? I mean, other than vegetarians, I guess. But as we have thoroughly established, vegetarianism is not my gig."

Ethan opened my car door. "No, Sentinel, it is not."

I'd climbed inside and he did the same, but he didn't start the car right away.

"Problems?" I asked.

He frowned. "I'm not sure I'm ready to return to the House. Not that I'd prefer to be at Creeley Creek, of course, but until I go back to Hyde Park, the drama hasn't quite solidified." He glanced at me. "Does that make sense?"

Only a four-hundred-year-old Master vampire would wonder if a grad student could understand procrastination. "Of course it does. Procrastination is a very human emotion."

"I'm not sure humans have a monopoly on procrastination. And, more important, I'm not sure this counts as procrastination."

He turned back again and started the ignition. "Unlike what you're doing."

"What I'm doing?"

He smiled just a little—a tease of a smile. "Procrastinating," he said. "Avoiding the inevitability of you and me."

"How long does 'inevitability' take when you're immortal?"

He grinned and pulled the Mercedes away from the curb. "I suppose we'll find out."

One summer night in Chicago. Three sets of battle lines drawn.

The protesters were still outside when we returned, their apparent hatred of us undiminished. On the other hand, their energy did seem to be a little diminished; this time, they were sitting on the narrow strip of grass between the sidewalk and street. Some sat in pop-up camping chairs. Others sat on blankets in pairs, one's head on the other's shoulder, given the late hour. Late-night prejudice was apparently exhausting.

Malik met us at the door, folder in hand; Ethan had given him a heads-up call in the car on the way back to the House.

Malik was tall, with cocoa skin, pale green eyes, and closely cropped hair. He had the regal bearing of a prince in training—shoulders back, jaw set, eyes scanning and alert, as if waiting for marauders to scale the castle walls.

"Militiamen and arrest warrants," Malik said. "I'm not sure it's advisable for you two to leave the House together anymore."

Ethan made a snort of agreement. "At this point, I'd tend to agree with you."

"Tate indicated the supposed incident was violent?"

"Exceptionally so, according to the firsthand account," Ethan said.

Once we were in Ethan's office and he'd closed the door behind us, he got to the heart of it. "The story is, the vamps lost control and killed three humans. But Mr. Jackson's description rang more of uncontrolled bloodlust than of a typical rave."

"Mr. Jackson?" Malik asked.

Ethan headed for his desk. "Our eyewitness. Potentially under the influence, but sober enough that Tate was apparently convinced. And by convinced, I mean he's threatening my arrest if we don't fix the problem, whatever it is."

Malik, eyes wide, looked between the two of us. "He's serious, then."

Ethan nodded. "He's had the warrant drawn. And that makes this problem our current focus. Tate said the incident occurred in West Town. Look through your rave intel again. Any connections to that neighborhood? Any talk about violence? Anything that would suggest the scale the witness talked about?"

That assignment given, Ethan looked at me. "When the sun sets, talk to your grandfather. Ask him to track down what they can about the Jackson incident—the vampires involved, Houses, whatever—and any new information they've gotten about the raves. This may not actually be one, but at the moment it's the best lead we've got. And one way or the other," he added, looking between us, "let's close these things down, shall we?"

"Liege," I agreed with a nod. I'd definitely visit my grandfather, but my circle of friends had grown a little wider over the last few months. I'd recently been asked to join the Red Guard, a kind of vampire watchdog group that kept an eye on Master vamps and the GP. I'd declined the invitation, but I'd made use of the resource, calling on the RG for backup during the attack on the House. This might be the time to make that call again. . . .

"And this McKetrick fellow?" Malik asked.

"He'll wait," Ethan said, determination in his eyes. "He'll wait until hell freezes over, because we're not leaving Chicago."

I'd visit my grandfather when the sun set. But first, I had a couple more hours of darkness and many hours of daylight to get through.

All the bedrooms in the House, which accommodated about ninety of Cadogan's three-hundred-odd vampires, looked like small dorm rooms. A bed. A bureau. A nightstand. Small closet, small bathroom. They weren't exactly fancy, but they gave us a respite from vampire drama. Given the messes we tended to get into, drama free was definitely a good thing.

My second-floor room—just like the rest of the House—still smelled like construction. New paint. Varnish. Drywall. Plastic. It smelled good somehow, like a new beginning. A fresh start.

The storm broke overhead just as I shut my door, rain beginning to pelt the shuttered window in my room. I peeled off my suit and toed off Mary Jane heels, then headed to my small bathroom, where I scrubbed my face. The makeup washed off easily. The memories, on the other hand, weren't going anywhere.

Those were the tough things to ignore—the sounds, the expressions, the sensation of Ethan and his body. I'd tried to lock the memories away, to keep my mind clear of them in order to get my work done. But they were still there. They stung a little less now, but you couldn't unring the bell. For better or worse, I'd probably always have those memories with me.

When I'd dressed again in a tank top and shorts, I glanced back at the clock. I had two hours to kill until dawn, which meant I had an hour to kill until my weekly date with my other favorite blond vampire.

My first task—taking care of basic vampiric necessities. I walked down the hallway to the second-floor kitchen, smiling at a couple of vaguely familiar-looking vampires as I passed them. Each of the House's aboveground floors had a kitchen, a very handy thing since vampiric emergencies didn't respect cafeteria hours. I opened the fridge and plucked out two drink boxes of type A blood (prepared by the lamely named Blood4You, our delivery service), then headed back to my room. Most vamps were fortunate enough to retain a pretty good hold on their bloodlust, me included. But just because I wasn't ripping at the seams of the boxes didn't mean I didn't need the blood. Most of the time, bloodlust in vamps was kind of like thirst in humans; if you waited to drink until you were truly thirsty, it was probably already too late.

While waiting for her highness's arrival, I poked a straw into one of the drink boxes and pored through the stack of books that was beginning to crawl its way up my bedroom wall. It was my TBR—my To Be Read stack. The usual subjects were there. Chick lit. Action. A Pulitzer Prize winner. A romance novel about a pirate and a damsel in a low-cut blouse. (What? Even a vampire enjoys a little bodice ripping now and again.)

Even though I'd spent the final hours of more than a few evenings in my vampire dorm room, my TBR stack hadn't gotten any shorter. With each book I finished, I found a replacement in the House's library. And I'd occasionally wake at dusk to find a pile of books outside my door, presumably left by the House librarian, another Novitiate vampire. His selections were usually related to politics: stories about the ancient conflicts between vampires and shape-shifters; biographies of the one hundred most vampire-friendly politicians in Western history; time lines of vampiric events in history. Unfortunately, no matter how serious the topic, the names were usually just silly.

Get to the Point: Vampire Contributions in Western Architecture.

Fangs and Balances: Vampire Politicians in History.
To Drink or Not to Drink: A Vampire Dialectic.
Blood Sausage, Blood Stew, Blood Orange: Food for All Seasons.

And the awfully named *Plasmatlas*, which contained maps of important vampire locales.

Maybe the managing editor of the vampire press was the same guy who wrote the chapter titles for the *Canon of the North American Houses*, my vampire guidebook. Both were equally punny—and just as ridiculous.

The names aside, let's be honest—with Ethan running around the House, there were definitely advantages to reading in my room. Was it Master avoidance? Absolutely. But when faced with the temptation of something you couldn't have, why not find something more productive to do?

Put another way, why order dessert if you couldn't take a bite?

So there I was—in a tank and boxers—cross-legged on my bed with *To Drink or Not to Drink* in hand, the rain pummeling the roof above me. I sighed, leaned back against the pillows, and sank into the words, hoping that I might find something moderately edutaining. Or infotaining.

Whatever.

An hour later, Lindsey knocked, and I dog-eared the book (a bad habit, I know, but I never had a bookmark handy).

The book had actually been informative, discussing the earliest recorded instances of a condition the author called hemoanhedonia—the inability to take pleasure from drinking blood. Vamps with the condition tended to demonize those who drank. Add that to the fact that being a "practicing" vampire was dangerous in its own right—humans didn't usually take kindly to being treated like sippy cups—and vampires began drinking together privately, away from the criticism. Abracadabra, raves are born.

With that historical nugget in mind, I put the book on the nightstand and opened the door.

Lindsey, fellow guard and my best friend in the House (assuming Ethan didn't count, and I don't think he did), stood in the hallway with a blond ponytail, killer figure, and silly smile on her face. She wore jeans and a black T-shirt with CADOGAN printed in white block letters across the front. Her feet were bare, her toenails painted gleaming gold.

"Hi, blondie."

"Merit. I like those duds." She cast an appraising glance at my ILLINOIS IS FOR LOVERS! tank top and shamrock-patterned Cubs shorts.

"Off-duty Cadogan Sentinel at your service. Come on in."

She hit the bed. I shut the door behind her.

One of our earliest dates as new friends had been a night in her room with pizza and reality television. It wasn't exactly cerebral, but it gave us a chance to be silly for a little while, to be concerned with which celebutante was dating which rock star or who was winning this week's crazy challenge . . . instead of worrying about which groups of people were trying to kill us. The latter was exhausting after a while.

I flipped on my tiny television (my Sentinel stipend at work) and changed the channel to tonight's reality opera, which involved male contestants solving puzzles so they could escape from an island of ex-girlfriends.

It was high-quality stuff. Classy stuff.

I joined Linds on the bed and pulled a pillow behind my head.

"How was the meeting with Tate?" she asked.

"Drama, drama, drama. Luc will fill you in. Suffice it to say, Ethan could be in Cook County lockup next week."

"Sullivan may have a heart of coal, but I bet he looks really good in orange. And stripes. *Rawr,*" she said, curling her fingers like a cat.

Lindsey was even less convinced that Ethan had had a legitimate post-breakup change of heart. But that didn't make him any less pretty.

"I'm sure he'll appreciate your compliments when he's climbing into that jumpsuit," I said. "Although Luc might get jealous."

As a guard, Luc was Lindsey's boss. He was tall and tousle-haired, his dark blond locks sun streaked from years, I imagined, as a boots-wearing cowboy on some high-plains ranch where cattle and horses outnumbered humans and vampires. Luc kept the boots after becoming a vampire, and he'd developed a monumental crush on Lindsey. Long story short, nothing had come of it until the attack on the House. Then they started spending more time together.

I didn't think it was überserious—more like a movie night here, a snack at sunset there. But it did seem like he'd finally managed to push through the emotional barriers she'd erected to keep him at a distance. I completely approved of that development. Luc had pined pretty hard; it was about time he tasted victory.

"Luc can take care of himself," Lindsey said, her voice dry.

"He'd enjoy it more if you were doing the caring."

Lindsey held up a hand. "Enough boy talk. If you keep harping about Luc, I'm going to hit you with a Sullivan one-two combination, in which case I'll be quizzing you about his hot bod and emotional iciness for the rest of the evening."

"Spoilsport." I pouted, but let it go. I knew she wasn't completely convinced about Luc, even if she was spending more time with him, and I didn't want to push her too far too fast. And to be fair, just because I thought they'd be good together didn't mean she was obligated to date him. It was her life, and I could respect that.

So I let it go and settled into a comfy position beside her, and then let my mind drift on the waves of prerecorded, trashy television. As relaxation went, it didn't exactly rank up there with a hot-rock massage and mud bath, but a vampire took what a vampire could get.

CHAPTER FIVE

DOWN BY THE RIVER

When I awoke again, I dressed in my personal uniform—jeans and a tank top over high-heeled boots, my Cadogan medal, my sword, and my beeper—and headed out.

I stopped at the House gate, intending to get a sense of the gauntlet I'd have to walk to get to my car. One of the two fairies at the gate guessed my game.

"They are quiet tonight," he said. "Ethan planned ahead."

I glanced over at him. "He planned ahead?"

The fairy pointed down the street. I peeked outside the gate, smiling when I realized Ethan's strategy. A food truck hawking Italian beefs was parked at the corner, a dozen protesters standing beside it, sandwiches in hand, their signs propped against the side of the truck.

Ethan must have made a phone call.

"Hot beef in the name of peace," I murmured, then hustled across the street to my ride, a boxy orange Volvo. The car was old and had seen better days, but it got me where I needed to go.

Tonight, I needed to go south.

You'd think a name as fancy as "Ombudsman" (which really meant "liaison") would have gotten my grandfather a nice office in some fancy city building in the Loop.

But Chuck Merit, cop turned supernatural administrator, was a man of the people, supernatural or otherwise. So instead of a swank office with a river view, he had a squat brick building on the South Side in a neighborhood where the lawns were surrounded by chain-link fences.

Normally, the street was quiet. But tonight, cars spilled across the office's yard and down the street a couple of blocks. I'd seen my grandfather surrounded by cars before—at his house in the midst of a water-nymph catfight. Those vehicles had been roadsters with recognizable vanity plates; these were beat-up, hard-driven vehicles with rusty bumpers and paint splatter.

I parked and made my way across the yard. The door was unlocked, unusual for the office, and music—Johnny Cash's rumbling voice—echoed throughout.

The building's decor was all 1970s, but the problems were modern and paranormally driven. So, I assumed, were the boxy men and women who mingled in the hallways, plastic cups of orange drink in hand. They turned and stared at me as I wove through them, their smallish eyes watching as I walked down the hallway. Their features were similar, like they might have been cousins related by common grandparents. All had slightly porcine faces, upturned noses, and apple cheeks.

On my way back to the office Catcher shared with Jeff Christopher—an adorable shifter with mad tech skills and a former crush on me—I passed a large table of fruit: spears of pineapple and red-orange papaya in a watermelon bowl; blood orange slices dotted with pomegranate seeds; and a pineapple shell full of blueberries and grapes. Snacks for the office guests, I assumed.

"Merit!" Jeff's head popped out from a doorway, and he beckoned me inside. I squeezed through a few more men and women and into the office. Catcher was nowhere in sight.

"We saw you on the security monitor," Jeff said, moving to the chair behind his bank of computer monitors. His brown hair was getting longer, and nearly reached his shoulders now. It was straight and parted down the middle, and currently tucked behind his ears. Jeff had paired a button-up shirt, as he always did, with khakis, his shirtsleeves rolled up to his elbows, presumably to give him room to maneuver over his monstrous keyboard. Jeff was tall and lanky, but what he lacked in mass he more than made up for in fighting skills. He was a shifter, and a force to be reckoned with.

"Thanks for finding me," I told him. "What's going on out there?"

"Open house for river trolls."

Of course it was. "I thought the water nymphs controlled the river?"

"They do. They draw the lines; the trolls enforce them."

"And the fruit?"

Jeff smiled. "Good catch. River trolls are vegetarians. Fruitarians, really. Offer up fruit and you can lure them out from beneath the bridges."

"And they prefer not to leave the bridges."

I glanced back. Catcher stood in the doorway, plate of fruit in hand and, just as Mallory had said, rectangular frames perched on his nose. They were an interesting contrast with the shaved head and pale green eyes, but they totally worked. He'd gone from buff martial arts expert to ripped smart-boy. The Sentinel definitely approved. I also approved of his typically snarky T-shirt. Today's read I GOT OUT OF BED FOR THIS?

"Mr. Bell," I said, offering a small salute to my former katana trainer. "I like the glasses."

"I appreciate your approval." He moved to his desk and began stabbing the fruit with a toothpick.

So, Catcher was a sorcerer, and Jeff was a shifter. Vampires were also represented, at least partly. Because Chicago's Masters were pretty tight-lipped about House goings-on, my grandfather had a secret vampire employee who offered up information—a vampire I suspected, largely without evidence, was Malik.

"Do they live under the bridges?" I wondered aloud, returning to the trolls.

"Rain or shine, summer or winter," Catcher said.

"And why the open house? Is that just maintaining good supernatural relations?"

"Now that things are escalating," Catcher said, frowning as he used the toothpick to push out the seeds from a chunk of watermelon, "we're working through the phone book. Every population gets a visit—an evening with the Ombudsman."

"Things are definitely changing," Jeff agreed.

"Things are getting louder."

We all looked back as a broad-shouldered river troll with short, ginger hair looked into the office. His wide-set eyes blinked curiously at us. He didn't have much neck to speak of, so his entire torso swiveled as he looked us over. A light breeze of magic stirred the air.

"Hey, George," Catcher said.

George nodded and offered a small wave. "It's getting louder. The voices. The talk. The winds are changing. There's anger in the air, I think." He paused. "We don't like it." He shifted his gaze to me, a question in his eyes: Was I part of the problem? Making the city louder? Adding to the anger?

"This is Merit," Catcher quietly explained. "Chuck's grand-daughter."

Awareness blossomed in George's expression. "Chuck is a friend to us. He is . . . quieter than the rest."

I wasn't entirely sure what George meant by "quiet"—I had the sense it meant more to him than simply the absence of sound—but it was clear he meant it as a compliment.

"Thank you," I said with as much sincerity as I could push into those two words.

George watched me for a moment. Thinking. Evaluating, maybe, before he finally nodded.

The act seemed to carry more significance than just an acceptance of my thanks—like I'd been approved by him. I nodded back, my act just as significant. We were two paranormal creatures—members of different tribes, but nevertheless linked together by the city's drama and an Ombudsman trying diligently to stem the tide—accepting each other.

The connection made, George disappeared again.

"Soft-spoken," I commented when he was gone.

"They are," Jeff said. "The RTs keep to themselves, except when the nymphs request it. And even then, they appear, they work the task, and they head back beneath the bridges again."

"What kind of things do they do?"

Jeff shrugged. "Generally they do the heavy lifting. Playing muscle for a nymph along her chunk of the river if there's a boundary dispute, maybe enforcing the peace, maybe helping clean up that chunk of the river if the waters are moving too quickly."

Apparently done with his explanation, Jeff stretched out to straighten a silver picture frame now on one corner of his desk. I'd previously seen the many-tentacled plush doll that sat atop one of his monitors, but the frame was new.

I walked over and peeked around his desk to get a glimpse of the picture. It was a shot of him and Fallon Keene. They'd apparently hit it off when the Keene family—and representatives of the rest of the Packs—had come to Chicago to decide whether to stay in their respective cities or head off to their ancestral home in Aurora, Alaska. The Packs had voted to stay, and the Keene family hadn't yet returned to their HQ in Memphis. That respite must have given Jeff and Fallon time to get to know each other.

In the picture, Jeff and Fallon stood beside each other in front of a flat brick wall, their fingers intertwined, gazing at each other. And in their eyes—something weighty and important. Love, already?

"You look very happy," I told Jeff.

Crimson rose on his cheeks. "Catcher's giving me crap about moving too fast," he said, keeping his gaze on the monitors in front of him. "But he's one to talk."

"He *is* already living with my former roommate," I agreed.

"Still in the room," Catcher said. "And speaking of things in the room, what brings you by?"

"Just the usual door-darkening crap. First item on the agenda— some kind of G.I. Joe–wannabe organization, led by a man named McKetrick. They set up a roadblock not far from the House. They had full military gear—combat boots, black clothes, black SUVs without license plates."

"No black helicopters?" Jeff asked.

"I know, right? McKetrick has styled himself as some kind of human savior from the vampire invasion. He thinks fangs make us a genetic mistake."

"A mistake he's going to remedy?" Catcher asked.

I nodded. "Precisely. He says his goal is getting vamps out of Chicago and, I assume, filling that vacuum with his sparkling personality."

"We'll do some digging. Find out what we can." Catcher tilted his head curiously. "How'd you get out of the roadblock?"

"Ethan called our favorite Pack members. Keene brought the family and then some."

"Nice," Jeff said. "Um, was Fallon there?"

"She was. But in a Cardinals cap. Can't you do something about that?"

He shrugged sheepishly. "I know how to pick my battles. So no. Oh—and did you hear? Tonya had the baby. A nine-pound boy. Connor Devereaux Keene."

I smiled back at him. Tonya was Gabriel's wife; she'd been quite pregnant the last time I'd seen her, and they'd already decided on "Connor" as a name. "Nine pounds? That's a big boy."

Jeff smiled knowingly. "That's what she said."

Catcher cleared his throat. "What's the second thing?"

"Raves."

They both looked up at me.

"What about them?" Catcher asked.

"That was actually my first question. At best, we have raves popping into the public eye—for real this time."

"And worst?" Catcher asked.

"We have something with the markings of a rave, but that actually involves psycho-vamps committing atrocities against multiple humans. Three supposed deaths so far, but there's no physical evidence."

There was silence in the office.

"You're serious?" Catcher asked, voice grave.

"Aspen serious." I gave them the details on Mr. Jackson and his experience, on the mayor's investigation, and on our visit to his home. It worried me that they didn't already have these details; my grandfather, after all, was the city's supernatural Ombudsman. He should have been the first person Tate called.

"Is it because of me?" I asked. "Is Tate keeping information from him because I'm his granddaughter? Because I'm in Cadogan?"

Catcher pushed away his plate of fruit, propped his elbows on the table, and rubbed his temples. "I don't know, and I really don't like that idea. But I do know Chuck won't be pleased at the possibility that we're a figurehead group, an office Tate keeps open to make sups think he gives a shit—"

"While he's keeping important information from us," Jeff finished.

"On the other hand," Catcher thoughtfully said, "it wouldn't be our job to investigate. That's the role of CPD detectives. But he'd normally give us a heads-up so we could make contact with the Houses or the Rogues." He shook his head. "We always thought Tate was a little cagey. I guess this proves you have to keep one ear to the ground even when you're supposedly in the loop."

"And speaking of keeping an ear to the ground, what's the word on raves? Anything new in the ether?"

He frowned. "I assumed you've talked to Malik or Ethan and you know about the three we tracked?"

"I've heard," I growled out.

With a nod, Catcher rose and went to a whiteboard newly installed on one end of the office, uncapped a green marker, and began writing. Accompanied by the squeak of the pen, he started by drawing what looked like an angled, limp fish.

"What's that?"

"Chicago," he said without turning around.

"Seriously? That's how you represent the city you work for? As a fish?"

"It really does look like a fish," Jeff said excitedly. "Oh, maybe it's an Asian carp. Are you making a metaphor about raves and invasive species?"

"Clever," I said with a smile for Jeff.

He leaned back in his chair, smiling proudly. "That's what the ladies say."

I rolled my eyes and turned back to Catcher, who was glaring at both of us above his Buddy Holly glasses. I had to bite my lip to keep from laughing aloud.

"As I was saying," he continued, before placing stars on the map in different locations, "we know about three new raves in the last two months."

"Intel from the secret vampire?" I wondered aloud.

"Two of them," Catcher admitted. "The third from Malik. All were second- or thirdhand reports."

Okay, so that pretty much blew my Malik-is-the-secret-source theory.

"There's also the rave we visited along the lakeshore," Catcher added, placing another star on the board.

We didn't find out about that one until after the rave was over and the vamps had closed up shop. As a result, we only walked away with a guess about the number of attendees and a clue as to who'd also investigated—the Red Guard and a shifter we later learned had been our blackmailer.

"There are also the raves we knew about before we visited that rave. And the one Tate identified. It was in West Town."

Catcher nodded, grabbed a blue marker, and filled in those stars.

I squinted at Catcher's "drawing," but still couldn't make heads or tails of it. Except that it still looked like a fish. "Could you at least show us where Navy Pier is?" I asked him. "I have no idea what I'm looking at."

Catcher grumbled, but obliged, and drew a tiny rectangle poking out from one side of the fish.

Jeff chuckled. "Is that Navy Pier, or is Chicago just happy to see me?"

I laughed so hard I snorted a little, at least until Catcher pounded a fist on the top of the closest table.

"Hey," I objected, pointing at him, "my Master might be in Cook County lockup by the end of the week, and that won't exactly be good for me. Sarcasm is my way of relieving stress, as you know, since you've seen me and Mallory at it."

Ironically, saying the jail bit aloud again made my stomach crumple with nerves. But Catcher's expression softened. He glanced back at the board, a smile at one corner of his mouth. "I guess it does look kind of ridiculous."

"And since you've acknowledged that, you may continue," I magnanimously offered.

"So the raves," he said without delay, "are sprinkled across the city. No apparent pattern. No apparent locus of activity."

"That's telling in itself," I said, sitting up. "That says there's no rave headquarters, not where the parties are held, anyway, and that the vamps are smart enough to move the party around."

"So no humans or Masters—if these are Housed vamps—get suspicious," Jeff added.

"Exactly," Catcher said.

"What about the size?" I asked. "The scale? Mr. Jackson was convinced there were dozens of vamps there, and that the entire thing was *American Psycho* violent."

"Just like the site we visited, our current intel says raves are a handful of vamps and a few humans. Small, intimate. Focused on the act of giving and accepting blood. To continue the movie analogy, this isn't *Fight Club*."

"More like *Love at First Bite*," Jeff said.

Catcher rolled his eyes again. "So this new incident we're

talking about is something unprecedented in terms of size and violence, without matching missing persons reports, and no actual evidence of a crime." He shrugged. "That suggests Mr. Jackson wasn't entirely honest. Problem is, we haven't talked to any vampires who were actually there. That would be the real coup—getting someone in from the beginning. On the ground floor. Figuring out who's there, how the information is being passed, who's participating, and whether they're participating willingly."

"Can you pull in data from the CPD?" I asked. "See what their files have to say?"

"Done and done," Jeff said, sitting forward and beginning to tap on his keyboard. "I might have to dig a little to find it—their IT architecture is for shit—but I'll let you know."

Of course, just because the Ombud's office didn't have information didn't mean there wasn't information to be had. It was probably time to tap my next source. . . .

"Thanks," I told both of them. "Can you give me a call if you hear anything else?"

"Of course. I assume Sullivan's going to send you out on some sort of crazy psycho-vampire-hunting field trip?"

"The forecast is strong."

"Call me if you need backup," Catcher said.

"Of course," I agreed, but I actually had an idea about that, as well. After all, Jonah had been offered up as a partner.

"And if you do go," Catcher added, "look for identifying information, listen for any word about how they're contacting vamps or identifying humans."

"Will do."

"You want me to find Chuck before you leave?" Jeff asked.

I waved him off. "No worries. He's busy. Let him handle his open house."

"I'm pretty sure I can manage a job and family both," said a gravelly voice at the door. I glanced back and smiled as my grandfather walked into the office. He was dressed up tonight, having traded in the long-sleeved plaid shirt for a corduroy blazer. But he'd stuck with the khaki pants and thick-soled grandpa shoes.

He walked over to where I sat at the edge of the desk and planted a kiss on my forehead. "How's my favorite vampire?"

I put an arm around his waist and gave him a half hug. "Are there any others in the running?"

"Now that you mention it, no. They tend to be rather high maintenance."

"Amen," Catcher and Jeff simultaneously said.

I gave them a snarky look.

"What brings you to our neck of the woods?"

"I was filling in Catcher and Jeff about our latest drama. Long story short, black ops and raves two-point-oh."

He grimaced. "That wouldn't thrill me even if I weren't your grandfather."

"Nope," I agreed.

"I hate to be the bearer of bad news myself," he said, "but your father tells me you haven't spoken in a few weeks."

I didn't care for my father, but I cared even less for the fact that he'd put my grandfather in the middle of our feud.

"Actually, I saw him leaving the mayor's home last night. We had a very pleasant exchange," I assured my grandfather.

"Good girl," he said with a smile.

I hopped off the desk. It was time to get the rest of the investigative show on the road. "I need to run, and you need to get back to your party, so I'll let them fill you in on the details."

"As if there's a chance I could avoid it," my grandfather said. He hugged me one more time, then let me go.

I said my goodbyes and walked back to the front door, the river trolls nodding at me when I passed as if I'd been vetted. Not as a vampire, maybe, but at least the granddaughter of a man they trusted.

Friends in high places definitely helped—especially if you had enemies in even higher spots.

My phone rang just as I was getting back into my car. I pulled the door shut and flipped it open. It was Mallory.

"Hey, Blue Hair. What's up?"

She didn't speak, but she immediately began sobbing.

"Mal, what's wrong? Are you okay?"

"Catharsis," she said. "It's one of those catharsis cries."

I blew out a breath. I'd been prepared to squeal tires in the rush to get to her if she'd been in danger. But every girl knows the importance of a cathartic cry—when you aren't necessarily crying over something specific, but because *everything* has worked itself into a giant, contorted knot.

"Anything you want to talk about?"

"Kind of. Not really. I don't know. Can you meet me?"

"Of course. Where are you?"

She sniffed. "I'm still in Schaumburg. I'm at the Goodwin's off I-90. I know it's far away, but could you meet me out here? Do you have time?"

Goodwin's was one of those ubiquitous twenty-four-hour restaurants that you saw in office parks and hotel parking lots. The kind frequented by senior citizens at four in the afternoon and teenagers at midnight. I wouldn't call Mallory a foodie, but she definitely had an interest in hip cuisine. If we were meeting at a Goodwin's, she wanted either bland food or anonymity.

I wasn't crazy about either option.

"I'm just leaving the Ombud's office. It'll take me about forty-five to get there. That okay?"

"Yeah. I'm studying. I'll be here."

The studying explained the choice of restaurants. We said our goodbyes and I looked back at the office door for a minute, wondering if I should head back in and warn Catcher that his girl was a stressball. But I was a BFF, and there was a code of honor. A protocol. She'd called me, not Catcher—even though he was in the office and clearly reachable. That meant she needed to vent to me, so that was what we'd do.

"On my way," I muttered, and started the car.

While I drove, I made plans for the second part of my investigation. And that part was a little bit trickier, mostly because I didn't think my source liked me. The first time we'd met, Jonah had been brusque. The second time I discovered him on the dark streets of Wrigleyville, having followed me around so he could get a look at me. Test my mettle, as it were.

The Red Guard had been organized two centuries ago to protect Master vampires, but now operated to keep a watchful eye on the Masters themselves. When Noah Beck, the leader of Chicago's Rogues, made the membership offer, he'd informed me that Jonah, captain of the guards of Chicago's Grey House, would be my partner if I signed up. I was flattered by the offer, but joining a group whose purpose was to keep an eye on Masters would have provoked World War III in Cadogan House. Ethan, if he'd learned of it, would have seen the move as a slap in his face.

I considered myself to be a pretty low-drag vampire; purposefully adding to my stockpile of drama wasn't really my cup of tea.

Jonah, having been singularly unimpressed with me, probably

wasn't bummed that I'd said no. I wasn't expecting this telephone call was going to go any better, but the RG had details on the raves—including the rave they'd cleaned up. And since my visit to the Ombud's office hadn't exactly been productive on an intel-gathering basis (albeit very productive on a river-troll-diplomacy basis), Jonah was a source I needed to tap.

He'd called me once before, so when I was on the move north toward Schaumburg, I dialed his number. He answered after a couple of rings.

"Jonah."

"Hi. It's Merit."

There was an awkward pause. "House business?"

I assumed he was asking if I was calling on behalf of Cadogan House—or our RG connection. "Not exactly. Do you have a minute to talk?"

Another pause. "Give me five minutes. I'll call you back."

The line went dead, so I made sure my ringer was turned on and put the phone in the cup holder while I made my way toward I-90.

Jonah was punctual; the dashboard clock had moved ahead exactly five minutes when he called back.

"I had to get outside," he explained. "I'm on the street now. Figured that would avoid the drama." Scott Grey's vampires lived in a converted warehouse in the Andersonville neighborhood, not far from Wrigley Field. The lucky ducks.

"What's up?" he asked.

I decided to offer up the truth. "Mayor Tate called us into his office yesterday. Told us he had an eyewitness account that a band of vampires had killed three humans."

"Damn." His curse was low and a little tired-sounding. "Anything else?"

"Tate suggested the violence was part of the rave culture. But based on our intel, this sounds different. Bigger. Meaner. If the witness, a Mr. Jackson, was telling the truth, this has the markings of some kind of attack. That it happened at a rave might be the minor issue. In any event, it's time to do something about them, and in order to do that, I need information."

"So you called me?"

I rolled my eyes. The question suggested he was doing me a favor—and that he'd ask for one in return. How very vampire.

"You're my best hope for answers," I matter-of-factly said.

"Unfortunately, I don't have a lot to tell you. I know about the last rave—the one the RG cleaned up—but only because Noah filled me in. I wasn't there."

"Do you think Noah might have any more information?"

"Maybe. But why not just call him directly?"

"Because you were offered up to me as a partner."

Jonah paused. "Is this call an indication of interest in the RG?"

It's a last-ditch effort to glean information, I thought, but offered instead, "I think this is big enough that it transcends Houses or RG membership."

"Fair enough. I'll ask some questions and get back to you if I learn anything. I assume you won't tell anyone we've talked."

"Your secret is safe with me. And thanks."

"Don't thank me until I dig something up. I'll be in touch."

The line went dead, so I tucked the phone away. There were more drama and complications with each day that passed.

Rarely did a night pass without more vampire drama.

Sometimes hanging out in pajamas with a good book sounded like a phenomenal idea.

The phone rang again almost immediately after I'd hung up. I glanced at the screen; it was my father.

I briefly considered sending him directly to voice mail, but I'd been doing that a lot lately—enough that my lack of communication hit my grandfather's radar. I didn't want my problems on his plate, so I sucked it up, flipped open the phone, and raised it to my ear.

"Hello?"

"I'd like to speak with you," my father said, apparently by way of greeting.

That was inevitably true. I'm sure my father had a number of topics in the queue for me. The trick was figuring out which particular topic was on his mind today.

"About?" I asked.

"Some things on the horizon. I've become aware of some investments in which I think Ethan might be interested."

Ah, that explained the good humor at Creeley Creek. If there was anything that made my father happy, it was the possibility of a capital gain and a fat commission. Still, I did appreciate that he was interested in working with Ethan—instead of trying to bury us all.

"We're in the middle of something right now. But I'll definitely advise Ethan of your offer."

"He can call me in the office," my father said. He meant his skyscraper on Michigan Avenue across from Millennium Park. Only the best real estate for the city's best real estate mogul.

With that bit of instruction, the line went dead.

If only we could have picked our family . . .

＊—＊ ❡❊❡ ＊—＊

CHAPTER SIX

SEASON OF THE WITCH

I pulled into the restaurant's almost empty parking lot. The restaurant's windows glowed, only a handful of men and women visible through the glass.

I parked the Volvo and headed inside, glancing around until I found Mallory. She sat at a table in front of a laptop computer and a foot-high stack of books, her straight, ice blue hair tucked behind her ears. She frowned at the screen, a half-full tumbler of orange juice at her side.

She glanced up when I came in, and I noticed the dark circles beneath her eyes.

"Hi," she said, relief in her face.

I slid into the booth. "You look tired." No need to equivocate when your BFF was in pain, I figured.

"I am tired." She closed the laptop and slid it out of the way, then linked her hands on the table. "Practicum isn't all it's cracked up to be."

I crossed my legs on the bench. "Hard work?"

"Physically and emotionally exhausting." She frowned over at the pile of books. "This is like sorcery boot camp—learning stuff I should have studied ten years ago, cramming all that into a few-month period."

"Is it useful stuff?"

"Yeah. I mean, I've gone over it with my tutor so much it's kind of second nature now."

Before I had time to blink, the plastic salt and pepper shakers were sliding across the table in front of me.

I glanced up and found Mallory completely still, her expression bland. I'd seen Mallory move things before—furniture, the last time—but I hadn't seen her so lackadaisical about it.

"That's . . . impressive."

She shrugged, but there was something dark in her eyes. "I can do it almost without thinking about it."

"And how do you feel about that?"

That was when the tears began to well. She looked up and away, as if the gesture alone would keep the tears from falling. But they slipped down her cheeks anyway. And when she brushed away the tears, I realized her fingers were red and raw.

"Talk to me," I told her, then glanced around. Our corner of the restaurant was empty; the only waitress in sight sat at a table on the other side of the room, rolling silverware into paper napkins. "It's practically just me and you in here."

That unleashed a new flood of tears. My heart clenched at the thought that she'd done or seen things in the last couple of weeks that had brought her to tears—and that I probably couldn't have stopped it.

I got up and moved to her side of the table, waiting until she slid down before I took a seat beside her.

"Tell me," I said.

"I don't know who I am anymore."

I couldn't help it; I smiled. If there was ever a problem I could understand as a newbie vampire, that was it. I bumped my forehead against her shoulder.

"Keep going."

The floodgates opened. "I was this girl, right? Doing my thing. Having blue hair, working my ad-exec mojo. And then you're a vampire, and Ethan Sullivan is touching my hair and telling me I have magic. And then there's Catcher and I'm a witch and I'm learning Keys and how to throw flaming balls of crap at targets so I'm ready when the vampire shit inevitably hits the fan."

She sucked in air, then started again. "I was supposed to be a partner at thirty, Merit. Have a condo on the lake. Have a Birkin bag and generally be satisfied with my very fancy lot. And now I'm doing"—she looked around—"magic. And not just magic."

Another tear slid down her cheek.

"What do you mean, not just magic?"

Her voice dropped an octave. "You know about the four Keys, right?"

"Sure. Power, beings, weapons, text."

"Right. Those are the four major divisions of magic. Well, turns out it's not that simple—those aren't the only major divisions."

I frowned at her. "So what are the others?"

She leaned in toward me. "They're black magic, Merit. The bad stuff. There's an entire system of dark magic that overlays the four good Keys." She grabbed a napkin and uncapped a pen. "You've seen Catcher's tattoo, right?"

I nodded. It was across his abdomen, a circle divided into quadrants.

She sketched out the image I'd seen, then pointed at the four pielike segments. "So each quadrant is a Key, right? A division of magic." She pulled another napkin from the holder and unfolded it, then drew another divided circle. When she was done, she placed the second napkin on top of the first one.

"It's the same four divisions—but all black magic."

This time, my voice was softer. "Give me something to go on, here. What kind of black magic are we talking? Elphaba, Wicked Witch of the West–type stuff or Slytherin-type stuff?"

She shook her head. "I can't tell you."

"You can tell me anything."

She looked over at me, frustration clear in her face. "Not *won't* tell you, *can't* tell you. There's Order juju at work. I know things, but I can't get them out. I can summon up the phrases in my head, but can't actually give voice to the words."

I did not like the sound of that—the fact that the already-secretive Order was using magic to keep Mallory from talking about the things that worried her. Dark things.

Regrettable things?

"Is there anything I can do?"

She shook her head, eyes on her hands on the table.

"Is that why your hands are so chapped?"

She nodded. "I'm tired, Merit. I'm training, and I'm learning what I can, but this—I don't know—it uses you differently." She clenched her hands into fists and then released them again. "It's a whole different kind of exhausting. Not just body. Not just mind. Soul, too, kind of." Her eyebrows knotted with worry.

"Have you talked to Catcher about any of this?"

She shook her head. "He's not in the Order. I can't tell him anything I can't tell you."

I suddenly had an understanding of why Catcher wasn't such a big fan of the Order—and why it mattered whether he was still a member or not.

"How can I help?"

She swallowed. "Could we just sit here for a little while?" She sighed haggardly. "I'm just tired. And I have exams coming up, and there's so much prep to do—so many expectations on me right now. I just don't want to go home. Not back to my life. I just want to sit in this crappy corporate restaurant for another couple of hours."

I put my arm around her shoulders. "As long as you want."

We sat in the booth for an hour, barely talking, Mallory sipping orange juice from her cup and staring out the window at the rare car that passed the restaurant.

When her tumbler was empty, I bumped her shoulder again. "He loves you, you know. Even if it feels like something you can't take to him, you can. I mean, I get that you can't give him the details, but you can tell him this is worrying you."

"You know that for sure?"

I caught the tiny thread of hope in her voice and tugged. "I know that for sure. It's Catcher, Mallory. Crazy stubborn? Sure. Gruff? Absolutely. But also totally in love with you."

She sniffed. "Keep going."

"Remember what you told me about Ethan? That I deserved someone who wanted me from the beginning? Well, Catcher Bell is your somebody. He would snap anyone who came at you in half, and that's been obvious since the second he met you. There's not a doubt in my mind that he's all in, and there's nothing you can't tell him. Well," I added with a smile, "unless you become a vamp. That would probably be a deal breaker."

Mal made a half laugh, half cry and wiped her face again.

"I assume you're not making secret plans to become a vampire?"

"Not right at this moment."

"Good. I think one vamp in the family is plenty enough."

"Concur on that one. It's just . . ." She paused, then started again. "There are very few decisions in my life that I regret. Not grabbing that vintage Chanel we saw at that consignment store on Division. Not watching *Buffy* until the third season. Minor stuff, but you know what I mean." She shook her head. "But this. Being ID'd as a sorcerer, agreeing to go along with this stuff, taking part in things—I don't know. Maybe I should have just ignored the whole thing. Kept on with the ad gig and ignored the vampires and the sorcery and Ethan touching my hair. I mean, who does that? Who touches someone's hair and pronounces they have magic?"

"Darth Sullivan."

"Darth goddamned Sullivan." She chuckled a little, then put her head on my shoulder. "Did you ever wish you could just walk away? Rewind your life back to the day before you became supernaturally inclined and catch an Amtrak out of town?"

I smiled a little, thinking of what Ethan had said. "The thought has occurred to me."

"All right," she said, putting her palms flat on the table and blowing out a breath. "It's time for a pep talk. Ready, set, *go*."

That was my cue to call adult swim at the pity pool and kick her out—and then offer up a little motivational magic of my own.

"Mallory Carmichael, you're a sorceress. You may not like it, but it's a fact. You have a gift, and you are not going to sit around a Goodwin's drinking fifty-nine-cent coffee because you've got concerns about your assignments. You're a sorceress—but you're not a robot. If you have concerns about your job, talk to someone about it. If you think something you're doing flunks the smell test, then stop doing it. Break the chain of command if that's what it takes. You have a conscience, and you know how to use it."

We sat quietly there for a moment, until her decisive nod.

"That's what I needed."

"That's why you love me."

"Well, that and we wear the same shoe size." She swiveled in her seat and pulled up a knee. Her foot, now propped on the seat, was snug inside a pair of lime green, limited-edition Pumas . . . one of the pair I'd left at Mal's house when I'd moved into Cadogan.

"Are those—"

"What they are is *so* comfy."

"Mallory Delancey Carmichael."

"Hey, Street Fest is this weekend," she suddenly said. "Maybe we could head down and nosh some meat on a stick."

Street Fest was Chicago's annual end-of-summer food bash. Restaurants and caterers put up their white vinyl tents in Grant Park to hawk their wares and celebrate the end of August's roasting heat and steamy humidity. Normally, I was a pretty big fan. Sampling Chicago's finest grub while listening to live music wasn't exactly a bad way to spend an evening.

On the other hand, "Are you trying to distract me with roast beast?"

She batted her eyelashes.

"Seriously, Mallory. Those shoes are limited edition. Do you remember how long I tried to find them? We staked out the Web for, like, three weeks."

"Epistemological crisis here, Mer. Seriously. One cannot tread lightly in cheap knockoff sneaks when one is enmeshed in a crisis."

I sighed, knowing I'd been beaten.

As it turned out, she didn't have two hours in her. She needed only twenty more minutes before she was ready to return to her life—to Keys and magic and Catcher. She decided to make an early night of practicum, and instead put in a call to Catcher that was sickly sweet enough that my blood sugar rose.

But however sickening, she was smiling by the end of the call, so I had to give props to Catcher. We exchanged hugs in the parking lot, and I sent her home to Wicker Park and the waiting arms of a green-eyed sorcerer.

Whatever worked.

Ironic, I guess, that I was heading back to the House of a green-eyed vampire, although definitely not—to his chagrin—his waiting arms. I was nearly back in that vampire's territory when my phone rang again.

"Merit," I answered.

"Something's going on tonight," Jonah said.

"A rave?"

"Might start out that way. But if these things really are as violent as you're hearing . . ."

He didn't need to finish the sentence, unfortunately. The implication was obvious—and bad.

"How did you find out?"

"Text message. A flashmob, just like the others."

"And this time we got in early enough?" I wondered aloud.

"This time we got lucky and found the phone," Jonah said. "Someone left it at Benson's."

"Benson's, as in across-the-street-from-Wrigley-Field Benson's?"

"Yeah. That's the Grey House bar."

One of the many bars around the stadium that had installed bleachers on its roof, Benson's was, in my opinion, the best spot in town to get a view of Wrigley Field without a ticket.

"Kudos on that one," I said. "I've spent many a fine evening in Benson's."

"And so you were in the company of vampires before you were even aware of them," he said. "How ironic."

I couldn't help but chuckle. He might be pretentious, but Jonah apparently had a sense of humor, as well.

"Anyway, I had the phone in my office, and we didn't think much of it until we got the text. Same format, same message as the others."

"Is the phone useful? Can we trace the number or something?"

"The phone was a disposable, and it hadn't been in use long. The outgoing calls were all to businesses that don't keep track of customer calls. The only incoming was the text. We called that number back, and it's already been disconnected. We haven't been able to find any other information."

Ah, but they didn't have a Jeff Christopher. "Can you give me the number? I've got a friend with some computer skills. Wouldn't hurt to have him look at it."

Jonah read me the digits; I grabbed an envelope and a pen from the glove box and wrote it down, making a mental note to send it to Jeff later.

"So where's the rave?"

"A penthouse in Streeterville."

Streeterville was the part of downtown Chicago that stretched from Michigan Avenue to the lake. Lots of skyscrapers, lots of money, and lots of tourists.

"I am not crazy about the idea of raving vampires in Streeterville."

"Although that would make a good horror-flick title. 'Vampires in Streeterville,' I mean."

A second joke in a matter of minutes. "I'm glad to know you have a sense of humor."

"I'm a vampire, not a zombie."

"Good to know."

"If you're in, meet me at the water tower. Two o'clock."

I checked the dashboard clock—it was barely past midnight, which gave me just enough time to get back to the House, change clothes, and head out again. "I'll be there," I assured him. "Weapon-wise, what should I bring? Sword or hidden dagger?"

"I'm surprised at you, Sentinel. Vampires generally don't use hidden blades."

He was right. Hidden blades were considered a dishonorable way to fight. I heard the question in his voice: *Are you an honorable soldier?*

Admittedly, carrying a hidden blade didn't pass the smell test I'd just told Mallory to use, but what could I do?

"The hidden-blade taboo was made before Celina got a wild hair and decided to out us to the world. I can fight without steel if necessary, but I'd prefer to have backup." I think I'd proven that point pretty well last night. And to think—only a few months ago, I'd been a graduate student in English lit. Go figure.

"Well put."

A thought occurred to me. "I can't tell Ethan I'm visiting a rave alone, and I certainly can't tell him I'm going with you if you want to keep your RG membership a secret."

"Maybe you should substitute Noah in the version you tell Ethan."

Since Noah was the de facto leader of Chicago's Rogue vampires, that made sense. Of course, I'd still have to lie to Ethan. I wasn't crazy about that idea, but it wasn't fair to rely on Jonah and his intel and then out his RG membership.

"Probably a good idea," I concluded.

"I'll give Noah a call and fill him in," Jonah said. "I'll see you tonight. Call me if you need anything."

I said my temporary goodbyes, sincerely hoping I could make it through the next few hours before meeting Jonah without having to call him for help.

Of course, even if I wasn't calling a vampire for help, I still had to ask a vampire for permission.

The food truck was gone when I returned to the House, and the humans looked tired again. Ethan probably hadn't counted on the truck's second benefit—the post-hot-beef food coma.

I walked past the protesters with a friendly smile and wave, then trotted into the House and headed for Ethan's first-floor office. I found the door open, the office abuzz with activity.

Helen, the House liaison for newbie vamps, stood in the middle of the room, pink binder in hand, directing the flow of sleek new furniture into Ethan's office. The room had been mostly emptied after the attack, the bulk of his furniture reduced to matchsticks. But that was being remedied by the men and women—presumably vampires, given Tate's human-free-House policy—who were carrying in pieces of a gigantic new conference table.

Another vampire I didn't recognize flitted around, offering suggestions to the movers about furniture placement. Since she wore a nubby pink suit that exactly matched Helen's, I assumed she was Helen's assistant.

Ethan sat behind a new desk, his chair pushed back, one ankle crossed over one knee, his gaze on Helen. He watched the two of them work with a mix of amusement and irritation in his expression.

I walked over and noticed the spread of glossy paper on his desk—home-decor catalogs, catering menus, lighting plans. "What's going on?"

"We're preparing."

Hands behind my back, I glanced down at one of the catering menus. "For senior prom? Let me guess—'A Night Under the Stars' is your theme."

Ethan glanced up at me, a line between his eyes. "For the imminent arrival of Darius West."

That floored me. Darius West was the head of the Greenwich Presidium. Since the GP was headquartered near London, I couldn't imagine Darius's arrival in Chicago portended anything good.

That took care of convincing Ethan not to join me and Jonah at the rave tonight. Darius gave me a perfect excuse to keep Jonah in the closet.

But that didn't mean I wouldn't take the opportunity to tweak Ethan. "Yet another surprise visit to Cadogan House?"

He kept his voice low. "As we've discussed, Lacey's visit wasn't a surprise, although it was somewhat accelerated." He looked up at me. "And as we've also discussed, you're the only one I'm interested in."

I wasn't up for this conversation in an empty room, much less a room full of vampires, so I changed the subject. "When will our esteemed leader be here?"

"Evidently in two hours."

I blinked, shocked Ethan wouldn't get a little more advance notice for the arrival of a man we had to call Sire. "And you're just discovering this now?"

Ethan wet his lips, irritation crossing his face. "Darius apparently believed it would be best if he visited the House au naturel, so to speak. No warning meant no time to fake conditions in the House, or some such concern. He wants to see us in our typical home environment."

"Being the knuckle draggers we usually are?"

He smiled thinly. "As you say. He's on a plane—has been since before sunset—and will be here relatively shortly. Helen is preparing an evening meal. There are ... traditions that must be followed."

"Virgin sacrifice?"

"The finest corn-fed, midwestern beef. In copious amounts for Darius and his entourage."

That word tightened my stomach. "When you say entourage—"

"I'm not including Celina. He won't be bringing any other GP members, just his usual traveling staff. He's already got an advance man in Chicago. They'll be staying at the Trump."

"I'm surprised he's not staying here if he wants to keep an eye on things."

Ethan scoffed. "The largest room we have available is the consort suite, and Darius's taste runs to something larger—and more refined."

I hadn't developed much respect for the GP in the relatively few months I'd been a vampire; this info wasn't doing much for my impression of Darius West, either.

Now that he'd explained the furniture shenanigans, it was time to give Ethan a second dose of fun news. I gestured toward Helen and her helpers. "Can I speak to you privately?"

"To discuss?"

"House business."

He glanced up, meeting my gaze for a moment while gauging my request. "Helen," he said, his eyes still on me, "could you give us a moment?"

"Of course." With a smile, she closed her binder. With a twirl of her hand, she rounded up her assistant and the movers.

"You have the floor," he said when the office door closed behind them.

"First matter of business, my father wants to involve you in some kind of investment. Feel free to call him back or not; I only promised that I'd tell you about it."

Ethan rolled his eyes. "That explains his chipperness at Creeley Creek."

"My thoughts exactly. As for the other Creeley Creek business, I visited the Ombud's office. They haven't heard any chatter about violent episodes." I steeled my will and offered up the lie I'd prepared. "Since we've suspected the raves are operated by Rogues, I called Noah."

Ethan paused, probably debating whether it was worth the trouble to scold me for making a call to the leader of the Rogue vampires without his permission. But after a moment, he relented. "Good thinking."

It was a lie, is what it was. And that did not sit well in my stomach or heart. But it had to be done.

"He called a few minutes ago," I added. "He was flashmobbed a time and place for some sort of event tonight."

"A rave?"

I shrugged. "He doesn't know. He only got time and place. A high-rent place in Streeterville. Two a.m."

Ethan pushed back his shirtsleeve and glanced down at his watch. "That's not much time. And with Darius coming in, I can't go, and I can't spare any guards."

"I know. Noah volunteered to go with me."

Ethan watched me for a minute. We'd usually, by circumstance, ended up on our various adventures together. This would be a first for me—an escapade with another vampire.

"I'm not crazy about this idea," he said.

"If Tate's information is correct, we're looking at something bigger and nastier than raves—maybe something the raves are evolving into. We have to figure out what it is. If we don't, you'll be wearing an orange jumpsuit."

"I know." He picked up a black pencil and tapped it absently on the desk before gazing up at me with translucently green eyes. "You'll be careful?"

"I have no interest in ending up on the wrong end of an aspen stake," I promised. "And besides, I took two oaths to serve your House. It wouldn't exactly be kosher of me to skip out just because I was afraid."

His expression softened sympathetically. "Are you?"

"I prefer to avoid violence."

"I know the feeling."

At the sudden knock on the door, we both looked up. Two vamps, unescorted by Helen, stood in the doorway, sharing the weight of a massive marble pedestal.

I glanced at Ethan, eyebrow lifted.

"It belonged to Peter Cadogan," he dryly explained. "We've had it in storage, but Helen thought it would add verve to the room."

"Far be it from me to disagree."

"We can move this in?" one of the vamps asked.

Ethan waved them in. "Of course. Thank you." As they scurried across the floor, marble in hand, he glanced back at me. "Good luck tonight. Report when you're back."

With that, he looked down at his papers, excusing me from his office.

It took me a moment to turn around and head for the door again. It was not that I'd expected a teary goodbye, but we had become de facto partners. I could understand his reticence to talk about raves in front of other vamps, but a few words of wisdom wouldn't have been amiss. I might have been a soldier, but I was still a newbie one . . . and even vampire soldiers were occasionally frightened.

As much as I loved casual, and as steamy as August had been so far, I knew jeans and a cotton tank top weren't going to cut it tonight. We were heading to a rave. At best, it was going to be a party for vamps, and I needed to look the part; at worst, it was going to be a battle of vamps, and I was going to need the protection.

No, tonight was a night for leather. Well, leather pants, at least, since it was much too hot for the full ensemble.

I know, stereotypical vampire. I had that thought every time I pulled the leather out of my closet. But you ask any Harley rider who's experienced road rash, and he'll explain why he wears leather. Because it *works*. Steel can slice, and bullets can pierce. Leather makes those things a little harder to get through.

I pulled a longish, flowy, gray tank top from the closet and paired that with the leather pants, then pulled my hair into a high ponytail, leaving a fringe of bangs across my forehead. I skipped the Cadogan medal—I was attempting to fly undercover, after all—but I pulled a long necklace made of strands of pewter-colored beads over the tank. With my black boots, the ensemble looked half-runway, half–party girl. It didn't scream vampire soldier, which I figured could only help. Element of surprise, and all that.

I slid my dagger, inscribed on one end with my position, into my right boot, then stuck my phone and beeper into a tiny clutch purse. I wouldn't take the purse or the beeper to the event, but at least I wouldn't have to carry a handful of gadgets to the car. En masse, they weren't exactly ergonomic.

I'd just added blush and lip gloss when there was a knock at the door. Luc, I assumed, having been sent upstairs by Ethan for a last-minute strategy session.

"About time," I said, pulling the door open.

Green eyes stared back at me. Ethan hadn't sent Luc upstairs; he'd come on his own. He scanned my outfit. "Date night?"

"I'm trying to fit in with the rest of the partygoers," I reminded him.

"So I see. You've got weapons?"

"A dagger in my boot. Anything else would be too obvious."

The emotion was clear in his eyes, but I needed to stay focused. I kept my voice neutral, my words careful. "I'll be safe. And Noah will have my back."

Ethan nodded. "I've updated Luc. The guards are all on standby. If you call, they come running, immediately. If you need anything, you call one of them. If anything happens to you—"

"I'm immortal," I interrupted, reminding him of the biological clock he'd stopped from ticking. "And I have no interest in taking liberties with my immortality."

He nodded, regret in his eyes. That look made it seem he was seeking a discussion between two lovers, not between boss and employee. Maybe he did have feelings for me. Real ones, unbound by obligation or position. But even if I was interested in pursuing that lead, now was not the time. I had a task to perform.

But before I could remind him of that and send him on his way, he cupped my face in his hands.

"You will be careful." It was an order that brooked no argument. That was convenient, since words failed me.

"You will be careful," he repeated, "and you will stay in touch with me, Luc, or Catcher. Darius will be here, so Malik and I may be indisposed. Get in contact with whomever you can. Take no unnecessary risks."

"I promise I wasn't planning on it. Not because you asked me to," I hastily added, "but because I like being alive."

He clearly wasn't dissuaded, and stroked my jawline with his thumb. "You can run. You can keep running to the ends of the earth. But I won't be far behind you."

"Ethan—"

"No. I will never be far behind you." He tipped up my chin so that I could do nothing else but look back into his eyes. "Do the things you need to do. Learn to be a vampire, to be a warrior, to be the soldier you are capable of being. But consider the possibility that I made a mistake I regret—and that I'll continue to regret that mistake and try to convince you to give me another chance until the earth stops turning."

He leaned forward and pressed his lips to my forehead, my heart melting even as my more rational side harbored suspicions.

"No one said love was easy, Sentinel."

And then he was gone and the door was closed again, leaving me standing there, dumbfounded, staring at it.

What was I supposed to do with that?

+ ◆═══◆ +

CHAPTER SEVEN

MORE HUMAN THAN HUMAN

The Chicago Water Tower sat like a wedding-cake topper in the middle of Magnificent Mile. It had survived the Great Fire, and now it served as a symbol of the city—and a background for tourist photographs.

Jonah leaned against the stone railing beside the steps into the building in trim jeans and a silvery button-up, his gaze on the phone in his hands. His hair was loose around a face that might have been carved by Michelangelo himself—if Michelangelo had sculpted a man who had looked like an Irish god. Perfect cheekbones, thin nose, square jaw, and long almond-shaped blue eyes framed by locks of his auburn hair.

Yes, Jonah was plenty handsome, even with the dour expression that marred his face when he looked up. He tucked the phone into a pocket and moved closer. I watched him look me over, taking in the leather and debating whether I'd be a help or a hindrance on this particular escapade.

"You're early," he said.

I reminded myself to pick my battles. "I prefer early to late. I thought we might want to talk strategy before we go in."

He gestured down Michigan toward the river. "Let's walk and talk."

And so we started down Michigan Avenue, two tall and well-dressed vampires, probably looking like we were on a date instead of planning to infiltrate a vampire blood orgy. And we looked normal enough, apparently, that no one made us out as vamps. Ah, the benefits of nightfall.

"How many vamps?" I asked him.

"I don't know. Raves are pretty intimate affairs, so if this is one, not many."

"If you found the phone with the invite at Benson's, are you thinking it belonged to a Grey House vamp?"

Jonah glowered. "I'm hoping, for the sake of the Grey House vamps, that it didn't. But as you said, the bar has an open-door policy, and we generally keep its House affiliation a secret. So it could have belonged to anyone."

I nodded. "Have you always been in Grey House?"

"I have not. I was born Rogue. Grew up in a rough part of Kansas City. Not the easiest place to come of age. I almost didn't make it out. And then along came Max."

"He's the one who made you a vampire?"

"He was. He helped me escape a bad scene. Well, to the extent inheriting vampire politics and drama is an escape."

"I can relate."

"I figured. No offense, but Sullivan's as political as they come."

I laughed aloud. "Truer words have never been spoken. He's a good Master. Cares deeply about his House." *But to the exclusion of all else*, I silently added.

"And you two—?"

I cut off the question. Most of the Cadogan vamps knew Ethan and I had shared a night together, so it didn't come as much of a surprise that Jonah, member of an espionage group, did, too. But while I appreciated that he was giving me the opportunity to clarify, it irked me that he assumed I'd be a liability, emotionally or otherwise. Starting off with a clean slate would have been nice.

"We are not an item," I assured him.

"Just checking. I like to get a line on any possible complications that might spill my way."

"None from this end," I assured him. Much to Ethan's disappointment.

We separated as a flock of teenagers bounded down Michigan. It was two in the morning, and the stores were long since closed, but it was also a summer night and school hadn't yet started. I suppose wandering Michigan Avenue was a relatively safe activity if you were a teenager with too much time on your hands.

"Anyway, Max was a vampire with Master-worthy power, but no House. The GP considered him unstable and wouldn't give him an official title. They were right about the instability. My guess? Max was bipolar as a human, and becoming a vamp didn't help."

"Can't be a good idea to have him running around Kansas City without oversight."

"And that was exactly the problem. The GP didn't think he was sane enough for a House, but that just meant an ego-driven psychopath was running around making one vamp after another. The creation of Murphy House was a way for the GP to rein in the Rogues and one-up Max. They gave Rich the House and grandfathered us in under some ancient *Canon* provision."

"How'd you end up in Chicago?"

"I transferred to Grey when Scott got his Masterdom. Each new House gets to steal a few Novitiates from the others to help fill it out. They're able to initiate new vamps, as well, obviously, but the trade gives them a start."

"Are you worried someone at the party might recognize you? I mean, you've been around for a while, and if anyone there is from Grey House . . ."

"If anyone there is from Grey House, they'll think I'm there to find them, enforce House rules, and drag them back to rationality—right before I kick their asses. Grey House is not Navarre House. We may enjoy sports, but we respect authority. We're a team—a unit. There's a clear chain of authority, and we follow it."

"And Scott's the coach?"

"And the general," he agreed.

While that might be theoretically true, I thought, Jonah was still a member of an organization whose mission was to secretly police the Masters. That didn't exactly fit the Scott-is-my-general analogy.

"Anyway, no worries on my end," Jonah concluded.

We passed a line of tourists burdened with restaurant leftovers and shopping bags. They looked exhausted, as if it was well past time for them to return to their hotel.

"I've never been to an actual rave before," I said after we passed them. I looked over at him. "Have you?"

"Near one, didn't go in."

"I'm nervous," I confessed.

"I have no objection to nerves before an op," Jonah said. "They keep you sharp. On your toes. As long as you won't freeze up—and from what I've heard about the attack on Cadogan, you aren't going to freeze up."

"I've been good so far."

"So far counts." He came to a stop at the light and pointed to the left. "We'll cross here, then a couple of blocks up."

When the light changed, we walked across the street and headed east, a couple of blocks off Michigan.

"This is it," Jonah said.

It was ... definitely something. The building looked like a gleaming black spear thrust into the banks of the Chicago River—at least up to the top three or four floors. They were still under construction, their skeletal structures wrapped in hazy plastic.

A plywood sign announced the building was the future home of a finance company.

With vampires like these, I thought, *who needs enemies?*

"Today," Jonah said, "we're playing invited guests. Act like you belong." He pushed through the building's revolving door. As I followed, Jonah smiled at the man behind the security desk and sauntered over, looking exactly like he belonged in a penthouse vampire party.

"We're here for the, er, mixer," Jonah casually said.

"Security code?" the uniform asked.

Jonah smiled. "Temptress."

For a second, I thought he'd gotten it wrong. The uniform looked at Jonah, then me, before apparently deciding we were in the building for legitimate reasons, and gesturing toward the elevator. "Top floor. Stay away from the edges. It's a nasty fall."

Jonah walked toward the elevator, then pushed the button. When the car arrived, we slipped inside.

"Are you ready for this?" he asked when the door closed.

"I'm not entirely sure."

"You can do it. Just remember, if this is a rave, our goal isn't to close them down tonight. We step in, and we figure out what Mr. Jackson might have seen. We identify perps, feuds, whatever we can. One step forward is good enough for our purposes."

"That sounds reasonable enough."

"The RG is a very reasonable organization."

"Not that it matters tonight," I pointed out.

"The RG always matters. Our welfare always matters."

The intensity in his voice made me ask, "Is this a test? An RG vetting process?"

The elevator zipped us to the top floor, and a female voice announced "Penthouse suite" as the doors *shush*ed open.

"Only coincidentally," Jonah finally answered, putting a hand at my waist. "Let's go."

I nodded, and we stepped out of the elevator.

To call it a penthouse was vastly overstating it. One day, it might get there. But today, it was a construction site.

The space itself was humongous, a giant, mostly empty rectangle with a center core of steel beams that I assumed marked the places where inner walls would eventually stand. The room itself was darkish, lit by a handful of hanging work lights and the lambent glow of the night-lit city through the plastic that wrapped the exterior walls. The floor was concrete and marked by construction debris, and boxes of materials sat in piles throughout the room.

Altogether, the effect was creepy, like the place in a horror movie where two lovers sneak off to make out—just before the killer bursts through the walls, knife in hand.

I didn't see any humans, but a couple dozen vampires stood in clusters throughout the space, their attire ranging from couture to casual, from Jimmy Choo to thrift-store flannel. With this many vamps in play, it seemed unlikely they were all Rogues without a House connection.

"Do you see anyone you recognize?" I asked Jonah, scanning the crowd for some sign of House affiliation—gold medals on chains for Navarre and Cadogan vamps, jerseys for Grey House vamps. But I didn't recognize any Cadogan vamps, and I saw nothing that gave me any sense of where they otherwise might have come from.

"No one," he absently said.

This magical mystery mix of vampires swayed as the whining guitar of Rob Zombie's "More Human Than Human" buzzed through the air, which was thick with magic. A haze of it, potent stuff, that immediately raised goose bumps on my arms.

"Magic," I murmured.

His fingers tightened at my waist. "A lot of magic. A lot of glamour. Will you succumb?"

I could feel the tendrils of glamour moving around me, checking me out, trying to seep inside. I'd sensed testing magic once before—the first time I met Celina, when she worked me over with magic to get a sense of my power.

But even with Celina, I hadn't sensed this much of it in a single place. I centered myself and forced myself to breathe through it, to relax and let the magic flow as it would. Generally resistance only made glamour harder to resist, like it welcomed the challenge to sway you to its side.

But I didn't think this glamour was trying to convince me of anything. I didn't sense any vampires trying to make me believe they were smarter, prettier, or stronger than they were, or to convince me to give up my inhibitions. Maybe this was just the collective swell of magic leaked from a roomful of vampires. Add that to the resounding bass and zingy guitar, and you had a recipe for a migraine.

I rolled my shoulders and imagined the magic rolling over me like a warm Gulf Coast wave. As it flowed and discovered I didn't offer a game to be won, the wave rolled past. The air still prickled with magic, but I could move through it, instead of vice versa.

"I'll be fine," I quietly told Jonah, my arms and legs tingling.

"You do have resistance," he said, gazing at me with appreciation in his eyes.

"I can't glamour," I confessed. "Resistance is the gift I got. But this feeling, this room, is still wrong. Still off."

"I know."

I made myself throw out the connection I'd already made. "Celina can work this kind of magic. Maybe not the quantity, but it does feel like her. The way it looks into you."

"Good thought. Let's hope we aren't running against her, as well." He released the grip on my waist, but entwined his fingers into mine. "Until we figure it out, stay close."

"I'm right beside you," I assured him.

He nodded, then guided me through the crowd.

A vampire or two glanced over as we walked, but most ignored us. They talked among themselves—their words inaudible, but their gestures making clear the emotion in their eyes. They were ready and waiting for something to begin. It was anticipatory magic.

As we passed one cluster, the vamp closest to us snapped his head to the side to gaze at us. His fangs had descended and his irises were silver, his pupils shrunken to tiny pinpoints, even in the moody lighting.

His upper lip curled, but another vamp in his knot pulled him back and into whatever argument they'd been having.

"I have to admit, this isn't exactly what I expected."

I looked around the space and noticed the plastic had been peeled back at one end of the room, and the opening led to a balcony. "Let's try out there," I suggested. "If humans are here, they're going to want to take in the view."

Jonah nodded his agreement and we maneuvered our way outside. The balcony was empty of furniture—but full of humans.

"Still not exactly what I expected," he muttered.

They were sprinkled here and there, mostly women, probably

under twenty-five or so. Like the vampires, the girls wore every-thing from party dresses and heels to goth ensembles with short skirts and big boots. One girl, a blonde who was a bit taller and curvier than the rest, wore a tiara with white streamers and a pink satin sash across her chest. When the crowd cleared, I could see BRIDE written across it in glittery letters. The girl beside her held her hand, both of them grinning in anticipation.

As nonchalantly as we could, we walked to the edge of the bal-cony, where a railing had been installed. The lake was spread on one side of us, the city on the other. Jonah slid an arm around my waist, and we continued the guise of two lovers enjoying a pre-bloodletting chat.

"A would-be bride looking for a final premarital adventure?" I said quietly.

"Quite possibly. They may be fully aware of what they're get-ting into. Check the wristbands."

I gave the girls another look. Around each of their wrists was a red silicone wristband. "What about them?"

"The bands mark them as vampire sympathizers. The ones who still think we're dark and delicious."

Like high-cocoa chocolate, I thought. "Even as the rest of the city begins to turn against us?"

"Apparently. I support the support, although a plastic bracelet doesn't exactly scream 'long-term political allies.'" He shrugged. "But here they are, and as much as Scott and Morgan may deplore it, drinking from humans isn't a sin."

"Brave words for a non-Cadogan vampire."

Jonah humphed. "I stand by my statement. In any event, we wait until we see something amiss—and then we move in."

I smiled up at him, then tugged playfully on a lock of his au-burn hair, playing the part in which I'd been cast. "Works for me."

He grinned, and the look was effective enough that it made even my hardened heart trip a bit. "And I thought you'd be stubborn and difficult to work with."

This time, I gave him a pinch on the arm I hope looked playful—and not spiteful. "In case you've forgotten, Ethan Sullivan trained me. And in case you didn't know, Catcher Bell schooled me in sword craft. I was raised on 'difficult to work with.'"

He chuckled. "Then you're forgiven."

"So magnanimous."

He put his hand on his heart like a man confessing love. "That's the nature of RG service."

I gave him a quick pat on the cheek. "Darling, I'll just have to take your word for it."

We wandered around the balcony for a while, fingers intertwined, occasionally sharing strategically furtive whispers. If this was a real rave, there was a lot less drum-and-bass and many fewer glow-in-the-dark necklaces than I'd have expected. But pills and powders were still passed around, and there was enough glamour in the air that my skin crawled with it, my neck beginning to ache from my constantly shaking off the peculiar tickle.

We kept an eye on the humans, and from our perch hundreds of feet above the city, we watched the play take shape. Vampires moved in and around the sprinkling of humans, plying them with alcohol and glamour. The vamps were clearly in touch with their predatory instincts—and they acted on them. Once glasses of champagne were passed out, the humans were separated and divided, then escorted, one by one, back into the penthouse. They were probably unaware they'd been singled out like calves from a herd.

On the other hand, we hadn't seen anything that looked remotely like crazed violence. This party was definitely bigger than prior raves, but it wasn't exactly the free-for-all Mr. Jackson had described.

When a tall, dark-haired vamp took one of the goth girls by the hand and led her back through the plastic, Jonah nudged me. "Let's head inside. I'll take her, make sure things stay aboveboard. You keep an eye on the rest of them."

"Will do," I said, ignoring the flutter in my stomach when he kissed my hand and walked back into the room.

I followed him, and I'll admit it: my boy troubles aside, I could appreciate a fine walk on Grey House vampire.

Unfortunately, I'd been doing just that when I found myself surrounded.

＋—◄━►—＋

CHAPTER EIGHT

THE ART OF WAR

It started with a bump, an obviously drunk female vamp stumbling backward. We were inside the would-be penthouse again when she ran into me, pushing me into two guys at my back.

She glanced cattily at me. "Sorry."

"No problem," I said with a tight smile. But when I turned around to apologize to the guys I'd run into, they were even less thrilled.

They were both vamps, both average-looking, both in button-down shirts and jeans, one slightly taller than the other. The taller vamp had dark hair; the shorter one was a blond. They boxed me in, close enough that I could smell their cheap cologne and the faint tang of blood that surrounded them. They'd taken blood recently—but from someone in the room?

I started with politeness. "Sorry. I got bumped."

"Yeah, well, watch where the fuck you're going."

Okay, bit of an overreaction, but we were at a party with a lot of people. Could be they'd been stepped on before and were sick of the crowd.

I smiled lightly. "Sure thing."

The blond guy grabbed my elbow. "That doesn't sound like much of an apology, you know. It doesn't sound like you were truly sorry for running into us."

Was this guy serious? I'd barely bumped him.

I pulled my arm away. "Again, sorry." I glanced casually around, checking both for Jonah and any sign of the girls, but the crowd seemed to have thickened, and neither was in sight. For the first time, I actually wished I'd been with Ethan instead of Jonah. At least he and I could have communicated telepathically.

"I don't appreciate your attitude," the blond guy said.

"I'm sorry?" I offered. "I was just trying to get out of your way." While batting my eyelashes, I looked him over, hoping to find some clue of House affiliation. But there was no medal, no jersey. Out of luck on that front.

"You know the password?" he asked.

"Um, temptress," I said, boredom in my voice. "I'm going to find my date." I turned to step away from the guys and toward the part of the room Jonah had headed into, but the vampires anticipated the move. The dark-haired one moved in front to block me, while the blond one took up point at my back.

"That's not all of it," mumbled the dark-haired guy.

The other one narrowed his gaze. His eyes were in the same shape as the fanged vamp I'd seen earlier—his pupils pinpricks of black amid a sea of silver. These guys were seriously vamped out tonight. Was that a side effect of all the magic in the air? Did my eyes look like that right now?

"What's the other half of the password?" he demanded.

My stomach went cold. Even if Jonah's text message had offered up the rest of the password, I had no clue what it was. I figured offering the wrong word was only going to piss them off more.

It was time to bluff, and since I was dressed for the part, I opted to play party girl.

I wrapped a strand of beads around my finger and leaned forward. "You guys don't seriously need the other half of the password from me, right? My boyfriend was the one who talked to the security dude. Have you seen him anywhere? Reddish hair. Really tall?"

"Everyone's responsible for the password," the dark-haired guy said. "If you don't know it, you don't belong here." I waited until he turned back to me to check his eyes: same as the other two. Completely silvered out, but the pupils constricted like the vamps were staring down the sun.

"And I don't know you," confirmed the blond one, his expression turning cold. That he didn't know me was a little miracle given my previous front-page antics. "I don't like vampires I don't know."

I winked. "Maybe you should get to know me. If my boyfriend approves, I mean."

The two of them exchanged a glance, and then they made their first mistake. The blond vamp wrapped an arm around my waist and yanked me back against him. "Enough with the games. You're coming with me."

I raised my voice to a girlie squeal. "Oh, my God, get your hands *off* me!"

"Aw, fighting's only gonna get him excited, sunshine," said the tall one.

"Not in this lifetime," I muttered, then dug the heel of my boot into the blond guy's foot. He yelled out a string of curses but released me. That's what I'd been hoping for. I took a step away, then looked over at the dark-haired guy with doe eyes.

"He hurt me."

"Yeah, well, it's gonna get worse." He lurched forward, arms outstretched to reach for me, but I wasn't about to get into a fight with some socially obnoxious, magic-drunk vamp at a party I was crashing. I was not, however, too proud to keep my shots above the belt. I put a hand on his shoulder and gave him a knee to the groin that dropped him to his knees.

"Jackass," I muttered, before adopting the squealy tone again. "And you keep your hands to yourself!" I poutily yelled, before stepping over him—curled on the floor, groaning—and hustling into the anonymity of the crowd. I figured I had a good minute or two before they barreled after me, which meant I needed to find Jonah and we needed to jet. I couldn't yet say whether Tate or Jackson had been right about the violence, but some of these vamps were definitely on a hair trigger—and I was in their line of sight.

I glanced around to find some sign of my would-be partner, but he was nowhere to be seen. Still keeping an eye on the girl, probably, but that wasn't going to help me. The crowd had thickened, which was great in terms of sheltering me from the thugs, but not for finding the needle in the vampire haystack.

I decided to make concentric circles around the space. With each turn, I'd move a little closer to the middle. I had to hit Jonah eventually, and hopefully I'd also confuse the guys who thought I was nothing more than a fanged party crasher.

I made my way over to the plastic wall, which was damp with humidity, and began to move forward along it, eyes peeled for any sign of Jonah. I had to bob and weave through the crowd to make progress, but still didn't see him.

What I did see were vampires and humans enjoying one another's company. Random bits of furniture had been placed here and there. Vampires were draped along the furniture, and humans, now brought into the vampire mix, were draped across the vampires. They seemed more than happy to be the center of fanged attention.

And I meant "fanged" literally. A few of the humans had already been tapped—with a vampire at a wrist or attached to someone's carotid. I worked to block out the perk of interest the blood prompted—wishing I'd had a prophylactic drink box before I'd left—and to fight the urge to shake the humans back to their senses. But their expressions fairly screamed consent . . . until I reached one of them who didn't look so interested. I stopped short.

She sat on the concrete floor, her back against a steel post. Her knees were up, her head rolled to the side, eyes slowly blinking, as if she was having trouble focusing on the world around her.

Glamour. A lot of it, if the tingle in the air was any indication.

Humans volunteering to dabble in the dark was one thing. But this looked like something different. Something much less consensual.

Ethan had told me once that glamour was about reducing a human's inhibitions. That a human wouldn't do anything he or she didn't ordinarily want to do. But there was nothing in this girl's eyes that spoke of pleasure . . . or consent.

I'd never drunk from a human before. Of course, I also hadn't really had the urge. My recent experiences with humans hadn't exactly been pleasant. And this girl? Suffice it to say I found nothing even mildly interesting, vampire or not, about biting a girl who seemed to be drugged beyond her capacity to consent to the act. I guess rationality could overcome hunger.

I crouched down in front of her and couldn't see any visible bite marks. While she might have been bitten in some hidden spot, there wasn't any blood in the air.

"Are you all right?" I asked her.

She looked up at me, her eyes orbs of black, her pupils almost fully dilated. The opposite of the vamps' eyes. "I'm perfectly content."

I was pretty confident she didn't actually believe that. "I think that's the glamour talking. Have you—have they—"

"Did they drink my blood, do you mean?" She smiled a bit sadly. "No. I keep hoping they will. Do you think it's because I'm not pretty enough?" She reached out a wobbly hand and touched the end of my ponytail. "You're very pretty."

But then her hand dropped, and her eyes fluttered closed. She looked pale. Too pale. I wasn't sure if glamour was strong enough to actually sicken a human; if not glamour, and not blood loss, maybe something slipped into her drink?

Whatever the reason, I needed to get her out of here.

Her eyes opened again, just a sliver beneath her lashes. "You'll live forever, you know. All vampires do."

"Unfortunately, probably not the ones who get into as much trouble as I do."

I should have knocked on wood after saying that, but at least I smelled old blood on the vampire behind me before he attacked.

I mouthed a silent curse before standing and spinning to face him. He was tall and muscular with dark, curly hair and a chin that fell on the wrong side of too square. There was blood at the corner of his mouth, and I'm proud to say I didn't have the slightest interest in it.

And his eyes—wholly silvered just like those of the other vamps I'd seen.

"Are you poaching, vampire?"

"She's sick," I told him. "This isn't the place for her. You want human blood, find it somewhere else."

The vampires around us began to glance our way, their gazes darting between me and him as if they were trying to work out whose side they should take. He looked around at them, a cajoling smile on his face.

"Aw, do we have a human sympathizer on our hands? Do you feel sorry for the little humans?"

Not so much sorry for as empathetic. I knew what it meant to be drunk without consent. With some luck, I'd made it through my attack, but I wouldn't wish it on anyone else.

Unfortunately, the vampires around me weren't yet convinced.

"I feel sorry for anyone who's not here by choice."

He belly-laughed, one hand pressed to his abdomen as he chortled. "You think any of these humans don't want to be here? You think they wouldn't pay to be here with us? Let the humans call us names. Let the press call us monsters. We are all that they aspire to be. Stronger. More powerful. *Eternal.*"

There were vague mumblings of agreement in the crowd. I'd apparently gone from anti-vampire demonstration to pro-vamp rally in a matter of hours.

You know what I thought? I thought people needed to stop holding on to their blind prejudices and do some rational think-ing. Stop forcing themselves into the mold of the lovers or haters. Some vamps had issues, as this guy was demonstrating, and there were plenty of humans in Chicago—some of them elected—who weren't exactly paragons.

"Enough," I said. "Enough talk. This girl isn't in a state of mind to consent to anything. I'm taking her out of here." I squeezed my hands into fists, preparing myself for battle, and rubbed my calf against the inside of my boot, feeling for the telltale bump of the dagger hidden there.

But the vamp wasn't buying my speech, and clearly wasn't

afraid of me. "You are not my Master, child. Find something else to do. Some pretty boy to bite."

"I'm not leaving her."

He narrowed his gaze and I felt the head rush of his glamour, the loosening of worry and fear, and the urge to find a spot on the floor and offer myself over to him, regardless of the circumstances.

But I kept my eyes trained on his and fought through the dizziness. I straightened my spine and gave him a questioning glance. "Were you trying to do something there?"

He tilted his head at me, interest in his expression. I fought the urge to slink back and hide from his intrigued stare, but as long as I was the target—and the girl wasn't—I figured I could stand it.

"You are . . . interesting."

I almost rolled my eyes, but then I realized the gift he'd handed me. I glanced slyly at him. "Would you like to find out how interesting?" Like a coquettish teenager, I twirled the end of my ponytail, then threw it back over my shoulder, revealing my neck.

As bait went, it might not have been much, but it worked well enough. He dropped his eyes—staring at me beneath hooded lashes—and began stalking toward me like a hunting lion. I'd seen a vampire stalk before—I'd seen Ethan in his prime, moving in my direction with lust in his eyes. This wasn't that kind of lust. This wasn't about love or connection—but control. Ego. Victory.

I stared right back, even as the intensity in his expression made my skin crawl. He would drink—but he wouldn't stop, not until there was nothing left of me or her. Maybe it was the magic in the air that pushed him toward the brink; maybe it was his own predatory instincts. Whatever the reason, I wanted no part of it.

In a silky-smooth move that would have filled Catcher with pride, I whipped a hand around and slid the dagger from its sheath.

And then it was up and in my hand, light pouring down the blade, the steel leaving a comfortable tingle in my palm. I tightened my fingers around the handle.

The vamp finally seemed to realize I was serious. His expression fell.

The dagger in hand, I looked down at the girl. "Can you get up?"

She nodded, tears slipping from her eyes. "I'm okay. But I want to go home."

I reached out my hand. When she grabbed it, I tugged her to her feet. Unfortunately, getting her to her feet didn't help us much. We were still surrounded—by one vamp pissed that I'd poached, and by a dozen more who didn't have a specific interest in the girl but seemed bizarrely eager for a fight.

Was this the violence Mr. Jackson had spoken about?

I swallowed down fear that knotted in my throat, and stood straight, gazing out at the crowd with forced bravery. "I'm taking her out of here right now. Anyone got a problem with that?"

I should have known better than to phrase it in the form of a question.

"Try me, cupcake," said the vamp who wanted me, and cold trickled down my spine. I was strong and fast and immortal, but the girl was not. Even if I fought my way through the crowd, I couldn't fight full out and protect her at the same time.

What I needed, I thought, was a distraction.

His timing couldn't have been better.

"Goddamn it!" I heard across the room, followed by the crash of glass that silenced the rest of the crowd.

The metallic tang of blood filled the air, and all the vamps in the vicinity turned toward the locus of the smell. I saw Jonah through the crowd, staring down a cowering vampire.

Blood had been spilled, maybe from a broken glass or pitcher. Not a bad way to get the attention of vampires—and to give me a way to get to the door.

I looked at the girl on my arm. "What's your name?"

"Sarah," she said. "Sarah."

"Well, Sarah, we're going to make a run for it. You ready?"

She nodded, and as soon as the brawler and the rest of the vamps began to move toward the waves of scent, we bolted.

I understood the draw of the blood. I was beginning to get hungry. We were nearing the end of the evening, and it had been hours since I'd eaten . . . or had blood. The smell was becoming undeniably delicious, so I gnawed on my lip to stay focused, the sharp sting of pain pushing back the hunger. As was so often the case, this wasn't the time or the place.

I guided Sarah through the vampires now rushing toward the blood, her arm over my shoulder, my arm around her waist. We weren't exactly graceful, but we got closer to the door and the edge of chaos.

And chaos had definitely erupted.

The room became a hurricane of violence as vampires stepped and crawled over one another to get to the blood. One angry vampire spurred a brawl with another, and that brawl pushed its way into someone else's conversation, which angered those vampires, as well. The violence traveled like a virus through the room, spreading as it made contact. And as the violence increased, so did the magic—spilling into the air and making the vampires even more predatory than they already had been.

"I thought you might need the cavalry."

I looked to my right, relieved to find Jonah at my side again. "Took you long enough. Thanks for the distraction."

"You're welcome. I didn't exactly expect you to have pulled

a blade and kidnapped a human." He glanced at Sarah. "What happened?"

"Don't know. Drugs? Glamour? I'm not sure. Either way, we need to get her out of here."

"I'm right behind you," he said with a nod, and we made our way to the elevators.

The doors were open when we got there; I helped Sarah inside while Jonah mashed buttons until the doors closed, muting the sounds of fighting behind us. I slipped the dagger back into my boot.

It wasn't until we were halfway down the building again that I let out the breath I'd been holding. I glanced over at Sarah. "Are you okay?"

She nodded. "I'm okay. But all those other people in there. We need to get them out, too."

Jonah and I exchanged a glance.

"Maybe you could call the police?" she asked. "Tell them about the party, and when they come, they can get the rest of the humans out?"

Jonah looked back at me. "If the cops come . . ."

I nodded, understanding his concern. If it took cops to shut this thing down, we'd be swimming in bad press and right back in the mayor's office—assuming Tate hadn't already issued Ethan's warrant.

But maybe we didn't need the cops. Maybe we just needed the fear of the cops. . . .

"We can beat them to it," I said as the elevator doors opened again. "Help her outside. I'll meet you there in a minute."

We shifted positions at Sarah's side, and while they shuffled to the front door, I hustled to the security desk. The guard's gaze followed Jonah and Sarah out the front door, his hand on the walkie-talkie on his desk.

"Hey," I said when I reached it, drawing his attention to me. "We just got a call—the cops are on their way to the top floor. You better head upstairs and make sure they clear out, or there's sure to be arrests and a gigantic mess. I know you don't want that in the papers tomorrow. Your, um, fanged clientele won't be happy about it."

The guard nodded with understanding, then picked up his walkie, turned a knob, and asked for backup. I hoped he had enough of it—and maybe some vampire repellent while he was at it.

I left him to his preparations, gulping in fresh, untainted air when I made it outside again. I watched Jonah and Sarah hobble across the street to a small square of green. He helped Sarah to a wrought iron bench; I stayed where I was until I was sure my mind was clear and my hunger was under control.

A minute or two later, I crossed the street.

"Evacuation in progress," I told Jonah, then crouched down in front of Sarah. "How are you feeling?"

She nodded. "I'm okay. Just really, really embarrassed." She pressed a hand to her stomach. Whatever haze had silenced her passed, and she began to sob in earnest.

Jonah and I exchanged an uncomfortable glance.

"Sarah," I softly said. "Can you tell us what happened? How did you end up there?"

"I heard vamps were having this party." She rubbed a hand beneath her nose. "I thought, oh, vampires, that could be fun, you know? At first it was okay. But then—I don't know. The tension in the room got kind of high, and then I started to feel really weird, and I sat down on the floor. I could see them out of the corners of my eyes. They'd move around and take a look at me, like they were trying to see if I was ready."

"Ready?" I asked.

"Ready to give blood?" She shuddered and sighed. "And then you came along." She shook her head. "I'm just really embarrassed. I shouldn't have been there. I shouldn't have gone." She looked up at me. "I really want to go home. Do you think you could find me a cab?"

"On it," Jonah said, stepping back to the road to scan for passing cabs. It was late, but we were still within a couple of blocks of Michigan, so it wasn't completely unlikely that we'd find one.

As he moved away, I looked down at Sarah again. "Sarah, how did you find out about the party?"

She blushed and looked away.

"It would really help us if you could tell me. It might help us put a stop to these parties."

She sighed, then nodded. "My girlfriend and I were out at a bar—one of those vampire bars? We met a guy there."

"Do you know which vampire bar?"

"Temple?"

My stomach sank. That was the Cadogan bar. "Go on."

"So, I went outside to get some fresh air—there were a lot of people in there—and there was a guy outside. He said a party was happening and we'd have a good time. My friend, Brit, didn't want to go, but I wanted to, you know, see what it was about."

So Sarah had gotten info about the rave at Temple Bar, and Jonah had found the phone at Benson's. That meant the folks who frequented the bars also knew about the raves. Ethan was going to be pissed about that one.

"The guy you talked to—what did he look like?"

"Oh, um, he was kinda short. Older. Dark hair. Kind of grizzled-looking? And there was a girl with him. I remember because she had on this, like, gigantic hat, so I couldn't see her face. Oh, but when I was walking back inside, he called her name. It was kind of old-fashioned, like Mary or Martha. . . ." Sarah squeezed her eyes closed as she tried to remember.

My heart thudded in anticipation. "Was it Marie?"

Her eyes popped open again. "Yeah! It was Marie. How did you know?"

"Lucky guess," I said. I may not have known a particularly short man, but I knew a vamp with a predilection for causing trouble. And once upon a time, she had been known as Marie.

Before I could ask a follow-up question, Sarah grimaced.

"Are you okay?"

"Just a headache. There was something weird in their air, I think."

Excellent segue to my next question. "Did you take anything while you were there? Maybe a drink someone handed you?"

She shook her head. "You're asking about drugs, but I don't do drugs. And I know not to drink anything I didn't pour myself. But I did see this. Another girl—a human—handed it to me."

She pulled a small paper envelope, the kind that might hold a gift tag, from her pocket. It was white, and there was a *V* inscribed on the front. I stuffed it into my pocket for later. And then I asked a question that made me hate myself a little bit, but it had to be asked. The stakes were too high.

I had to know if she posed a risk to Cadogan.

"Sarah, are you thinking about going to the police?"

Her eyes widened. "Oh, God, no. I shouldn't have gone to the party, and if my parents found out, if my boyfriend found out, they would *freak*. Besides," she shyly added, "if I called the cops, you'd get in trouble, too, right? You're a vampire, too, but you helped me."

I nodded, relief in my chest. "I am a vampire," I confirmed. "My name's Merit."

She smiled a little. "Merit. I like that. It kind of describes you. Like you were always meant to be good, you know?"

This time, I was the one sniffing back a sudden errant tear.

The clack of a car door opening pulled my gaze to the street. Jonah stood beside a black and white cab, door open. "Let's get you home."

Sarah nodded. She still wobbled on her feet, but we made it the dozen or so feet to the cab. At the door, she turned back and smiled at me.

"Will you be okay?" I asked.

She nodded. "I will. Thank you."

"You don't have to thank me. I'm sorry about what happened. I'm sorry they made you feel uncomfortable."

"It's forgotten. But I won't forget this," she said, "not what you did tonight."

When the door closed, we watched the cab pull away.

Jonah glanced back at me, and then at the eastern sky. "Dawn will be here soon," he said. "We should get home." He gestured down the street. "I actually parked pretty close. You want a ride back to your car?"

"That would be great," I agreed, the adrenaline giving way to exhaustion.

We walked in silence a few blocks, then stopped at a hybrid sedan.

"Thinking about the environment?"

He smiled ruefully. "If the climate goes bad, we're going to be here for it. Might as well plan ahead."

When he unlocked the doors and we climbed inside, I gave him directions to my own parking spot, then closed my eyes and dropped my head back to the seat.

I was out in seconds.

✦ ✦ ✦

CHAPTER NINE

BE IT EVER SO HUMBLE . . .
UNLESS YOU'RE IMMORTAL AND
UNDERSTAND COMPOUND INTEREST

I shuddered awake, blinking in the glow of unfamiliar lights. I was curled into a ball atop a giant sleigh bed that smelled like woodsy cologne and cinnamon. I sat up and took in unfamiliar surroundings. A massive bed, topped by a pile of taupe bedclothes. An equally large flat-screen television at the end on a facing bureau. And leaning against the bureau, arms crossed over his chest, was Jonah. He was dressed more casually today in a V-neck T-shirt, jeans, and sneakers.

"Good evening, Sentinel."

"Where are we?"

"Grey House. My room."

"Grey—," I began to repeat, but the night began to replay. I fell asleep in his car, and he must have brought me here. No, not just brought me—carried me—into Grey House while I was out.

"I wasn't comfortable dropping you off at your car. You were completely out, and your being here was easier to explain than my showing up with you at Cadogan House. Dawn was moving in; I had to make a call."

That made sense, although I wasn't thrilled that I'd been carried around like a hapless girl in one of my favorite bodice rippers.

"Thanks. Did anyone else see me come in?" If so, since I'd spent the night in Jonah's room, I could imagine well enough myself what they'd been thinking. I felt the rising blush on my cheeks.

"Nope. Everyone else was bunked in by then."

I swung my feet over the bed and buried my toes in expensive, thickly piled carpet. "Where did you sleep?"

He hitched a thumb over his shoulder. "Sitting room. I'm a gentleman, and there's nothing about seducing an unconscious vampire that appeals to me." He shrugged. "Besides, the sun was nearly up. We were out. I could have slept right beside you, and no one would have been the wiser. We'd both have been angels."

I was on enough of a boy hiatus to agree, but appreciated that he'd given me space. It was a gentlemanly thing to do, and not something I'd take for granted.

"Thank you."

He shrugged. "I borrowed your phone. Sent a message to Ethan to let him know you were okay. I thought you'd probably have checked in when you returned, and a call from me would have been really suspicious."

I nodded my agreement. Of course, just because he hadn't outed himself to Ethan didn't mean there weren't going to be questions. Ethan was still going to wonder where I'd spent the day.

I glanced into the sitting room where he'd slept. A plush couch and love seat were poised near another enormous flat-screen television mounted to the wall. The rest of the room was equally nice. Luxe carpet, rich colors, crown molding, and wainscoting. An arcade video game stood against one wall, and a framed Ryne Sandberg jersey hung on the other.

This place could have been featured on vampire *Cribs*.

"This is a pretty sweet place."

"New House, new digs. Well, relatively new House, anyway. Only eight years old, which isn't much when immortality is the context." He walked to a mini-fridge built into a cabinet on the far wall and opened it, revealing tidy rows of longneck bottles. He plucked one out and walked my way.

"I don't think hair of the dog is going to do it for me today."

"It's not beer." When he held it out, I looked it over. It was blood. Traditional beer bottle, but definitely not the traditional brew. It was another Blood4You product—the unfortunately named LongBeer. They really could use Mallory's marketing expertise.

"You looked like you could use it."

I nodded my agreement and twisted off the cap, my fingers shaking with the sudden hunger. The blood was cold and had a peppery zing to it, like it had been doctored with a dash or two of Tabasco.

As blood went, it was delicious. But, more important, it satiated the need. I finished the bottle in seconds flat, then lowered it again, chest heaving.

"Guess you needed that?"

I nodded, wiping my mouth with the back of my hand. "Sorry. Sometimes the hunger takes me."

Jonah reached out and took the bottle from my hand. "It can do that. And you had a big night last night."

"Not as big as it might have been, but big enough. I got hungry at the party, and I was lucky not to flip out like everyone else there."

He dropped the bottle into a bin beside the refrigerator. "Speaking of, you certainly got the vamps fired up."

"It wasn't me," I assured him. "A female vamp bumped me, and I ended up with two vamps in my face trying to take me out."

Jonah frowned. "There did seem to be a lot of aggression in the air."

"And did you notice their eyes?" I asked. "Totally silver, barely any pupil. They were seriously vamped out."

"There was also a lot of magic in the room. You put those two things together and you get vamps itching for a fight."

I shook my head. "This couldn't just be volume—all the vampires in a room together. The Houses couldn't exist if just being near other vampires made them predatory enough to fight for no reason. Maybe it's a mob-mentality thing? One vamp sanctions violence and the rest of them fall into line?"

Jonah shook his head. "I've got another theory. What if the magic wasn't just leaked by the vamps—what if it was directing them?"

"You're suggesting someone was using magic against us? Fueling the aggression?"

He nodded. "Making the vamps super predatorial."

"Okay," I allowed, "say it is magic. But who does that implicate? Sorcerers? They usually try to stay away from vamp drama, and there are only, like, three in the Chicago area. I know two of them, and making vamps play gladiator isn't exactly on their to-do list." Granted, I'd never met Mallory's tutor, but I had a pretty good idea how he was spending his time—training her.

"Okay, so probably not sorcerers. How did you find Sarah?" Jonah asked.

"She was sitting on the floor, looked completely spaced-out. No visible bite marks, so something else had to be going on. Is it possible to glamour someone into illness? I mean, to make them physically weaker just from the glamour?"

He frowned, considering it. "I've never seen it. But that's not to say it's not possible. Did you learn anything from her? How she found out about the party?"

I passed along the information she'd given me about Temple Bar and the man she'd seen outside. "She also gave me this," I said, digging the envelope from my pocket. I pulled it out, then opened the flap and emptied the envelope's contents into my hand.

Two white pills fell into my palm.

"Well," he said, "that might explain why she was so out of it."

I held one tablet up to the light. The same curvy *V* was pressed into its surface.

"She said she didn't take anything."

"She was also embarrassed about what happened."

"True," I agreed. "Tate said Mr. Jackson had been arrested for drug possession. So maybe vamps are drugging humans to make them, what, more susceptible to glamour?"

"Given the crowd you saw last night, would that seem far-fetched to you?"

Unfortunately, it didn't. Of course, we also didn't have any evidence of it. Sarah could have been glamoured—not that vamps manipulating humans was a big improvement over drugging them.

Whatever the case, it was worth looking into. I put the pills back into the envelope, then tucked it into my pocket again. "I'll take them to the Ombud's office," I told him. "Maybe they can find out more."

The debriefing done, Jonah let me freshen up in his small bathroom. I rubbed at mascara smears and hitched up my ponytail again.

When I came out, he was pulling a buzzing phone from his pocket. He glanced up at me. "I'm going to take this. I'll be right back. Make yourself at home. There's more blood if you need it."

I nodded at him. "Thanks."

He stepped outside and closed the door behind him, leaving me alone in the cool comfort of his suite.

I rounded the corner, moving into the sitting room and toward a group of framed papers on the wall. They were diplomas for four doctorates: three from state schools in Illinois (history, anthropology, and geography) and one from Northwestern (German literature and critical thought). Each diploma bore a variation of his name—John, Jonah, Jonathan, Jack—and their dates were spread in time across the twentieth century.

I guess graduate school was possible for a vampire.

The door opened. "Sorry," he said behind me. "It was Noah. He is now aware you spent the night at his condo last night."

"Good call," I said, assuming Ethan didn't quiz me on the finer points of Noah's home—or any other details about Noah other than the little I already knew.

I pointed at the degrees. "You're quite the student."

"Is 'student' a euphemism for 'geek'?"

"It's a euphemism for 'man with four PhDs.' How did you manage all this?"

"While hiding the fact that I'm fanged, you mean?"

I nodded, and he grinned and walked toward me. "Very carefully."

"Lot of night classes?"

"Exclusively. All of these were before online classes were an option." He smiled secretly as he looked over the certificates. "In earlier days, grad school was still a place for eccentrics. It was easy to play the lone genius—the one who only took evening classes, slept during the day, et cetera."

"Did you TA any?" Being a TA, a teaching assistant, seemed like it would have been harder.

"I did not. I got lucky with some fellowship money, and I liked researching, so they kept me away from the classrooms. Otherwise, it would have been hard to arrange." He tilted his head at me. "Did you do time in grad school?"

"Before I was changed, yeah."

He must have heard the regret in my voice. "I'm guessing there's a story there?"

"I was in grad school at U of C before I was made a vampire. English lit. Three chapters into my dissertation." Before I could stop myself, the entire story was out. "I was walking across campus one night, and I was attacked." I looked over at him. "One of the Rogues Celina hired."

He put two and two together. "You were one of the park victims. The one who was bitten on campus?"

I nodded. "Ethan and Malik happened to be there. They jumped out, scared the attacker away, and Ethan took me home and began the Change."

"God, that was lucky for you."

"It was," I agreed.

"So Ethan saved your life."

"He did. And made me a Cadogan vampire and House Sentinel." I frowned. "He also pulled me out of school. He didn't think I could go back as a vamp." That was right before the North American Vampire Registry outed my Initiate class in the paper, so he'd probably been right.

"He had a point," Jonah said. "School as a closeted vampire wasn't an easy task. It was a little easier, I think, as an older vamp who knew the rules, knew how to play the game. For an Initiate still learning the ropes?" He shrugged. "It would have been difficult."

"Said the man with four doctorates."

"Fair point. But you seem to have adjusted to being a vampire, even if the transition wasn't exactly by choice."

"It wasn't easy," I admitted. "I had my moments of irritating whininess. But I eventually reached the point where I had to accept who I was and deal with it—or leave the House and pretend to be a human again." I shrugged. "I opted for the House."

Jonah wet his lips, then looked at me askew. "I should give credit where credit is due. You did well last night."

"That would be more flattering if there wasn't so much surprise in your voice."

"My expectations were low."

"Yes, I'm aware of that." I thought of the first time we'd met, of the disdain in his voice. "And why is that exactly? Why the anti-Sentinel sentiment?"

He smirked. "It's not so much anti-Sentinel—"

"As anti-Merit?" I finished for him.

"I know your sister," he said. "Charlotte. We have mutual friends."

Charlotte was my older sister, currently married with two children and engaged as a full-time charity soiree attendee and fundraiser. I loved my sister, but I wasn't a part—by choice—of the fancy circles she ran in. So it didn't exactly impress me that he knew her.

"Okay," I said.

He sighed, then looked up at me a little guiltily. "I'd assumed—your being a Merit—that you were her clone."

It took me a moment to gather up an answer. "What, now?"

"I just figured—since you're sisters and all. And both Merits . . ." He trailed off, but didn't need to finish the rest of it. Jonah wasn't the first vampire who'd confessed he'd judged me based on my family name—and the baggage that accompanied wealth and notoriety. I'm not saying money doesn't have its advantages, but being judged on one's own merits—pun very much intended—isn't one of them.

On the other hand, that did explain why he'd been so cold the first couple of times we'd met. He'd expected a bratty new vampire from new-money Chicago.

"I love my sister," I told him. "But I'm far from being her clone."

"So I see."

"And now you believe what?"

"Oh. Well." He smiled, and there was pride in his eyes. "Now I've seen you in action. I've seen this avenging angel—"

"I prefer Ponytailed Avenger," I dryly said. That was the nickname ascribed to me by Nick Breckenridge (aka "the blackmailer").

Jonah rolled his eyes. "This avenging angel of a vampire," he continued, "coming to the rescue of humans and roaring through the folks who cross her. And now I'm wondering if you wouldn't be such a bad addition to the RG."

"As opposed to the train wreck I would have been a couple of months ago?"

He had the grace to blush.

"I know you weren't impressed by me. You didn't exactly hide it. And I wouldn't call myself an avenging angel. I'm Sentinel of my House, and I do what I can to protect them."

"To protect *only* them?"

I met his steady gaze. "For now, only them."

We stood there for a moment and let the phrase stand between us. I was again passing up the opportunity to become his partner, but admitting that I wasn't ruling it out completely. Immortality, after all, lasted a long time.

He nodded. "I should probably get you back to your car."

"That would be a good idea. I need to get home." Back to the House, back to Ethan. Back to a routine that didn't involve my fighting crazed vampires—but now involved lying to him about them.

Jonah grabbed up keys, and we left his room.

The sight outside it was unbelievable.

Grey House was located in a converted warehouse near Wrigley Field, and they'd definitely made use of the space. His door was one of many along the wall, each evenly spaced like in a hotel. The hallway was open on the other side, a railing made of steel posts and thin wire giving way to a four-story atrium. Across the atrium, at the same level on which we stood, was another line of doors. Bedrooms, I supposed.

I walked to the railing and glanced down. The middle of the space below us was filled by a forty-foot-tall tree and a lush island of greenery. There were also plants and trees along a path that wound through the space. Black posts stood at intervals along the path, each bearing a vertical flag of a Chicago sports team.

It was unlike anything I'd seen before—and certainly unlike anything I'd seen in the realm of vampires.

"This is spectacular," I said when Jonah joined me at the rail. I glanced up at the ceiling, which was all glass. But that couldn't work in a House of vampires. "How do the trees grow? I mean, don't you have to close up the skylights during the day?"

Jonah made a circle with his hands. "The roof has a parabolic canopy that rotates to close during the day." He swiveled his fingers. "They close just like a camera shutter, so it leaves a gap in the middle for the tree. And the mechanism is photosensitive, so the circle follows the sun as the earth rotates to ensure the tree always has light."

"That is amazing."

"The technology is pretty impressive," he agreed. "Scott's taken the time to try new things, which we can't always say about Masters."

"They do tend to be a little stodgy."

He made a vague sound of agreement. "The rest of the foliage gets light as the shutters turn."

"And if a vamp has an emergency and needs to move through the atrium during the day?"

"They don't," Jonah said simply. "The interior architecture of the House is organized so you never have to cross the atrium space to get to any living quarters or exits." He pointed below. "The rooms on the sides of the atrium are nonessential—offices and the like—and there are shaded walkways in any event."

He turned and began walking down the hallway, and I followed him to an elevator and a basement parking level that was pretty similar to ours: long concrete vault, lots of expensive cars.

I stopped short when we passed a platinum silver convertible. It was small and curvy, with round lights, a hood vent, and wire wheels, and it looked exactly like the kind of car James Bond would drive.

"Is this—is that an Aston Martin?"

He glanced over. "Yeah. That's Scott's car. He's been alive for nearly two hundred years. A man accumulates prizes in that time."

"So I see," I said, clenching my hands to fight back the urge to run my fingers across the spotless paint. I'd never seen one in person. Never seen one at all outside the movies. But it was stunning. I didn't consider myself to be a car person, but it was hard not to like long lines and sweet curves. And what I'd imagine was a pretty fast engine.

"Lots of, you know, horsepowers or whatever?"

He smiled and unlocked his hybrid's door, and was still grinning when we climbed inside. "Not much of a car buff?"

"I can appreciate a beautiful thing. But cars are only a skin-deep infatuation for me."

"Duly noted."

We drove from Wrigleyville back to Magnificent Mile and my car. And I totally lucked out—my car had been parked in the same spot for nearly twenty-four hours, but while there was a ticket under the wiper, there was no boot on the tire. Street parking in Chicago was a hazardous activity.

"Are you going to get hassled for sleeping over?" he asked through the open window as I unlocked my door.

Only if Ethan thinks I'm sleeping with Noah, I thought to myself.

"I'm good," I told Jonah. "Besides, it's not like you could escort me home. You'd blow your cover."

"True. We should probably plan to talk again. I expect this isn't the last time we'll hear about what went down last night."

"Probably not." My stomach turned over. I wasn't thrilled at the possibility of heading back into another "rave," if that's what we were calling it. I had the skills for war, but not the stomach for it. It was easy to help someone in need, but it would have been nicer if the need didn't exist in the first place.

"I'll talk to the bartenders at Temple Bar, see if they've noticed anything suspicious. And I'll let you know if I find out anything about the phone number. I'll also talk to them about the drugs. They'll want to know if illegal substances are being spread around, and what the effects are."

"Sounds like a plan. Keep me posted."

"I will. Thank you again for the help."

Jonah smiled thinly. "That's what partners are for."

"Don't jump the gun. We aren't partners yet."

With a final, knowing smile, he pulled away from the curb, leaving me on the sidewalk beside my lonely Volvo. What had Mallory said about not wanting to go back to your life again? And what had I told her? Something about accepting the choices you were presented with and getting the nasty stuff done regardless?

I climbed into the Volvo and shut the door behind me, blowing the bangs from my forehead as I started the car.

"Good times," I muttered, as I turned the wheel into traffic. "Good times."

When I was parked in front of the House, I took a moment to get the next part of the investigation in motion. I dialed up Jeff's number.

His answer was enthusiastic. "Merit! We heard some shit went down last night. You okay?"

"Hey, Jeff. I'm good. I'll fill you in later. But for now I need a favor."

"The Jeff abides. What's up?"

I rattled off the phone number Jonah had given me. "It's the number that sent out a text about the party, which may or may not have been a rave. Can you trace it?"

"On it," he said, and I heard the rhythmic *clack* of keys. "Nothing in the first round," he said after a moment. "Give me a little bit of time. I'll find it."

"You're a doll."

"You and I both know it. I'll call you."

"Thanks, Jeff."

That done, and the phone tucked away again, I glanced up at the House. Probably best to get the hard part over with. I headed inside—this time through a gauntlet of personal epithets from the protesters—and straight for Ethan's office.

The office door was open, and he sat at his desk, a phone at his ear.

I waited until he put the phone down, and then started in. The words came out in a rush.

"It was in a high-rise in Streeterville, but it wasn't an intimate rave, not like we think of them. This was at least two dozen vamps. A lot of magic, a lot of glamour, and a lot of fighting. Everyone was on a hair trigger, like they were waiting for an excuse to rumble. There were plenty of humans, and some bloodletting. There's also a possibility they're being drugged to make them susceptible to glamour."

Ethan's eyes shifted to something behind me.

"Sire," he said after a moment, "this is Merit, Sentinel of Cadogan House. Merit, Darius West. Head of the Greenwich Presidium."

Oh, snap.

CHAPTER TEN

LIKE A BOSS

I froze, realizing for the first time—and much too late—that we weren't alone in the office. I clenched my eyes closed, embarrassment rising on my cheeks. So much for keeping our infiltration of the raves under wraps.

A few seconds later, I finally opened my eyes again, expecting to see fury in Ethan's. Instead, he offered a gently chastising look.

Maybe he had changed.

"I'm so sorry," I mouthed, before turning to Darius. He stood with Malik and Luc, in the office's sitting area in front of leather furniture that hadn't been there on my last visit. Helen did efficient work.

Darius was tall and lean, with a shaved head and blue eyes. His features were sharp and nearly arrogant—straight nose, wide mouth, aristocratic chin marked by a perfect cleft.

"That's a very interesting tale you weave," he said. Darius's accent was clearly English; his diction would have made the queen proud. "Come have a seat. Ethan, won't you join us, as well?"

I had a sense the request was actually an order, so I took a seat on one of the leather chairs that faced the couch. As Ethan followed me over, Luc and Malik took seats on two end chairs. Ethan took the chair beside me.

Darius sat on the couch, then reached into his pocket and removed a slim, silver case. He popped it open and pulled out a thin black cigarette. It wasn't until he'd lifted it to his mouth that he looked at Ethan for permission.

"Be my guest," Ethan said, but it was clear he wasn't thrilled about Darius smoking in the House.

Cigarette at the corner of his mouth, Darius tucked the case back into his pocket and pulled out a book of matches. He lit one, leaving a sulfurous sting in the air, and touched it to the end of the cigarette before putting it out with a flick of his wrist. He dropped the wasted match into a heavy crystal dish on the coffee table that sat in the middle of the ring of furniture.

He puffed for a moment, then lifted a single eyebrow—I guess we now knew where that tic of Ethan's had come from—and blew a stream of fragrant smoke from the side of his mouth.

"In this political climate," he began, "with these challenges, you sent your Sentinel to a *rave*?"

"I'm not sure it was a rave," I put in, trying to salvage what I could. "We believed it might be a rave—or something calling itself a rave—but this is on a different scale. Very large, and very violent."

"Raves are always violent," Darius said. "That is the nature of a rave."

I opened my mouth to disagree, but thought better of it. After all, since I'd seen only one rave, he'd definitely know better than I whether the bloodlust was unusual.

"What is atypical," he continued, "is an official House staff member being utilized to infiltrate such things."

"Infiltration was our only option," Ethan said.

Darius's face radiated disbelief, and his tone was deadpan. "Your only option."

Ethan cleared his throat. "Seth Tate informed us that he'd learned of the alleged murder of three humans by vampires. He has a warrant for my arrest in hand, and has threatened to execute that warrant within the week if we don't solve the problem. The opportunity to investigate arose, and we took it."

"Did he execute the warrant?"

"Not yet, but he—"

"Then you had *options*," Darius said, in a tone that brooked no argument and reminded us all that while Ethan was Master of the House, Darius was master of the *Houses*.

And then he turned his cold blue gaze on me. "You're the Sentinel."

"I am, Sire."

"You look rather a mess."

I had to work not to smooth down my hair and my wrinkled tank top. I'd slept in my clothes, and while I'd cleaned up a little at Grey House, I'm sure I still looked pretty awful. On the other hand, I looked awful because I'd been working, not because I lacked basic hygiene skills.

"I was on an assignment, Sire."

"Such as it was," Darius muttered. "And you're just now returning to the House? You have traversed Chicago looking like this?"

I waited to give Ethan a chance to offer silent suggestions, to tell me what I was or was not supposed to tell Darius—although the cat was mostly out of the bag. When he stayed silent, I assumed that was permission enough and told the truth—and nothing more.

"It was late, Sire. We were running close to sunrise."

The cigarette in his fingers, Darius wet his lips, and slowly shifted his gaze to Ethan. "Now is the time to perfect the public image, to sweeten and sharpen it, not send it rumpled and trashed through the city like some kind of well-used party girl."

I went stiff at the insult; Ethan stirred in his chair. "She is a soldier. That her battlefield is unusual doesn't make it any less a battlefield, nor does it make the uniform any less a uniform."

I appreciated that he'd taken the hit for me, stood up for what some believed was my "mere" status as a soldier for the House. And, honestly, what more honorable service was there? Making decisions from a continent away in a dress shirt, smoking cigarettes from a silver box?

I lifted my chin and met Darius's gaze. "I am a soldier," I confirmed. "And I have no qualms about that."

His eyebrows lifted with interest. "And you've returned from a battle."

"In a manner of speaking."

Darius sat back in his chair again. "You said tonight's event, whatever it might have been, was unusually violent." He took another puff, the suspicion clear on his face. "You've been to another rave? You have a basis for comparison?"

"I haven't," I admitted. "The comparison is based on information from other sources, and the one site I visited after the fact. Our intelligence says raves in Chicago are few and far between, and that—perhaps to avoid risk of detection—they're usually very intimate affairs. A few vampires at most. That's not what we saw last night."

"Although I disagree with your conclusions, that's not a bad report." He turned to Ethan. "I can see why you like her, Ethan."

"She's more than capable," Ethan agreed. "But I assume an update on our Sentinel's work is not what brought you across the pond?"

Darius leaned forward and mashed the rest of the cigarette into the ashtray. "Matters in Chicago are, as you know, escalating. Shifters. Rogues. The attack on your House."

Ethan crossed one leg over another. "As you've seen, those things are in hand."

"Those *things* suggest a decided lack of organization and political control among the Illinois Houses. When Celina was removed, you became the most senior Master in Chicago, Ethan. It is your responsibility, your duty to the Presidium, to maintain stability within your domain."

And he would have, I thought, *if you'd managed to keep Celina in England where she belonged*.

"What does that mean?" Ethan asked.

"It means there's a significant chance that Cadogan House will be placed into receivership by the Presidium until Chicago is under control."

I didn't need to know the details of a "receivership" to get the general idea—the GP was threatening to take over the House.

The room went silent, as did Ethan. The only sign he'd even heard Darius's threat was the telltale line of concern between his eyes.

"With all due respect, Sire, there's no need for impetuous action." Ethan's tone was carefully neutral, his words carefully modulated. I knew he was bursting with emotion—there was no way Ethan wasn't boiling over at the possibility that the GP was going to step in and take over his House. But he was doing an impressive job of keeping his emotions under control.

"I'm not entirely sure that was duly respectful, Ethan. And as I'm sure you'll appreciate, placing one of the American Houses into receivership isn't something the Presidium takes lightly. It raises uncomfortable memories."

"Uncomfortable?" I asked. I probably shouldn't have spoken, being the least-ranking vampire in the room, but sometimes curiosity won out.

Darius nodded. "The American Revolution was a difficult time for the British and American Houses, as you might imagine. The GP hadn't yet been formed—that was still decades down the road—and the Conseil Rouge retained power. Being French, the Conseil supported the colonies' freedom. Being British, we did not."

I nodded my understanding. "And immortality being what is, some of those colonists are still alive in the American Houses."

"Indeed."

"An excellent reason," Ethan put in, "to preclude discussion of receivership."

"The discussion is already under way, Ethan. I know you don't approve of the Presidium or the actions we've taken, but we have rules and processes for a reason."

So Celina can ignore them? I wondered.

There was a knock at the door, which opened a little. A man tidily dressed in cuffed trousers, button-up shirt, and suspenders—only his wavy brown hair askew—looked inside. "Sire, your call with New York Houses is ready." His voice was equally British and posh; he must have been part of Darius's retinue.

Darius glanced up and over. "Thank you, Charlie. I'll just be a moment."

Charlie nodded, then disappeared through the door again. When he was gone, Darius stood up. The rest of us did the same.

"We'll chat later," Darius said, then nodded at me. "Good luck with your continued training."

"Thank you, Sire."

When he was gone, and the door was closed again behind him,

silence reigned. Ethan put his elbows on his knees and ran his hands through his hair.

"Receivership," Luc repeated. "When was the last time that happened?"

"Not since the financial meltdown before World War II," Malik answered. "Many, many years."

"He's being unreasonable," I said, glancing around at them. "None of this is Cadogan's fault. It's Adam Keene's fault. It's the GP's fault—Celina's fault. We're reaping the consequences of their bad acts, and now he wants to put the GP in charge of the House?"

Ethan sat up straight again. "That's the long and short of it. A receiver would come into the House, begin an investigation of House procedures, and have the authority—the GP-granted authority—to approve every decision that's made in this House, regardless of how big or small. A receiver would report every decision back to the GP, including Darius, including Celina."

Ethan looked up at me, his green eyes icy cold. "And I have to wonder whether he'd be raising the issue if our Sentinel hadn't just informed him that Chicago was heading to hell in a handbasket." So the calm, unruffled, forgiving Ethan had been an act for Darius.

Unfortunately for him, we'd come too far for me to be intimidated by a snarky phrase or nasty look. I'd gone out and faced danger for him and the House, and I wasn't about to shrink away because he didn't like the consequences. I gave him back the same stare.

The room went silent, until Ethan barked out an order, his gaze still on me. "Excuse us, please."

When no one budged, he glanced around the room. "I wasn't asking for permission."

That was enough to send Luc and Malik scurrying out the door, both of them offering me sympathetic looks.

It wasn't until we were alone, the door shut behind them, that Ethan finally looked away. For a full minute, he sat quietly, his back rigid.

Finally, he walked back to his desk and settled himself behind it, putting space—and furniture—between us.

I'd known him long enough to call it "typical Sullivan." It was the kind of action we could have added to the Ethan Sullivan drinking game, falling somewhere between his imperious eyebrow arching and his habit of referring to any Novitiate in his House by position, rather than by name.

"Sentinel," he finally said, linking his fingers on his desk.

I took a step forward, intent on making him believe how much I regretted what I'd inadvertently told Darius. "Ethan, I am so sorry. You were on the phone, and it didn't even occur to me to see if anyone was behind me."

He held up a hand. "You told him where you'd been. I am not sure whether to throttle you now or simply hand you over to the Presidium and let them do it."

If I were him, I'd throttle me, too. I just nodded.

When Ethan finally looked at me again, there was desperation in his eyes.

"A receiver. In my goddamned House. A House I have watched, guided, parented when necessary. Do you know what an insult that is? To have an administrator—some organizational specialist who couldn't guide vampires with a map and compass—replacing me? Telling me what I've done right or wrong, how I should 'fix' the things I've broken."

My heart clenched sympathetically. It must have been hard to hear that not only was the supreme leader of vamps not happy with your work, but he was considering sending someone across the pond to make sure the work was done correctly. It wouldn't have thrilled me, either.

And the worst part? This was at least partly my fault. I mean, it seemed unlikely Darius would have traveled this far if he didn't have concerns about the House, but that didn't mean I hadn't pushed him over the receivership edge.

"This House is old, Merit. It is a respectable House. The appointment of a receiver is a slap in the face." He looked away, shaking his head ruefully. "How can I not take that as an insult to all that I've done since Peter's death?"

That Peter was Peter Cadogan, the House's namesake and first Master. The man who'd held the reins until his death, when Ethan took over.

"I would take it personally, too."

Ethan barked out a laugh. "It's hardly that I take it personally, Sentinel. It's that it's a slap against me and Malik, Luc, Helen— the entire staff. Every Initiate Commended, every Novitiate who has served. Every sacrifice made. You essentially told him we don't have things in hand."

"We don't if what we saw last night is commonplace. This wasn't half a dozen vampires and a couple of humans, Ethan. There were dozens of vamps, dozens of humans. The party was huge, and it was loud, and it wasn't just about a little private sip."

"So it wasn't a rave."

"Not the kind of raves we knew about before. The vamps were on edge, the magic thick. Vamps were picking fights all over the place."

"Did you and Noah have to defend yourselves?"

I hated lying to Ethan. *Hated it.* But it wasn't fair of me to clear my conscience at Jonah's expense, so I sucked it up and played out the story.

"Defend ourselves, yes. We weren't involved in any fighting of consequence, although things got nasty when we made our exit. I'd found a human who needed help—drugged or glamoured; I'm not sure which. She needed out, and there were a few vamps who weren't happy to see her go. Noah spilled blood as a distraction, and the vamps went crazy. The place erupted with fighting, but we got her out and sent her home. She was grateful enough—embarrassed enough—that I don't think she'll cause us problems down the road."

I sighed and looked away. "I hate saying that, Ethan. It mortifies me that I have to think about a woman who's been in a bad position as a liability. She was made a commodity by those vampires. That shouldn't happen twice. Not by us."

I looked back at him, and appreciated the sympathy in his eyes.

"You are a very human vampire," he affectionately said.

"So you say."

"I once considered it a liability. And for some vampires, I still do. But for you—let us hope they don't bleed it out of you."

We were quiet for a moment, just looking at each other. I finally broke the silence. I reached into my pocket, pulled out the envelope, and handed it to him. "This is why we think the humans may have been drugged."

Ethan inspected the envelope, then dropped the pills into his hand. "What's V?"

"Don't know. I'm assuming it stands for 'vampire.' And the punch line? The human who gave this to me, Sarah, had learned about the rave at Temple Bar."

His gaze went cold. "Someone is using the Cadogan House bar to solicit humans?"

"That would appear to be the case."

A muscle in his cheek twitched, but after a moment, he seemed to relax again.

"At least you managed not to tell Darius about that."

There was a smirk in his eyes that made me smile.

"We'll thank God for small miracles," I agreed. "Sarah said she heard about the rave from a short guy . . . and a woman named Marie."

Ethan froze, before slipping the pills back into the envelope. "There are probably thousands of women in Chicago named Marie."

"That is true," I agreed.

He handed the envelope back to me. "There's no way to know that it was Celina. She hasn't gone by that name in two centuries."

"That is also true," I said, tapping my fingers against the envelope.

"You're usually much more argumentative at this point."

"I usually have more evidence to go on."

He smiled. "We may make a Sentinel out of you yet."

Of course, while I did usually have more evidence that Celina was involved in something obnoxious, that didn't change the facts. . . . "It is still quite a coincidence that the rave pusher was using one of Celina's former aliases."

"An alias that led us to a saboteur the last time she used it," Ethan reminded me. He had a point—Celina sent incriminating e-mail messages to Peter as "Marie Collette." But he'd forgotten a key fact.

"Celina doesn't know we traced that particular e-mail address; she was using half a dozen others. And she doesn't know that's how we found out about Peter. She just knows he stopped showing up to do his bidding. And, more important, she probably didn't think she'd get caught. What are the odds that particular girl would tell me that someone calling herself 'Marie' was soliciting humans outside a bar?"

"What are the odds Celina would use an alias we could identify outside a bar we own?"

Okay, put like that, it didn't sound so convincing.

"Just because I don't currently have all the evidence doesn't mean there isn't evidence to be found."

"And so it begins," he muttered, then lifted his gaze, no longer amused. "Merit, the head of the GP is steps away from us right now. I am ordering you not to bring up her name again—"

When I opened my mouth to object, he held up a hand.

"Until you have more evidence than a name she may or may not have used. I now consider the subject to be dropped. Understood?"

"Understood," I said, then wet my lips. "Do you trust me?"

His gaze went a little more seductive than I cared for. "Do I *trust* you?"

"It doesn't sound like Darius wants me getting my hands dirty. But this is my job, and frankly, I'm kind of good at it."

"Much to everyone's surprise."

I gave him a petulant face. "We know something weird is going on out there. If the rave scene is the way we get in and shut it down—the way we make sure vamps aren't out there slaughtering humans en masse—then we go the rave route. I need to get out there again, and we need to keep pulling this string."

"You cannot make an enemy of the GP. And not just because you're a member of this House," he preemptively added at my narrowed gaze. "I understand your impatience and I honor your commitment. But if they believe you stand against them, they will bring you down, Merit. Their sovereignty is important. Celina lives because she hasn't challenged that sovereignty; if you challenge it, you pose a direct threat to Darius and the others. And that will be the beginning of the end of you."

"I know. But that's not reason enough to allow them to tear the city apart."

His expression—half sorrowful resignation, half pride—mirrored my own emotions. "I didn't train you, invest in you, so that you could give yourself over to the GP as some kind of Windy City sacrifice."

His voice was soft, earnest, but there was emotion in his eyes. Real emotion.

"I don't intend to be a sacrifice. And I don't intend to let you be one, either."

He looked away. "They have an eye on the House. They'll know what we're doing."

Here comes the kicker, I thought, bracing myself. "Not if you're not involved."

He paused, obviously startled, then leaned back in his chair. He might be nervous about the idea, but I'd piqued his interest. "Meaning?"

"Meaning I have powerful friends. Mallory. Catcher. Gabriel. My grandfather. Noah." Not to mention Jonah and the rest of the Red Guard. "I can work with them to accomplish what the GP won't allow you to do."

Frowning, Ethan sat up again and absently shuffled papers on his desk. After a moment, he shook his head. "If you're working outside my authority, you also work outside my protection. And if you do get caught, the GP won't like the idea of an uncontrolled Sentinel running around Chicago."

"But they'll allow an uncontrolled former Master to run around Chicago?"

"She only killed humans," he dryly reminded me. "You're talking about challenging the GP."

"I'm talking about doing what's necessary, and what's right. We've got humans picketing outside and a mayor who's going to try God knows what against you and the House so he can make a name for himself. We've also got really pissed-off vamps who'll start a fight without provocation just for the fun of doing it. Do you want them running around Chicago? Besides," I quietly added, knowing what he needed to hear, "I'm stronger now than I was before. I'm more skilled now than I was before."

He looked up at me, worry tightening his eyes.

God, I hated to see that worry. I hated what I'd done to put it there. And so I went to him, all reasons to the contrary. I slipped between his chair and the desk, and when he leaned toward me and rested his forehead on my abdomen, I slid my fingers into the thick golden silk of his hair.

"I'll be careful."

Ethan grunted and wrapped his hands around my waist. I ran my fingers through his hair—the same motion over and over again—and then traced my fingertips down his back. Gradually, I felt the tension leave his shoulders.

He looked up again, his eyes now lambent pools of green.

I smiled down at him. "You look drunk."

"I feel . . . relaxed."

I didn't trust that I wouldn't cross any more lines than I'd just vaulted, so I loosed his hands and stepped away, then moved around his desk and took a seat on the other side.

I figured I'd see irritation in his eyes when I looked back at him. For the second time, he surprised me. He was smiling—a kind of honest, humbled, sweet smile.

"Maybe I'm getting better at this?" he asked. "Better at wooing you in the manner in which you should be wooed?"

I crossed one leg over the other and met his gaze. "My job is to ensure the sanctity of this House. Ensuring the sanity of its Master seemed like a good start."

"Is that the story you're sticking with?"

"That's my answer."

"I don't buy it."

I smiled thinly, eyes half-hidden beneath my lashes. "You don't have to."

"Hmmph," he said, but he was clearly pleased by the repartee.

This time, he was the one who took the offensive. He stood and moved around his desk and toward me. I straightened up, every nerve in my body on alert as he approached. When he reached me, he took my hands, the same move Mayor Tate had used a couple of nights ago.

"I'm self-aware enough to admit that I prefer to be in control," he said. "It is a consequence, I think, of the responsibility of maintaining this House. But I told you how I felt about you—"

"You didn't, actually."

He blinked. "Excuse me?"

I gave him a smile. "You told me you were beginning to remember how it felt to love someone. You didn't make a confession specific to me."

His lips tightened, but he was smart enough to ask the pertinent question. "Will it make a difference if I say that?"

"No. But a girl likes to feel appreciated."

The only warning I had was the flash in his eyes before he moved, got down on his knees.

I froze, my stomach seizing. My teasing aside, a boy on his knees meant stuff I wasn't going to be prepared to hear.

Ethan reached forward and slid a hand around my neck, his thumb tracing the pulse point he found there. "Merit, I lo—"

"*Don't.*" I knew I'd goaded him to it, but that didn't mean I was ready for the words. I could hear the pleading in my voice, but I managed to stop him before he got out the *L* word. "Don't say it. Putting it out there is only going to make it harder for both of us to actually do our jobs."

"I'm not flattered by the fact that you aren't sure whether I mean it or not."

"Do you?"

He gave me a flat look, but then his expression changed to something much more appraising. And that made me worry.

"What?" I asked him.

"We're vampires."

"I'm aware."

"As vampires, we bargain, we negotiate, and we honor our agreements."

I lifted my eyebrows. "And what agreement do you intend on forming?"

"I want a kiss. One kiss," he added, before I could question him, "and I'll keep the declarations to myself. One kiss, and then I'll cease all flirting, as you call it, unless and until you come to me with your own declarations."

I slid him a glance to check his expression. Reverse psychology wasn't beyond him, and the deal didn't make much sense otherwise. I wouldn't deny the attraction between us, but I felt pretty confident I could manage not to make sexual overtures to my boss.

"One kiss?" I reiterated.

"One kiss."

"Deal," I said. Hoping to jump the gun, I closed my eyes

and offered puckered lips. Ethan chuckled, but ignored me long enough that I opened one eye.

"Don't think you're going to get by that easily." The hand on my neck slid down, his thumb resting in the hollow at the base of my neck, the rest of his fingers splayed across my collarbone. His eerily green eyes stayed trained on mine, at least until his tangled lashes dropped and he moved in.

But he didn't kiss me.

His mouth hovered just beyond mine, out of reach only so long as I refused to make that plunge forward—and he refused to execute the bargain.

"You're cheating," I murmured. I was torn about whether I was glad of it or not. I was afraid that if his lips touched mine, I'd lose the will to resist, and I was afraid that if I gave in, I'd lose my heart again.

Ethan shook his head. "I said one kiss, and I meant it. One kiss, my terms, to be claimed when the time is right."

Suddenly, he shifted his mouth to my ear, his teeth grazing the lobe. I shuddered at the spark that trilled down my spine, my eyes rolling back at the ridiculous pleasure of it.

"This isn't a kiss," he whispered, his lips at my ear.

"Nor is it in the spirit of the bargain."

"Let's not focus on the formalities, Merit." And then his lips were back again, hovering against my jaw, teasing me with the possibility of what he might do.

With the anticipation of it.

I fought back the urge to step forward, to push my lips against his to be done with it. To push my lips against his because he'd incited me to it.

"I'll have you in my bed again, Sentinel. And at my side. That is a promise."

"You mean to tease me into a seduction?"

"Is it working?"

My answer was less a word than a frustrated grumble. I was self-aware enough to know that the only thing I enjoyed more than getting what I wanted was not getting what I wanted. In my experience, wanting was often more fun than having.

On the other hand, this was a game that could easily be played by two.

I lifted a hand and pushed a lock of hair behind his ear, then traced the line of his eyebrow and jaw with a fingertip, my gaze drinking in each part of his face, from perfect cheekbones to long lips.

This time, he froze.

Flushed with feminine power, I traced the line of his neck, then curled a fist into the top of his shirt and tugged him forward.

His eyes widened; I bit back a smile.

This time, I tortured him, skimming my lips along the line of his jaw, and then to his ear. I bit him delicately, just enough to hear his heavy sigh. I wasn't sure if I meant it, if I was torturing him because I thought he deserved to be teased just like he'd teased me, or if I wanted the joy of doing it on my own.

My heart pounded, the rhythm sped by fear and trepidation and simple desire.

"Do you like being teased?" I whispered.

"I enjoy previews," he said, the words confident, but his voice rough with arousal.

I took the gravelly edge to his voice as my cue. I wanted to tease him, not push us both past the point of no return. I put my hand flat against Ethan's chest and pushed him backward. He rose unsteadily to his feet, looking down with me with frustration in his eyes.

A taste of his own medicine, I thought. To be so close to something you wanted . . . and yet so far away.

I stood up and walked around my chair and toward the door, then blew out a breath and straightened my ponytail.

"That's it?"

My heart was beating like a timpani drum, the blood rushing through my veins faster than it should have. "One kiss, you told me. You had your chance to take it."

Ethan wet his lips, straightened his collar, and moved back to his desk. He sat down in his chair, then looked up at me, something soft in his eyes. "One kiss," he promised. "And after that, the next time we touch, it will be because you ask me."

I wasn't naïve enough to tell him I wouldn't ask, to deny that I'd ever seek him out again. I knew better; we both knew better.

"I'm afraid," I finally confessed.

"I know." His voice was quiet. "I know, and it kills me that I put that fear into your eyes."

We were both silent for a moment.

"Next steps?" I asked, turning him back to business once again.

"A stiff drink?"

I opened my mouth to respond, but then something occurred to me. I thought about what Sarah had said, and then gestured toward his shiny new furniture. "You know, a stiff drink may not be such a bad idea."

"Have I finally driven you to alcohol, Sentinel?"

I grinned back at him, a sparkle in my eyes. "We're nearing the end of the construction. Maybe I should round up some Novitiates for a drink at Temple Bar."

His eyes widened appreciatively. "Offering an opportunity to casually investigate whether someone is using my bar to recruit human victims. Good thought, Sentinel."

"I don't know what you're talking about, Sullivan. I'm just talking about a few drinks with my girlfriends."

We sat quietly for a moment, the new deal between us solidifying. I was Ethan's eyes and ears, his tool to solve the problem Tate had presented. But in order to keep him safe, he couldn't have any more information than necessary. I wasn't crazy about taking on the GP, and I hadn't had much experience playing Sentinel without Ethan at my side, but I did like the idea of playing Sentinel without constantly fighting the chemistry between me and Ethan and the danger that brought with it.

He glanced down at his watch. "In case you're vaguely curious, Darius will undoubtedly be back for additional threats, but he'll eventually retire to the Trump. Some combination of jet and vampire lag. If you were to head to the bar at, let's say, three o'clock, you'd probably miss him entirely."

"How unfortunate." The deal struck, I headed for the door. "I'll keep you posted on any pertinent drink specials."

"Sentinel?"

I glanced back.

"Next time you're feeling chatty, don't forget to check the room first."

✦ ⊱⊰ ✦

CHAPTER ELEVEN

PARTY GIRLS

I t wasn't healthy, I could admit. I knew sponge cake and marsh-mallow cream weren't the cure for physical frustration, that a long run through Hyde Park or a training session with Luc would have cured me better than calories might have.

But that didn't make my fourth Mallocake—a processed and hydrogenated log of chocolate sponge cake filled with marshmal-low cream so sugary it left your teeth gritty—any less delicious than the third had been.

Mallory had discovered Mallocakes one night at a convenience store in Bucktown. There were only a few stores in Chicago that sold them, which made her burgeoning love for the things—sparked in part because of the similarities in their names—that much more inconvenient. Mallocakes were made by a mom-and-pop bakery in Indiana that shipped them out only once a month, which made them harder to find. But pain in the rear that they were to acquire, I couldn't fault her taste.

They were *ridiculously* good.

The chocolate sponge cake was just the right balance of tangy chocolate and not-too-sweet cake, which matched up perfectly against a cream filling that reeked of sugar. There were a few hundred calories in a single dose, and each box boasted half a dozen cellophane-wrapped cakes. They were a self-pity sesh just waiting to happen.

On the other hand, I was a vampire. They couldn't hurt me. Whatever criticisms you might level against Ethan for making me a vampire, I had a crazy-fast metabolism and no obvious means of weight gain.

A smarter vampire might have tried blood, satiated the need with a bag or two of type O or AB. But Mallocakes were so very human. And sometimes a girl needed to stay in touch with her humanity. Sometimes a girl needed breakfast that didn't involve flax or wheatgrass or organic free-range cruelty-free whole grains. Besides, we were the only beings alive who could eat processed sugar and carbs with impunity—why not go for it, right?

Mallocakes, it was.

Really, it was a celebration prompted by the fact that the day's paper didn't reveal word one about last night's rave. Things may not have gone smoothly in the House when I'd returned, but a quiet press was still a victory we needed.

And so, one small victory and two thousand calories later, I stuffed empty cellophane wrappers into the trash and grabbed my phone from the nightstand. I'd had my snack, so it was time to get back to work.

Jeff answered before the first ring was complete. "Merit!"

"Talk to me, Jeff. Any news on that phone number?"

"Not a damn thing. It was assigned to a disposable phone, and the account has no other outgoing messages or calls. Just the one text. And I didn't find any record of purchase in my merchant-data file for the minutes or the phone itself, so it was probably cash on both those transactions."

"Hmm. That's a bummer. And for the record, I'm very disturbed you've got merchant-data records."

"It's only mildly illegal. Hey, you want me to make you disappear from the financial system? I can do that. Even the Fed couldn't find you. They are such noobs over there."

There was too much enthusiasm in his voice for my comfort. I was the granddaughter of a cop, after all. On the other hand, Jeff worked for that cop.

"No, thanks. And if you're committing felonies, let's make sure it's for the good of the city."

"You're no fun," Jeff complained.

"Aw, that's not true. I'm plenty fun."

"Vamps are really only like ten percent fun at any given time. The other ninety percent is largely fretting. And bloodletting."

"You've been spending way too much time with Mr. Bell. Hey, while I've got you on the phone, can I talk to him? I've got a question."

"Absotively," he said, and then I heard his request. "Catch, the grandkid's on the phone."

I heard shuffling, which I imagined was the sound of Jeff carrying his phone to Catcher. That gave me time to adjust to the fact that I'd been deemed "the grandkid." So much for my vampire suaveness.

"Yo gabba gabba," Catcher said. "What's up?"

"Drugs."

"We're in the third-biggest city in the country. You're going to need to be more specific."

I picked up the envelope and looked it over. "White tablets. Dose is maybe two at a time, and they're delivered in a little white envelope. There's a *V* on the pill and also on the outside of the package."

He was quiet for a moment. "I'll have to check the database, but it doesn't sound familiar. Why do you ask?"

I gave him the rundown, substituting Noah's name for Jonah's again, and hating that the lies were beginning to layer on top of one another. Pretty soon I was going to need an app just to keep everything straight.

"Is there a chance humans were being doped with it?" I wondered aloud. "To make them more susceptible to glamour?"

"So they'd be more willing to give blood at a party? That doesn't ring for me." I imagined him leaning back in his chair, hands behind his head, ready to dish out some wisdom. "Kind of a lot of trouble to do something glamour would do anyway. I mean, that is the point of glamour, after all."

"True."

"And besides, I don't want to blame the victim here, but if they're showing up at a vamp party, they probably have some idea that bloodletting's going to happen. That doesn't mean they're consenting to it happening to them—playing pro-vamp at a party isn't the same thing as sitting down and offering up a vein—but the point is they may not need a double dose of convincing. You know about the wristbands?"

"The red ones? Yeah, I saw them. There were a few there."

"Then it doesn't sound like the vamps needed to convince anyone. And, frankly, humans sitting down and presenting a vein doesn't exactly offer much challenge. I'm not sure that's the kind of thing testosterone-laced vamps would even enjoy."

"This one doesn't," I confirmed. "There was a lot of magic floating around. Any chance the magic was external? Not vampire, I mean?"

His voice went flat. "You're asking if a sorcerer would knock out a human so a vampire could go at her? Even if there were

Order schlubs in Chicago other than Mallory and her tutor, which there aren't, no. There's no way a sorcerer would do that."

"What about aggression? Would a sorcerer be interested in making vamps more aggressive, giving them a hair-trigger temper, that kind of thing?"

"I hate to dash your dreams, Merit, but your testosterone levels aren't really of interest to the Order."

So much for Jonah's sorcerer idea, not that I'd been a big fan of it anyway. "Then I'm flummoxed. I was hoping you'd have insights."

"I always have insights. You said there were violence, glamour, and drugs, right?"

"It was Ghouls Gone Wild in there. The biters had fangs out, and I saw a lot of really silvered eyes. Not the usual irises-turned-silver bit. There was enough magic, enough glamour, enough blood floating around, that their pupils were narrowed down to nothing." I nearly outed Jonah, and had to remind myself to use his cover—"Noah created a distraction with some blood, and the vamps went batshit crazy."

"It's blood. You're vampires. Batshit crazy is pretty basic math."

"Not just First Hunger bloodlust. More, I don't know, angry?" I thought about what Ethan had said. "It was like the whole event wasn't about sensuality; it was about fighting. Aggression. Adrenaline. We're not talking a few vamps drinking in some hole-in-the-wall hiding place. We're talking a big party with a lot of magic, a lot of glamour, a lot of susceptible humans, and a lot of very angry vampires ready for a fight."

Catcher sighed. "I don't mean to be the bearer of bad news, but maybe that's just a side effect of the popularity. Maybe that's just how vamps are partying these days."

"If so, they're doing the recruiting at Temple Bar. And the phone that received the text was found at Benson's."

I heard the creak of his chair.

"They're recruiting at House bars?" he asked.

"From what we've heard. Word is, the recruits at Temple were a short guy and a woman. We think her name was Marie. Did I ever tell you Celina's given name? Marie Collette Navarre," I said, without waiting for his answer.

"Now, that is interesting. It's shitty evidence, but it's interesting."

"I live to infotain."

"I don't suppose you have plans to head to Temple Bar and investigate?"

"I'm leaving within the hour."

"Good girl. In the meantime, I'll talk to our vamp source and see if I can find out anything about the recruiters. Besides, I owe you a favor."

"You do?"

"I do." He cleared his throat a little nervously. "Mallory and I talked last night."

"Is she okay?"

"She's not her best. But she's feeling a lot better after a little conscience clearing. You did good by her, Merit, and I appreciate it. A lot. I talked her down," he assured me. "The rest will come with time."

My eyes welled a little at the corners. "Thanks, Chief. I was worried. I love her, too, you know. Just not in the grotesquely physical way that you do."

"The sex is phenomenal."

I made a faux gagging sound. "Spare me the details and call me if you learn anything."

"On it," he said, and the line went dead.

I hung up the phone and stared at the receiver for a minute, not quite ready to make the next connection in tonight's call-athon.

Ethan might not have bought my argument, but I still suspected Celina had some part in this: at a minimum, hiring vamps—or perhaps a short guy—to do her dirty work. It was too much of a co-incidence that "Marie" was running around inciting vamps to treat humans like disposable convenience food.

I made myself a promise—whatever it took, she was mine. She'd caused me trouble, she'd caused Ethan trouble, and she was lining up trouble for the House and the city. Even if I had to hide it from Ethan and the GP, I was going to bring her down.

Of course, I still needed evidence. I could admit the use of an old alias wasn't exactly strong support for my theory. And if I wanted to confirm whether she'd been involved, who had the best access to Celina?

Morgan Greer. Newish Master of Navarre House, former (brief) boyfriend, and former Celina booster. I wasn't exactly looking forward to the call. But he'd been Celina's Second, and that made him my best source for info about her current whereabouts. I couldn't trust he'd voluntarily call up Scott and Ethan and offer them information.

I punched in Morgan's number—which was still in my phone just waiting for a drunk dial—and hung on for the ring.

"Greer," he threw out. There was something pretentious about his answering with his last name. He'd gained it back when he became Master of Navarre House; apparently he wanted to remind callers about that change in position.

"Hey, Morgan. It's Merit."

"Oh. Hi." Suspicion snuck back into his tone.

"I'm sorry to call you, but I need a favor."

"A favor?"

"Yeah, and I need you to promise not to freak out."

"No one ever says that unless the odds of freaking out are pretty high."

"True." I paused for courage, then spit it out. "I need to talk to you about Celina." I gave him the details, from the would-be rave to the woman named Marie outside Temple Bar.

There was a long pause. "And what, exactly, do you think she's doing?"

"I'm not sure yet. Maybe soliciting humans for some kind of vamp anger-management sessions?"

He made a disdainful sound. "Merit, even if I conceded the point, which I don't, the GP isn't going to put her behind bars."

"Maybe not. But if we have enough information about what she's really doing here, we tip the odds. And if nothing else, we gain a better understanding of what she's up to and how we can keep her from destroying the city."

"So, let me get this straight—you want me to help you investigate my Master, the woman who made me a vampire, whom I gave two oaths to serve, against the wishes of the GP, and you don't have any evidence of whatever it is you think she might be involved in?"

"'Investigate' is a really strong word. I prefer 'keep apprised of.'"

He went quiet.

"Look," I said, "I know it's a lot to ask, especially from you, especially from me. But she's tried to kill me twice, she's tried to kill Ethan, and God only knows if she's really staying out of Navarre business."

That last one was a stretch, but given the quick hitch in his breath, I figured I was on to something.

"She's got friends," I reminded him. "At least a couple from

Cadogan, and that's not even her House. Have you lost any members lately?"

I had to give it to him. His tone changed, from adolescent angst to vampire in charge.

"No," he said. "But they loved her. And I haven't made any vamps yet. Won't until the spring, so their allegiances are to her. Would it surprise me if they'd been in touch? And that they hadn't told me about it? Eh. I wouldn't put great odds on it, but stranger things have happened."

"If she is mixed up in this—getting humans to vamp parties—why would she do it? What would her motivation be?"

"Well, she did have the crown whipped out from under her, so to speak. If she can't play the vamp heroine, maybe she's ready for a stint as the antagonist."

"The humans don't like her anymore, so she'll happily feed them to the wolves?"

"Like I said, stranger things have happened. But I seriously, seriously doubt she's playing it that loose. Showing up at a Cadogan bar where folks might recognize her? That doesn't play for me."

And now Morgan and Ethan were thinking alike. That was a frightening development. But they'd both forgotten something important about Celina.

"But those folks might include me. And she's taken the chance for a showdown with me whenever it's presented itself." The woman had it in for me, although I wasn't entirely sure why.

"I don't know. I'm just not feeling that argument."

"Well, if you start to feel it any more strongly—or maybe you hear anything concrete about Celina or her whereabouts—could you give me a call? And if you don't want to do it for me, consider the fate of the city."

"You think she would cause that much trouble?"

"Yes, Morgan, I do. Celina is very smart, very savvy, and, from what I've seen, very unhappy about the way things went down. She expected to play the martyr with humans as well as vamps. She might have a few vamps on her side—"

"And Cadogan vamps at that," he interrupted.

I rolled my eyes, but continued. "She might have a few vamps on her side, but she doesn't have humans anymore. And that's the thing that bothers her."

"Get me some evidence," he said, "and we'll talk."

He hung up the phone.

Why did everyone keep demanding "evidence" and "facts"? I swear, cop and courtroom dramas were ruining the good name of gut instinct.

Well, either way, I was going to have to get more info. Might as well get started.

My attempt at Temple Bar espionage couldn't get started without a little introductory chat, so after I showered and donned more club-worthy clothes—my black suit pants and another tank, this one in red, matched with red Mary Jane–style heels—I headed to the basement.

The House was four stories of vampire wonder: dorm rooms and Ethan's suite on the top floor. Dorm rooms (including mine), the library, and the ballroom were on the second floor. The first floor held administrative offices, the cafeteria, and the sitting rooms. The basement, however, was all business: training room, the Cadogan House arsenal, a gym, and the Operations Room. The Ops Room served as Luc's office and the HQ for the Cadogan House guards, including Lindsey and, on rare occasions, me.

The Ops Room door was cracked open, and this time I had the good sense—and the patience—to peek inside before storming in.

Juliet and Kelley sat at computer stations along the wall, which meant Lindsey was probably outside patrolling the grounds. Luc sat at the conference table that took up the middle of the room—but he was wearing a suit.

Across from Luc sat a tall, slightly gawky-looking man in a suit at least a size too large. He was talking at full speed about his video-gaming hobby.

"And I try not to use cheats, but you can't always rely on the designers to have created a game that progresses logically through any particular portion of the world, so occasionally you have to compromise your standards and find a cheat code in order to move forward, because you really don't want to lose the inertia of forward progress or you'll completely lose interest in the quest."

When he paused for breath, I found myself sucking in air, too. This guy, whoever he was, did not know when to stop.

"Thank you, Allan. I think that's an interesting answer, although it doesn't entirely speak to how you could contribute as a House guard."

Oh, my God, Luc was *interviewing* this guy. We were a man down since Peter's betrayal, so he must have been looking for a replacement. I hoped this one was a safety pick and not Luc's first choice; otherwise, we were in trouble.

Allan's expression was withering. "It goes to the times in which I, as a House guard, would need to rely upon my own fighting instincts and occasionally disobey the standard procedure—the standard protocol, if you will—rather than following the dictates of a Guard Captain who—"

"Wow," Luc interjected, "that is an excellent clarification, and I think that will do it for us today, since we've got another meeting coming up—oh, and look, here's our Sentinel now!"

I muttered a silent curse, but put on a fake smile and pushed through the door. "Hi, there."

Luc jumped up and headed for the door, then put a hand at my back. "Thank sweet Christ, Sentinel," he murmured, then smiled broadly at Allan.

"Allan, have you met our Sentinel? Merit, Allan is interviewing for the open guard position. He's a Cadogan vamp living outside the House, and he's looking to join our little family."

That explained why I'd never seen him before. I offered a little wave. "Nice to meet you, Allan."

But Allan had no time for niceties. "Is there really a reason to have a Sentinel in this day and age, given the state of current security technology?"

"Okay, then," Luc said, then moved Allan toward the door. "Just head right up those stairs to get back to the first floor. Thanks so much for coming in."

"When will I find out when I start?"

"Well, we're just at the beginning of our interview process, but we will absolutely let you know when we're ready to fill the position."

"I'll be on vacation in a week. I'm going to Branson. So you might not be able to reach me. But I have a sat-phone. I could take that with me."

"That is exceptional," Luc said, all but shoving him out the Ops Room door. "I'll be sure to get that information. And say hello to Andy Williams while you're down there."

Luc shut the door, then proceeded to bang his forehead against it.

"Interviews not going well?"

Forehead still pressed against the door, he glanced over. "I want to stab myself in the eye with a pencil. This kid's smart, but his head's in the wrong place, and he doesn't exactly have people skills."

"Then maybe he'd be good on the computers," I pointed out. "Even Jeff Christopher has a Warcraft fixation."

"You are ever the optimist. And I'm not busting his balls for the gaming. I may have cut my fangs in a different time, but I own every current gaming system on the U.S. market." He leaned in. "And a couple from Taipei no one knows about yet."

He shook his head. "Nah, I object to the attitude. We're asking this guy to step in front of a stake for the rest of us if necessary, and he's waxing philosophical about when it's okay to disobey orders? No, thank you. Would you trust him to do that for you?"

"Good point. And no."

"Unless a booth babe was throwing the stake," Kelley dryly threw out, her gaze still scanning the black-and-white closed-circuit security images on her computer screen.

"You hit that one on the head, Kels," Luc said. "Now, Sentinel, what brings you downstairs, other than your hella good timing? Did Darius scare you down here?"

"Actually, I need to give you a heads-up about something. Could you give Malik a call? Ask him to come down, as well?"

Luc arched an eyebrow. "Got a bee in your bonnet?"

"Not exactly. But I might have a former Navarre Master soliciting humans outside Temple Bar."

Luc's brows lifted. "Let me get him on the phone."

CHAPTER TWELVE

OVER THE RAINBOW

Ten minutes later—and presumably an excuse to Ethan and Darius—Malik joined us in the Ops Room. We put Lindsey, who'd been outside patrolling the grounds, on speakerphone so she could listen in.

"I'm on," Lindsey said. "Get to it, Hot Shit."

She really did love me.

"So you know the basics," I told them. "We previously saw small raves—a handful of vampires, a few people, some drinking. Now we're talking full-on parties with lots of vamps, lots of humans, and lots of potential for violence. I didn't see the kind of violence Tate talked about while we were there—but we pulled the plug as quickly as we could. We know humans are being pretty severely glamoured, maybe helped in part by a drug being passed around. And we think the human invites are originating from the House bars."

The room went silent, everyone exchanging looks of concern.

"Your evidence?" Malik asked.

"The phone that got the text about last night's shindig was left at Benson's, the Grey House bar. And another human told us she found out about the party when she met a short man and a woman named Marie outside Temple Bar."

Malik's lip curled. "Someone is using our place to hit on humans."

"That appears to be the case."

There was only one word for the look in his eyes—determination. "And what's your plan?"

"Well, in a perfect world, the plan would be not pissing off the GP. But as we know, this is clearly not a perfect world."

There were general grumbles of agreement around the room.

"Darius wants us safe and sound inside Cadogan House—where, for now, he can keep an eye on us—not stirring up trouble outside the House. But there's already trouble brewing out there, and if we don't get a handle on it, things are going to go south very quickly. We can't just sit here and watch the city fall around us.

"I know I'm young," I continued, "but I also have an obligation to do the things I think are necessary to protect the House. Even if Darius doesn't approve . . . and even if Ethan doesn't know about them."

I let that implication sink in for a minute, and then dropped my voice. "I've given him a general heads-up, but I'm not giving him details, and he's not going. The less he knows—"

"The less Darius can use him as a scapegoat," Malik said.

I nodded in agreement. "Precisely. The short of it is, he gave me a thumbs-up to make the best decision I could, and I want to give you all the same courtesy. The GP is putting enough pressure on the House without me adding to it. If you want to know what I'm doing, I'll tell you. If not"—I held up my hands—"no worries. You can deny you knew anything was going on, and hopefully that will shield you from Darius if worse comes to worst."

My piece said, I glanced around the room again.

Luc kicked a booted foot onto the tabletop. "Are you seriously asking us if we're not going to take your side against the GP? Seriously, Sentinel? I thought I taught you better than that. We are a team—and you're a member of it."

"And you're getting better at the speechifying," Lindsey said. "I think Sullivan's going to your head. Oh, and I'm totally in."

Juliet and Kelley smiled at each other, then at me.

"We're obviously in, too," Kelley said. "We've known Ethan a lot longer than we've known Darius. He may not be perfect, but he's concerned about the House, not just the politics."

"Agreed," Juliet said.

We all looked at Malik, the only one I wasn't quite sure of. It was not that I doubted his allegiances, but he was quiet enough that I wasn't entirely sure where I stood with him.

"Your heart is in the right place," he said. "That's all I need to know."

I smiled at him, then nodded at the group. "Okay, then. Here's the plan."

Fast-forward forty-five minutes to a gaggle of vampires emerging from a cab into the dark, muggy street in front of Temple Bar, not far from Wrigley Field. Me, Lindsey, and Christine—Christine Dupree, before she lost her name to join the House, another vamp from my Novitiate class—dressed to the nines in chic shades of black, gray, and red and makeupped within an inch of our immortal lives.

We probably looked like the new cast of *Charlie's Angels*. I was the spunky brunette, Lindsey was the sassy blonde, and Christine—formerly a brunette—was now rocking a sleek bob of russet hair.

Christine wasn't a guard, and she and I weren't exactly close friends. Since we were bringing her into something that could get her in trouble—and demanded her loyalty—Luc gave her a lecture on duty. We didn't give her all the details about the raves; she only knew that we were looking into bad acts at Temple Bar. She seemed eager to help, which was good enough for me.

As for the bar itself, I'd decided on a new plan—playing the bait.

The Cadogan vamps knew me as Sentinel and Lindsey as guard. But they also knew that Christine was the daughter of Dash Dupree, a notorious Chicago lawyer, and that I was the daughter of Joshua Merit, Mr. Chicago Real Estate Bigwig.

I'd realized at the Streeterville party that I could fake party girl pretty well, so I was going to try it again. And with creds like mine and Christine's, no one was going to question two socialites mixing it up at Temple Bar, asking questions about new kinds of excitement.

There was a line outside the door. Although humans hadn't been allowed in the House, Tate hadn't extended the ban to the bars. Colin and Sean had gotten creative, installing neon signs above the door to help visitors keep track. Tonight, the HUMANS and CADOGAN lights were lit, which meant vamps from Navarre or Grey were out of luck.

The human part was fine by me, as it would help us accomplish part one of my Temple Bar Infiltration Plan, or T-BIP. Unfortunately, the ban on Grey and Navarre vamps wasn't going to help. I'd hoped I could use the night to get info from the other Houses about the raves and drugs. Oh, well. Jonah could get me into Grey House. As for Navarre, I'd cross that bridge when I came to it.

Christine, Lindsey, and I sauntered in like we owned the place, then stood in the front of the bar for a moment . . . to see and be seen.

I took a moment to appreciate the locale. Temple Bar was practically a shrine to the Cubs, my favorite sports team. The walls were lined with uniforms and pennants, and Cubs memorabilia covered every free spot in the bar. The bar was run by two redheaded vampires, also brothers, Sean and Colin. They kept all things Irish and Cubbie alive and well in Wrigleyville.

"First stop in T-BIP," I told my accomplices, "identifying humans who might have gotten an invite to a once or future rave so we can identify the host."

"Or hostess," Lindsey added. "Let's not forget the Celina possibility."

"Can we please stop calling it T-BIP?" Christine put in. "I get that you enjoy acronyms, but that sounds ridiculous."

"Unfortch," Lindsey said, "I have to agree. Unless the acronym is a helluva lot more rugged. Like 'DANGER' or 'KILLFACE' or 'STUN GUN' or something."

I slid her a questioning glance. "And what, exactly, would 'DANGER' stand for?"

"Um." She looked up at the ceiling while she made up an answer. "'Dedicated, angsty Novitiate girls examining risk'? Or maybe, 'drugs are never good entertainment, right?'"

"*Lame,*" I muttered.

"Aw, sadface. I came up with that totally off the cuff. No props for off the cuff?"

"Ladies," Christine said, holding up a hand. "Let's act our ages and stay on target."

Lindsey and I exchanged a guilty glance. I'm honest enough to admit that sarcasm and silliness were my preferred methods of dealing with stress. But I had a lot of it, and it wasn't like I could just break out a Mallocake mid-katana-fight.

Coolly, Christine surveyed the crowd like a lion eyeing a herd of water buffalo—dedicated to finding the weakest link. We figured any humans at a vamp bar were more likely to remember a socialite turned vampire and trust her with their vamp-party information.

"There," she finally said, pointing with a carefully manicured finger to a couple of human guys in fraternity shirts who, by the look of the empty pitcher on their table, had already done some imbibing.

"I start there," she said, then sauntered across the room toward her unsuspecting victims. The guys' heads lifted as she neared them, their eyes going a little glazy, although I wasn't sure if that was because the two of them had finished a pitcher or because she was throwing out some serious glamour.

"Strong Psych?" I asked Lindsey. That was the measure for a vamp with a lot of glamouring capability.

"Nope," Lindsey said. "Those dopey expressions are one hundred percent about her lovely lady lumps."

If so, those lumps were proven winners; one of the boys hopped up and offered Christine a chair. She took it, demurely crossing one leg over another, then leaning forward to chat with the boys. If they had any pertinent information, I had no doubt she'd ferret it out.

"She is surprisingly good at this," I said, glancing over at Lindsey. "Is Luc interviewing her for a job?"

"I'm not sure she works," Lindsey said. "She's more the trust fund type—which comes in very handy in situations like this. On the other hand, no complaining if we start having dinner in the Dash Dupree Memorial Cafeteria a decade from now."

I chuckled, then looked over at the bar. "Since her work is under way, let's get moving on ours."

"Humans—check," Lindsey agreed, moving her finger in the shape of a check mark. "Now, shall we hit up the bartender?"

I winked at her and moved toward the bar. "Just try and keep up, okay?"

Lindsey snorted. "Honey, you may have the steak, but I got the sizzle."

Only Colin, who was a little older and taller than Sean, was working the bar tonight.

"If he's solo, it might not be a good time to tear him away," Lindsey said as she followed me over.

I took her point, but countered with my own. "We're nocturnal, and he probably works the bar until sunup. I'm not sure there would be a good time to tear him away, and we need to find out what's going on."

We bypassed the two-deep crowd of humans and vamps in front of the bar and went directly to the end of it. I waited until Colin moved toward us, wiping his hands on a towel stuck into his belt, before I popped the question.

"Can we talk in private for a few minutes?"

With a dubious expression, Colin turned to grab two beers out of a small refrigerator, then put them on the bar and grabbed the cash a vamp had dropped there. "Busy tonight. Can it wait?"

"Um, hello?" Lindsey asked, moving beside me and propping an elbow on the bar. "I'm here. I can watch the bar."

Colin frowned at her. "Are you up for it?"

"Honey, I spent a decade of my rather glorious life pouring shots in the East Village. These people will be both drunk and entertained by the time you get back, or I'm not one of the top ten hotties of Cadogan House. Seriously," she added with a glance at me. "There's a list, and we're both on it."

"Nice," I said. Not bad for a former library-bound grad student.

From hottie to barmaid, Lindsey didn't waste any time sidling behind the bar and slapping a white towel over her shoulder.

"Ladies and gentlemen," she announced, "who needs a drink?"

When the crowd let out an appreciative hoot, Colin put his hand at my back and steered me toward the other end of the bar. "Let's go to the office. It's a little quieter back there."

I followed as he made a loop through the bar. He worked the room like a seasoned politician: checking on drinks, kissing pretty girls on the cheek, recommending pizza toppings at the joint next door, and inquiring after the parents of apparently human friends. I didn't know Colin much at all, but he was clearly well liked, as much a fixture of the bar as the Cubs gear and vampires.

When we made it across the room, we stopped in the photograph-covered back hallway—and past a picture of Ethan and Lacey Sheridan, his former flame—and into a small room at the end.

Colin pulled a key ring from his pocket and unlocked the door. The office was small—barely large enough to hold a metal desk and beat-up file cabinet. Every free surface was covered in papers—magazines, notes, checks, tax returns, pages from yellow legal pads, folded newspapers, sports programs, invoices, take-out menus.

The walls were also covered, although the content was much less kid-friendly. Posters and calendars featuring pinups from the last seventy years were plastered like wallpaper across the room, busty blondes and brunettes in tiny shorts and three-inch heels smiling down at us coquettishly. It looked like the office you might find in a service station or quick-lube shop. Not exactly the kind of place that made it comfortable to be a woman, but then again, I wasn't the target audience.

"Nice digs," I politely said.

"We like it," he said. "Get the door, would you?"

I closed it, which lowered the volume just enough to allow us to talk instead of screaming.

Colin slid around the desk and pulled open the top drawer of the file cabinet. He slipped a small metal flask out of the drawer, unscrewed the cap, and took a sip.

"Booze?" I wondered aloud.

"Type O. My own special concoction." He offered it to me, but I shook him off. I needed a clear head, and I wasn't confident Colin's "special concoction" was going to keep me in a business-minded place.

"No, thank you."

The flask still in one hand, he pulled out an ancient desk chair, the back cushion covered by more duct tape than fabric, and took a seat. "Now, Ms. Sentinel, what can I do for you?"

"Have you noticed anything out of the ordinary around here lately?"

He made a sarcastic sound. "Once upon a time, this was a bar for vampires. For the fanged and their kith and kin. Since we came out of the closet, I've been serving humans who think male vamps are brooding, romantic heroes and female vamps have a secret weight-loss formula. I'm also occasionally serving humans who think vamps are trash and the harbingers of the apocalypse. So out of the ordinary? Yes, Sentinel. I'd say so."

By the end of the rant, his words had sped up, and the faster he talked, the more pronounced his accent became. I'd never been to Ireland, but I could hear green hills in his voice.

He also had a point, but I was looking for something a little more specific, so I got to mine. "We think vamps are using the bar to find humans for a new kind of rave. Anything like that ring a bell?"

He took a sip from his flask. "Like I said, plenty of humans want to spend time with vampires. I'm not sure I'd recognize the difference between a vamp hitting on a human and a vamp inviting a human to attend a drinking party of some type."

"Fair enough." I gnawed my lip for a moment, disappointed he hadn't given me any breakthrough information. "Okay, how about drugs? Something called V? It might be used to make humans susceptible to glamour."

His brows lifted with interest. "You don't say. Are we so unskilled at glamour these days that we have to resort to pharmaceuticals to do the job?"

"We're not sure yet about how it works—just that it's been found at a party."

He shrugged one shoulder. "This is a bar; drugs are par for the course. I haven't heard about any new drugs being passed around, but that doesn't mean it's not happening."

Strike three for the Sentinel, but I tried again. "What about familiar characters? Anyone hanging around the bar a lot more than usual? Anyone out of place, or anyone who pops up over and over?"

Colin leaned back in his chair and crossed his arms over his chest, the flask nestled beneath his arms like a doll. "I don't want to rain on your parade, and I appreciate everything you do for the House as Sentinel. But to be frank, I spend my time trying to ensure the vampires and humans in this bar are well tended and entertained and have an opportunity to burn off a little of the steam that builds up through the workweek. But if you're asking me if I've seen anything suggesting Temple Bar is the new HQ for some kind of rave movement? Then no, I have not."

Deflated, I sighed. I'd figured the guy who spent most of his time at the bar was going to have the best insight into what Sarah had thought was going on at Temple Bar. But he had a point; he might have had the access, but he also had plenty else to do.

I nodded. "Thanks for the honesty. Get in touch if you think of anything?"

He offered a wink. "Rest assured, Sentinel."

With no more information in hand, I excused Colin and headed back into the bar.

And that was when I got surprise number two.

I knew Lindsey had been born in Iowa. I knew her father was a pork producer. I knew she'd lived in New York and had an allegiance toward the Yankees that I, as a loyal Cubs fan, could only assume was the result of some sort of low-grade vampire insanity.

I did not know she was bartender extraordinaire.

I found Lindsey behind the bar and a crush of vamps four-deep, dollars in hand, shouting her name like she'd just won them a pennant.

Girl was a *phenomenon*. She spun a cocktail shaker horizontally in one hand and a bottle of blue alcohol in the other. The crowd let out a "Woot!" when she flipped the bottle over her shoulder and caught it again in the palm of her hand, then dumped the contents of both containers into a martini glass. The bottle and shaker hit the top of the bar, and then the glass was in her hand and headed for the vampire in front of her. She tidily plucked cash from the vamp's extended fingers and pushed it into a jar.

The crowd around her let out a round of applause; Lindsey made a little bow and then began prepping a drink for the next vamp in line. The vamps at the bar watched her movements with shifting eyes as if they were waiting for a once-in-a-lifetime sip of rare and limited wine. Personally, I didn't understand the appeal, but I wasn't much of a drinker.

I turned at the tap on my shoulder and found Christine at my side.

"Anything to report?"

She gestured toward the boys. "Our new favorite fraternity brothers are here at least once a week, usually on weekends. Last Friday, they were smoking in the alley when a man approached them, made some overtures about trying out a new vampire experience. As it turns out, while our fraternity brothers were brave enough to venture into a vampire bar, they weren't quite brave enough for anything more than that." She gave me a knowing smile. "Drinking at a bar with vamps apparently gives them a taste of danger without the calories, so to speak. They didn't get a good look at the man, but—"

I held up a hand to stop her, satisfaction warming my blood. I really did enjoy the moment when the puzzle pieces began to fall into place. "Let me guess—he was short, older, dark hair?"

Her eyes widened in surprise. "How did you know?"

"My witness was taking a breather outside when she was approached by a man with the same description."

"And he's using Temple Bar as his own personal recruiting ground?"

"That might be the case."

Rowdy applause split the air near the bar. I looked over just in time to see Lindsey finish up another drink and clap her hands together like a Vegas dealer.

"And now, for my next trick," she said, sliding me a glance, "something vampires never get to see. I will make your House social chair do my bidding!"

With the encouragement of the crowd, she beckoned me over. I rolled my eyes, but the crowd apparently appreciated the humor, so I did my part and slid behind the bar.

She immediately began bossing me around, pointing to medium-sized glasses. "Give me seven of those and line 'em up along the bar."

When I did as directed, Lindsey grabbed a clean cocktail shaker and began pouring alcohol into it. After she'd layered five or six kinds of booze, she put the bottles down again and capped the shaker.

"You know what I miss?" she asked the crowd. "Clouds. Sunshine. That weird moment when it rains but the sun's still out. Sunrises. Sunsets—until after the fact, of course."

The crowd chuckled appreciatively.

"But you know what I miss most of all?" she continued. "Rainbows, like a handful of Skittles thrown across the sky. So for all of you lovely Cadogan vamps, here's a rainbow, one color at a time."

With a flick of her wrist, Lindsey began pouring the liquid in a cascade over the glasses. She filled the first glass with blue and, as soon as each glass was full, switched to the next. Like magic, the alcohol she'd layered into the cocktail shaker became a rainbow across the glasses, from turquoise to a bright shade of pink. When she was finished, there were seven glasses of liquid that stood on the bar like a perfect, wet rainbow.

"And that," she said, putting the shaker back on the bar, "is how vampires make rainbows."

The bar burst into applause. I had to admit, it was a pretty sweet trick. The drinks might not taste especially good—they looked like sci-fi movie props, to be honest—but they looked phenomenal.

Lindsey glanced over at me and grinned. "Not bad for a Yankees fan, eh?"

"Not bad at all," Colin said, stepping behind the bar again. "You did us proud."

He apparently hadn't been the only one impressed. The vamps along the bar, a mix of men and women, began jostling for position to get at one of the seven drinks.

"It's just booze, ladies and gents," Colin said with a chuckle, wiping up the excess alcohol Lindsey had spilled.

"There is plenty more where that came from," she added, "and I'm sure Colin would be happy to take your money for it."

Colin chuckled, but the jostling for Lindsey's drinks hit me as odd. Essentially, they were booze poured by a member of the House whom the vamps could have seen any night of the week—and in a bar they could have visited any night of the week.

My senses on edge, I moved back to the end of the bar, and caught Lindsey's glance from the corner of my eye. She'd watched me move, and ever the savvy guard, she gave the vamps the same once-over, saw them nudging one another to get to the alcohol.

That meant we were both watching the moment a little pushing erupted into a full-blown fight.

CHAPTER THIRTEEN

THE REVOLUTION WILL BE TELEVISED

"I saw it first," said a vamp at the end of the bar with dreadlocks pushed back under a beret-style hat.

"I was reaching for it when you put your meaty hand out there," said a second, a slender, brown-haired man wearing a dark T-shirt and khakis. They looked more like poetry-slam or coffeehouse guys than Temple Bar scrappers . . . until they began punching each other in the face.

"What the shit?" Lindsey exclaimed as I jumped around the bar to pull them apart. I grabbed T-shirt by his arm and yanked him backward. He stumbled a few feet before hitting the bar floor on his butt. Dreadlocks—still in the heat of passion—swung out at me—but I caught his fist and swung his arm around, leveraging his weight so that he went to his knees.

And then I looked into his eyes. His pupils were tiny, his silvered irises diamond-bright rings around them.

I muttered a curse. They were acting like the rave vamps had acted—trigger-happy and anger-prone—and they had the same enlarged irises. My stomach sank in warning, and I feared the worst. Was this the next stage of a vampire mass hysteria?

I gave Dreadlocks a shot to the neck that cut off some oxygen and put him out on the floor. Unfortunately, by the time I made it to my feet again, a dozen more vamps had succumbed to whatever ailed them. Furious fists and insults were hurled around, the vamps pounding at one another as if their lives—and not a cheap glass of cheaper alcohol—were on the line.

The irritation spread like a virus. Each vamp that lashed out and inadvertently bumped another started a second round, and the violence rippled through the crowd accordingly.

With no better option than to jump into the fray, I looked at Lindsey, shared a nod of agreement with her, and made my move. My goal wasn't to win the fight, but to separate the fighters. I began by jumping between the two closest to me. I took a punch in the shoulder for my trouble, but managed to rip the two vamps away from each other. I tossed them in opposite directions and headed for the next pair.

Lindsey did the same, hopping over the bar—spilling the rainbow drinks in the process—and pulling vamps apart.

Unfortunately, they weren't willing to go. Whatever had possessed them took them over, kept them raking their nails at one another, eager to continue a fight over nothing substantial.

Fortunately, the ones who weren't affected—a handful of men and women that I'd seen around the House—helped us separate the contenders. We became a team. Fighting against our own, unfortunately, but still fighting for the good of the cause.

I appreciated the effort, even if it wasn't enough. With each pair I separated, another seemed to pop up, until the swell of fighting vampires crashed through the door to the bar. Over the background roar of brawling, I could hear the nearing wail of sirens. Someone had called the cops about the fight. This was about to get even uglier; it was time for a new plan.

I glanced around, looking for Lindsey, and found her at my left, dragging a squalling vampire by the ankle.

"Lindsey, I'm going to get the humans out of the bar!" I yelled, pushing one vamp off me and turning to avoid another's boot stomp.

Cops wouldn't be thrilled if vamps were fighting other vamps, but they'd be downright pissed if humans got caught in the cross fire. With Tate already on the warpath, I'm not sure we could make it through that kind of scandal with the House intact, much less without a receiver.

"I'm on my way," she replied, dumping her vamp a few tables away. Another Cadogan vamp took over for her, holding that vamp back while she rushed back to me and yanked back the vamp who'd tried to kick me into submission.

"You're a doll," I told her, hurdling a knot of wrestling vampires as I ran for the door. I started by building a vamp chute by grabbing the nearest table and sliding it toward the door. Three more made a faux retaining wall between the exit and the rest of the bar, which kept the fighting vamps corralled and gave the humans a clear path.

I looked back at the crowd, and first spied a couple squeezed back into a booth, eyes wide. I ran to them, hustled them to their feet, and pointed them toward the now partially secured exit.

"Out that way," I said, and as they headed for the door, I rounded up the rest of them. The humans were pretty easy to spot. The few vamps who hadn't been affected by the violence were trying to help; the humans mostly cowered, probably shocked by the violence and trying to stay out of the way. I located as many as I could and sent them toward the door, police sirens getting louder as they ran outside.

When I'd cleared out the last of the humans, I moved to the

door and found the street awash in blue and red lights as humans ran from the bar like hostages released from a bank robbery.

Cops began to emerge from their vehicles, and I began to fear the worst—that we'd all be arrested for inciting public mayhem. Of course, that would make Tate's arrest-warrant threat moot.

I moved slowly toward the sidewalk, not eager to be shot by cops who thought I was an emerging perp. Adrenaline began to pulse again as I prepared to face round two—the aftermath. But when a familiar Oldsmobile rolled to the curb, I breathed a sigh of relief.

My grandfather stepped out of the car's passenger side, wearing khaki-colored pants and a butter yellow, short-sleeved button-down shirt.

Jeff stepped out of the backseat, and Catcher popped out of the driver's side in a dark T-shirt advertising "Bang Bang Home Repair." His wearables might have been kitschy, but his expression was all business.

The three of them nodded at the cops they passed. I walked their way.

"Problems?"

"Violence," I said. "Lindsey was mixing drinks at the bar, and the vamps started fighting over who was going to get which drink. The aggression spread like a virus after that."

"Same thing you saw at the rave?" Catcher asked, and I nodded my agreement.

"Looks like it. Something in the air, maybe, or slipped into their drinks? I don't know." I gestured to the cluster of humans. "We got the humans out of the bar, but things are still tense inside. They're still going at it, and pulling them off each other hasn't really worked."

"How'd you get them calm at the rave?" Jeff asked.

"We didn't. We basically faked a fire alarm and fled the scene. Since it didn't make the news, I assumed they'd calmed down on their own."

A bar table suddenly flew through the open doorway and crashed on the sidewalk outside, rolling to a stop at the front tire of one of the CPD cruisers.

"We may not have that kind of time," Catcher said.

"Get in there," my grandfather prompted, gesturing to get the attention of one of the CPD cops. They exchanged some sort of secret cop code, the other officers standing down while Catcher jogged toward the bar and disappeared inside.

It was only a moment before Lindsey and the rest of the non-fighting vamps were jogging out onto the sidewalk. Colin was last in line, a dour expression on his face.

"What's Catcher going to—" was all I managed to get out before the bar went silent. No more crashing glass, no more screamed epithets, no more flat *pop*s of flesh against flesh.

Although I knew it probably wasn't possible, my first thought was that Catcher had somehow taken out every vamp in the bar with his mad fighting skills. But Jeff leaned in with a more likely answer.

"Magic," he whispered. "Catcher got the happy vamps out of the bar. That gave him room to work the Keys on the rest of them."

"By putting them to sleep?" I asked.

"Nah, probably just a little calming juju. He's good at that— willing folks to chill the eff out. It's a skill that comes in handy with sups on occasion."

I wasn't entirely sure how I felt about that juju. Although I trusted Catcher, I wasn't thrilled a sorcerer was using his abilities to sedate vampires. I would have preferred to be in there with him, keeping an eye on things and providing a little oversight.

But before I could even give voice to the concern, it was over. Catcher appeared in the doorway again and waved a hand toward the rest of the cops. By now, there were a dozen milling around our corner of Wrigleyville. Most wore uniforms, but a few were detectives in button-downs and suits, their badges clipped to their waists or on a chain around their necks.

"We'll head in," my grandfather said. "My hope is that no one will be arrested until we sort this out. These officers know this isn't just a drunk and disorderly call—but that there's more going on here supernaturally."

"And we'll keep an eye on the vamps until they come to their senses," Jeff added, putting a hand on my arm. "That's part of our job description—occasionally playing guardian angels."

"I would appreciate that."

"We'll be in touch as soon as we can," my grandfather said. "You stay out of trouble until then."

I looked back at the bar and thought about my investigation. Our frat boys and Sarah might have been solicited by the same guy, at least based on their minimal descriptions. That was worth a few more questions. "Actually, I think I'm going to take a look around."

My grandfather frowned. "I'm not sure I'm crazy about your wandering around out here when there's something strange in the air."

"I have a dagger in my boot, and I'm surrounded by cops."

"Fair point, baby girl. Just do me a favor—be careful? I'll take a lot of heat if the uniforms end up arresting my granddaughter, not to mention the phone call I'd have to put in to your father."

"Neither one of us wants either of those options," I assured him.

While my grandfather and Jeff headed back to the bar, I scanned the block.

Lindsey and Christine had corralled the unaffected vamps at

the corner opposite me. The humans, now witnesses, were milling around inside the perimeter of yellow tape. Paparazzi had already gathered at the edges, snapping photographs like they were going out of style. The *click* of their shutters sounded like a plague of descending insects.

Darius and Ethan both were going to have a conniption about this one. And speaking of, I pulled my cell phone out of my pocket. I hated being the bearer of bad news, but I needed to update Ethan. I settled for a text message with a quick recap ("FIGHT AT TEMPLE BAR. COPS HERE.") and a warning ("PHOTOGS ON LOOSE. DON'T LET DARIUS NEAR A TV."). A text would have to do for now.

That done, I looked down the street in the other direction. The block was segmented by an alley that ran alongside the bar. If our rave solicitor had been scoping out Temple Bar, would he have moved through the alley? That seemed as reasonable a step as any, so I decided to check it out.

I wrinkled my nose as soon as I'd moved a few feet into the alley. It was a warm summer night, and it smelled like most urban alleys probably did—garbage, dirt, and urine from unknown sources. It was dark, but wide enough for a car to pass through. A sign on one wall that had once read NO BIKES OR SCOOTERS now read NO IKES OR COOTERS. I managed to hold in a juvenile laugh, but still smiled a little.

About halfway down the alley, I reached the bar's service entrance. The heavy metal door was red and rusted and marked by DELIVERIES ONLY and PROTECTED BY AZH SECURITY signs. Flattened beer boxes were stacked in a neat pile beside the door. Beyond that, there wasn't much to see.

For the hell of it, I walked to the other end of the alley. There were a couple of Dumpsters and two more service entrances to other businesses, but that was about it.

I frowned with disappointment. I'm not sure what I'd expected to see, although a short, dark-haired man standing beneath a floating neon arrow that read BAD GUY HERE would have been nice. A suspect and quick confession wouldn't have been amiss, either.

This was a lot harder than in the movies.

Oh, *lightbulb*. That was it.

My heart suddenly pounding with excitement, I jogged to the bar's back door. Sure enough, poised above the door was a security camera. The area was dark and grubby, so the camera may not have captured anything Oscar-worthy, but at least it was a lead. First things first, I needed to find Jeff.

I ran back through the alley, but Jeff hadn't yet emerged from the bar. Since I wasn't about to head inside and jump into the middle of CPD drama, I decided to check in with Lindsey.

I hadn't gone two feet when I felt a tap on my shoulder.

"Is everything okay?"

The voice was familiar, but he'd startled me enough to merit a full-body shiver. I turned around and found Jonah standing behind me in a snug T-shirt and jeans. Two vampires I didn't know stood beside him. One wore a blue and yellow jersey with a number on the front. The Grey House uniform, I assumed.

Jonah was here with friends, which meant we were playing Sentinel and captain, minus the RG connection. And in those roles, since no one had seen us together at Grey House, we hadn't met. I could play along with that.

"You're Merit, right? Cadogan Sentinel."

"Yeah. And you are?"

"Jonah. Captain. Grey House." He glanced back at the bar. "You need help here?"

"I think we're okay. There was a fight at the bar."

Jonah's eyes widened. "A fight?"

I glanced back to the guys behind him. I might give Jonah information, but these two were complete strangers. "I don't know your friends."

"Danny and Jeremy," he said, pointing to each of them in turn. "They're Grey House guards."

Danny smiled and nodded his head; Jeremy offered a half wave. "What's up?" he said.

"You can be candid," Jonah said, and I had a sense he was talking to me as a potential RG member, not just a witness to chaos.

In that case, "There were a lot of vamps in there. They got riled up over relatively nothing, then went crazy. The bar practically exploded with it."

"We've heard there've been some gatherings. Violent ones."

"I've seen it with my own eyes." I glanced from him to the guys behind him. "What are you guys doing out here?"

"We were in the neighborhood, but we're heading back to the House." He pulled a white card from his pocket and handed it to me. It was a business card with his name, position, and phone number on it. "My landline's on there. Feel free to call me if you need anything."

"Thanks. I appreciate the offer."

"Nothing like a little inter-House cooperation," he said. "Best of luck."

"I appreciate it."

With a nod, the captain of Grey House and his employees moved on and disappeared into the crowd. It would have been nice to ask him for help again—but what could he have done tonight?

I tucked the card into my pocket and, when I turned around again, found Catcher behind me.

"You know Jonah?"

"I do now," I said, my stomach clenching at the lie. "He's the Grey House captain."

"So I've heard." He stared at me for a moment.

"What?" I asked, my own curiosity aroused. Did he suspect I knew Jonah? Did he suspect Jonah knew more than he was admitting?

But Catcher stayed silent, keeping whatever suspicions he might have had to himself.

That's when I saw him—only a shadow at the edge of my eyesight at first, but then a distinguishable man standing across the street, one of his soldiers behind him.

It was McKetrick, dressed in black running pants and a black T-shirt. No obvious weapons, but with all the cops nearby, it was impossible to tell if he was carrying something concealed. He did have a small pair of binoculars in hand, and the man behind him scribbled in a small notebook. Apparently our friendly neighborhood anti-vampire militiaman was working a little recon tonight. He scanned the crowd, apparently unaware that I was nearby with a couple of vampire sympathizers. I can't imagine he'd have had anything pleasant to say about that.

I leaned toward Catcher. "Across the street on the corner. That's McKetrick and one of his goons."

With all the slickness of a CIA operative, Catcher pointed at a building in McKetrick's direction. "Did you know that building was created by a monkey that lived in the top of Tribune Tower?"

"I did not know that. A monkey, you say?"

"Fur, bananas, crap throwing, the whole bit." He turned back again and stuffed his hands into his pockets. "Don't know the face. But he's in black, and he's got binoculars and an underling. Former military?"

"Given the way he was outfitted the other day, that was my guess. What do you think he's doing out here?"

"He probably has a police scanner," Catcher said, the grumble in his voice giving me all the info I needed about his opinion of them. "He probably heard the call and decided to come out and see what kind of trouble vamps were getting into tonight."

"Damn vampires," I muttered.

"Always getting into something," he agreed. "Since he's focused on the vamps, I'll run a Chicago Shuffle and get eyes on him."

"Chicago Shuffle?"

"I'll head in the opposite direction and catch him from the back."

"Sure thing, boss," I said. "Just watch out for the brass and any dames with nice gams."

Catcher gave me a dark look. "Sometimes, I don't know why I bother."

"Because I'm awesome, and you supplanted me in my own home."

He smiled slyly. "That does lessen the sting. You keep an eye on him from here and give me a text if it looks like he's planning on joining in the fun."

"Will do."

Catcher pulled down his ball cap, then slunk into the darkness of the street in the opposite direction.

"Chicago Shuffle," I quietly murmured, just wanting to say the phrase aloud. I decided all future operations needed names as slick as that one.

Jeff popped back over as soon as Catcher disappeared. "Where's he off to?"

"We saw McKetrick—the vamp hater—across the street. Catcher went to gather some intel. What did you find out inside?"

"There're a lot of dopey vamps in there, and the cops aren't thrilled they're causing trouble in public. They're going to want to pin this on Cadogan, you know."

"I know. I'm not looking forward to talking to Ethan about it."

"I wouldn't be, either. The cops were talking to Chuck about calling Mayor Tate, advising him of what's up."

"Kind of a small-beans matter to bother the mayor with, isn't it?"

"Apparently not when vampires are involved." He gestured toward the paparazzi, still snapping photos, now of the humans who'd been inside the bar.

"Not much we can do about it now," I said. "But there is something you can do for me." I held up a hand before he could remind me about Fallon again. "And it's nothing prurient. But it will require your technological prowess."

"That's my second-favorite prowess."

"There's a camera at the back door of the bar. Can you check with Colin and find out if they're recording the video?"

"Will do. If I find it, what am I looking for?"

"Anything at all. Suspicious activity, drug kingpins, stuff like that."

"That's not very specific."

I patted him on the arm. "That's why I came to you, Jeff. Because you have mad skills. And keep an eye out for a short guy with dark hair. You find him, you get the big prize."

Jeff rocked back on his heels. "Define big prize."

It took me a moment to imagine a prize that wouldn't get him in trouble with Fallon—or me in trouble with the North American Central Pack. But Jeff was an all-American, red-blooded shifter, so I had an idea.

"I'll call my grandfather's favorite butcher and order his deluxe holiday special for the office."

His brows lifted, a gleam of predatory appreciation in his eyes. "We're not supposed to, you know, accept gratuities—city employees and all—"

"I'm pretty sure there are half a dozen filets in there, probably some sirloins, burgers, chops, franks. But if you think it's inappropriate, I'll skip it. I don't want you to get in trouble."

Jeff nodded with absolute certainty. "If there's video, I'll find it. We'll get you your man."

"Appreciate it."

Assignment in hand, Jeff headed back to my grandfather's Olds, where he climbed into the backseat and opened a black laptop.

I smiled at the enthusiasm, glad I had friends who were on the side of truth and justice. Being Sentinel would have been much harder without Jeff, Catcher, my grandfather, Mallory, and everyone else who kept info moving in my direction. You really couldn't underestimate the value of a good team.

And now I was starting to sound like Jonah. Maybe his talk about the RG was getting to me, after all.

CHAPTER FOURTEEN

THE BUCKET LIST

As dawn neared, the rest of the vampires began emerging from the bar, stumbling a little amid the strobelike lights of the police cruisers and the snap of camera flashes. They were covered in bruises that were already green, the result of the speedy vampire healing process. I bet the community wounds would take longer to heal, unfortunately.

My grandfather and Catcher talked to the cops, probably sharing notes and theories. Jeff eventually carried the laptop into the bar, probably to find out what he could about the security tapes.

When the police removed their tape and the cruisers began to depart, I headed to the spot where Lindsey and the unaffected vamps were waiting.

She stood up as I approached. "Do you know anything?"

"Not yet. Crime scenes apparently involve a lot of waiting and standing around. You?"

Lindsey glanced back at the vamps, who looked shell-shocked by the combined drama of cops, detectives, rainbow alcohol, and paparazzi. "Nothing yet. I heard from one of the EMTs that your grandfather brought in a counselor to talk to the humans."

"It was a bar fight," I grumbled. The humans were certainly entitled to their feelings, but none of them had actually been injured—they hadn't even really been involved.

"But it was a bar fight with crazy, scary vampires," she exaggeratedly said, wiggling her fingers like a menacing monster.

I humphed, but recognized it wasn't an argument I was going to win, not when the humans were surrounded by reporters and cameras. I glanced back at the bar. "Maybe we should head back inside. Clean up a little. Do you want to round up the troops?"

"God, yes, please. Luc wanted us to stay put until the cops gave us the all clear, so I've been here and bored. I'm going to consider your request the all clear."

That rationalization worked for me. "Give me a minute head start. I want to take a look around." She nodded, so I headed back inside.

The floor of the bar was in shambles, not unlike Cadogan after the shifter attack, albeit with more casual decor. The Cubs memorabilia, thankfully, made it through the onslaught, although the tables and chairs were mostly upended. I scanned the room for anything that might give me a clue as to why our vamps were losing it, but assumed anything that would have helped had long since been picked up by the cops. And there was no short man with rave invites to be found.

If Celina was involved and she was somehow leading the vampire mass hysteria, she'd managed to get us kicked out of our own bar. It was just the kind of thing she'd have enjoyed. As I stood there alone, I imagined Celina popping up from behind the bar, awash in balloons, arms raised in victory.

"Ah, the power of fantasy," I murmured, and began picking up overturned bar tables. Lindsey came through the door, her flock of vampires behind her.

"All right, boys and girls," she said. "Let's get this place back into fighting shape. So to speak."

The vampires grumbled but obeyed, righting chairs and tables. Colin groaned as he walked back through the door as he surveyed his place. He glanced over at me. "You gonna figure this out?"

"I'm working on it," I assured him. "And speaking of, I need one more favor. I don't suppose you can whistle?"

He put two fingers in his mouth and let out a high-pitched trill. It took only a moment before I had the attention of all the vampires in the bar.

"Discretion is the better part of valor," I said, "so I'm going into the back office. If anybody's got information, this would be a good time to come talk to me."

Like an irritated elementary school teacher, I stared them down until I began to see a few sheepish expressions crossing their faces. This probably wasn't going to do anything for my popularity, but it needed to be done. Playing social chair was secondary to playing Sentinel and actually keeping the House intact.

I glanced over at Colin and held out a hand until he offered up the office keys. When I had them in hand, I headed back for the office. I unlocked it and moved immediately to the file cabinet. I could use a drink, and I didn't think he'd mind if I sampled his flask. I popped open the top drawer, pulled out the flask, and gave the contents a warning sniff.

My nose wrinkled. Whatever was in his secret mix, it smelled pickled. I squeezed my eyes shut and took a sip.

It was . . . not that bad, actually. It wasn't a taste I could easily describe—"pickled" came closest, but there were also the tang of blood and a sweet edge that balanced out the taste, not unlike raspberry vinaigrette. Of course, I didn't want to drink down raspberry vinaigrette, so I put the cap back on and promised myself an extra Mallocake when I finally made it home.

I noticed her in the doorway just as I closed the file cabinet again. She was a vamp I'd seen around the House but didn't really know, a cute brunette with long, wavy hair and a curvy figure.

She looked right and left down the hallway as if afraid she might be seen darkening the teacher's door.

"You can shut the door if you want," I told her.

She stepped inside and closed the door behind her. "I'm Adriana," she said. "I'm on the third floor of the House."

"Nice to meet you."

She got right to the point. "I don't like playing tattletale, but I'm loyal to my House, and I'm loyal to Ethan." There was no doubting the ferociousness of that affection in her gaze. "And someone threatens that, or the House, it's time to speak up."

I nodded solemnly. "I'm listening."

"I saw it the first time a few weeks ago. I was at a party—no humans—and a Grey House vamp was using it. He tried it, and twenty minutes later he was pounding someone he said had made a pass at his girl."

Adriana paused, seemed to gather her courage, and then looked up at me again. "And then, tonight, I found this in the bathroom." She held out a clenched fist, and then opened her fingers. In her palm sat a small white envelope with a *V* inscribed on the front. I didn't need to look inside to know what it would hold.

I squeezed my eyes shut, irritated with my own stupidity. The drugs hadn't been for the humans. They hadn't been used to make humans more biddable; that was just good old-fashioned glamour.

They were for *vampires*. It wasn't the spill of magic or a virus or some sort of mass hysteria that was making them aggressive—it was a drug they'd apparently been stupid enough to take. Maybe it weakened their inhibitions toward violence; maybe it increased their testosterone. Whatever the chemistry, this was the reason the vamps at the rave had been willing to fight over my stumbling, the reason the vamps at the bar were fighting over rainbow booze . . . and probably the reason why Mayor Tate thought three humans had been killed in West Town.

"Thanks," I said, opening my eyes again and holding out my hand. She handed over the drugs.

"If it's any consolation, immortality makes some of them bored," Adriana said, "so they do things—they try things—that they wouldn't ordinarily try. But now it's making the rounds through Temple Bar, and I don't want to see it infiltrate the House."

"Excellent call. Did you ever meet the seller?" I asked.

She shook her head. "These things move from vamp to vamp. Unless you're looking to score, which I'm not, you don't even come in contact with the seller."

Another miss, but at least I'd put some information together. Someone out there was selling V to Cadogan vampires. Another someone—maybe the same someone?—was soliciting humans for raves.

Whoever was orchestrating it, put the two together and you had an explosive situation.

"Thanks for letting me know. I'll see to it Ethan finds out about the V so we can put a stop to it, but I won't tell him who told me."

I could see the relief in her face, but she quickly squared her shoulders again. "You find out," she said. "You find out who is putting this out there, who is putting us at risk."

"I intend to," I promised her.

By the time I made it back into the bar, the chairs and tables were right side up again. Christine was sweeping up broken glass while another member of our Novitiate class held the pail for her. Colin was back behind the bar, cleaning up overturned booze and broken beer bottles.

Heads turned as I walked in, vamps looking at me curiously. They probably wondered what I now knew—and how much trouble they were going to be in because of it.

It was a good question. 'Cause right now, on behalf of me, Ethan, the House, I was *pissed*. I could have been sympathetic to the brawlers when I'd imagined this was some kind of traveling hysteria. But this was something they'd *chosen* to do. All this trouble—the cops, the bad press we were inevitably going to receive, Tate's rampage, the raves—was caused because idiot vampires had decided to take drugs.

They'd made a choice to wreak havoc, and I had no sympathy for that.

I stalked to the bar and vaulted over it, then grabbed the rope of the giant bell that hung behind it. It was used for vampire silliness, usually to signal the start of a drinking game based on Ethan's idiosyncrasies.

But now I used it to signal something more serious.

I grabbed the rope and slung it back and forth until the bell pealed across the room. Then I pulled an ice bucket from a shelf and put it square in the middle of the bar. I scanned the crowd to make sure only vamps were in attendance, and when the magic checked out, I let the vitriol flow.

"So this is about drugs," I said, and felt a little better when some of the unaffected vampires looked surprised; at least they hadn't been using. But they were apparently the only ones.

"Some of you have been using," I said. "I don't know why, and I'm not sure I care. Either way, you couldn't have picked a worse time. Darius is in town, and Ethan is already in trouble. The House is on the hot seat with Tate, and this certainly isn't going to help."

I let that sink in for a moment, taking in the hushed whispers and worried looks.

"Things are changing," I said, my tone softer. "Our House has been through hell recently, and the future isn't looking much brighter. I'm not going to tell Ethan which of you were here tonight."

There were looks of obvious relief around the room.

"But we can't let this happen again. We cannot—I cannot—allow V into the House. Besides, since I have to tell the cops about the drugs, there's a pretty good chance everyone will be frisked before they leave."

I held up the ice bucket to show them I meant business, then put it down on the bar. "If you've got V on you, it goes in the bucket. I'll take it out of the bar myself and turn it over to the cops. It will be better coming from me than all of you individually. We can't let things get worse. So for the sake of the House, do the right thing."

I turned and faced the wall, giving them the privacy to make their deposits. It took a few seconds, but I finally heard footsteps and shuffling of chairs, and then the *ping* of a tablet or the quiet *thush* of an envelope hitting the side of the bucket.

The sounds of conscience clearing.

After a moment, Colin called my name. "I think they're done," he quietly said when I glanced at him.

I nodded, then looked back at the crowd. "Thank you. I'll make sure he knows that you helped, that you understood your responsibilities. And you can always, always come to me if you have problems."

With that said, but still feeling like a total narc, I grabbed up the bucket and headed for the door. I now knew why this was happening, knew why the raves were bigger and meaner than before. I'd hopefully been able to keep the chaos out of our House.

Now I had to find the pusher and put a stop to the chaos everywhere else.

I made my way outside and found my grandfather, Catcher, and Jeff. My grandfather sat at the curb, his expression somber.

He stood up when I approached. I guided him behind one of the cruisers—and out of the way of the paparazzi—before handing over the bucket.

"This is V," I said. "The same stuff we saw at the Streeterville party. Apparently it spread from Benson's to Grey House to Temple Bar, where Cadogan vamps were stupid enough to try it." I looked at Catcher. "This is why they've been so violent. It's not the glamour or the magic—"

"It's the drugs," he agreed with a nod. "Not for humans, but for vampires."

"I'd guess you're probably right about that," my grandfather said, pulling two small, clear plastic evidence bags from the pocket of his jacket. There were pills and envelopes in each.

"Where did you find those?"

"On the floor of the bar," he said. "Someone must have dropped it in the confusion. Maybe the *V* stands for 'vampire.' Or 'violence'?"

"Whatever you call it," Catcher said, "it's bad. V is in the clubs, it's in the parties, it's in the vampires."

My grandfather glanced back at the paparazzi, who were flashing pictures from behind the police tape, their gray and black lenses zooming in and out as they tried to capture each bit of the scene.

"I can't keep them from taking pictures," he said, "but I'll hold on to the V issue as long as possible. At this point, the drug's only targeted at vampires, and there doesn't seem to be an obvious risk to humans."

"I appreciate that, and I'm sure Ethan does, too."

A beat cop approached my grandfather, making eyes at me as he did it. Catcher, Jeff, and I were silent as my grandfather stepped aside, chatting quietly with the officer and, when they were done, passing him the bucket.

When my grandfather walked back over again, his brow furrowed, I assumed nothing good was heading my way.

"How do you feel about coming down to the precinct and giving a statement?"

My stomach curled. He was doing me a favor by letting me do the talking—letting me control the House's destiny, so to speak—but that didn't mean I was crazy about the idea of going voluntarily to a police station.

"Not great, to be real honest. Ethan will have a fit."

"Not if the other option is a random Cadogan vamp without your training or allegiances. We need to talk to a Cadogan vamp," he said, "and it's better you than anyone else."

I sighed. Not only was I now the bearer of bad news; I was the rat fink tasked with reporting all the dirty details to the CPD. But my grandfather was right—what better choice did we have?

I nodded my agreement, blew out a breath, and pulled out my cell phone again.

I might not be the bearer of good tidings, but at least I could give him a little forewarning—and hope to God he wasn't waiting to strip me of my medal at the end of the night.

I rode in the front seat of my grandfather's Oldsmobile, adrenaline turning to exhaustion as we drove to the CPD's Loop precinct.

He parked in a reserved spot and escorted me into the building, a hand at my back to keep me steady. Given the task at hand, I appreciated the gesture.

The building was relatively new and pretty sterile—the peeling paint and ancient metal furniture of cop dramas replaced by cubicles and automated kiosks and shiny tile floors.

It was nearly four in the morning, so the building was quiet and mostly empty but for a handful of uniformed officers moving through the halls with perps in handcuffs: a woman in a short skirt and tall boots with undeniable exhaustion in her eyes; a jittery man with gaunt cheeks and dirty jeans; and a heavyset kid whose straight hair covered his eyes, his oversized gray T-shirt dotted with blood. It was a sad scene, a snapshot of folks having undoubtedly miserable evenings.

I followed my grandfather through what looked like a bull pen for detectives, rows of identical desks and chairs filling a room bordered by a ring of offices. Detectives lifted their gazes as we passed, offering nods to my grandfather and curious—or just plain suspicious—glances at me.

On the other side of the bull pen, we moved down a hallway and into an interview room that held a conference table and four chairs. The room, part of the renovation, smelled like a furniture showroom—cut wood, plastic, and lemon polish.

At my grandfather's gesture, I took a seat. The door opened just as he took the chair beside me. A man—tall, dark-skinned, and wearing a pin-striped suit—walked inside and closed the door. He had a yellow notepad and a pen in hand, and he wore his badge on a chain around his neck.

"Arthur," my grandfather said, but Arthur held out a hand before my grandfather could stand up in greeting.

"Don't bother on my account, Mr. Merit," Arthur said, exchanging a handshake with my grandfather. Then he looked at me, a little more suspicion in his eyes. "Caroline Merit?"

Caroline was my given name, but not the name I used. "Call me Merit, please."

"Detective Jacobs has been in the vice division for fifteen years," my grandfather explained. "He's a good man, a trustworthy man, and someone I consider a friend."

That was undoubtedly true given the respectful glances they shared, but Detective Jacobs clearly hadn't made up his mind about me. Of course, I wasn't here to impress anyone. I was only here to tell the truth. So that's what I tried to do.

We reviewed what I'd seen at the rave, what I'd learned from Sarah, and what I'd seen tonight. I didn't offer analysis or suspicions—just facts. There was no need, no reason that I could imagine, to insert Celina or GP drama into events that were already dramatic enough.

Detective Jacobs asked questions along the way. He rarely made eye contact as we talked, instead keeping his eyes on his paper as he scribbled notes. Much like his suit, his handwriting was neat and tidy.

I'm not sure he was any less suspicious by the end of my spiel, but I felt better for having told him. He might have been human, but he was also careful, analytical, and focused on details. I didn't get the sense this was a witch hunt, but rather his earnest attempt to solve a problem that just happened to involve vampires.

Unfortunately, he didn't have any information about V or where it might be coming from. Like Catcher had said, as the third-biggest city in the country, Chicago wasn't exactly immune from drug problems.

Detective Jacobs also didn't share any strategies with me, so if he had plans to do his own infiltrating, I wasn't aware of it. But he did give me a card and asked me to call him if I discovered anything else, or if I had anything I thought he could help with.

I doubted Ethan would want me involving veteran CPD vice detectives in the investigation of our drug problem.

But that's why I'd been named Sentinel, I thought, tucking the card into my pocket.

Ethan sat in a plastic chair in the hallway. He was bent over, elbows on his knees, hands clasped together. He tapped his thumbs together, his blond hair tucked behind his ears. It was the kind of pose you'd have seen on a family member in a hospital waiting room—tired, tense, anticipating the worst.

His head lifted at the sound of my boots on the tile floor. He stood up immediately, then moved toward me. "You're all right?"

I nodded. "I'm fine. My grandfather thought it would be better to get the story from me."

"It seemed like the fairest decision," said a voice behind me.

I glanced back to see my grandfather moving down the hall toward us. Ethan extended his hand. "Mr. Merit. Thank you for your help."

My grandfather shook his hand, but he also shook his head. "Thank your Sentinel. She's a fine representative of your House."

Ethan looked at me, pride—and love?—in his eyes. "We're in agreement there."

"I'm tired," I said, "and I don't have a car. Could we go back to the House?"

"Absolutely." Ethan's gaze shifted to my grandfather. "Did you need anything else from us?"

"No. We're done for now. Enjoy the rest of your night—to the extent possible."

"Unlikely," I said, patting his arm. "But we'll do the best we can."

But before we could take a step toward the exit, the doors at the end of the hallway pushed open. Tate walked through, followed by a squadron of suit-clad assistants. They looked drowsy, and I sympathized; it was a crappy job that required hangers-on to wear suits at five fifteen in the morning.

Tate strode toward us, both sympathy and irritation in his expression. I figured the irritation was offered up by his strategic half, the political leader anticipating nasty commercials about "the vampire problem." The sympathy was probably offered up by his baby-kissing half.

He looked at my grandfather first. "The situation is contained?"

"It is, Mr. Mayor. Things at the bar are in hand, and Merit came in and provided us with a very detailed statement so we can get a handle on the issue."

"Which is?"

"We're still figuring that out, sir. You'll have my report as soon as I can type it."

Tate nodded. "Appreciate that, Chuck." He glanced at Ethan. "Is this related to the problem I asked you to address?"

"It may be," Ethan vaguely said. "Merit is spending most of her free time investigating it, including this evening."

Tate's expression softened and went all-politician. "I can't tell you how much I appreciate that."

Oh, I could tell, I blandly thought. *You probably appreciated it ten to fifteen points in the polls.*

Tate reached out and shook my hand, and then my grandfather's. "Merit, let's stay in touch. Chuck, I look forward to your report."

He reached out to shake Ethan's hand, but instead of a simple shake, he leaned toward Ethan and whispered something in his ear. Ethan's shoulder's stiffened, and he stared blankly ahead, barely controlling his anger, when Tate walked away.

Ethan's car was parked in a secured lot beside the station. I barely made the short walk. The drama was beginning to take a collective toll; for all my extra vampire strength, I was tired. My brain was fuzzy, my body was exhausted, and my temperature was that strange deep-seated cold that you get before the flu starts up.

Ethan opened the door for me and shut it again when I was inside. I checked the clock on the dashboard; it was nearly five forty-five, about twenty minutes before dawn. Another late night—and another race against the rising sun.

Silently, Ethan climbed into the car and started the motor.

I made one final play at being the dutiful Sentinel. "Do you want to debrief now?"

He must have seen the exhaustion in my eyes, because he shook his head. "Luc filled me in on the major points, and the morning news programs are already on the case. Rest for now."

I must have taken the direction literally, because I remember nodding in agreement—but not the rest of the ride home. As soon as he pulled out of his parking spot and began spiraling back down through the parking garage, I dropped my head onto the headrest. I woke up again as the car descended into the Cadogan parking lot.

"You *are* tired," he said.

I put a hand over my mouth to hide the burgeoning yawn. "It's nearly dawn."

"So it is."

We sat there awkwardly for a moment, like a couple at the end of a first date, neither quite sure what's expected of the other.

Ethan made the first move, opening his door and stepping outside. I did the same, wobbling a little as I exited the car, but staying on my feet. I could feel the tug of the sun, my nerves itching with exhaustion, my body screaming that it was time to find a soft, dark place to wait out the day.

"You going to make it upstairs?" he asked.

"I'll make it." I concentrated on putting one foot in front of the other, blinking to keep my eyes focused.

"The sun does a number on you," Ethan said as he typed in the code to the basement door, then held it open while I walked through like a near zombie. I was conscious enough to realize that he didn't seem to have the same trouble.

"You're less affected?" I asked as we walked to the stairs.

"I'm older," he explained. "Your body is still adjusting to the genetic change, to the differences between being diurnal and nocturnal. As you get older, you'll find the pull easier to manage. More a gentle suggestion than a grab-and-go."

I was capable only of muttering a sound of agreement. By some miracle I made it to the second-floor landing without falling over.

"We'll talk tomorrow," Ethan said, and headed for the stairs. But I called his name to stop him. He glanced back.

"What did Tate whisper in your ear?"

"He said, 'Fix this, goddamn it, or else.' We'll talk about it tomorrow."

He didn't have to tell me twice.

CHAPTER FIFTEEN

ALL THAT GLITTERS

As Ethan had pointed out, one obvious downside of being nocturnal was the fact that the sun exerted more power on me than I cared to admit. On the other hand, I didn't need caffeine to wake up. I might have spent a few minutes being groggy, but the haze blew off quickly enough, leaving a wide-awake (and usually starving) vampire in its wake.

I started the evening with a bowl of crunchy cinnamon cereal and as much blood as I could stomach. I'd done a lot of fighting last night, and my stress level had been pretty high. Fighting and stress generally tripped my hunger trigger faster than anything else.

Well, maybe other than Ethan. I could confirm the bagged stuff didn't compare in taste to the real thing, but that didn't make it any less satisfying. Nutrition was all well and good, but the emotional comfort also paid off.

I showered and dressed in my Cadogan black. I wasn't sure what the night held in store, but I was confident that after last night's escapades Darius would be involved at some point. It was probably best to dress a bit nicer than I had been the last time he'd seen me.

I brushed my hair until it shone and added my Cadogan medal and Mary Jane shoes. I'd been so busy with vampire drama that I'd forgotten about Mallory's sorcery drama, so before I went downstairs I flipped open my phone. I found a message from my father, probably another entreaty to allow him to help Cadogan House. Joshua Merit was nothing if not persistent.

I sent Mallory a message checking in, and got back a quick response: "BETTER TONIGHT. PRACTICUM ON HEALING MAGIC. FUN!"

I wasn't sure if her "Fun!" was sarcastic, but "healing magic" sounded a lot better than dark magic.

My phone buzzed again just as I was shutting my door. This time, it was a text from Lindsey, and not a promising one.

"WE NEED TO TALK," she'd texted.

I hated hearing that. My fingers were fast on the keys. "HOUSE TRAUMA?"

"BOY TRAUMA," she replied, and my shoulders unknotted a bit. "DRAMA OF MY OWN MAKING."

I wasn't entirely sure how she'd managed to have boy trauma or drama. She'd been with me last night, and it wasn't yet an hour after sunset. I couldn't resist asking.

"HOW COULD YOU HAVE BOY DRAMA THIS EARLY IN THE EVENING?"

"JUST FIND ME LATER," she responded. "THE DEVIL'S IN THE DE-TAILS."

Wasn't that always true?

A potentially distressing conversation with Lindsey on my agenda for later, I made my way downstairs to Ethan's office. I found him alone, the door open, adjusting the knickknacks he'd salvaged from the battle on his new bookshelves.

"A little interior decorating to start the night?"

"Trying to make my office feel like my office again."

"Procrastination can be very satisfying."

He laughed ruefully. "As you pointed out, it may be a very human emotion, but there's undoubtedly something satisfying about pretending the world is fine and your problems will keep until you're ready to deal with them."

"It's a lovely coping mechanism," I agreed. "I'm glad you've made it to our side. Where's Darius tonight?"

"Scott won the lottery this evening; Darius is at Grey House." He turned and glanced at me. "Tell me you learned something last night. Tell me this mess will have some good end."

"How much should I tell you? I mean, I don't want to put you into an awkward position with Darius."

Ethan made a sarcastic sound. "You clearly haven't seen last night's local news."

I hadn't, and by the tone of his voice, I probably wouldn't want to. "That bad?"

"It's so bad, Darius hasn't called me yet."

I grimaced. The only thing worse than being yelled at by a boss was having screwed up so royally, he'd moved right into silent treatment.

I decided not to sugarcoat it. There were details I didn't need to give—information about the vamps who'd actually bought and used the drugs, for one—but I wasn't going to give him a false sense of the problem.

"It all comes down to V," I began. "It's a drug for vampires, not humans. It's somehow making them more aggressive. The House bars, at least for Grey and Cadogan, have been used as distribution points. I'm not sure about Navarre."

I gave him a moment to process that information; by the look of him, he needed it. He put an elbow on the shelf, then rubbed his temples with a hand.

"I have put up with a lot in this House," he said. "Unfortunately, vampires aren't any more immune to stupidity than humans." He dropped his hand and looked away, the corners of his eyes wrinkled with disappointment. "I would have hoped that they respected the House—and me—more than this."

"I'm sorry, Ethan."

He shook his head, and shook it off. "Tell me about the bar."

"Colin hadn't seen anything out of the ordinary. I asked Jeff to pull the security footage so we can figure out how it's getting in. It's definitely getting in, although I had everyone hand over their stash so they couldn't bring it back into the House."

"And so it wouldn't be found on them if the cops patted them down."

"Exactly," I agreed. "But my grandfather had already found it in the bar, so he'd already put two and two together. I gave him the rest of the drugs, and that's when they brought in Detective Jacobs."

"Your theory?"

"Still working it out. In terms of the overall picture, we've now had two instances of extra-violent vamps and drugs in the same place at the same time. As for the why of it . . ." I shrugged. "Who's pushing the drugs? Someone who wants us in trouble? Someone who wants vamps bringing down the Houses on their own? Someone who wants to take us down one pill at a time?"

"That doesn't sound like Celina," he pointed out.

"Not unless she's decided all vamps have to suffer for her crimes," I agreed. "Morgan didn't think that was likely, but I wouldn't put it past her."

"Until you have more evidence, I'm not conceding that point.

What about McKetrick? He's focused on forcing us out of Chicago. Perhaps he's pushing V to rile up vampires and pressure Tate into deporting us?"

"McKetrick was outside the bar last night," I said. "I saw him, then pointed him out to Catcher. He was going to tail McKetrick and get what info he could." I made a mental note to follow up with him later. "That said, McKetrick may hate us, but making vamps extra-aggressive risks a lot of collateral damage. I don't see it being part of his master plan."

"Whoever is behind it, we need to find them and stop the distribution before things get any worse."

"Coincidence—those are the first two things on my to-do list."

"I have item three for you. Dinner at Grey House this evening with Darius and the Masters. Darius also invited Gabriel and Tonya. One o'clock. We'll leave from here. And it's formal, of course."

Since Darius seemed like a rules stickler, the formal bit didn't surprise me. But I was curious about his invitation to Gabriel and Tonya, Gabriel's wife. Vampires and shifters had a historically nasty relationship—a lot of distrust and angst by vampires, a lot of eye rolling and denial by shifters.

"Why invite Gabriel and Tonya?" I asked.

"If I was being generous, I'd say Darius was interested in improving inter-sup relations. But he's more likely attempting to micromanage our relationship with the Packs. It would be bad for the Chicago Houses to completely alienate the Packs. But in Darius's mind, it would be altogether worse to become too cozy with them. There've never been official allegiances with a Pack before. If we pulled it off, it would indicate a definite shift in power in our direction."

At his mention of the potential Pack allegiance, I looked

away. Ethan's fear that our relationship—or our future breakup—would endanger our burgeoning friendship with the North American Central was the reason he'd given for the breakup he now regretted.

"Come on," Ethan suddenly said, walking toward the door.

I glanced up again, moved from my reverie. "Where are we going?"

"Ops Room. I was supposed to have you downstairs fifteen minutes ago."

I followed him obediently to the basement stairs and toward the Ops Room. The door was open; Luc, Juliet, Kelley, Malik, and Lindsey were already assembled around the conference table. Luc, in a faded denim shirt and jeans, was an interesting contrast to the rest of the guards, who were all dressed in black.

Ethan closed the door. I took an empty seat at the table, and he took the chair beside me.

I glanced between Luc and Lindsey, who sat on opposite ends of the table, trying to read the tea leaves regarding her message earlier. But she wore her usual expression of mildly amused boredom; Luc was scanning the paper on the Ops Room table, a steaming mug in his hand. If they were at odds, I couldn't tell, and there wasn't any obviously negative magic in the air.

"Finally, they join us," Luc said, sipping his drink. Normally, that kind of comment would have been a tease coming from him. This time, it sounded like a rebuke, and Luc didn't normally err toward grouchiness. Maybe he and Lindsey *had* gotten into something.

"We were on our best behavior," Ethan advised him. "Merit was filling me in on last night's investigation."

"Do tell," Luc said.

"Long story short, it's the V that's been causing the violence."

Luc frowned, sat up, and put his mug on the tabletop, hands wrapped around it like it was providing necessary warmth. I'd been cold as a newbie vampire, and it had taken some time to ward off that chill. But it was August and probably ninety degrees outside. I didn't understand people who drank coffee in the heat of summer.

"Why would some lowlife sell drugs to vamps and get them together for parties? What's he trying to accomplish?"

"Merit thinks McKetrick might be involved," Ethan said, "that maybe it's a ploy to get vamps out of the city."

I put up a hand. "That was actually Ethan's idea," I said, giving credit where credit was due . . . or distributing the blame accordingly.

Luc tilted his head back and forth while he considered it. "Whoever came up with it, it's not a bad idea, although manufacturing the drug, distributing it, organizing the parties, and everything else in the chain means a lot of work just to get rid of a population. There are easier ways."

"Agreed," Malik said. "And at the risk of jumping on one of our favorite bandwagons, the first witness saw a woman named Marie. Any votes for Celina?"

"But we haven't heard anything about her since then," I pointed out. "So if she is involved, she's staying under the radar. I'm having Jeff Christopher check the bar's security tapes, so if there's any sign of her—or any more details about the seller—we'll find them."

Luc nodded, then picked up a remote that sat beside his mug. "In that case, a little more good news to brighten your evening." He held up the remote and mashed buttons until the clip on the screen began to play.

It was a recorded news program. We caught the end of a story about international warfare before the headline switched to read, "Vamp Violence in Wrigleyville." The female anchor—polished in her jewel-toned suit, her stiff hair a helmet above her head—offered up the rest.

"In this morning's top local news," she said, "an uptick in violence in the city is deemed the result of a drug called 'V' that's circulating among the city's vampire community."

They cut to an image of a white V tablet in someone's hand, and then to a shot of Temple Bar.

"One such event was last night's disturbance at a Wrigleyville bar with ties to Cadogan House. We were live on scene last night, and here's what one local resident had to say."

They cut to video of the two frat boys from Temple Bar.

"Oh, those traitorous little shits," Lindsey muttered. "Those are the humans Christine talked to."

"It was awful in there," said the taller of the two boys. "All those vamps just wailing on each other. It was like they just went crazy."

"Did you fear for your life?" asked an offscreen reporter.

"Oh, absolutely," he said. "How could you not? I mean, they're vampires. We're just humans."

"The atom bomb was invented by 'just humans,'" Malik muttered. "World War II and the Spanish Inquisition were perpetrated by 'just humans.'"

We were clearly not a receptive crowd for muckraking journalism.

"Aldermen Pat Jones and Clarence Walker issued statements this morning calling for investigation of Chicago's vampire Houses and their role in this new drug. Mayor Tate responded to events this morning after meeting with his economic council."

The newscast cut to a shot of Tate shaking hands with a

woman in an unflattering suit. Beside a plain-looking bureaucrat, he looked that much more like a romance-novel hero: seductive eyes, dark hair, wicked smile. You had to wonder how many votes he'd gotten because voters just wanted to be near him.

When reporters began peppering him with questions about the bar fight, he held up both hands and smiled affectionately. That smile, I thought, walked a thin line between empathy and condescension.

"I have made Chicago's Houses well aware of their responsibilities, and I'm sure they'll take whatever precautions are necessary to put an immediate stop to the spread of V and the violence. If they don't, of course, steps will have to be taken. My administration is not afraid to take those steps. We've done a lot of work to remake this city into one that Illinois can be proud of, and we will continue to ensure that Chicago remains a place of peace and prosperity."

The anchor popped on-screen again. "Mayor Tate's approval rating remains consistently high even in light of the recent violence."

With that, Luc reached up with the remote and stopped the video again.

The room went silent and heavy with concern. I guessed I now knew why my father had called. He was probably dying to berate me for being a vampire and sullying the family name—despite the fact that I'd had no say in becoming fanged, and I was trying my best to keep the peace in Chicago.

Unless his tone had changed about that, as well.

"Well," Ethan finally said. "It does comfort me so to know that Mayor Tate's approval ratings remain strong."

"Tate must be feeding the anchors with information," I offered. "We only barely know about the uptick in violence, and my grandfather promised to keep V out of the press."

"So Tate's using vamps to make political hay?" Luc offered. "I guess it's not the first time a politician's taken advantage of chaos, but it sure would be nice if it wasn't at our expense."

"And if he didn't have an arrest warrant ready," I agreed.

"Way to put the city first," Lindsey said.

Luc glanced over at Ethan, concern in his expression. "Anything from Darius?"

"He's still on radio silence."

"It's not going to go over well."

"Drugs and violence in my bar? Drugs and violence covered by local paparazzi that will probably spread to national coverage, if it hasn't already? No, I don't imagine he will be pleased, and there's a good chance the House will suffer for it."

"Tell him the other part," Kelley said.

"The other part?" Ethan asked, his gaze shifting from Kelley to Luc.

"The other part," Luc confirmed, picking up the tablet and tapping its screen. The image on the projector shifted from the newscast to a black-and-white live feed of a dark neighborhood street. During my stint as an on-duty House guard, I'd seen that feed enough times to be familiar with it.

"That's outside Cadogan House."

"Good eye, Sentinel," Luc complimented. "Indeed it is." He tapped the tablet again and zoomed into the feed, fixing on a boxy sedan that held two passengers. Both wore suits.

"Kelley went for a run. She noticed the sedan when she left, and she noticed the sedan when she came back."

"Twenty-six miles," Kelley put in. "It took me an hour and twenty-four minutes."

Not bad for a marathon-length run. Chalk one up for vampire speed.

"That's a long time for two guys in suits to be sitting in a car outside the House," Ethan said, then looked back at Luc. "It's an unmarked CPD car."

"That's our thought. Neither the car nor the suits seemed like McKetrick's crew, so we figured detectives. We called the Ombud's office to confirm, but they had no idea about the car."

I muttered a curse. "They had no idea about Mr. Jackson's rave, either. Tate isn't being entirely candid with the office right now."

"A lack of trust?" Ethan wondered.

"Or perhaps a fear that the Ombud's office is tied too closely to Cadogan House," I suggested. "Tate's office doesn't give the Ombud's office all the information, which acts like a check and balance on my grandfather."

Lindsey grimaced. "That's a slap in the face."

"Yes, it is," I agreed. "I guess the cop car signals Tate's lack of trust in us, too?"

Ethan shuffled in his chair. "Given the fact that he's got a warrant for my arrest ready to go, I'd say so."

My cell phone buzzed. I pulled it out and checked the caller ID. "Speak of the devil. It's Jeff." I flipped it open. "Hey, Jeff. Got anything for me?"

Jeff chuckled. "Of course, I do. But I'm strictly off-limits now. You know, 'cause of the little lady."

"No disrespect meant to you or yours. Hey, I'm in the Ops Room with Ethan and everyone. Can I put you on speaker?"

"Knock yourself out. Probably helpful for all to hear."

I put the phone down in the middle of the table, then pressed the speaker button. "Okay. You're live. What do you have?"

"Aw, if only I'd prepared a monologue."

We heard Catcher's voice in the background. "Focus, kid."

"Well," Jeff said, and I heard the clacking of keys, "it turns out the security cameras are live, and Colin and Sean do record the video. It's stored in the bar on a dedicated server, and there are also external backups just in case some bad stuff goes down. I was actually pretty impressed. You don't expect bars to have that kind of security protocol."

From the looks of the crusty back room, Temple Bar definitely did not seem like the kind of establishment with a "dedicated server," not that I could differentiate a dedicated server from an undedicated server.

"So, anyway, I grabbed the video and uploaded it."

I leaned forward, linking my hands together on the table. "Tell me you found something, Jeff."

"It took some spooling," he said. "Trucks use the alley quite a bit to make deliveries. There's also the occasional catering-truck pickup, garbage trucks, taxis, bar drop-offs, et cetera, et cetera. But beginning two months ago, every couple of days, usually in the wee hours, a vintage Shelby Mustang—wicked car—pulls into the alley. Sometimes the car sits there for a few minutes, nothing happens, the car drives away. Sometimes a driver gets out."

My heart began to beat in anticipation. We were getting closer, I knew it. "What did the driver look like?"

"Well, although the backups are impressive, the video is for shit. Very grainy. But I did manage to pull a still for you. I'm going to send you a pic."

"Use this e-mail," Luc said, reading off an address to Jeff and picking up one of the tablets from the desktop. "That way we can project the image."

"Done and done." Jeff had barely gotten out the words before Luc's tablet dinged, signaling a new message. His fingers danced across the tablet, and an image popped onto the screen.

The guy was short—maybe five feet in shoes—older with

slick, dark hair and bulbous features. There was nothing especially remarkable about his face, but I would have sworn I'd seen him before.

"Does he look familiar to anyone?" I asked, but got muttered "no's" around the room.

The others might not have recognized him, but I had a sense Sarah would have.

"He matches the description of the guy Sarah—the human at the Streeterville party—met," I said. "Make my night and tell me you got a license plate on the car, Jeff."

"Because I am, in fact, awesome, I was able to zero into the video. I got the license of the car, then ran it through the DMV system. The car is registered to one Paulie Cermak." Jeff read out an address. "The interwebs say his address is near the Garfield Park Conservatory."

I made plans to pay Mr. Cermak a visit. I also opened my eyes again and smiled at the phone. "Jeff, you are a paragon of man."

"The funny thing is," Jeff continued, "the car's title shows a recent sale—only a few months ago to our Mr. Cermak. But there's no information about the prior owner or who he purchased the car from."

I frowned at the phone. "That seems weird."

"Definitely weird," Jeff agreed. "When we're looking at records, too much data usually signals a plant. Not enough data signals a scrub. Vehicle sales are almost always in the system; there's no reason not for them to be. This file had scrub all over it. Oh, and that's not all."

"We're listening."

"Because I am, in fact, not just supremely awesome, but also all that and a bag of chips—preferably kettle-cooked jalapeño of some kind—I checked Mr. Cermak's criminal record in the Cook

County DB. I mean, probably not supposed to go into their system without permission, but what else is a boy to do when his favorite vamp makes a call?"

"Indeed. What did you learn?"

"Factually, not much. There's one sealed criminal record in the file, and that's it."

"Do you think that file was scrubbed, too?"

"Eh, not necessarily. You can seal criminal files for all sorts of legitimate reasons. To protect the victim, because the perp's underage, because the perp's a brains-eating mind-dead zombie with no mens rea whatsoever—"

"Sealed record?" Ethan prompted.

"Yeah. So, the file is sealed, and I can't access any data. They're actually rocking some pretty good encryption on the sealed records. I'd need the access key or password, or you'd have to get a court order to pull the file."

"So a dead end there?"

"Ha! You made a joke. But yes. Very dead. Dead as a doornail. Dead as a doorknob even, although I'm not sure I know what the difference is between those two things."

"We got it."

"Oh, one final thing." I heard more key tapping, the sound overlaid by Jeff's humming. It sounded like "White Christmas."

"Little early for Christmas carols, isn't it, Jeff?"

"Never hurts to get into the holiday spirit, Merit. Okay, so the video isn't great, and the alley by the bar door isn't very well lit. But occasionally, on a full moon, the light shines just right. . . ." As he trailed off, I heard more tapping. "Okay," he said again. "I'm going to send you another image."

This one was a fuzzy black-and-white shot of a car in the alley. Jeff was right—the image was grainy, but the vehicle it showed was undeniably a classic Mustang, complete with racing stripes and side vents. And that wasn't all.

I squinted at the picture, trying in vain to bring it into focus. "Is that a woman in the passenger's seat?"

"It appears to be so," Jeff said. "It's more of a shadow, but it does appear to be a woman. Curves, ya know?"

"We know," Ethan said dryly.

"Anyway, I was checking out the shadow of the lady in the video, right? I'm running the film at like half speed, and I find something else. I've got a close-up, and I'm going to send it to you."

Again, the tablet beeped, and a new black-and-white image replaced the previous one on our screen.

I squinted at it, but predatory eyesight or not, I still couldn't get a good read on the woman in the car. In fact, I couldn't get a good read on anything other than pixels.

"What are we supposed to be looking at?" I wondered aloud.

"Check the middle of the image," Jeff said, "approximately where her collar would be."

I'd just opened my mouth to protest that I couldn't see anything—and that was when I saw it—around her neck, an undeniable glint of light.

"Jeff, that looks like a House medal." Not unlike the one I'd seen Celina wearing the night she returned to Cadogan House.

"That's what I thought, too."

"Can you zoom in any closer?" Ethan asked.

"Unfortunately, I can't give you any more details. The camera's sensor just didn't record any more data. But that's something, isn't it? It kind of suggests you've got a House vamp involved in this drug business."

Malik and Ethan exchanged a heavy glance.

"It does suggest that," Ethan agreed. "But for now, let's keep this between us, shall we?"

"You're the boss," Jeff pleasantly said.

"Thanks, Jeff. We appreciate it."

"Unfortunately, I've got bad news to go along with the good news."

"What's that?" I asked.

"Paulie Cermak's the only suspect we've got for distributing V. I narrowed down the video late last night, and had to turn it over to the CPD this morning."

"Of course," I said. "Detective Jacobs would have been interested in the video."

"Is and was. They sent detectives to Cermak's house this morning."

Ethan frowned at the phone. "Did they find anything?"

"Not a thing. The house was clean. The car was clean. They're still processing some of the stuff they lifted for trace evidence, but there's nothing that ties him to the drugs or the raves. As far as we know, he's just a guy in a public alley. He had every right to be there."

Be that as it may, my gut said Paulie Cermak was more than a passerby, and I'd bet that if we called up every Cadogan vampire who'd been in Temple Bar in the last month, they could pin him as the guy who'd been loitering outside and pushing V. Of course, that would require calling out each Cadogan vamp. I wasn't willing, at least at this point, to drag the individual vampires into it.

"Thanks, Jeff. Any objections if I pay Mr. Cermak a visit on my own?" At my suggestion, Ethan's head shot up, but he didn't voice an objection.

"Not from us. And CPD doesn't have to know. Hey, Chuck's paging me, so I've gotta go. We've got a couple of fairies who want him to mediate a property dispute, and I need to upload some docs. We'll be in touch."

"Thanks, Jeff," I said, then tapped off the phone.

The Ops Room was quiet for a moment.

I looked up and around at the vamps in the room. "Any thoughts before I visit our apparent drug pusher?"

"How opposed are you to capital punishment?" Luc growled out.

"I'd prefer not to play judge, jury, and executioner," I said. "But if you have any strategic or diplomatic suggestions, I'm all for them."

Ethan patted my back good-naturedly. "Good Sentinel."

✦━═◆═━✦

CHAPTER SIXTEEN

THE PERP

Lindsey escorted me to my room so I could change back into boots and grab my sword. I usually skipped bringing it along on public outings, but Paulie Cermak was quite possibly a drug kingpin, and I was heading to his home turf. No way was I going on that field trip without steel.

It wasn't until we were inside with the door shut, Lindsey on my bed while I sat on the floor, sword unsheathed before me to ensure it was in fighting shape, that she made the confession she'd apparently been holding in.

"We made out," she said.

I wiped the blade down with a sheet of rice paper. "I don't recall making out with you."

"I made out with Connor."

I looked up at her and couldn't help the disappointment that crossed my face. Connor was a vamp from my Initiate class, a sweet kid with whom Lindsey had been flirting since our Commendation into the House. He was cute and charming in his way . . . but he was no Luc.

"When did that happen?"

"I got back from Temple Bar, and a bunch of us were talking in the downstairs parlor, and then everybody got tired and left. Everybody but him, I mean. And then one thing led to another. . . ."

The blade clean, I resheathed the sword again. "One thing led to you making out with a newbie vampire?"

"That would appear to be the case."

What was new, I thought, was the fact that she was chagrined about it. Lindsey wasn't much of a worrywart, and it wasn't her style to Monday-morning-quarterback her own decisions. Maybe Luc was making progress.

I tilted my head at her. "So why do you seem weird about it?"

Hands in her lap, shoulders slumped forward guiltily, Lindsey looked away.

I thought of the edge I'd heard in Luc's voice earlier, and figured out the reason for it. "Luc found out?"

She nodded.

"Crap, Linds."

"Yeah, crap." When she looked back at me, a tear slid down her cheek. She wiped it away nonchalantly, but there was no mistaking the guilt in her eyes.

"This thing with Connor—was it a fling? Just because you'd had a really long night?"

"I don't know what it is. That's kind of my problem. I'm just—I don't know—I'm not ready to be in some big"—she swirled her hands in the air—"committed relationship thing."

"Not ready? You're over a century old."

"That is so *not* the point. Look, Luc and I met a long, long time ago. He had a girlfriend; I had a beau. He's hot, sure. Obviously he's hot. But we started off friends, and I'd just rather we stay friends than become some kind of mortal enemies."

I gave her a dubious look. "How could you and Luc become mortal enemies? I'm not sure he even has mortal enemies. Well, other than Celina. And Peter."

"Definitely Peter," she agreed, then shrugged. "I don't know. It's just—immortality is a long time. I could be alive a long time, and I'm having a hard time imagining only one guy being a part of that."

My sword in hand, I stood up, moved to the bed, and sat down beside her. "So bottom line is, no big commitment thing right now."

"Yeah," she said sadly.

I hated that for both of them—her for the guilt, him for the heartache. "So what are you going to do?"

"What can I do? Break his heart? Tell him I'm not interested in settling down?" She flopped back on the bed. "This is why I avoided it for so long. Because he's my boss, and if we tried it and it didn't work—"

"It was that much more awkward for everyone."

"Precisely."

We sat there quietly for a moment.

"So, how about them Cubbies?" she finally asked, fake cheer in her voice.

"Name one current Cubs player."

"Um, that hot one with the broad shoulders and the soul patch?"

"And that's what I get for being friends with a damn Yankees fan."

"I am useless," she muttered, then pulled a pillow over her face. A muffled, frustrated scream escaped it.

"You're not useless. Hey, if nothing else, you're one of the top ten hotties in Cadogan House, right? I'd put you at least in the top three."

She lifted a corner of the pillow and blew hair from her face. "Really?"

"Really."

She smiled a little. "You're the best Sentinel ever."

Yeah, sometimes I wondered.

Luc and Ethan met me on the first floor again.

"You've got your phone in case you need us?"

"I do," I assured him, patting my jacket pocket. "If the cops didn't find anything at his house, he probably won't be territorial enough to start anything. But I will definitely call you if the need arises. Don't worry—"

"She rather likes being alive," Ethan finished for me.

"I do," I said with a smile.

"Keep an eye out for accomplices," Luc offered. "If he's truly clean, someone must be doing the dirty work for him. They could be on alert after the CPD sweep."

"It's also possible he changed protocols afterwards," Ethan said.

"I'll get a good look before I go in. He knows he's on the watch list, so he probably won't be that surprised to see me. The bigger question is—if I find him, what do I do with him?"

Ethan arched a suspicious eyebrow.

"I'm not suggesting homicide," I explained. "But if the CPD couldn't find anything, it's not like I could bring him in."

"Just get the information you can," Ethan said, "and stay safe. Don't worry about engaging him. We know where he is and how to find him."

"At least until he bolts," Luc said.

"And do be back in time for dinner," Ethan reminded me.

"I remember. I'll even be back in time to clean up and dress respectably." I had to—I was heading into a meeting with three House Masters and the head of the GP. There's no way I was going in there without being dolled up.

Ethan smiled back. "That would be much appreciated."

At the sound of footsteps on the hardwood floors, we all turned around. Malik stood at the edge of the hallway, his expression wan.

"Darius is on the phone," he announced. "He'd like to speak to us."

Luc and Ethan exchanged a glance that made me nervous, even though it was one of those looks that commanding officers share so they don't have to speak the words aloud and freak out the soldiers. "My office," Ethan said, then glanced at me. "Work your magic, Sentinel—and close this thing down." He followed Malik back down the hallway, and they both disappeared into Ethan's office.

I glanced at Luc. "You wanna walk me to my car?"

"Happy to."

I led the way down the sidewalk to the Cadogan gate. As per usual, two fairies stood at attention as we passed, but this time, one of them was a girl. She had the same straight, dark hair as the male mercenaries, and her face was sculpted and gaunt in a European supermodel kind of way. She also wore the same black ensemble as her counterpart and gave me the same look of disinterest as I passed.

"Have the mercenary fairies gone egalitarian?" I asked Luc as we headed down the street, ignoring the screams of the protesters. There were more camped out this evening, probably because of the morning's news report, and they led with the new classic: "No more vampires. No more vampires."

"Apparently we'd previously had male fairies because no women applied for the job. She did."

"What's her name?"

"Not a clue," Luc said. "I don't even know the names of the guys who stand there, and we've had the mercs on contract for years. They prefer to stay professional."

We walked past a boxy sedan parked across the street from the House. Both guys in the front seat munched on sandwiches. Binoculars and paper coffee cups were stashed on the dashboard. I assumed those were our cops.

"Not exactly subtle, are they?" I murmured to Luc.

"About as subtle as vampires on V."

"Ouch."

"Too soon?"

"Let's wait until we aren't under threat of indictment." And speaking of uncomfortable topics, "About Lindsey . . ."

"She's killin' me, Sentinel."

"I know. I'm sorry."

"I saw her kiss him."

"Honestly? I don't think she has feelings for Connor. I just don't think she's ready to settle down."

He stopped on the sidewalk and looked at me. "Do you think she'll come around?"

"I certainly hope so. But you know how stubborn she is."

Luc laughed mirthlessly. We'd reached my orange car, and he popped a fist gently on the trunk. "I definitely know that, Sentinel. I suppose I decide to wait her out, or I don't. Not a whole lot else I can do."

I gave him a sympathetic smile. "I guess so."

"By the way, do you have any plans to tell me which vamps were using V? They need to be interviewed."

I shook my head. "No dice. I turned my back when they handed over the drugs, and I promised not to offer up their identities if they did. I made a promise, and I won't break it. I won't reveal my source."

I'd expected irritation or a lecture about duty to the House and its vampires, but I didn't get one. He almost looked proud.

"Well played, Sentinel."

I nodded at him, then adjusted my sword and stepped into the car. "While I'm gone, make sure Ethan doesn't murder Darius."

"I'll do my best. Good luck," Luc said, closing the door.

I hoped I wouldn't need it.

I wasn't fancy enough to have a GPS unit, which would have seemed odd in the Volvo anyway. So I found Paulie Cermak's house the old-fashioned way—with a street address and directions printed from the Internet, offered up by Kelley before I left the House.

Jeff had been right—Cermak's place wasn't far from the Garfield Park Conservatory. The conservatory was an amazing place, but this area had definitely seen better days. Some chunks of the block were empty of houses, the little remaining grass strewn with trash. Many of the buildings—grand stone apartment houses and World War II–era homes—had seen better days.

Cermak's house was nondescript—a narrow, two-story building with gray shingles and a highly pitched roof. The yard was neat, the grass clipped, but with no real landscaping to speak of. The remains of a paper fast-food bag were sprinkled across the lawn, probably caught in a mower blade, and no one had cared enough to clean up.

He was lucky in one respect—unlike the rest of the houses on this side of the block, Cermak's had a side garage. It wasn't attached, but it was a garage nonetheless, and it gave him a way to avoid what thousands of other Chicagoans had to face every day—residential on-street parking.

I parked my car a few houses down the block, then grabbed my sword and a small black flashlight from the glove box. Once outside, I belted on my sword and pushed the flashlight into my pocket. I locked up the car, took a good look around for any errant McKetricks or unmarked police cars, and started walking.

I'd been standing Sentinel for a few months now. While I wasn't thrilled about the battles, I was getting used to them. But the part of the work that still made me nervous was the walk-up. I'd been nervous walking down Michigan with Jonah, but at least I'd had someone to keep me company and keep my mind off the task ahead. Now I was alone in a dark, quiet neighborhood with nothing but my thoughts.

I hated the anticipation of violence.

I stopped beside the house's black plastic mailbox. The red flag was raised, but I resisted the urge to open the box and see what he was mailing out. I had enough problems without adding mail tampering to the list.

Cermak's garage was dark, as was the top floor of the house. The first floor glowed with light. The security door was open; the screen door was closed.

"Start with the garage," I murmured, tiptoeing through the grass on the far side of the lot. The driveway, such as it was, consisted of two thin lines of concrete, just enough to give a car tire a bit of protection from the mud. I stuck to the grass to muffle the sound of my boots. While I planned to knock on the front door at some point, I wanted to check out the lay of the land first, and that required sneakiness.

The garage was narrow, an old style with a pull-up door and a row of windows across the top. I pulled out my flashlight, twisted it on, and peeked inside.

A thrill shot through me.

A gleaming Mustang was parked inside, the same car we'd seen on the security feed—a coupe with white racing stripes and the telltale Mustang side scoops. The car was gorgeous. Whatever Cermak's problems, I couldn't fault his taste in vehicles.

I snapped an image with my camera phone, and considered the "confirm vehicle" box checked. Next stop, the house.

I crossed the lawn and headed for the small concrete porch. A television show from the eighties—complete with laugh track— blared through the screen door.

When I reached the porch, I wrapped my left hand around my sword handle, squeezing it for comfort. I could see through the house to the kitchen and the avocado green stove and refrigerator. The house inside was simply decorated with motel-style furniture. Plain and thrifty, but serviceable.

"Can I help you?"

I blinked when a man stepped up to the door—the man from the Temple Bar video. He wore a Yankees sweatshirt that had seen better days and a pair of well-worn jeans. He smiled, revealing a mouthful of straight, white teeth. And he might have lived in Chicago, but the accent was all New York.

I decided to get to the point. "Paulie Cermak?"

"You got him," he said, head tilted to the side as he took in my features . . . and then my sword. "You're Merit."

He must have seen the surprise in my eyes, as he chuckled. "I know who you are, kid. I watch television. And I expect I know why you're here." He flipped the lock on the screen door and pulled it open a little. "You wanna come in?"

"I'm good where I am." I might have been curious, but I wasn't stupid. I'd rather stay out here with the city at my back than willingly go into the home of a suspect.

He let the door shut again and crossed his arms on the other side of it. "In that case, why don't we get to it? You were looking for me—now you found me. What do you want with me?"

"You've spent some time at Temple Bar lately."

"That a question or a statement?"

"Since we both know you parked your car outside the bar, let's say it's a statement."

He shrugged negligently. "I'm a small businessman, just trying to make my way in the world."

"What's your business, Mr. Cermak?"

He smiled grandly. "Community relations."

"Is Wrigleyville the relevant community?"

Paulie rolled his eyes. "Kid, I got interests all over this city."

All these questions, and I was beginning to feel like a cross between a cop and an investigative reporter—with none of the credentials or authority. "Is it any coincidence that you start popping up outside Temple Bar and a new drug hits the streets?"

"In case you ain't already aware, the men and women in blue have been through my house from top to bottom. You imply that I've been distributing drugs, but don't you think they would have found something if I had been?"

I sized him up for a moment. "Mr. Cermak, would you like to know what I think?"

He smiled slowly, like an eager hyena. "As it turns out, yeah. I would like to hear what you think."

"You had the forethought to keep any trace of V out of your

house. I think that makes you an incredibly smart and resourceful man. The question, then, is where you're keeping the drugs . . . and who you're getting them from. How'd you like to fill me in on that?"

Paulie Cermak stared at me, wide-eyed, for a moment before erupting with laughter, the belly-aching kind that soon had him coughing uncontrollably.

When he finally stopped guffawing, he wiped tears from the corners of his eyes with fingers that were longer and more delicate than I'd thought they'd be. Like the fingers of a pianist, but attached to a shortish, barrel-chested drug pusher.

"Oh, Jesus," he said. "You are gonna give me an embolism, kid. But you are a kick, you know that? And you aren't exactly shy, are you?"

"Is that a no?"

"The business world is a very delicate place. You've got higher-ups. Middlemen. And everyday, run-of-the-mill vendors."

"Such as yourself?"

"As you say. Now, if I draw too much attention to those other levels, the entire balance gets thrown off, and that makes management unhappy."

"Is McKetrick your management?"

He went quiet for a moment. "Who's McKetrick?"

I couldn't be certain, but I had a sense his confusion was legitimate, that Cermak really didn't know who McKetrick was. Besides, he'd all but admitted he was selling drugs. Why start lying now?

A thought occurred to me—and not the kind of thought that was going to help me sleep better at night. I was the granddaughter of a cop, and a vampire with connections to Cadogan House. Why wouldn't he lie to me, unless he thought vampires couldn't touch him . . . or whomever he worked for? And who was the only woman the GP wouldn't let us touch?

I had to inquire, but I didn't want to make him—or Celina—skittish.

"Do you work alone?" I asked him.

"Most of the time," he carefully said, as if not sure where the question was headed.

"With vampires?"

"Honey, I've got a carotid. Given the nature of the merch, I prefer to get in and get out with as few fangs as possible."

"You were spotted with a vamp named Marie."

Paulie stared back at me, refusing to respond. Maybe he hadn't noticed the security camera.

Brave as he might have been about the V, Cermak apparently wasn't willing to admit to Celina's involvement. I wasn't sure what that signaled, if anything. And I was running out of ideas.

"I know what you think it stands for," Paulie said.

"What?"

"V," he said. "The name of the drug. You think it means 'vampire,' right?"

I paused for a moment, surprised he was willing to be that overt about it. "It had occurred to me," I finally got out.

He pointed a finger at me. "Then you'd be wrong. Stands for *veritas*. That's a Latin word meaning 'truth.' Idea is, it's supposed to remind vamps what being a real vampire feels like. The old-school, flying-bats, Transylvania, horror-film bloodlust. The good kind of bloodlust. And battling. No wussy, pansy human bullshit. Getting out there and mixing it up. It's a gift, V, to the vampires. *Veritas*. Truth," he repeated. "Personally, I appreciate that."

That was an awfully philosophical explanation. "And what makes you so generous toward vamps?"

"I'm not generous, kid. I'm not saying I've seen V, but if I had, it ain't the kind of thing I'd get involved in out of the goodness of my heart. It's more the kind of thing I'd consider making a living from."

"Who would?"

Paulie snorted. "Who do you think would have the motivation to do something like that? To make vamps crazy for blood, to make them want to act like 'real vampires'?" He shrugged. "All I can say is, you gotta go higher in the chain than me, doll."

Another hint about Celina? Or maybe another higher-up in Chicago's Houses? I needed more info. "You wanna point me in the right direction?"

"And take the chance of reducing my income? No, thanks, kid." An old-school telephone rang from somewhere in the house. Paulie glanced back at it, and then at me. "You need anything else?"

"Not at the moment."

"In that case, you know where to find me." He stepped away and closed the door, and the house shook a bit on its foundations as he walked back to the phone and silenced its ringing.

I closed my eyes and closed out some of the extraneous neighborhood noise, focusing in on the phone call.

"Wrong number," I heard him say, the phone's bell ringing as he put it back on its cradle again.

I walked back down the stairs and across the yard to the driveway, then turned back to face the house. I gnawed my lip for a moment, trying to figure out my next move. Even in the dark, it was obvious the paint was peeling in sizable chunks away from the shingles. The roof looked awful, and the screen in the door was ripped across the bottom.

I glanced back at the garage. Paulie's house was in pretty miserable shape—but he had a perfect vintage Mustang? If he couldn't even afford to fix up the house, how could he afford to pay for the Mustang?

I didn't know the answer, but I thought it was worth exploring. I pulled out my phone and sent a message to Jeff. "NO DICE AT THE CERMAK HOUSE. KEEP LOOKING AT THE CAR."

I'd just gotten back into the car when Jeff called back.

"That was fast," I said.

"We were on the same wavelength. I've been poring through databases since we talked earlier, and I've got nothing about the sale of the car. If this thing was actually sold—I mean if money exchanged hands—it was an off-the-grid sale. The only way we're going to be able to trace it now is if Cermak happened to tell you who sold it to him."

"Negatory on that one. I guess that makes the car a dead end."

"Unless you randomly bump into the guy who sold it to Cermak."

"In a city of nearly three million? Unlikely." But he did give me an idea. While I couldn't exactly cuddle up to Celina and ask her if she knew Paulie Cermak, I knew someone else who might.

I checked my watch. It was only eleven o'clock. I had time for a little trip east . . . and some Zen deep-breathing exercises before I got there, because I was going to need all the patience I could muster.

"Do me a favor, would you, Jeff? E-mail me the picture of Cermak from the video footage?"

"You got it."

Once I'd received his e-mail, I put away the phone. I considered calling Ethan to give him an update, but the idea made my stomach roil. He'd just been on the phone with Darius, and I really didn't want to know how that conversation had played out.

Ethan probably also wouldn't have approved of my next trip.

No—a visit to Navarre House seemed like one of those things for which it would be easier to apologize later than get permission in the first place, especially with a grouchy GP leader in the city.

Decision made, I pulled away from the curb. It was time to visit the Gold Coast.

CHAPTER SEVENTEEN

TWO MASTERS AND ONE BAD ATTITUDE

I was halfway to Navarre House when the phone rang again. It was Jonah, so I flipped it open and nestled the phone between my ear and shoulder.

"Hi, Jonah. What's up?"

"Just checking in. How's the investigation progressing?"

"Well, we were able to ID the short man Sarah saw outside the bar. Found video with his car on it. Guy named Paulie Cermak. I just paid him a visit."

"Get anything interesting?"

"Not really. He's got a crappy house and a fabulous vintage Mustang. He's not exactly shy about his work, but his story is that he's a bit player. He says he's got management running the show. The police didn't find anything to pin on him, so I don't think we'll have much luck, either."

"Any chance McKetrick's in charge?"

"He seems to have no idea who McKetrick is. He also says V stands for *veritas*."

"Truth?"

"The very same."

"That's awfully deep for a pill pusher."

"That's exactly what I thought."

"Great minds and all," he said, with an amusing tone in his voice. "You coming to the shindig tonight?"

"I am. You?"

"With bells on . . . and a fine Italian suit I have no choice but to wear."

"Just be glad you only have to pull it out on special occasions," I told him. "You guys get jerseys—we get fine Italian suits every night."

He chuckled. "Very true. Hey, speaking of Ethan, a heads-up—my story is that we met for the first time outside Temple Bar after the incident."

"Fine by me. Have you talked to Darius this trip?"

"Not yet. I've been with the guards today. We were training. Why?"

"Just a heads-up, he's kind of an ass." I regretted the words the instant they were out of my mouth. Sure, Jonah had done me a solid, but did I really know anything about him? Other than his pretty-boy looks and ridiculous overabundance of graduate degrees?

"Well aware," Jonah said. "He and Scott went a round about the jerseys, actually. Darius found them unbecoming of Housed vampires."

I couldn't help but chuckle. "That does sound like something he would say. I guess Scott won the battle eventually?"

"I wouldn't say he won it per se. More like he wouldn't give in and Darius eventually lost interest in the argument."

"That's a risky strategy with an immortal," I said. "They've got all the time in the world to argue."

"Speaking on your own behalf?"

"Me? Of course not. I'm not at all stubborn and completely flexible."

"Liar," he slyly said. "Well, I'll stop harassing you and let you get back to it. Call me if you need me."

"Will do. Thanks."

I tucked the phone away again, a little weirded out by the phone call. It was nice of Jonah to check in—to work from the assumption V was a problem vamps needed to face together. All hands on deck, as it were, instead of the Sentinel going it solo.

On the other hand, the conversation had sounded a little . . . datey. He was checking in, asking what I was doing later. Maybe he hadn't meant anything by it. Maybe he really was warming up to me and my various charms. But there was a flirty, friendly edge to his voice that I hadn't heard before . . . and I wasn't entirely thrilled to hear now. Flattered? Yes. But I didn't need the complication.

I also wasn't thrilled that I'd just given Jonah an update I hadn't yet provided to Ethan. I didn't like deception, especially not when it came to deceiving someone who'd saved my life once upon a time. I knew why I was withholding information from him, but that didn't make it any more comfortable.

The irony? I'd railed against Ethan for withholding information from me. Not that it had stopped him, but it still drove me crazy. And here I was, doing the same thing. Were my reasons any better? Had his been any worse?

And although we weren't a couple, the dishonesty felt wrong. Like a breach of the trust we'd earned, a kind of trust that went beyond Sentinel and Master. I was also missing out on using Ethan as a sounding board about Jonah and the RG. If there was any possibility he could be neutral, a second opinion would have been helpful.

But as a Master, he couldn't be neutral. So as much as I didn't like it, there was no clear path to the truth right now.

I nibbled on that conclusion for a while, working it over and over in my mind. I lost myself in my thoughts and the drive.

It wasn't that vampires were antithetical to mansions. The vampire design aesthetic was far from chains, skull candles, and black lace, and it wasn't as if Cadogan House was a hovel. It had been elegant before the attack, and it was becoming elegant again.

But Navarre House set a new standard for vampire opulence. First, it was tucked into the Gold Coast neighborhood, one of Chicago's ritziest areas, full of Gilded Era mansions and celebrity retreats. Second, the interior was awe inspiring. Giant spaces, weird art, and the kind of furniture you saw in design magazines. (The kind of furniture you thought was neat in a museum kind of way, but wouldn't actually want to sit on when watching a game on the flat screen on a Saturday afternoon.)

Did I mention Navarre had a reception desk?

Having parked the Volvo and freshened up as much as possible in the rearview mirror, I went inside and prepared to face the three dark-haired women who controlled access to Navarre and its Master.

Ethan and I had dubbed them the three Fates, à la Greek myth, because they exercised a similar amount of power. They looked petite, but I had the sense that one false move—or one unauthorized step past the reception desk—and you'd be in trouble.

Today they mostly seemed overwhelmed. The House's lobby was swamped with people. None fit into obvious categories—no reporters, no vampires, no one who seemed like a member of

McKetrick's crew doing a little in-House surveying. Most wore standard black suits, more of the accountant variety than the Cadogan House variety, and they carried notepads or nondescript black bags.

I maneuvered through them to the reception desk and waited until I got the attention of the Fate on the left.

After a moment, she looked up at me, obviously frazzled, her fingers flying across the keys even as she made eye contact.

"Yes?" she asked.

"Merit, Sentinel, Cadogan, here to see Morgan if he's available?"

She blew out a breath, finally glanced down at her screen, and continued her marathon typing. A man bumped beside me at the desk and looked down at her.

"I had an appointment fifteen minutes ago."

"Nadia is working as quickly as possible, sir. She'll be with you shortly." She pointed a long-fingered nail at the benches behind the desk. "Have a seat."

The man clearly didn't like her answer, but he bit his tongue and squeezed back through.

I leaned forward a bit. "What's going on in here today? I thought Tate wasn't allowing humans in the Houses?"

She rolled her eyes. "He's offered an exception to that rule. We're in the process of selecting our vendors for the next calendar year. The mayor suggested Nadia talk with representatives of the human businesses in town to get their bids."

Nadia was the Navarre Second, Morgan's vice president. She was also supermodel gorgeous, which was a shocking thing to learn the first time you walked into your ex-boyfriend's abode.

The Fate cast an unhappy glance out across the crowd. "I seriously doubt they can meet our needs."

I'd assumed we had a cleaning crew and a grounds staff, and I knew one of the House chefs. But it hadn't occurred to me that vampires needed vendors. But someone had to stock the House kitchens, keep folders and highlighters in the Ops Room, and ensure the crystal decanters in Ethan's office were filled with fine liquor. Here, that duty fell to Nadia and a boatload of vendors vying for the privilege of selling their wares.

I wondered if Malik did the same thing for Cadogan House, interviewing vendors, considering bids and quotes, and reviewing contracts. It certainly would have made sense. Ethan was the House's chief executive officer, which made Malik its chief operating officer.

A blonde with tightly hot-rolled hair and a lot of black eyeliner stepped up to the desk. "Is Mr. Greer available? Perhaps I could just speak with him if Nadia is too busy?"

Expression flat, the Fate glanced at me. "Do you remember where his office is?"

"I can find my way up," I assured her, walking away to the unhappy squeals of the woman I'd displaced in line.

Not that she'd had any chance.

I walked across the House's gigantic first floor to the arching staircase that led to the second floor. Morgan's office was there, a modern suite with a garden view. The door was closed, so I rapped my knuckles against it.

"Come in."

I stepped inside . . . and nearly lost my breath.

Morgan was half-naked, clad only in black trousers, pulling a short-sleeved white undershirt over his head, the muscles in his stomach clenching and bunching with the effort. When he was clothed, he pulled his dark, shoulder-length hair back and tied it at his nape.

It wasn't until then that he glanced over at me. "Yes?"

I opened my mouth, then shut it again, having completely forgotten the speech I was prepared to make. Honest to God, my mind was completely blank, all rational thought having fled at the sight of his body. God knew, physical attraction was never the problem. Nothing about Morgan was the problem. I was the problem. *Ethan* was the problem.

I had to shake my head to clear it. His expression went smug; I assumed he was happy he'd been able to fluster me.

"Not expecting company?" I finally managed.

Morgan sat down on the edge of a chair, pulled on socks, then lifted fancy square-toed shoes from the floor and slid his foot into one. "I just finished a workout, and we've got the dinner in an hour. What do you need?"

Realizing I was still standing in the doorway, door askew, I stepped into the room and closed it behind me.

"I wanted to update you on the investigation."

Halfway through the second shoe, his hands stilled, and he looked up at me. That's when I noticed the blue shadows under his eyes. He looked tired. It couldn't have been easy for him to fill Celina's shoes, especially given the unrest. I didn't envy a Second forced into the role of a Master . . . and I'd helped put him there.

"Then by all means, update me."

I managed not to roll my eyes, and repeated what we'd discovered in Streeterville, what we'd learned at the bar, and what we'd learned from Paulie. By the time I was done, Morgan was fully clothed and was sitting back in the chair, fingers linked across his stomach.

"You came across town to tell me all that?"

"We've identified the guy who's been selling V to vampires. His name's Paulie Cermak. I need to know if he looks familiar."

"Yeah, well, I don't generally hang around with addicts."

The attitude wasn't unexpected. That's why I'd asked Jeff for the picture—this was about evidence, not irritation. I pulled out my phone and called up Paulie's picture. "He's not an addict. He's a salesman, at least as far as I can tell."

I walked closer and held out the phone, then watched to make sure he glanced over at it.

I'd expected Morgan to roll his eyes and tell me he hadn't seen Cermak. I'd expected him to wax sarcastic about my investigation.

I hadn't expected the wide-eyed expression. He tensed, his shoulders squaring, his jaw clenching. He knew something.

"You've seen him," I said, before he could deny it or make his features blank again. But it still took him a minute to answer.

"Six months ago. Celina never allowed humans in the House, even before Tate issued the mandate. I was on my way up here to talk to her—I don't remember what we were meeting about. He—Cermak—was on his way out of the office. I asked her who he was. It was . . . strange that he was in the House."

So Celina had met with the man who sold V in her own House. That was all well and good, but it was completely circumstantial.

Circumstantial or not, Morgan was clearly flustered, clearly bothered by the links he was beginning to put together. Morgan closed his eyes, then scrubbed his hands over his face and linked his hands over his head. "It really, really pisses me off when you're right."

"I don't want to be right," I assured him. "I want to be the one with ludicrous theories. I don't want Celina making your job—or mine—harder."

He grunted and looked away, not ready to share the details of whatever he knew. I gave him space, walking to the other side of the office where a giant window overlooked a smartly designed courtyard.

"What did Celina say about him?" I asked after a moment.

"That he was a vendor for the House."

And things had come full circle. "And as Second, selecting vendors was your job, right?"

Morgan glanced back and nodded ruefully. "That's another reason it was strange that he was here. I just guessed it was a special project. I checked the books—they were fine. All the House's funds were accounted for. But there weren't any extra vendors listed."

"So she hadn't actually gotten anything from him. On the books, anyway."

Morgan nodded.

"What else would she want with Paulie Cermak? I mean, even if they were in the drug game together, why would she want to be involved in selling drugs to vamps? Does she need money?"

Morgan shook his head. "She gets a stipend from the GP for being a member, and she's been alive for a very long time."

"Compound interest?"

"Compound interest," he confirmed.

No dice there, then. "Maybe it's the drug itself," I suggested. "Cermak said it stood for *veritas*, which is Latin for 'truth.' He said it's supposed to make vampires feel more like themselves."

Morgan furrowed his brow, considering. "Celina has always believed relations between humans and vampires were going to come to a cataclysmic end. She just thought she'd come out on top."

"Which is why she'd worked to ingratiate herself to humans—to usher in the end of their reign?"

He shrugged. "Maybe. But as for V, I don't know. If she wanted 'truer' vampires, why not allow Navarre to drink?"

Because if she'd allowed drinking, I thought, she wouldn't have been able to demonize Cadogan. In any event, we could ferret out her motivations later. Right now, we needed evidence.

I stared at the floor for a minute, trying to figure out if I was missing anything. But nothing occurred to me, as much as I wanted there to be an ultimate answer to all my V-related questions. When I looked up at Morgan again, I found his gaze on me, his expression surprisingly unguarded.

"What?" I asked him.

He gave me a flat look, the implication being that he'd been reminded of the affection for me that I didn't share. No time like the present to cut off that train of thought.

"I should get going," I said. "I need to get changed."

"You bringing a date?"

"Is there ever going to be a time that you don't ask me about Ethan?"

"Only when it stops irritating you to ask."

"Unlikely to happen."

"And there you are."

We stood there for a moment, and I caught the hint of a smile on his face. If he could manage to work through his anger, I could manage to have a good attitude about it.

I headed for the door. "You're such a comedian."

"I try, Merit. I really do."

"Good night, Morgan."

"Only for an hour," he reminded me as I closed the door and walked back to the stairs.

When I reached the first floor, the cadre of vendors still stood in the lobby, milling impatiently about as they waited for their turn with Nadia. I hoped they had more patience with the Navarre House staff than I did.

When I returned to the House, Ethan and Luc met me at the door.

I looked at Ethan, prepared to tell the tale one last time. Frankly, being a proactive Sentinel involved repeating the same information over and over and over again. But the tale needed to be told, so I sucked it up and did my duty.

"Paulie Cermak is probably involved in the drug trade, and he's not especially shy about it. He says he's only a bit player. His digs are in pretty bad shape, but there's a shiny, vintage Mustang in the garage."

I almost spilled out the rest, but thought ahead enough to glance at Ethan, a question in my eyes: Could I tell him? Could I implicate a member of the GP after the tongue-lashing I assumed he'd received from Darius? Or was I putting him in an even worse position?

"At this point," he said quietly, "there's no harm in candor."

"In that case, I went to Navarre House and showed Morgan the picture of Cermak. Six months ago, Morgan saw Paulie coming out of Celina's office. She called him a 'vendor.'"

I watched Ethan's expression carefully, and I'm still not sure whether I saw relief or anxiety there. The news was equally bad and good—we had a witness who could link Celina to the man who sold V, but it was Celina. She was hands-off as far as the GP was concerned.

Luc glanced around warily, then lowered his voice, as if expecting Darius to come waltzing in at any moment, receivership papers in hand. "So Celina and Paulie are acquaintances," Luc said. "That makes it more likely Celina was the 'Marie' seen by the human, and the woman in the car."

"But we can't prove that," Ethan said, tucking his hands into his pockets. "And as much as it pains me to say it, that Paulie and Celina had a meeting half a year ago doesn't mean she's actively involved in setting up the raves or distributing V."

"And it's unlikely she's going to come forward and offer the evidence on a platter," Luc said.

"True," I agreed, a plan already forming. "Which is precisely why we need to draw her out."

Ethan's gaze snapped to me. "Draw her out?"

"Prove that Paulie and Celina are connected. Use him to get to Celina, to draw her out, and to prove that she's involved in distributing V and organizing the raves to help that endeavor."

"And how do you propose to do that?" Ethan asked. "What bait could we offer that would entice Celina?"

The answer was easy. "Me."

Silence.

"You have certainly grown into your position," Ethan dryly said. "And your willingness to take risks on behalf of the House."

"I'm well aware that she can thoroughly kick my ass. That makes it less a risk—if more of an inevitability."

"You are stronger than the last time you met," he pointed out. "You've bested shifters since then."

"She knocked me out with a single kick to the chest," I pointed out, my ribs aching in sympathy. "But that's not the point. For whatever reason, as we've discussed, she's fascinated by me. If Paulie tells her I'll be waiting, she'd probably take advantage."

Ethan frowned. "That is probably true."

"I have to do it," I told him. "We've identified Paulie, and we know he's involved with Celina. But we can't close down V—halt the distribution—until we have proof, at least enough evidence to take to Tate. We don't have to take it to the GP," I reminded Ethan.

"We only need to give Tate enough information to nail Paulie and Celina so the CPD can close the loop. If we can't rely on the GP to bring her down," I quietly added, "then let's help Tate do it."

"She has a point, hoss," Luc quietly agreed. "She's our best means to pull Celina out."

After a moment, Ethan nodded. "Work your plan, Sentinel." He tapped his watch. "But first, go get dressed."

I only just realized that he was already prepped for dinner in a slim-fit black suit and narrow black tie. That meant he'd be waiting on me.

"I'll go change," I agreed. I was also going to head upstairs and use the phone number Jeff had given me to send a message to Paulie Cermak.

One way or another, I was going to find her. GP be damned, I was going to bring her down.

Much to my surprise, I found no dress hanging on my door when I returned upstairs. The last couple of times I'd had to make social appearances with Ethan, he'd given me decadent couture gowns, presumably so I wouldn't embarrass the House with my usual jeans and tank tops. At first, I'd been offended by the gesture. But even a girl who cut her fangs on denim and Pumas could appreciate good design when it presented itself.

This time, the door was empty of all but its small bulletin board, and the closet bore only the usual pieces of my wardrobe.

Oh, well. It was probably for the best. I didn't really have time to be the girl who needed Lanvin just to leave the House.

Without a new option, I cleaned up and stepped into one of the other dresses Ethan had supplied. It was a knee-length, black cocktail dress, with a sleeveless bodice and swingy skirt, the fabric tucked into horizontal pleats from top to bottom.

I opted for the black heels Ethan had provided with the dress, as well as a holster that went beneath the skirt and held my dagger in place against my thigh. My Cadogan medal was my only accessory, and I left my hair down, my bangs a dark fringe across my forehead.

When I was made up, I sent a message to Paulie Cermak.

"TELL MARIE I'M READY TO MEET HER."

The message sent, I slipped the phone into a small black clutch. It was time to go play with the boys.

———◆◆◆———

CHAPTER EIGHTEEN

V IS FOR VALOR

Ethan was waiting on the first floor by the newel post and looked up as I stepped onto the final stair. "You look lovely."

"Thank you." I smoothed my hands over the skirt self-consciously. "No objection to the fact that I'm wearing this dress again?"

Ethan's smile was teasing. "Don't tell me you were looking forward to receiving another one?"

"That would be ridiculous. I'm well above such juvenile concerns."

His smile turned a little more philosophical. "You like the things you like. You take great joy in those things, and you should never be ashamed of that. The pleasure that you take in simple things—food, clothing, architecture—is a very attractive quality."

I looked away from the warmth in his eyes. "Are we ready?"

"You have your dagger?"

"I rarely leave home without it."

"Then to the Batcave, Sentinel."

He was in a rare, jovial mood, a mood lighter than I would have expected given the event we were about to attend. Ethan could definitely do formal; he looked good in a tux and knew how to schmooze a crowd. But the audience wasn't likely to be receptive.

When we were in the car and buckling our seat belts, our gazes caught.

"Do you think McKetrick will attempt to waylay us this time?"

He snorted and started the car. "Given our luck, quite possibly."

Fortunately, he was wrong. We made it to Lake Shore Drive without incident other than a nasty snarl that slowed traffic to a crawl. It was late, but that didn't preclude a solid case of gaper's block—the near standstill of traffic caused when drivers slowed to check out a wreck. In this case, there wasn't even a wreck, just a couple of club-going girls who pouted beside their car while a cop wrote up a ticket.

We were somewhere near Navy Pier when I broached the topic he hadn't yet. "Are you going to tell me about your call with Darius?"

I'd decided I'd rather have him punching trees than holding things back. At least with tree punching I could gauge how much trouble we were in. With silence, I had no clue.

It took Ethan a moment to answer. "There's no need to get into it."

"No need to tell your Sentinel what the head of the GP thinks about the House?"

"Suffice it to say, he had choice words about my leadership."

I glanced over at him. "And that's all you're going to tell me? No venting?"

"There are times when politics invade the House. Sometimes it's unavoidable. But my job, as a Master, is to insulate you from those things. Not from the consideration of strategy and alliances and the like, but from political pressure from the top. You are to undertake the tasks appropriate to your position—and worrying about my job or Darius's aren't some of those tasks."

"Thank you. Except it doesn't exactly help me prepare for the inevitable GP kick in the face."

He paused. "Sometimes you're too smart for your own good, you know."

I smiled toothily. "It's one of my better qualities."

He humphed. "Well, to spare you the sordid details, he is quite convinced our investigation of the raves is only making the problem worse—and drawing more attention to it. He is of the opinion these are matters for the GP to handle, and if and when the GP feels action is appropriate, they will do so."

"Wow," I sarcastically said. "That's not at all shortsighted and naïve."

"Attention to detail has never been Darius's strong suit. Call it the farsightedness of immortality—he often misses the trees for the forest." Ethan drummed his fingers against the steering wheel. "I don't know what to say to convince him otherwise, to make him understand the gravity of the situation."

"Maybe we should arrange for McKetrick and Darius to have a chat."

He chuckled. "Not an altogether bad idea. Although I'm not sure who'd win—the British bully or the American one."

"I wonder if, four months ago, you'd be thinking such things?"

He slid me a glance. "Meaning what, Sentinel?"

I thought for a moment, trying to figure out how to give voice to the idea. "On our good days, I think we make each other better. At our jobs, I mean," I quickly clarified. "You remind me of the House, of the thing we fight for."

"And you remind me what it's like to be human."

I nodded, now feeling a little silly for voicing the sentiment.

"We are a good pair," he said, and I didn't disagree.

We'd reached a détente. We seemed to be working well together right now—as if we'd found that delicate balance point between friends and lovers.

I didn't want to be one of those girls that became more attracted to things I couldn't have. But that was not really what this was. Against all odds—and every bit of relationship advice handed down by mothers and girlfriends through the centuries—he honestly seemed to be *changing*. He'd moved from taking advantage of the chemistry between us to wooing me with words, with trust, with respect.

That wasn't something I'd expected, but that made it all the more meaningful . . . and frightening. As a girl with good sense, how was I supposed to react to a boy who'd done the unthinkable and actually grown up?

It was a hard question. While the thought of our being together was kind of thrilling . . . I still wasn't ready. Would I be ready eventually? Honestly, I didn't know. But as Ethan had once told me, he had eternity to prove me wrong.

He found on-street parking outside Grey House. It was weird to approach the building for the second time in the guise of a dinner guest who'd never seen the inside. I decided to play surprised and impressed—but however I tried to spin it, it was still a lie to Ethan.

With a Master at my side, I walked back into Grey House. Charlie, Darius's assistant, stood just in front of the lush greenery in the atrium. He wore navy slacks and a khaki blazer, a pale blue shirt beneath. His feet were tucked into loafers, no socks. It was an odd ensemble for August in Chicago, but the formality suited him.

Charlie didn't leave his task to the imagination. "Darius would like to speak with you."

Ethan and I exchanged a glance. "Where?" he asked.

Charlie smiled grandly. "Scott has offered up his office. This way," he said, extending an arm.

We followed him through the atrium to one of the doors beneath the walkway—one of the rooms Jonah had said was nonessential. He opened the door and waited while we walked inside.

The room was gigantic, nearly as large as a football field. It looked like an old warehouse—with well-worn plank floors and painted brick walls, a post-and-beam ceiling overhead. There were desks sprinkled throughout the space. I guessed Scott and his staff shared an office.

But if so, they weren't in sight now. Darius sat beside Scott on a low, modern couch. Both of them wore suits. Jonah stood behind him and gave me a small nod of acknowledgment . . . and then what looked from the corner of my eye like a more lingering glance. I was probably imagining it, but when I involuntarily met his gaze, he looked swiftly away like he'd been caught midstare.

Like I'd said, complications.

Morgan stood a few feet away, arms crossed over his chest, wearing the shirt and trousers I'd seen him in—and not in—earlier. He glanced up when we walked in, but wouldn't make eye contact.

My stomach sank, and I knew exactly what was coming. I risked making telepathic contact with Ethan.

Be ready, I told him. *I think Morgan told Darius about Paulie Cermak.*

Charlie walked out again and closed the door behind him. Darius started in as soon as the door was closed.

"Mr. Greer has advised me that you've been investigating Celina."

This time, it was my mental connection with Morgan that I activated—it wasn't a connection we were supposed to have, since he hadn't made me a vampire, but it was handy when he needed a bit of surreptitious berating.

I trusted you, I told him. *I trusted you with information, and you decided to take it to Darius?*

He didn't respond, just shook his head. It was the move of a coward—or a child. And it didn't exactly help diminish my own anger.

Ethan might have been surprised the last time Darius had gone on the offensive, but this time he was prepared for the on-slaught. "As you know, Sire, we are required by *Canon* to follow the laws and dictates of the city in which we are Housed. Mayor Tate required us to investigate the nature of the new raves. We have done so."

"You have implicated a member of the Presidium."

"We have followed the information where it led."

"And it led to Celina?"

Ever so slowly, Ethan turned his frosty gaze on Morgan. "I believe Mr. Greer was the vampire who confirmed Celina's re-lationship with a man believed to be distributing V across the city."

Morgan looked back at Ethan, teeth bared, magic suddenly spilling into the room as his anger obviously blossomed.

Ethan's reaction was nearly instantaneous. His eyes silvered, his own fangs descended, and his own magic—cooler and crisper than Morgan's—spilled out, as well. Ethan took a step forward, menace in his eyes, and me at his back.

I'd seen Ethan pissed before—even at Morgan—but never like this.

"You will remember your place," Ethan said, calling on the fact that he'd been Master longer than Morgan had been alive. Hell, I'd been a vampire longer than Morgan had been Master, and that wasn't saying much.

But this time, Morgan wasn't swayed. He took a step forward and stabbed a finger in his chest. "*My* place? Mine is the oldest American House, Sullivan. And don't you forget it. And I'm not the one embarrassing all the Houses by stirring up drama that doesn't need to be stirred."

"Are you insane?" Ethan asked. "Do you understand what's going on out there right now? The trouble—the risks—the Houses are facing because of what your former Master did? Or because of what she's doing right now?"

"Enough!" Darius said, jumping to his feet. "Enough of this. You are Masters of your Houses, and you're acting like children. This conversation is an embarrassment to all American Houses and the GP—without whose generosity they would not exist."

That was putting it a bit strongly, I thought.

"As of this instant, you will both begin to comport yourselves like Masters. Like the princes you were meant to be. Not squabbling like human children."

Darius looked up, icy eyes drilling into me. "Your Sentinel is off the streets. She is not to be engaged in any further investigation of whatever issues your mayor imagines to exist."

Ethan's eyes could hardly have been wider. "And if the warrant for my arrest is executed?"

Darius's gaze slipped back to Ethan. "The mayor of the city of Chicago is surely intelligent enough not to think that a man-made prison can hold you. However much he may enjoy using the threat of incarceration to coerce you into solving his problems for him, those problems are still his to solve. And, more important, have any of you seen evidence that the three girls your mayor believes were killed are actually dead? Have you seen any evidence three girls were missing in Chicago?"

Catcher had promised he'd look into the girls' deaths, but hadn't passed any information along to me. But just because they hadn't solved the crime didn't mean a crime hadn't been committed.

I spoke up. "The eyewitness believed that three women were killed. And the things he described were accurate—vampires who were trigger-happy, doped on violence, ready to fight."

"In other words," Darius began, his manner supremely smug, "just like vampires?"

Let it be, Sentinel, echoed Ethan's voice in my head. *Battling six hundred years of entrenched belief is not a fight you can win.*

He's wrong, I protested.

That's as may be. But our fight is for Chicago, not Darius West, whatever his power. Fight the fight you can win. For now, he added in classic Ethan style, *be still.*

"And the fact that raves are becoming larger and more violent?" Ethan asked.

"Vampires are acting as vampires have always acted. If a few errant vampires break the rules of their home city, let the city respond."

"And if that's not enough?"

"Then the GP will discuss it, and the GP will act. Maintain control over your own House, Ethan, and leave the GP to its work. You are not to consider this issue any further."

A heavy silence filled the room.

"Sire," Scott said, finally speaking up. "I'm informed our guests have arrived. As you have presented your directives, perhaps Ethan can acknowledge receipt and we can move into dinner?"

Darius tilted his head at Ethan, the move more canine than vampiric. "Ethan?"

Ethan moistened his lips, and I knew he was stalling. Given the spiel he then offered up, I knew why.

"Sire, I acknowledge receipt of your directives and . . . will act as commanded."

He might as well have been crossing his fingers behind his back for all the rebellion in his body language. But you couldn't fault his answer. He sounded completely obedient—in word and tone.

Those words, probably holdovers from some feudal ritual, were enough, for Darius nodded. "Let us eat, drink, and be merry."

He walked to Ethan, arm extended. In a move similar to one I'd seen Ethan and Malik make, Ethan extended his arm, as well, and they grasped forearms and shared a manly half hug. Whispering followed, quiet enough that I couldn't make out the words.

When the gesture was complete, Ethan and Darius exited the office. Morgan followed, then Scott. I was last out the door, but I didn't make it very far.

Morgan cornered me in the hallway, putting his hand on my arm to stop me. "She was my Master. I had to tell him."

I pulled my arm away. "No," I whispered, "you didn't *have* to tell him. You knew we were handling it, that we were investigating. What you apparently *had* to do was sell me—and my House—down the river because our relationship didn't work out and you're still pissed about it."

His eyes widened, but he didn't comment.

"I'm done helping you," I told him. "We're the ones fighting to keep the Houses, the city, together. I thought I could count on you as an ally, which is why I gave you the information. I thought it would help if we were all on the same page. I was obviously wrong about that, because you'd rather act like a stung fourteen-year-old than a grown-up."

"I am still a Master," he said, puffing out his chest a little.

"For Navarre, that remains to be seen, 'cause you're letting Celina keep control. And as for me?" I leaned forward a little. "You're not my Master." I walked away, undoubtedly leaking a trail of magic behind me.

I'd thought when Morgan took over Navarre that at least we wouldn't have an enemy in place, someone who used people whenever the whim struck her. But as was the case with so many other things since I'd become a vampire, I'd been wrong.

CHAPTER NINETEEN

RED, RED WINE

Our dinner party was assembled in another room accessible through the atrium, a space in the warehouse nearly as large as the joint office had been. This one looked like a room for special events; tonight, a single, rectangular table was set in the middle of the room, a handful of modern-style chairs surrounding it.

Gabriel Keene, head of the North American Central Pack of shape-shifters, stood beside the table with his wife, Tonya. The Masters were already moving toward their chairs, having apparently already offered their introductions, which left the shifters to me.

I walked toward them, ignoring the vampire behind me and the others in the room. I wouldn't call Gabriel and Tonya friends per se, but Gabriel certainly had more foresight than Darius, which I could respect.

"I understand congratulations are in order," I said, offering them both a smile.

Gabriel was as manly as they came—big, brawny, tawny-haired, and honey-eyed with a love of leather and fine Harleys—but his face beamed with paternal pride. "We have a beautiful baby boy at home," he confirmed. "We appreciate the sentiment."

"It was nice of you to join us tonight," I said with a teasing smile. "I can't imagine you'd normally prefer vampire company to your newborn son's."

Gabriel cast a suspicious glance at Darius and the others. I understood the feeling. "There are things in life we need to do," he said, "and there are things in life we must do. Although I don't anticipate we'll stay very long."

Smiling, Tonya fished a tiny wallet out of her clutch. "Who could leave this face for long?" She held out a small photo of an admittedly adorable baby in a blue onesie. Gabriel smiled at the sight of the picture. He was clearly smitten.

There was a wealth of pride and love in his eyes, but when he raised his gaze to me, I could see the hint of fear behind it. The fear that comes from loving something so much you feel weighted down with it, nearly crushed by it. The fear of potential loss, of potential heartbreak, that you might fail the thing you worked so hard to bring into the world.

Parental fear, I suppose, made worse by the fact that being leader—Apex—of the Pack was hereditary. Connor was born a prince among wolves. He'd been born beneath a mantle of power, but also bearing the mantle of a responsibility he couldn't even begin to fathom. It must have been a lot for Gabriel to bear, knowing the responsibility he'd one day hoist upon his child's shoulders.

"You'll do right by him," I whispered. I wasn't sure if the words were elegant enough, but they seemed right enough. And Gabriel's small nod told me I'd said just the right thing.

"How are things otherwise?"

"Well, we aren't being used as scientific experiments," Gabriel said dryly. "That's a small victory." One of his concerns about announcing shifters' existence to the world was the fear they'd become fodder for military or medical research—the kinds of things you saw in monster movies and horror flicks. It wasn't exactly a pleasant thought, and I was glad to hear it hadn't come to pass.

"It's not that I think humans don't believe we're threats," he added. "They just aren't entirely sure what to do with us."

Shifters were generally considered the most powerful supernatural beings, at least of the groups I knew about so far. I considered humans' ignorance on that point a benefit.

"And the shifters who attacked the House?"

His expression darkened. "They're working their way through the penal system just like any average human criminal."

While I grimaced, Scott clapped his hands together. "Welcome, all, to Grey House. I appreciate your attendance here, and hope this can be a step toward friendship among us. Shall we dine?"

Before we could answer, men and women in chef's whites began pouring into the room bearing silver dome-topped trays. I took a seat beside Ethan as the trays were deposited before us. Two vampires traveled around the table with carafes of lemon water and bottles of a deep red wine, pouring as the vampires requested. Only Ethan, Jonah, and I opted for the wine; I guess we needed a drink worse than the others.

Other vampires lifted the domes, revealing a meal that might have been described as "Predator's Delight." Loins, roasts, cutlets. Sausages, steaks, filets. All laid out with artistic perfection. Oh, to be sure, there were sides, as well. Small fingerling potatoes, corn, and a grain salad of some kind. But in a room of vamps and shifters—predators among humans—the carnivorous urge was undeniable.

My stomach chose that moment to growl in a rumble that nearly echoed across the room.

As my cheeks heated, all eyes turned to me. I smiled lightly.

Gabriel smiled back, then lifted his water glass when the chefs disappeared from the room again. "Thank you, Mr. Grey, for the opportunity to share grain and beast with you. This is a meaningful gesture to us, and we hope our families can continue to commune in peace in the years to come."

"Hear, hear," Darius said, raising his glass, as well. "We are now neighbors in this fine city, and we hope that our days of strife are behind us, and that we can work together in peace and allegiance for millennia to come."

Gabriel offered a polite nod and gestured with his glass again, but didn't exactly commit to the "allegiance" bit. Vamps collected formal allegiances like baseball cards; shifters weren't exactly crazy about that kind of thing.

"And since I'd truly rather Merit focus on her meal than on me," Gabriel said with a wink, "let's stop talking and start eating."

But, of course, that would have been much too simple.

I don't know why it surprised me that Scott offered up a mean feast. The man loved the Cubs, he had an amazing warehouse turned House, and Benson's was his House bar. Those facts screamed "Quality Master."

The food was no exception. The meats were choice cuts that even my particular father might have served to dinner guests. They were tender enough to make a knife irrelevant, and seared to perfection on the outside. He couldn't have done better, especially for a group of predators.

Honestly, if I'd been a guy, I would have finished my plate, relaxed in my chair, and unfastened the top button of my pants. Food that good deserved undisturbed digestion.

Unfortunately, it wasn't to be.

I'd just taken another sip of wine—grimacing at how dry it

was—when the door at one end of the room burst open. Five vampires rushed in, some in black street clothes, but a couple wearing blue and yellow hockey-style jerseys with GREY HOUSE in capital letters across the front. They all had swords in hand and malice in their expressions.

"This is how you treat us?" asked one Grey House vamp who wore number thirty-two. "Some fucking shifter and his bitch get fed like kings?"

The Grey House vamp on the other side wore number twenty-seven. "And the GP, too? Shit is falling down here in the States, and we're serving steak to a vamp from the UK? Does that seem right to you?"

Within seconds, my dagger was in hand. And I wasn't the only one on alert.

Scott Grey jumped out of his chair and marched to the end of the table. "Matt, Drew, back the fuck off. Drop the swords, and march right back to the door."

The Grey House vamps wavered, probably the result of some mental Master juju Scott was throwing their way. But the rest of them didn't seem to be affected at all.

I carefully got to my feet and moved toward them, spinning the dagger in my palm as the anticipation built. All five vamps wobbled a little on their feet, their movements erratic, their eyes darting around the room. As I moved incrementally closer, I could see the cause in their eyes—they were almost wholly silver.

"Scott, it's V," I warned him.

"Any easy solution for handling them?" he called back.

"Not without a sorcerer," I told him. "We'll have to knock them out the old-fashioned way."

"Then that's what we'll do," Ethan said, stepping beside me, a knife from the table in his hand.

"Nice of you to join us, Sullivan," I teased, my gaze following the vamps as they spread out in a line, ready to rumble, whatever the cost. And with Darius, an Apex, and three Masters in the room, the cost would be high. . . .

"Let's go, old man," Thirty-two said. "You want to fight your own vampires? You want to take his side over theirs?"

"Liege," Jonah said, "as your captain, I'm going to request you move into a safer position."

"Request it all you want, Red," Scott told him, a mirthless smile on his face. "But that's not going to stop me from putting these dumbshits in their places. That's what they get for doing V."

Ditto what he said, Sentinel, Ethan silently told me. I suppose he wasn't going to let me argue he should just sit this one out.

The Grey House vamps seemed equally eager to brawl. "Oh, go to hell, man," Twenty-seven said.

"Only if you join me," Scott said pleasantly, and before another second passed, the room erupted into violence. Jonah and Scott took the Grey House vamps. Gabriel, Darius, and Tonya were sitting this one out. That left the Rogues to me, Ethan, and Morgan.

"I got the one in the middle," I called out.

"That leaves the other two for us," Ethan said. "Greer, take the one on the left."

And with that, we moved. I slipped between the in-House squabble to the angry-looking Rogue behind them, his eyes just as silver as the Grey vamps' had been. He was a big guy, and beads of sweat formed at his temple as he fought the rush of the drug. But this guy didn't care whether it was rage or drugs fueling his attack. He bared his teeth and moved in.

I had to give him credit—he was faster than I would have imagined given his bulk. He moved like a spider—his weight carried delicately on small, mincing feet.

He slashed, stepping into the movement like a trained fighter. I blocked the knife with my dagger, but miscalculated his speed and felt the cold burn of pain on the back of my hand. My own blood scented the air, pushing my vampiric instincts into overdrive.

I glanced down and saw the thin line of crimson. Only a couple of inches long and not terribly deep. It was a glancing blow, but that didn't ease the burn.

"Not cool," I said, moving into a spin, the dagger in my hand slicing through the front of his shirt. He muttered a few choice phrases but jumped back again. I stayed on the offensive, my intent to make this guy as uncomfortable as possible—to keep him as off balance as possible—while watching for a chance to knock him out.

"You think you're any better than the rest of them?" he muttered, raising the sword over his head and slashing down. I jumped back and out of the way, but my heel caught in a knot in one of the planks. I stumbled backward and into one of the room's giant wooden posts, catching myself with a hand.

Ethan's concerned voice echoed through my head. *Sentinel*.

I'm fine, I assured him, then kicked off my shoes. A vamp didn't need to fight in stilettos, anyway.

When I was upright again, I recentered the dagger in my hand and stared back at the vamp. "You were saying?"

"Bitch," he called out, swinging his katana in an awkward cross-body slice that would have been better suited for a broadsword than fine Japanese steel. And I cringed on its behalf as I ducked, and felt the echoing shudder of the column as his katana made contact—and stuck there. What a waste.

I spun out from beneath him as he loosened his grip on the handle and began stepping backward, eyes widening as if suddenly aware that the Sentinel from Cadogan House was on his case.

Maybe the drug was beginning to wear off.

"I'm going to do you a solid," I said, holding my dagger out to the side. "I'm going to toss this away, so we can have a fair fight."

I saw the relief in his expression as I chucked the steel. And when his eyes shifted to watch it spin across the floor, I made my move. I threw out a roundhouse kick that connected with his head. He went down hard, like a sack of vampire potatoes, then bounced a little before finally rolling to a stop.

Sure, roundhousing someone while wearing a cocktail dress wasn't exactly ladylike, but it certainly was effective.

With my Rogue out of commission, I glanced over at Ethan. He was in the process of putting his on the floor with a twisting judo-style drop that rattled the floorboards. When he was down, Ethan used an elbow at the neck to knock him out.

When the guy was still, he looked up at me, then noticed my guy was down. *Roundhouse?* he silently asked.

It is a classic, I said, glancing up. The rest of the party crashers had been bested, as well, all five of them out cold on the floor.

Jonah looked around the room, his gaze stopping when he reached me. "You okay?" he mouthed.

I nodded back. That definitely seemed personal.

"Scott," Darius called out, "What the fuck was that?"

Before Scott could answer, I filled in the blank. "With all due respect, Sire—those are your errant vampires."

Scott's guards, including Jonah's friends Jeremy and Danny, stormed the room not a moment later, pulling out the unconscious users. But they left the katana in the column—a visible sign to others in the House who might be stupid enough to try V.

We said goodbye to Gabriel and Tonya, who, understandably, left the House as soon as the coast was clear. Scott escorted the rest of us into the atrium while the remains of dinner were cleaned up. Charlie and Darius stood quietly together; Morgan stood alone. I was standing near Ethan when Scott and Jonah moved our way.

Scott looked between us. "Thanks for the assist."

Ethan nodded graciously. "It happens to the best of us, unfortunately."

"How are the vamps doing?" I asked.

"They're still out. They're in the infirmary under guard for the moment. When they're awake again, we'll have a lengthy conversation about drugs and responsibility."

"Did you know them well?" I asked.

"Only as applicants to the House," Scott said. "They're relative newcomers. Members of your Initiate class."

"What's a 'newcomer' in immortal terms?" I asked.

A smile perked at one corner of Scott's mouth. "Anything less than a decade."

Which made me a baby vamp.

Ethan slid a glance to where Darius stood, now offering up some sort of instructions while Charlie tapped at a tablet computer. "Do you think he'll consider the threat any more real now?"

"The GP has an odd attitude about things like this. I'm still not sure he sees us as anything other than troublemakers at this point. Squeaky wheels taking him away from real business in the UK."

"Are you going to investigate?"

Scott blew out a breath. "That's a tough one. This is a problem in my House. It has to be addressed."

"And if you discover Celina had anything to do with it?"

"Then we didn't have this conversation, but the Chicago Houses agreed to quietly deal with the problem as it exists."

Scott and Ethan looked at each other until Scott extended a hand. Ethan shook it, the deal struck.

Scott gestured toward his office. "I'm going to have a chat with my guards for a moment. I assume Darius will want to speak with us before you leave."

"We'll wait here," Ethan agreed.

"I think Luc was right," he added when they were out of earshot. "I can hardly take you out anymore."

"I just took out a vamp twice my weight while wearing a cocktail dress and three-inch heels. I think I deserve some credit for that."

"Is that so?" he asked.

That's when I first felt it—that rumble of warning from somewhere deep in my bones, telling me something wasn't right. But I ignored it and challenged him anyway.

"Yes," I baldly said. "You're fortunate I was there to help."

"Fortunate? I believe I bested my own foe, Merit. Perhaps you should thank me for my assistance." He raked his gaze up and down my body. "I'm sure I can suggest some small measure of gratitude."

The blood began to pound in my ears, my skin prickling with sudden heat. I had no doubt my eyes were silver, but I didn't care. I slipped a finger into one of the belt loops on his trousers and tugged him closer. "What did you have in mind?"

His eyes changed, his pupils mere pinpricks of black against the swirling quicksilver of his irises. He began moving forward, pushing me backward, and he didn't stop until my back was literally against the brick wall of the atrium.

Before I could object, his hands were on my face, his mouth against mine. His lips pulled at my mouth, kissing me hungrily, greedily.

In some satellite part of my brain, it occurred to me that it was odd that Ethan was kissing me in someone else's House. And yet, even as I thought it was weird, my blood began to warm and boil with a heat I'd never experienced before. It itched beneath my skin, adrenaline pushing through my veins as if I were still mid-battle with the Grey House vampires.

"Ethan," I managed, calling his name in warning, even while I let him kiss me there in the middle of Grey House. He changed tactics and kissed me slowly, languorously, before finally opening his eyes and looking at me. There was an apology in his eyes.

"Something is . . . wrong."

I nodded my head, knowing that he'd meant this wasn't just love or lust, but a different kind of force, but the thought was distant, and the burning need was here and now.

It was *immediate*.

Intense.

I rolled my head to the side, my eyelids fluttering, the invitation overt.

"Do you need something from me?" His voice was low, more like the warning growl of a tiger than the question of a vampire.

I swallowed . . . and nodded. I felt like a teenager at a first dance. I didn't know the music, wasn't savvy to the steps, but the emotions were so basic, so fundamental, that it wasn't possible to dance them incorrectly.

Ethan lifted a hand to my neck, the bare touch of his fingertips nearly buckling my knees. And before I could ask why he was apologizing, he kissed me. His kiss was firm, insistent, and questing. He moved closer, wrapping his arms around my back and deepening the kiss. His tongue explored as he pressed harder against me, the sudden length of his unmistakable erection pressing against my stomach.

I should have been shocked. Should have reminded him that this was neither the time nor the place, that we'd seen how bad things could get.

But with each possessive rumble in his throat, our own magics twined together. I was drawn in—by the magic, by the kiss, by the possessive bite of his fingers. I pulled him toward me, my fingers slipping into the belt loops on his trousers, and leaned up to deepen the kiss. I was as hungry for him as I'd ever been for blood, but this hunger was *now*. It was immediate, and it demanded to be sated.

Love was a dangerous drug.

Oh, God. That was it. Ethan wasn't overpowered by love or lust or the sudden, romance-novel-esque realization that *He Had to Have Me Now*. This was unprompted aggression, albeit of a slightly different variety than we'd seen before. . . .

"Ethan, I think we've been drugged."

He ignored me, instead growling and tangling his fingers into my hair. My heart tripped, not out of lust this time, but out of fear because the growl had changed, become meaner.

I switched tactics, giving him a telepathic order that I hoped would push through the haze of drugs to the part of his brain that was still functioning. *Ethan, stop.*

He lifted his head, and I saw the conflict in his eyes. His brain ordered him to stop, but his body was propelling him forward—evidenced by his eyes. They were nearly all silver.

"What?" he asked.

"I think we've been drugged. Someone slipped us V. Maybe in the food?"

A wave of hot, itchy anger rushed through me. I squeezed my eyes shut and my fingers into fists, pressing until the pain in my palms helped slow the spinning of my mind.

"The anger found a different outlet," he said, his voice hoarse. "Perhaps a different dose. Maybe in one of the meats?"

I shook my head. "The wine," I answered. "I think it was in the wine. It had an odd taste. Really, really bitter."

"Who else drank the wine?"

I thought back. I'd had wine, as had Ethan. And the only other person who'd had wine was Jonah. But I was saved the trouble of telling Ethan.

We both looked up as Jonah burst through the foliage in front of us. His eyes, already silver, became fierce as he stared Ethan down.

"It isn't nice not to share."

Ethan growled, low in his throat, a warning to Jonah. "I don't share."

Jonah clucked his tongue. "You should. Life is so much more interesting, don't you think, when all of us get a taste?" I'd heard of girls being thrilled to be fought over before, but I didn't like feeling like a piece of property.

"I'm no one's to offer up," I said.

"But you could do so much better," was Jonah's retort.

It's just V, I silently reminded Ethan. *He had the wine, too.*

"Regardless the cause, he'd best behave himself," Ethan gritted out. He stared Jonah down, fangs bared. They were nearly the same height, close to the same build. Ethan was fairer than Jonah, but they'd have made equally matched opponents, if not for Ethan's position, which surely would have reaped Jonah more trouble than the fight would have been worth.

"Jonah," I warned, standing up, as well. "Back off."

But instead of backing off, he bared his fangs at Ethan, hissing in warning that he'd found a prize and didn't plan to give it up.

I wasn't sure where the sudden interest had come from, but seriously doubted it had anything to do with me. More likely, Jonah had been drawn in by the magic that Ethan and I had spilled into the room. And in classic V fashion, he'd become unreasonably angry.

"Jonah, come on," I urged. "You need to back off. You don'
want to fight a Master, especially not when Darius is here."

My voice was pleading, and he threw me a glance. His brow
were drawn together, as if he was trying to puzzle out exactly why
he was standing in the atrium, ready to fight for a girl he'd only
recently come to respect, much less actually like.

But Ethan apparently hadn't noticed the self-reflection, and
took a menacing step forward. "She is *mine*."

Jonah shook off rationality and faced him down. "That decision is hers to make, and it doesn't look like she's made it yet."

"She sure as fuck won't be choosing you," Ethan growled out.

Jonah lifted his arm. My own instincts kicked in, protecting
Ethan at the top of my list.

"*Step back*, Jonah," I warned him, but he still hadn't managed
to push through the V. He cocked back to swing. I reached forward
to pull him off, but he swung blindly out. As if time had slowed
down, I watched his fist move toward me, a swat to push me away
He made contact.

The lights went out.

CHAPTER TWENTY

—————— ❦ ——————

THE HANGOVER

I blinked and waited for the room to stop spinning. I was look-ing up at an industrial ceiling, the fronds of plants and ferns at the edges of my vision. Still Grey House, I guessed.

Green eyes appeared in my frame of vision. "How's your head?"

"Throbbing."

I began to sit up, but Ethan put a hand on my shoulder. "You've been out for a few minutes. Take it slow."

"What happened?"

"You tried to keep Jonah from punching me, and he inadver-tently nailed you."

Now I remembered. I'd gotten in the way of Jonah and Ethan's battle, and I'd ended up the worse for it.

Ethan held out a hand. "Give me your hand," he said, then slid his other one behind my back. I sat up, closing my eyes until the vertigo passed.

When I finally opened them again, Ethan tipped back my chin, gazing into my eyes. "Look to the left," he said, and when I did, added, "And the right." I did that, too.

"He rang my bell," I said, touching a finger gingerly to the knot on the back of my head. Given the speed of vampire healing, it wouldn't last much longer, but for now, it smarted.

"Yes, he did," Ethan agreed.

"Where is he?"

"Jonah? Scott's got him locked down until he's satisfied the drug's worn off. It was the wine," Ethan added. "According to the Grey House vamps, they obtained the V from Benson's, where they collegially shared it with a group of Rogues."

"Undoubtedly in the name of inter-House cooperation," I said dryly.

"I'm sure. The Grey House vamps also passed along that Darius would be dining here tonight. They then managed to rile each other up about the injustices of the GP."

"Probably an easy argument for Rogue vamps to make," I observed. "Especially if they're all on V."

Ethan nodded. "They came back to the House intent on giving Darius a piece of their minds. They also snuck into the kitchen with an extra dose and hit up the wine. They wanted him to experience the effects of being a true vampire."

"Ironic that Darius didn't drink any."

"Very. Although he is now keenly aware of V's effects."

A long shadow appeared over me, and then an English voice spoke. "How is she?"

I glanced up. Darius stood at my side.

"She'll make it," Ethan concluded, "although I think bed rest would be a good way for her to spend the rest of the evening."

"I think that's a capital idea," Darius agreed. "A few pints of blood might also speed the healing."

Ethan nodded. "And our investigation of V?"

"I've made the GP's position clear."

"Sire—," Ethan began, but Darius silenced him with a hand.

"There is more to consider, Ethan, than the game you are playing with your mayor. You take care of your House; allow Mr. Grey and Mr. Greer to take care of theirs. The rest is none of your concern, and that includes any current GP members. Is that clear?"

Ethan's jaw twitched, but he managed a nod. "Of course, Sire."

Darius nodded officially, then offered a weak smile for me. "Heal quickly, Merit," he said, and then he was off again, Charlie stepping into line behind him.

"I'd like to go home," I quietly said.

"The sentiment is definitely mutual," Ethan said, his gaze still following his political master as he disappeared into the man-made jungle. "Let's go home."

Ethan insisted on carrying me to the car, which felt equal parts ridiculous and romantic. As a self-assured woman, it wasn't exactly comfortable being carried like a child. On the other hand, Ethan had made me a vampire, and the link between us remained. The scent and feel of him was soothing, and I managed to enjoy being swept up in his arms, no matter how guilty the pleasure.

When we reached the House again, I protested enough that he let me walk back upstairs to my room, but he refused to let me leave it. While Ethan retrieved blood from the kitchen, I changed into yoga pants and a Cubs T-shirt and lay down on my bed, a pile of pillows behind my tender head.

Ethan returned carrying a giant plastic cup with a handle, the kind a trucker might buy to provide an all-day dose of caffeine for the road.

"Was that the smallest container you could find?"

"I prefer not to underestimate your potential for grumpiness," he said, sitting down on the edge of my bed and offering the vessel.

I humphed, but accepted the cup and began to sip through the hard plastic straw stuck through its top. After a moment, I pulled back. "Is there chocolate sauce in the blood?"

His cheekbones pinked a bit. "Since you weren't feeling well, I thought a little chocolate might do you good."

Unfortunately, chocolate and blood weren't a tasty combination. But he'd gone to such trouble that I couldn't bear to disappoint him.

"Thank you," I said, taking another heartening sip. "That was really thoughtful."

He nodded, then sat quietly while I drank. I sipped until I felt the latent hunger ease, then put the cup on the nightstand beside me. I closed my eyes and sank back into the bed, my head against the backstop of pillows. As soon as I was still again, exhaustion overwhelmed me.

"I'm tired, Ethan."

"It's been another long evening," he said.

But I shook my head—just a little, so my head didn't throb with it. "It's not just the concussion. It's the work. I wouldn't want a cop's job. I'm not entirely sure I want my job right now."

"And miss all the fun and excitement? The chance to review security footage and fight drug-addled vampires?"

"Don't forget about pissing off the head of the Greenwich Presidium."

"Ah, yes. Who'd have thought, less than a year ago when you were grading papers, that your life would come to this?"

"Certainly not me," I said. I opened my eyes again and looked over at him. "Are we going to finish this? Or are we going to do as he asked?"

"I don't know. I certainly prefer not to put my fate in Tate's hands." Ethan sighed and rolled his shoulders. "Tate called the

House while we were gone. Informed Malik he was tired of the delay, and said I had forty-eight hours before my warrant was issued."

"Awesome," I muttered.

He looked back at me, his eyes glowing emeralds. "We should talk about the kiss."

This time, I was the one who blushed. "Is there anything to talk about? We were high."

He gave me a flat look; I looked away.

"At least admit that there's more to it than drugs," he quietly said.

I looked away, gnawed the edge of my lip, and pondered the irony. I'd kissed Ethan, and he wanted to discuss our relationship. We'd now completely switched roles.

"There's more to it," I finally agreed. "But you know how I feel."

"And you still aren't convinced my intentions are noble?"

I was becoming more convinced, I thought to myself, but how could I tell him that? How could I confess it without sounding cruel for not believing him completely—and without risking my heart by telling him he'd managed to halfway convince me?

An awkward silence descended. Thankfully, he changed the subject. "In my position, what would you do about V?"

"I'm not in your position."

"Assume that you were," he said. "Assume that you had a House of vampires under your protection. Assume that a bureaucrat had decided you weren't allowed to solve an immediate problem facing your House for fear it would draw undue attention to the existence of the problem."

I sat up, crossing my legs beneath me. "You've answered your question, haven't you? You have an immediate risk to the safety of your vampires, and a political risk that might occur down the road. Solve the immediate risk first. Apologize, instead of asking for permission."

"And if the end result is the House in receivership?"

"Then we hope the receiver has more sense than the leader of the GP."

Finally, Ethan cracked a half smile. I was struck by the urge to lift his burden, to make the smile complete, to give him the kind of relief he'd tried to give me—however unsuccessfully—with chocolate-flavored blood.

"I have an idea," I said.

"What's that?"

I paused, still thinking it through, before offering, "Meet me outside in five minutes—out near the fountain."

He arched a crisp eyebrow. "Because?"

"Because I said so. Trust me."

He debated for a moment, then nodded. "Very well. Five minutes." He stood up and walked to the door, glancing back before walking out. "And never doubt it, Merit—I do trust you."

He disappeared through the door. I climbed off the bed, my headache beginning to dissipate, and set to work.

The Cadogan House gardens were spectacular, from the running trail to the brick barbecue pit to the formal French garden behind the House. A fountain sat in the middle of the garden, bubbling water for the enjoyment of any vampires who might be seated on the benches around it.

I took off my shoes after I crossed the brick patio at the back of the House, closing my eyes at the luxurious feel of soft, cool grass beneath my feet.

Your five minutes are drawing to a close, Ethan silently said. I smiled as I padded back to the fountain.

Aren't you always lecturing me about patience?

An overrated virtue, he replied, and I could all but hear the sarcasm in the thought.

I found him in a genteel sprawl on one of the benches, the only vampire in the vicinity, and clearly doing a little luxuriating of his own. Eyes closed, he was slouched comfortably across the seat, one foot on the bench, the other on the ground. One arm was slung across its back, his other hand on the flat of his stomach. In his white button-down and trousers, he looked more like a Regency rake than a Master of vampires.

Maybe he was reliving history.

I sat cross-legged on the ground beside him, the box in my lap.

"What do you have there?" he asked, not bothering to look up.

"Quid pro quo," I said. "Chocolate for chocolate. But there will be a price to pay."

"Is the treat worth it?" His voice was a low, amused drawl.

I answered in the same honeyed tone, both of us knowing full well that a flirtation in the middle of the backyard was just that—an enjoyable flirtation. "It absolutely is."

Ethan chuckled. "In that case, Sentinel, be my guest."

"What was your favorite time period? What period did you enjoy the most?"

His brows lifted, as if surprised by the question. He opened his eyes and shuffled a bit on the bench, then stilled as he thought it through. "There's no denying today's mechanical conveniences. Humans are on the cusp of momentous discoveries that would have been impossible even twenty years ago. And yet," he began, then quieted again.

"And yet?" I prompted after a moment.

He sighed. "There have been times that were dangerous, but invigorating. Scenes from history I was fortunate enough to witness firsthand. The birth of this republic—the vigor of the debate, the fervency of the belief that man could do better than monarchy. Moments during the Civil War in which men and women—even in times of great peril—were brave enough to remind us of the best of ourselves. D-day in London, when Whitehall was filled with heart-bursting joy . . . and grief."

Ethan sighed. "Immortality affords you the opportunity to witness history in the making. Humanity's triumphs and its cruelties, both. It is both a high price to pay and a priceless gift, to carry the weight of that knowledge."

He turned over a bit, propping his head on his fist and glancing down at me. "Now, having walked through my lifetime, Sentinel, what's my treat?"

I lifted the box for him to see and thoroughly enjoyed the vaguely dismayed expression on his face.

"You're joking."

"I never joke about Mallocakes. Sit up."

He didn't look any less suspicious, but he did as I asked, shuffling down to the end of the bench to give me room to join him. But I was fine on the ground. It put space between us and kept the interaction casual. It let me pretend the emotional boundaries I'd put between us were still firmly intact . . . even as I sat on the ground quizzing him about his life and preparing to feed him cream-filled sponge cake.

But when denial was your safety net, denial was what you worked with.

I pulled off the paper zip strip on the box and pulled out two cellophane-wrapped snacks. I handed one to him, put the box aside, and cradled mine in my hands.

"Behold the glorious marriage of cake and cream."

Ethan looked unimpressed by the sugar log I'd placed in his hand. "Really, Sentinel."

"Trust me. You won't regret this." I opened my packet and held up the cake. "Now, there are various theories of the best way to eat a Mallocake."

Finally, a hint of a smile. "Are there, now?"

"Our favorite sorceress, Mallory Carmichael, prefers to dunk them whole in milk. It's not a bad treatment, but I think it makes them soggy, and I have this thing about wet bread."

"You are a constant source of wonder."

"And thus appropriate that I prefer the 'fishes and loaves' method. Behold," I said, pulling the cake in half lengthwise, then holding up the two chocolate slabs. "I've doubled the number of cakes!"

"You have a strong tendency for silliness, you know that?"

"It's one of my better qualities," I said, nibbling on the edge of the cake. And as if the chocolate sponge was a drug itself, the flavor almost instantly sent a calming pulse through my blood.

Ethan took his own bite. "Not bad, Sentinel."

"I have any number of issues," I admitted. "Taste in food is not one of them."

For a moment, we ate our snacks silently in the garden.

"I told you once that you were my weakness," he said. "But also my strength. I said it before betraying your trust. I know that now, and I am so very sorry." He paused. "What would I have to do to convince you to give me another chance?"

His voice was just more than a whisper, but the sentiment was strong enough that I had to look away, tears brimming in my eyes. It was a legitimate question—but not one for which I had an easy answer. What would it take for me to believe in Ethan again? To believe that he'd chosen me, for better or worse, and regardless of the politics?

"I'm not sure you could convince me otherwise. I'm too fast a learner."

"And I taught you that I would betray you if the opportunity arose?"

This time, I met his gaze. "You've taught me that you will always be concerned with next steps and appearances, with strategy and alliances. You've taught me that I could never be sure you really wanted me for me—and not just because I helped you meet some end, or because it was convenient. You've taught me that I could never be sure you wouldn't change your mind if breaking things off gave you a strategic advantage."

Ethan's smile drooped, and for the first time, he faced the possibility that his actions would have unalterable repercussions. "You don't think I can change?"

I softened my tone. "I don't think a relationship is any good if I have to ask you to change. Do you?"

He looked away, then sighed haggardly. "This feels like a battle I cannot win."

"Love shouldn't be a battle."

"And yet, if it wasn't worth the fight, what would be the point?"

We were quiet long enough that crickets began to chirp in the garden plots around us.

"Is there anything you'd like to tell me about Jonah?"

I nearly jumped at the question, my heart suddenly thudding at the potential my secret had been discovered. "No," I answered. "Why do you ask?"

"He seems to have some interest in you. Are you well acquainted?"

Thank God I already had at least part of an answer prepared. "We talked outside Temple Bar the night of the attack." Absolute truth.

"Anything else?" His gaze was suspicious, his eyes tracking across my face as if trying to gauge my sincerity.

"No."

"Don't lie to me, Merit."

"Are you asking me not to lie to you because we're friends, because we were lovers, or because I'm a vampire of your House?"

His eyes widened. "I expect your honesty for all three reasons."

"You expect—you are owed—my loyalty. That's not entirely the same thing."

This time, his eyes narrowed. "What's going on? What haven't you told me?"

"Nothing that I can share right now." And there it was. I may not have told him about the Red Guard, their invitation to me, and Jonah's role in the organization, but I'd now confessed that I hadn't been honest with him, that I'd held things back.

He blinked back shock. "You have information you won't share with me?"

"I have information that isn't mine to share," I clarified. "The information belongs to others; I know it only coincidentally, and I won't do them the disservice of making the decision to share it. Not when they've chosen not to."

His gaze was calculating. Evaluating. After a moment, he nodded. "So be it," he said. While his capitulation was a victory for me as Sentinel, I still felt like I'd lost something, like I'd broken some personal bond. I'd placed being House Sentinel over being his friend and confidante.

I'd done the same thing for which I'd chided him.

Ethan stood up and balled the cellophane in his hand, moving around me and stepping back onto the path. He stopped for a moment, before glancing back over his shoulder. "It's a difficult balance, isn't it, to put others before your own needs?"

I didn't care to have my own hypocrisy pointed out to me. I looked away.

When I glanced back at the path again, he was gone.

———

My mood wasn't any better when I returned to the second floor. My head was beginning to throb again, this time for different reasons. I put the box of Mallocakes back in the kitchen, then walked back to my room. My hand was on the door when I heard a voice behind me.

"He's not as cold as he seems, you know."

I glanced back. Charlie, Darius's assistant, stood in the hallway, arms crossed over his chest.

"Excuse me?" I asked.

He gestured toward the door. "Can we go inside?"

"Um, sure," I said, then opened the door. Charlie walked inside. I followed, then shut the door behind us.

He sat on the edge of my bed and linked his hands in his lap. "Darius is dedicated to the Houses, and he has no greater interest in drama here in the States than he does in the UK. The problem is," Charlie said, looking down at the floor, "he is a strong believer in hierarchy. The Masters should control the Houses. Problems beyond the Houses are the concerns of the GP, and only the GP."

I liked Charlie's honesty, but I had no doubts about where his loyalties lay. "Be that as it may, the GP hasn't actually taken any steps to control Celina or keep peace in Chicago. We are doing what we can to keep the city together in spite of what she's doing."

Charlie shook his head. "Has it occurred to you that you're playing into her hands? That by acknowledging Celina and bringing her activities to light—instead of ignoring her antics—you end up giving her the very thing she wants?"

"Which is?"

"Attention. By the Houses, the GP, humans, the press. Celina wants to be seen, to be heard. She wasn't getting sufficient attention as a Master, so she sabotaged that relationship in order to exchange it for something different—the attention of humans. And when she learned that she wasn't the beloved of humankind, she acted out again. Each time you seek her out, each time you fight back, you give her a reason to come back again."

"You're saying we enable Celina?"

He answered with nothing more than a challenging look. The question in his eyes was obvious—*Don't you?*

Shaking my head, my arms crossed, I leaned back against the closed door. "That theory assumes that if we ignored Celina, she wouldn't act out. That's simply not true. Each time things settle down in Chicago—like when we get a confession from her about the park murders and send her away—she pops up again. Believe me, Charlie, she forces us to act."

This time, he shook his head. "I'm sorry, Merit, but we have to disagree with you. *I* have to disagree with you." He frowned, then looked up at me. "I don't like saying this, making this accusation. Darius won't say it—it's not his position to do so—but I think it bears consideration."

"What's that?"

"None of this started until after you joined Cadogan House."

My heart beat like a timpani drum in my chest. *"Excuse me?"*

He held up a hand. "Hear me out. For better or worse, Celina seems to have an obsession with you. You move into the House, you elicit a confession from her, and as a result she apparently decides you, and perhaps Ethan, are her new targets."

I forced myself to bite my tongue. Ethan clearly hadn't told him that I'd been Celina's intended victim, that he'd brought me into the House because a Rogue she'd hired hadn't done his job completely. I wasn't sure why he'd made that call, but I wasn't going to be the one to break the news to the GP. I had no objection to the GP knowing as little about me as possible.

"We're aware of the Breckenridge situation," Charlie continued, "of the fact that she attacked you outside the House. Would you deny that you appear to be one of her keenest targets?"

"No," I said. It would be impossible to deny that. On the other hand, "I'm not the only target. Cadogan House is a target. Chicago is a target."

He was saved a response by sudden, high-pitched beeping. He lifted his wrist, revealing a square calculator watch circa 1984.

After tapping its buttons, he smiled guiltily. "I was amazed by the technology when it was revealed, and I haven't found anything that compares since then. Simple, efficient."

"Kudos," I said, trying to stuff the snark as far down as possible.

Charlie stood up again and walked toward me, heading for the door now that he'd concluded his lecture. "I hope it doesn't seem that I'm trying to irritate you or blame you for her actions. Clearly, she is a woman with free will and the ability to make decisions for herself. But consider the possibility that the actions you undertake—as Sentinel of your House, with all of its appurtenant responsibilities—bear upon her actions, as well."

I stepped aside, giving him access to the door.

"We do truly wish you the best with your House. We want all the American Houses to succeed, to flourish."

"I will relay that sentiment to Ethan," I said politely. Although my silent thoughts were much less polite, as I guessed would be the case for Ethan's, as well.

"Excellent. Good evening, Merit."

"Good evening, Charlie."

He walked out again, an efficient smile on his face and a hop in his step. And in his wake . . . insecurity.

Was he right? Had we prompted Celina's antics by responding to them? Were vampires drugged and humans dead because we'd encouraged her to act out, to rebel against Cadogan House like an angsty adolescent?

It wasn't fair to lay the responsibility for Celina's actions at our door. We'd tried to do right by Cadogan and Chicago, and ultimately she was the one who'd solicited the murders of humans, who'd blackmailed us, and who was now probably behind selling drugs. Those decisions were her own.

Still. Charlie's accusation gnawed at me. Even if she'd perpetrated the acts, it wasn't unfathomable to think she'd done it, at least in part, because she was reacting to me and Ethan, trying to rile us up, trying to score in the vampiric chess game she'd created.

I hated the idea of it, hated the thought that the battles we fought on a daily basis were somehow our fault, no matter how good our intentions.

On the other hand, what else could we have done? We couldn't exactly leave her to her own devices, creating chaos across Chicago just to fulfill her childish craving for attention. We couldn't have ignored the blackmail attempt or Tate's threats against us even if we wanted to. It wasn't like Ethan and I were out and about searching for something to rail against.

Of course we wanted peace and quiet. Of course we wanted to wake in the evening and spend our time training, researching, working to ensure the success of the House—instead of playing defense against the marauders at the gate.

Whatever the drama, whatever her motivations, there was only one thing that was going to solve the Celina problem. Getting her out of Chicago, once and for all.

—◆✠◆—

CHAPTER TWENTY-ONE

DEEP-FRIED PLAUSIBLE
DENIABILITY ON A STICK

I needed a break from vampires. I also hadn't checked in on Mallory in a while, and that definitely needed to be remedied. So when I woke and dressed, I texted her for an update and learned that she and Catcher were training at his gym. Translation: I'd get to watch Catcher torture someone other than me, and I'd get to see Mallory work her magic.

Easy call. I left the House and headed to the Near North Side, where Catcher's workout space was tucked into another old warehouse. (Converting former warehouses into playrooms for vampires and other sups was apparently the new trend in Chicago.)

I hardly needed to sneak out of the House. Darius had pulled us off the V investigation, so there wasn't going to be much need for me to stick around. And my conversation with Ethan last night had raised uncomfortable questions about me and my hypocrisy that I wasn't keen to face. I knew we'd talk eventually; there was likely no avoiding it. But it didn't have to be right now.

But avoider though I might have been, I wasn't so immature that I didn't take my beeper; I also put my dagger and sword in the car. Even if I was on investigatory hiatus, it wasn't impossible Paulie had passed along my message to "Marie," who planned on paying me an unscripted visit. On that front, better to be prepared.

The drive was pretty quick by Chicago standards—a surprisingly speedy jaunt along Lake Shore Drive—but it did give me a few minutes to reflect and gain a little perspective. Not that I was going to find a lot of resolution in a fifteen-minute drive or even a few hours away from the House, but the space was necessary. I needed to recharge around people who knew me only as Merit . . . not as Sentinel.

I'd apparently burned through my parking luck; a new bar had opened across the street from Catcher's gym, so the neighborhood was full of long-legged girls and overcologned boys ready to head into the bar for flirtations and overpriced appletinis. I found a space three blocks away and walked back to the gym, then headed inside.

The interior of the building was shaped like a giant T, and the gym—the place where Catcher had taught me to use a sword— was down the central hallway. I felt the electric sizzle in the air as soon as I reached the doorway. Rubbing the uncomfortable prickle along my arms, I peeked inside.

Catcher wore his fancy new glasses, track pants, and a T-shirt; Mallory wore yoga pants and a sports bra, which was actually more clothing than he'd let me train in. The lucky duck.

That said, her training was a different duck altogether. I'd known Catcher was amazing with a sword, and I'd known sorcerers—in addition to bending the universe to their wills—could throw balls of what looked like magical fire. But I'd never seen anything like this.

It was a like a game of magical handball. The two of them stood at opposite ends of the room, throwing and dodging brilliantly colored orbs at each other. Catcher would heft a ball of magic toward Mallory, and Mallory would avoid it or toss out her own shot. Sometimes the shots would hit each other and burst into a fall of sparks; sometimes they'd miss and explode against the walls with a crackle of sound.

That explained the tingle in the air—each time a ball exploded, it sent a cloud of magic pulsing through the room. I guess that was the risk of watching sorcerers practice.

Mallory looked over and offered a quick wave before lobbing a ball of blue fire back at Catcher.

"Hey, you!"

I glanced over. Jeff sat in a plastic chair on the other side of the door, a bowl of popcorn in his lap.

"Cop a squat," he said, patting the seat behind him. "I was actually going to call you."

"No need to call now," I said, taking a seat and grabbing some kernels of corn. It was kettle corn, which I adored. A little bit salty, a little bit sweet, and probably plenty better for me than a box of Mallocakes.

"So, I did a little more digging into the criminal record of our friend Paulie Cermak."

"I thought you said his file was sealed."

Jeff threw up a piece of popcorn, then caught it in his teeth. "Oh, I did. But 'sealed' and 'no longer in the system' are two different things."

"Is this the appropriate time for a lecture on computer hacking?"

"Not if you want me to give you the information I found."

I was becoming less of a stickler for the rules. "Lay it on me."

"So, to put it in layman's terms, while the file has officially been sealed for court purposes, an image of the file's contents was cached before it was sealed, so all the data's still out there. Now, as it turns out, there was only one item on the guy's record—he got a citation for punching someone in the face. A simple assault kind of deal."

I tried to play back my memory. I thought I'd seen Paulie Cermak before. Had it been on television? A report of the assault on the evening news? But I couldn't remember anything specific. "Who was the victim?"

"No clue. The guy never pressed charges, and his name was redacted from the file before it was scanned."

I sighed. "So Paulie Cermak punches a guy. The cops get called, but the vic doesn't press charges, and the file gets sealed anyway."

"That sums it up."

"That's weird. Why seal his file if no one pressed charges?"

Jeff shrugged and tossed another piece of popcorn in the air. This one bounced off his lip and hit the floor—or would have hit the floor, had it not bounced just as a pulse of magic moved through the room. It hovered for a moment a few inches above the floor, and then exploded into tiny popcorn shards.

Jeff and I both ducked, then looked up at Catcher. He stood with his hands on his hips, staring us down. "Popcorn? Really?"

"What?" Jeff said slyly. "This is like the best tennis match ever. We needed a snack."

Catcher's lip curled, and he lobbed a shot of blue that had us both dropping in our chairs. It hit the wall behind us and burst into a shower of sparks. I sat up, frantically brushing sparks from my hair.

"Hello! I'm here to be supportive. Let's ix-nay on the hitting me with agic-may."

"Yeah, Catch," Mallory said. "She's trying to be supportive." She threw a ball of magic that had him jumping to avoid the sparks and letting out a string of curses.

"Good times," I said, giving Mallory a thumbs-up.

"So, before we were so rudely interrupted," Jeff said, "I was going to say that it's not exactly a common thing to do—to seal a record when there's no charges pressed or whatever—but there could be lots of reasons. Most likely, Paulie Cermak had friends in high places." He chuckled.

I made a sarcastic sound. "Paulie doesn't exactly seem like someone who hangs with suits. Maybe Celina had him rough someone up."

"It's an idea. I'll keep digging."

"You're doing a great job," I told him, bumping him with my shoulder. "I appreciate the hard work."

Jeff blushed little. "Even Catcher said I was doing some pretty good investigation on this one."

"Well, Catcher never met a topic he didn't have an opinion on. Speaking of which, any developments on the V? I assume the CPD does testing and such."

"Yeah—they do, and did. Turns out, V's chemical structure is similar to adrenaline."

"That explains why it gets vamps so hyped up."

Jeff nodded. "Exactly. But that's not even the most interesting part. Catcher did a little magical sniffing of his own, and he thinks there's another component to the drug beyond the chemistry—magic."

I frowned. "Who else could have added the magic?"

"That's what's got him worried."

It had me worried, too. Even if we could pin V on Paulie and Celina, we now had an unknown source who was throwing gratuitous magic around. And speaking of unknowns: "Did you ever glean any more information about the assault Mr. Jackson saw?"

"Only the info you already knew. There haven't been any developments as far as I'm aware. Case is going cold."

I wasn't sure if that was better or worse than bodies having been located. That question in mind, my phone buzzed, so I pulled it from my pocket, expecting a question from Ethan: "Sentinel, where are you?" or the like.

I didn't recognize the number, but I answered it anyway. "This is Merit."

"Kid, I got something I think you'll be interested in."

The New York accent was unmistakable. "Paulie. What do you want?"

"A certain someone wants to meet with you."

"A certain someone?"

"Marie," he said. "You asked her for a meeting, and it turns out she's amenable."

Of course she was. We knew Celina wouldn't pass up the chance, and even if this "Marie" wasn't Celina, a meeting would almost certainly answer some of our questions. "Where and when?"

"Street Fest. Tonight. Meet beside the Town booth."

Town was a chichi café in the Loop that regularly topped the annual "best of" lists. It was a place for socialites to see and be seen, a place that required reservations weeks in advance—unless you knew someone . . . or you were the daughter of Joshua Merit. Pork saltimbocca? Yes, please.

Although I didn't figure Celina for a Street Fest participant, Town was just the kind of place she'd choose.

"What time?"

"Eleven o'clock."

I checked my watch. It was a quarter till ten. Street Fest ended at one o'clock, so the meeting time would hit the crescendo of bands, foods, and imbibing Chicagoans.

"I assume I won't need to wear a carnation in my lapel so she recognizes me?"

Paulie coughed out a laugh. "She'll find you. Eleven p.m. sharp."

The line went dead, so I tucked the phone away again and nibbled on my thumb as I thought it through.

Celina—well, someone I thought must be Celina—wanted a meeting in a public place. And not just a public place—a public place where thousands of humans would be milling about. Was she hoping the crowd would give her anonymity, or was she planning on causing trouble in the middle of them?

She had to have an ulterior motive, something she wanted to pull off. Maybe a trap she hoped to spring. It was just a matter of figuring it out—or planning for all contingencies.

When I finally looked up again, I found Catcher, Jeff, and Mallory staring at me.

"Paulie Cermak," I explained. "'Marie' wants to meet me at Street Fest tonight."

Catcher and Mallory walked toward us. "You're going?"

"Do I have a choice? Darius is pissed, and so's Tate." I rolled my shoulders, muscles aching against the joint irritation of magic and tension. "We could pretend this isn't our problem, but that's not going to make V go away, and it's not going to keep our House together."

"So what's the downside of meeting with her?" Mallory asked.

"Other than the possibility she'll kill me? Darius ordered me and Ethan to stop investigating."

Catcher's expression was incredulous. "On what basis? Vamps are fighting in public. How could he possibly deny that there's a problem?"

"Oh, he knows something's going on." I filled them in on the escapade at Grey House. "Darius just thinks it's Tate's problem to solve. He also apparently thinks we're the ones creating the problem—that Celina's acting out because we keep giving her attention."

"Not impressed with Darius so far," Mallory said.

"Tell me about it," I agreed.

"Am I interrupting?"

All heads turned to the doorway. A cute guy in a T-shirt and jeans smiled back at us.

"Who's he?" I whispered.

"That," Mallory tiredly said, "is Simon. My tutor."

I'll be honest—when Mallory had said she had a tutor, I'd expected the nerdy type. Someone with an academic bent and maybe a pocket protector.

Simon was about as far from the stereotype as they got: buff and cute in a boy-next-door way, with nary a pencil to be seen. His hair was closely cropped, with blue eyes peering out beneath a strong brow.

"Well done," I whispered to her.

"You wouldn't say that if he was making you levitate a two-hundred-pound lead weight for the sixty-seventh time." But she smiled politely. "Hi, Simon."

"Mallory," Simon said, then looked at Catcher. "It's been a while."

Catcher's expression stayed blank. He apparently wasn't interested in a warm reunion with a member of the Order. "Simon. What brings you to the city?"

Simon gestured toward Mallory. "We're going to take a ghost tour."

I glanced at Mallory. "You're going on a ghost tour?" It's not that Mallory wasn't interested in the occult. She was the girl with the Buffy fixation, after all. But she'd always refused when I'd asked her to go, calling the idea of a ghost tour the "fauxcult."

"Simon," Mallory said with an absent wave of the hand, "this is Merit and Jeff. She's a vampire, but I'm still friends with her because I'm awesome that way, and he's a computer nerdling extraordinaire who works with Catcher."

Simon smiled at me, but the effect wasn't nearly as friendly as you might have imagined. "So, you're Sullivan's Sentinel."

"I'm the Cadogan House Sentinel," I politely corrected.

"Of course," he said, in a tone that suggested he didn't quite buy my clarification.

"So you're going on a ghost tour?" Jeff asked. "Is that some kind of magical research?"

"In a manner of speaking," Simon said. "The hauntings aren't all wives' tales. Some of the locales are legitimately infested. Mallory's task tonight will be to separate fact from fiction. It's part of her practicum."

Mallory frowned. "Is that today? I thought that was tomorrow."

"Do you need to reschedule? There are some other things I could take care of while I'm in town."

Mallory waved him off. "No, today's fine. It's going to be on the exam, so I might as well do it."

"Oh, my God, you *are* Harry Potter," I said, pointing a finger at her. "I knew it!"

She rolled her eyes, then looked at Catcher. "I guess I need to get cleaned up and go?"

Catcher frowned, clearly not comfortable sending Mallory off into the city with Simon. I couldn't tell if the animus was all Order related or not.

Catcher looked at Simon. "Could you give us a minute?"

"Of course," Simon said after a moment. "I'll wait in the car. Jeff, nice to meet you. Merit, we'll have to talk sometime. I'd love to hear more about Cadogan House."

I gave him a noncommittal smile.

Simon walked out again. I looked back at Mallory and Catcher. "He seems pleasant enough."

"He's a member of the Order," Catcher grimly said. "They're always 'pleasant enough' until they're calling you a troublemaker and stripping you of your membership."

"Sounds like the Order and the GP have things in common," I said.

Catcher grunted his agreement.

"Simon's . . . okay," Mallory said. "But speaking of the GP, you need to get out there and mix it up." She reached out her arms, and I stepped forward into her hug. "Just like you told me," she said, "you do what you have to do. You know right from wrong, and your instincts are good. Trust them."

"And if I still can't pull it off?"

She pulled back, her expression fierce. "There's nothing you can't do if you put your mind to it. You just have to decide that you can. You go and find Celina Desaulniers, and you kick her ass this time."

Let's hope it ended that way.

There was a limo parked outside the House when I returned, as well as the usual gaggle of protesters. I recognized two or three— the same protesters were camped out night after night, their hatred of us apparently taking priority over any other activities.

I figured the limo belonged to Tate or Darius, which didn't thrill me. Neither was going to make my current task easier. I double-parked in front of the House and moved carefully inside, tiptoeing toward Ethan's office.

No Ethan. But Malik stood in the middle of the room, reviewing papers. Darius was in the sitting area, chatting on a cell phone.

I smiled politely at Darius and walked toward Malik. His gaze lifted as I moved closer, and he must have noticed my frazzled expression. "What now?"

I slid my gaze toward Darius. "In light of the GP's directive, I thought I'd take the evening off. Head to Street Fest. Meet some friends."

Malik's expression was blank only for a second before realization dawned.

"I thought I'd see if Ethan wants me to bring anything back. You know how much he loves greasy food. The man cannot get enough of battered and fried."

Malik smiled slyly. "That he does, Sentinel. I believe you'll find him in his apartment. He and Darius plan to meet in a few minutes, but perhaps I could entertain him while you discuss the menu?"

At my nod, Malik walked toward Darius. I headed for the door again. Darius must have ended his call, as I heard Malik ask, "Sire, have you had a chance to see the grounds? The gardens are spectacular in late summer."

Good man, I thought, taking the stairs two at a time until I reached the third floor.

Ethan was just walking into the hallway when I reached him. Without bothering to ask permission, I moved past him into his bedroom. When I turned around again, he was still in the doorway, eyebrow arched.

"Malik is taking care of Darius. I need five minutes."

"I have the distinct sense that I'm not going to enjoy those five minutes."

"Quite possibly not."

Either way, he walked inside and shut the door behind us, then crossed his arms over his chest.

"Tonight will be tricky," I said.

"Because?"

"Because she may be wreaking havoc in a very public place."

He dropped his arms, alarm in his expression. "How public?"

"Street Fest."

Ethan closed his eyes for a moment. "Do we have defenses?"

"Yours truly."

Ethan's eyes flashed open. He opened his mouth to object, then closed it again.

"Wise decision," I complimented, "since I'm the only defense you've got at the moment."

"Is this a trap?"

"Quite possibly. And it may be the kind of trap that puts us square in the public eye. But I'm going to do everything I can to prevent that—or at least make sure it's the right kind of publicity."

We stood there quietly while he reached his verdict.

"I assume that's all you're going to tell me?"

"For your sake and mine. Two words, Sullivan: plausible deniability."

"I think I liked you better when you were a nerdy graduate student."

"You didn't know me as a nerdy graduate student," I reminded him. "Well, not while I was conscious, anyway." Technically, he'd known me as an unconscious graduate student, since he'd nursed me for three days following my transition to vampire, but I didn't remember it. "Anyway, if you've got a better idea, I'm all for it."

He looked at me for a moment, that line of worry between his eyes. "Unfortunately, I do not."

"Your confidence is inspiring, Sullivan."

He gave me a flat look. "You know better than that. I trust

you, Merit—implicitly—even if you don't tell me everything. I wouldn't let you leave the House if I didn't—there's too much at stake."

"At stake. Ha-ha." At his frown, I winced. "Sorry. I kid when I'm nervous."

"Are you nervous?"

I sighed and crossed my arms. "We are talking about Celina. Am I stronger than before? Yes. But she's still hundreds of years older than me, and I've barely seen what she's capable of. Plus, we'll be in public. Even if I can take care of myself, how am I going to take care of everyone else who's there?"

"We could give you a perimeter of guards around the festival," Ethan suggested.

"No," I said, shaking my head. "That's too risky for the House. If Darius finds out I was there, you can say I acted alone, went off on a whim. And I do have a plan in mind."

I'd called on Jonah before; if Cadogan House was barred from acting, maybe Noah would be willing to plant a few Red Guards into the crowd.

"Anything you can share?"

I glanced up at Ethan. There was curiosity in his eyes, but no rebuke. He wanted to know what I had in mind, but he'd leave the decision to me.

"Plausible deniability," I reminded him. "You master the House from here. Let me protect us out there."

Ethan sighed, then put a hand on my cheek. "I don't tell you this enough, but I am incredibly proud of the vampire you've become. I want you to know that."

He leaned his forehead against mine. I closed my eyes and breathed in the cottony scent of his cologne. "Be careful."

"I will. I promise." I pulled back and saw the flash of guilt in his eyes, but I shook my head. "You're doing your job," I assured him. "Now let me do mine."

I offered a little prayer that I had the chance to do it right this time.

It was unrealistic to think I'd find parking near Street Fest, and I didn't have time to wait for the El. While I gave Luc the five-minute précis, Lindsey called a cab and promised to move my car. They'd all heard about Darius's ban on my activities; they'd all agreed to help me carry them out regardless. There were times when the work needed to be done, the consequences be damned. This was one of those times, and they were all on board.

Once in the car, I messaged Noah and asked him for backup. Noah agreed almost instantaneously and told me the crew of guards would be recognizable by their clothing: they'd be wearing faux-retro MIDNIGHT HIGH SCHOOL T-shirts.

Clever boy.

I'd considered calling Jonah, but this was a public event. That risked outing his RG membership and putting him in the same position as me—bearing the wrath of Darius West. No, thank you.

The cabdriver didn't stop glancing back at me, his brown eyes popping up in the rearview mirror every few seconds as if he was waiting for me to breach the plastic wall between the seats and chomp on his neck.

I'll admit, the idea of taunting him occurred to me. But I wasn't Celina. I had a conscience and a job to do, and fang-teasing the cabdriver wasn't part of that job.

"This is fine," I told him, sliding cash into the small door in the plastic when he reached the southern edge of Grant Park. I slipped out of the cab, waving the driver off when he continued to stare at me through the window.

"Humans," I muttered, and set off toward the tents and crowds. This part of the park was empty, which gave me the chance to prepare . . . and get panicky.

I was well trained enough to put on a brave front to Ethan, Luc, and Malik. But let's face it—I was scared. Celina was more powerful than me, and I'd agreed to meet her in a place and at a time she'd selected. This was her game, and there was a good possibility that I wasn't going to win . . . or make it out in one piece.

I walked through the trees, dagger in my boot, my stomach churning with nerves, even as the smells of food drew nearer.

I reached an orange vinyl fence that surrounded the festival. I hopped it, then mingled into a group of drunken bachelorette partygoers as they made their way toward the main thoroughfare. That gave me my first view of the battleground. Columbus Drive was lined with white tents. People walked in the wide lane between them, food and drinks in hand. The air was thick with the smells of batter and beer and people and sweat and trash, and the sound of a thousand conversations and sizzling food and the country band on the make-do stage was nearly enough to overwhelm my senses.

I maneuvered out of the lane of traffic and stopped beside a booth, closing my eyes until the world settled back down to a dull roar.

"Coupons?"

I opened one eye.

A woman balancing a wailing, pink-cheeked toddler on one hip held out a stack of food coupons. "We have extra, and it's getting late, and Kyle is just freaking out, so we need to go." She smiled sheepishly. "Would you want to buy them by any chance? They're still good."

"Sorry," I kindly said. "I don't need anything."

Obviously disappointed, she sighed heavily and lumbered awkwardly away, the baby now beginning to squall.

"Good luck," I called out, but she was already looking for someone else to tempt.

I didn't always get to play the hero.

I walked around the tent and back into the flow of people, and I was nearly overdone again. My stomach growled at the smells; there was only so much blocking that a vampire could do. I silently promised myself a deep-fried candy bar and a paper tray of bacon-wrapped Tater Tots if I made it through the night unscathed. Not a good nutritional combo, but I figured the odds were low anyway.

I walked to a sign that identified the tents' locations, found the Town booth, and checked my watch. It was about ten minutes until eleven. Ten minutes until showtime.

A hand suddenly gripped my arm. I jerked, expecting to see Celina. For better or worse, I got a different kind of surprise.

"Hello, there," said the man at my side.

It was McKetrick, having traded in his fatigues for jeans and a snug black T-shirt. The better to blend in with the humans, I assumed. He smiled grandly at me. He might have been handsome, but the effect was still creepy.

I pulled back my arm. "If you're smart, you'll walk away right now and go about your business."

"Merit, you are my business. You're a vampire, and I'd be willing to bet you're carrying a weapon here in this public place. It would be irresponsible of me to let you go on about your merry way, don't you think?"

It would save me a lot of trouble, I thought, because there was no way I could explain why I needed him to leave me alone. He'd go ballistic if he knew I was here to entertain Celina. And speaking of, time was ticking down, and I needed to get to the Town tent.

"If you're smart," I told him, "you'll be on your own merry way."

He tilted his head. "You seem a little preoccupied. You aren't planning to start trouble, are you? That would be most unfortunate."

"I never start trouble," I assured him. It just usually seemed to pop up in my vicinity. Case in point: "Since I was minding my own business before you grabbed me, you're the one causing trouble."

"If you minded your own business," McKetrick retorted, "you'd be home among your own kind."

I was saved the trouble of responding to his prejudiced idiocy by the sound of an argument moving toward us. I looked up. A man and woman bickered as they walked, each clearly irritated by the other.

"Really, Bob? Really?" asked the woman. "You think the best course of action is to spend an entire week's salary on food tickets? That's what you think? Because you want to eat gyros and fried cheesecake for the rest of the week? Not that I should be surprised. It's just the kind of harebrained thing you'd do."

"Oh, yeah, Sharon. Lay it on. Lay it on thick. Right here in public where everybody can see!" The man, who was only a couple of feet from me, lifted his arms and moved in a circle. "Did anyone not hear my lovely wife berating me? Anyone?"

The people around us chuckled nervously, not sure whether they should step in and put an end to the dramatics, or ignore them.

I had the same question—until the man made the full turn and I could see the red T-shirt beneath his thin jacket. MIDNIGHT HIGH SCHOOL was written in faded white letters across the front. These were my RG helpers.

The guy winked at me, then stepped directly between me and

McKetrick. "I mean, really, sir, is this the kind of behavior you'd expect from your wife? What happened to 'for better or worse' and all that?"

The woman stepped up and poked a finger into the guy's chest. "Oh, just another thing for you to criticize me about, huh, Bob? I'm shocked. Really shocked. I should have listened to my mother, you know!"

"Oh, yeah, Sharon. Bring your mother into this. Your poor, woebegone mother!"

A crowd began to gather around the couple, creating a thicker human barrier that put more space between McKetrick and me. Two security guards also ambled over, adding two more humans— and two more weapons—to the fray.

I got while the getting was good.

I found the Town booth and camped beside it, but fifteen minutes, and then half an hour, passed with no action. I cursed McKetrick, positive that he'd scared Celina away.

For the twentieth time, I stood on tiptoes to get a better look at the grounds, nearly falling over when a dark-haired woman nudged past me.

Absently, I watched her dark ponytail bob as she walked, but it wasn't until she was nearly gone that I felt the tingle of magic in the air. I hadn't recognized her—and wouldn't have, but for the power that lingered behind her. My heart began to thud with anticipation.

Before she could escape, I grabbed her wrist.

CHAPTER TWENTY-TWO

DEVIL IN A BLUE DRESS

Celina slowly turned to face me. She wore a one-piece, royal blue jumper with ankle boots, her hair in a ponytail. Her eyes widened in apparent shock.

Okay, now I was confused. Why did she look surprised to see me?

Her arm still in my hand, she moved a step closer. "If you're smart, child, you'll let go of my hand while you still have yours to use."

"I was told you wanted to meet me," I informed her. "By a mutual friend."

Almost instantaneously, her expression changed. Her eyes narrowed, her nostrils flared, and her magic rose in an angry, peppery cloud. The humans still moved past with fair food and plastic cups of beer in hand, completely oblivious to the magical reactor who was throwing off enough power to light the Loop.

"That little shit," she muttered, followed by a few choice curses.

I assumed she meant Paulie, but if she hadn't been expecting me . . .

"Who did you think you were meeting?"

Her expression went haughty. "As you are well aware, and as the GP has reminded you, my life is none of your concern."

"Chicago is my concern. Cadogan House is my concern."

She scoffed. "You're a vampire in a fourth-rate House. And sleeping with its Master isn't exactly a coup."

I resisted the urge to do the nail raking and hair pulling I'd complained about only a few days ago. Instead, I gave back the same pretentious look she gave me. It wasn't that I was naïve about Celina or her power—or the damage she could do to me. But I was tired of being afraid. And if the GP was going to act like she wasn't a threat, then I was, too.

"My life is none of your concern, either," I countered. "And I don't care how well you've managed to convince the GP you're a good citizen and have nothing to do with the havoc in this city right now. I know it's bullshit, and I am not afraid of you. Not anymore. I'm also not afraid of the GP, so I'm going to give you one chance to answer this question." I pressed my nails into the flesh of her arm. "Did you put V on the streets?"

Celina looked around, seemed to realize that the people around us were beginning to stare. And of all the reactions I might have imagined, the one she handed back wasn't even on the list.

"Maybe I did," she said, loud enough for all to hear. "Maybe I helped put V on the streets. So what?"

My mouth opened in shock. Celina had just announced to a few thousand humans that she'd helped put V on the street. It was a coup for me, but there was no way she'd make that kind of announcement if she didn't think she had an out. What was her game?

The humans around us stopped, now staring full out. A couple of them popped out phones and were taping the scene.

"What's your connection to Paulie Cermak? I know you talked to him at Navarre House."

She barked out a laugh. "Paulie Cermak is a little worm. He's got a warehouse in Greektown that houses the V, and he's been handling the distribution from there. That's why there wasn't any V in his house." She gave me an appraising gaze. "What's more interesting is how you learned about it. Morgan told you, no?" She looked me up and down. "Did you offer yourself for a little information?"

In addition to feeling disgusted by the suggestion, I felt a little sympathy for Morgan. Celina's craziness didn't excuse the fact that Morgan wasn't reliable, but it sure did explain why he wasn't trustworthy. If he'd learned to be a Master by following in Celina's footsteps, there'd probably been no hope for him.

"And the raves?"

"The raves were the linchpin," she said. "The key to the entire system. They were means to get V—and humans—into the hands of vampires."

Celina looked around, realized she had a captive audience of humans who'd recognized who she was—and the fact that she was supposed to be locked away in England, not standing in the middle of Street Fest confessing to crimes against the citizens of Chicago.

If I'd been in her position, I would have balked. I'd have lowered my head and ducked through the crowd, seeking escape. But Celina wasn't your average vampire. With nothing close to regret or fear in her eyes—and while I stared at her, shocked at her audacity—she began to address the crowd.

"For too long, I bought into the notion that humans and vampires could simply coexist. That being vampire meant tamping down certain urges, working in communion with humans, leading humans."

She began to turn in a circle, offering her sermon to the crowd. "I was wrong. Vampires should be vampires. Truly, completely vampires. We are the next evolution of humans. V reminds us who we are. And you, too—all of you—could have our strength. Our powers. Our immortality!"

"You killed humans!" shouted one of the humans. "You deserve to die."

Celina's smile faltered. She'd changed positions in a second attempt to ingratiate herself with humans, and it still hadn't worked. She opened her mouth to counter the assertion, but the next words weren't hers.

Four uniformed CPD officers stepped around her. Three pointed weapons; the fourth grabbed her wrists and cuffed them behind her back.

"Celina Desaulniers," he said, "you have the right to remain silent. Anything you say could be used against you in a court of law. You have the right to an attorney. If you cannot afford one, one will be appointed to you. Do you understand the rights I've read to you?"

Celina struggled once, and she was strong enough that the man who'd cuffed and restrained her had to fight to keep her on the ground. But after a moment she stopped, her expression going pleasantly blank.

That wasn't a good sign.

"She'll try to glamour you," I warned. "Stay focused, and fight through it. She can't make you do anything; she'll just try to lower your inhibitions. You might want to have the Ombudsman meet you at the station. He's got staff who can help you."

Three of the cops ignored me, but the fourth nodded with appreciation. It couldn't have been easy to get a lecture from a skinny vamp with a ponytail.

"There's no need to glamour them," Celina said, her blue-eyed gaze on me. "I'll be out before you can warn your lover that you found me here. Oh, and enjoy your conversation with Darius. I'm sure he'll be thrilled to find out about this."

She went willingly. After a moment, the crowd completely dissipated, leaving no evidence of Celina's recapture or the proselytizing speech she'd just given.

That gave me a minute to focus on the bigger question: What the hell had just happened?

I stood there for a moment, still trying to wrap my mind around Celina's confession and arrest.

Long story short: I had to be missing something. The entire thing was way too easy and felt like a giant setup. Celina clearly didn't know she was going to meet me, but she'd nevertheless confessed to the entire crowd that she'd been helping Paulie distribute drugs and arrange the raves. And then she tried to convince them to join the vampire bandwagon.

How did that make sense?

It simply didn't. While I wasn't unhappy Celina was off the streets and back in the hands of the CPD, I couldn't figure out her angle. She had to have one. There was no way a woman as egotistical as Celina makes a confession without thinking she'll get something out of it. Maybe that was it. Did she think she could get out of it? Did she think she was immune from trouble because she had GP protection? Unfortunately, that possibility wasn't entirely unrealistic.

I didn't know what game she was playing, but I knew this wasn't the end of the story. Vampire drama rarely wrapped up so easily.

I sighed and pulled out my phone, preparing to give Ethan a

quick update before I searched for a cab. I'm not sure what made me glance up or over, but there he was—right in front of me. Paulie sat at a small, plastic café table inside a beer tent. Two empty plastic cups sat on the table in front of him, and a third, half-full cup was in his hand. He lifted it to me, a toast to my participation in whatever con he was running.

At least to Paulie, this had been a game. He'd set up Celina, but why? To get her out of the way? So he could lose the vampire middleman—the woman bringing unwanted drama to the entire operation—and gain access to her share of the profits?

I shifted my body weight forward to launch myself toward him. But before I could move, I was stopped by the same thing that had kept McKetrick from me—humans.

This time, a family moved in front of me. Mother and a double stroller of sleeping children in the lead; father with a sleeping infant on his hip pulling a red wagon that held a third sleeping toddler. The entire family was tethered together with ribbon. It was a wagon train of family.

By the time they'd moved their caravan out of the way and I looked up again, Paulie was gone.

CHAPTER TWENTY-THREE

◄ ◄ ═╪═ ► ►

DEMERITS

I wasn't entirely sure how to break the news to Ethan. How did you tell your boss that for no apparent reason, your enemy had confessed her evildoings and gone willingly into the arms of the Chicago Police Department?

Turned out, I didn't need to. After picking through the protesters to get into the House, I found half the House's vampires in the front sitting room, eyes glued to a flat-screen television that hung above the fireplace.

Tate stood in front of a podium in a charcoal gray suit, every hair in place, and a soothing smile on his face.

"We've discovered today that Celina Desaulniers, thought to be in the custody of officials in the UK, made her way back to Chicago. While here, she continued to create the chaos she'd begun before her first capture. We've also learned that she was responsible for the increase in violence we've seen in the city. Now, finally, the city of Chicago can breathe a sigh of relief. Life can return to normal, and vampires can return to being a part of the city, not antagonists. Rest assured, Ms. Desaulniers will stay in the custody of the Chicago Police Department in a facility we created just for the purpose of keeping the public safe from supernatural criminals. I also need to give credit to Merit, the Sentinel of Cadogan House."

"Oh, shit," I said aloud, half a dozen of the vamps in the room turning to stare at me, finally realizing I'd stepped into the room behind them, probably smelling of kebabbed meats and deep-fried candy bars.

"She was a crucial part," Tate continued, "of efforts to locate and apprehend Celina Desaulniers. Whatever your opinions of vampires, I ask—on behalf of the city—that you not judge all the individuals based on the actions of a few."

My beeper began to buzz. I unclipped it and glanced at the screen. It read, simply, OFFICE.

I blew out a breath, then looked up at the vamps in the room and offered a small wave. "It was lovely knowing you," I assured them, then turned on a heel.

I hustled down the hallway. The office door was cracked, so I pushed it open and found Darius, Ethan, and Malik inside. They were all seated at the conference table—Darius at the head, Malik and Ethan on the window side.

I didn't like the symbolism there, and my already-raw stomach began to churn again.

"Come in, Merit," Darius said. "And close the door."

I did as I was told and took a seat opposite Ethan and Malik. Ethan's expression was completely blank. My stomach tightened, but I'd already decided I wasn't going to be afraid any longer. It was time to talk.

"Sire," I said, "may I speak candidly?"

I heard Ethan's warning in my head, but I ignored it. There was a time to be meek, and a time to take a stand. At this point, I had nothing to lose.

Darius regarded me for a moment. "Speak."

"V was moving through the city. It was hurting our vampires, it was hurting humans, and it was hurting our relationship with the city. With all due respect to the concerns of the GP, we have to live here. We don't have the luxury of returning to another continent, and we couldn't simply ignore the problem. Shifters and humans were already turning against us. If we didn't act, we'd be in the middle of the war the sorcerers have predicted. I stand Sentinel for this House, and I acted in a manner consistent with the House's best interest, even if that interest, in your opinion, does not coincide with that of the GP."

When I was done, Darius looked at Ethan. "Tonight's events do not reflect well upon the North American Houses or the Greenwich Presidium. We should not be involved in altercations in a public festival in one of the largest cities in the United States." He looked up at me. "We do not need the publicity, nor the heroics. What we need is respect for authority, for hierarchy, for chain of command. Assimilation is how we've done that for centuries. Assimilation is how we'll continue to do it."

His gaze went ice-cold, as did the blood in my veins.

"Merit, consider yourself officially reprimanded by the GP. Your file will be annotated to reflect what you've done today. I hope you appreciate the seriousness of that action."

I actually didn't have any clue how serious it was, but that didn't matter. It felt like I'd been slapped in the face, every sacrifice and decision I'd made since becoming a vampire called into question.

I tried to obey the warning look Ethan shot me from across the table, but I was done playing GP doormat and blame magnet.

I stood up and pushed back my shoulders. "Will my file be annotated to reflect the fact that I followed the leads to Celina, and hat she admitted spreading V around the city? Will it reflect the act that she helped arrange the raves so she could institute her new world order—which it sounds like she plans to institute without the GP? Will it reflect the fact that today we closed her down and saved the city and the GP a lot of trouble down the road?"

Darius was motionless. "Celina is a member of the GP and must be afforded the respect due to a member of the GP."

"Celina put dangerous drugs into the hands of vampires, drugs that could only lead to their destruction and incarceration. She is a murderer and an aider and abettor of murder. GP member or not, she needed to be stopped. I was a Chicagoan before I was a vampire, and when I have an opportunity to help this city—to do right by this city—I'm going to. GP be damned."

Silence.

"Your file will be annotated, your demerits noted. And while I find your bravado intriguing"—he slid his gaze to Ethan—"I strongly recommend you learn to control your House and your vampires."

When I looked back at Ethan, his expression was stony, his gaze on Darius.

"With all due respect, Sire," he bit out, "I do not control my vampires. I *lead* them. Merit has acted with my permission and in the manner befitting a Cadogan vampire and a Sentinel of this House. She has acted honorably to defend Cadogan, its Master, and its vampires. She has acted to protect this city from the criminals the GP has seen fit to let roam free. If you have a problem with her actions, then it's my file, not hers, that should be annotated. I trust her, fully and completely. Any action of hers bears on my leadership, not her abilities as a Sentinel nor her loyalty to the Presidium."

He looked at me with eyes that were radiantly green, this man who'd just stood up for me, defied his own master for me, trusted in *me*.

I was floored. Speechless. Moved to tears, and suddenly very, very nervous, both at the sentiment and its political cost.

But regardless of the surprise of Ethan's words, their generosity, his defense of my actions, Darius wasn't buying. He maintained the party line, and the House would suffer for it.

"Appointment of a receiver is clearly an inevitability," he said. "There is no way to avoid GP oversight of Cadogan House at this juncture. I expect you will give the receiver the same access and respect that you would give me. Is that understood?"

Ethan bit out words. "Yes, Sire."

"In that case, Charlie has a car waiting and I need to get to the airport." He pushed back his chair and rose, then started for the door. "I can see myself out."

The room was silent as he crossed it, but a few feet from the door, he stopped and looked back. "One way or the other, with your approval or without it, the receiver will put this House in order. I suggest you get used to that idea."

And then he turned and walked out the door, closing it firmly behind him.

Ethan put his elbows on his knees and ran his hands through his hair. "We did what we had to do. The GP will act as it deems appropriate."

"They're acting like naïve children." We both looked at Malik. His expression was fierce. "I understand your according them due respect, Ethan, but this is completely irrational. They should be thanking Merit for what she's done. Darius should be thanking the House for taking a threat off the streets. And instead, they're sending in a receiver? They're punishing this House for Celina's acts?"

"Not for her acts," Ethan said. "For the publication of those

cts. It's less the action than the embarrassment he apparently be-
ieves we've caused the GP." He blew out a breath. "If only you'd
taked her when you had the chance."

I had staked her, I thought to myself. I just hadn't hit her heart.

"This isn't the end of it," I warned. "Celina confessed too eas-
ly, and Paulie is still on the streets. I'm sure she's given him up
o the cops at this point—she does usually love a scapegoat—but
either way, it's not over."

"It's over enough," Ethan said. "We've done all we can do for
his city on this particular issue. Tate has been satisfied, and that
vas the point."

I nearly argued with him, but I could see the exhaustion and
disappointment in his eyes, and I didn't want to add to his burden.

"Take the rest of the evening off," he said, rising from the con-
erence table without making eye contact. "Sleep this off, and we'll
egroup tomorrow and create a plan to get through the receivership."

We nodded obediently, watching as he moved across the room
and through the office door.

I'd done nothing more and nothing less than my job had re-
juired. But why did I feel so miserable?

I tried to find space. I joined Lindsey in her room for a round of
mindless television. That helped fill the evening, but it didn't
calm the nerves in my stomach, or the flutter in my chest.

Two hours later, silently, I stood up, picked through the crowd
of vampires who filled the floor, and went for the door.

"Going somewhere?" she asked, head tilted curiously.

"I'm going to find a boy," I said.

I was nervous as I made the trip to his room, afraid that if I
stepped inside—both of us emotionally drained—he'd be able
o slip past defenses I should keep intact. And worse—that we'd

never be the same for it. That the House would never be the same for it.

I stood outside his door for a full five minutes, clenching and unclenching my hands, trying to build up the nerve to knock.

Finally, when I couldn't stand the anticipation any longer, blew out a breath, pulled my fingers into a fist, and wrapped my knuckles against the door. The sound echoed through the hallway, oddly loud in the silence.

Ethan opened the door, his expression haggard. "I was just about to head to bed. Did you need something?"

It took me seconds to speak, to find courage to ask the question. "Can I stay with you?"

He was stunned by it, clearly. "Can you stay with me?"

"Tonight. Not anything physical. Just—"

Ethan slid his hands into his pockets. "Just?"

I looked up at him, and let the fear, frustration, and exhaustion show in my eyes. I was too tired to argue, too tired to care what the request might mean tomorrow. Too tired to fight back against the GP and him.

I needed companionship, affection. I needed to trust and be trusted in return.

And I needed that from him.

"Come in, Merit."

I stepped inside. He closed the doors to his apartments and turned off the lights, his bedside lamps glowing through the door to his bedroom.

Without another word, he put his hands on my arms, and pressed his lips to my forehead.

"If 'just' is all you can give me now, then 'just' is what we'll do."

I closed my eyes and wrapped my arms around him, and I let the tears flow.

"If he decides I'm his enemy?" I asked. "If he decides taking me out—or letting Celina take me out—is how he maintains control of the Houses?"

"You are a Cadogan vampire, by blood and bone. You have fought for this House, and you are mine to protect. My Sentinel, my Novitiate. As long as I am here to do it, I will protect you. As long as this House exists, you will have a home here."

"And if Darius tries to tear it down because of something I've done?"

Ethan sighed. "Then Darius is blind, and the GP is not the organization it has set itself up to be. It is not the protector of vampires it imagines itself to be."

I sniffed and turned my cheek into the coolness of his shirt. His cologne was clean and soapy, like fresh towels or warm linens. More comforting than it should have been, given the knot of fear still in my heart.

Ethan pulled away and moved to the bar on the other side of the room, then poured amber liquid from a crystal decanter into two chubby glasses. He put the top back on the decanter, then walked back and handed me a glass. I took a sip and flinched involuntarily. The liquor might have been good, but it tasted like gasoline and burned like dry fire.

"Keep drinking it," Ethan said. "You'll find it improves with each sip."

I shook my head and handed the glass back to him. "So it finally tastes good when you're completely drunk?"

"Something like that." Ethan drained his glass and deposited both on the closest table.

He took my hand and laced our fingers together, then led me to the bedroom, where he closed the bedroom doors. Two sets of doors, of finely honed and paneled wood, between us and humans and shifters and the GP and drug-addled vampires.

For what felt like the first time in days, I exhaled.

Ethan pulled off his jacket and placed it across a side chair. I toed off my shoes and stood there for a moment, realizing that in my haste to find him I hadn't bothered to think about clothing.

"Would you like a T-shirt?" he asked.

I smiled a little. "That would be great."

Ethan smiled back, unbuttoning his shirt as he walked across the room to a tall bureau. He opened a drawer and rifled through before pulling out a printed T-shirt and tossing it to me. I unfolded it, checked the design, and smiled.

"You shouldn't have."

It was a "Save Our Name" T-shirt, printed as part of a campaign to ensure Wrigley Field kept that name. It was also very much my style.

Ethan chuckled, then disappeared into his closet. I slipped out of my clothes and into the T-shirt, which fell nearly to my knees. I chucked decorative pillows from his massive bed, then slid into cool cotton and closed my eyes in relief.

It may have been minutes or hours before he returned to the room and turned out the lights. I was already in and out of sleep, only vaguely aware of the press of his body behind mine. His arm snaked around my waist and pulled me tight against him, his lips at my ear. "Be still, my Sentinel. And sleep well."

He'd promised me that he'd be patient, that he'd wait for me, that he wouldn't be the one to kiss me again.

He followed through on his promise.

I woke in the middle of the day, the metal shutters still banking any light from the windows, but unusually aware of his body beside me . . . and of the craving that nearness inspired.

We'd moved apart in sleep, but I curled into him again, vaguely xpecting him to react to the sensation with a kiss. He traced a nger through my hair, the act more comforting than erotic.

And it wasn't enough.

"Ethan," I muttered, my heart suddenly racing even as the sun lared down from its cradle in the sky. But as much as I wanted im, I couldn't take that next step. I couldn't force myself to move, o kiss him. Some of the hesitation was born from exhaustion, by ne fact that I should have been unconscious until the sun sank gain. But the rest was pure, unmitigated fear. Fear that if I made a nove, kissed him, I'd be offering up my heart again, risking heartreak again.

Instincts warred, because equally as powerful was the urge to tep forward, to take what I wanted, to make the most of the kiss ven if it wasn't the smartest thing I'd ever done.

As if he knew my struggle, he smoothed a hand over my hair. Sleep, Sentinel. The time will come when you're ready. Until nen, be still and sleep."

CHAPTER TWENTY-FOUR

CHERCHEZ LA FEMME

I dreamed it was the first day of high school and I was an awkwardly tall twenty-eight-year-old walking down a hallway with a new notebook and pen in hand. I'd somehow forgotten to register for classes, and even though I had two and a half college degrees, I'd also apparently forgotten to finish tenth grade.

I sat down at a desk too small for me and stared at a chalkboard filled with handwriting—quadratic equations too complicated for me to solve. When I looked around the room, everyone else was busily filling out the stapled pages of a test.

One by one, the other students looked up and at me and began pounding their fists on the desk.

Thump. Thump. Thump.

A girl with long blond hair looked over at me. "Open the door," she said.

"What?"

"I said, open the—"

I jolted awake, sitting straight up in bed, just in time to see Ethan disappear from the room.

I rubbed my hands across my face until I was in his room again—not a helpless sophomore out of place in a high school I was too old to attend.

I heard his door open and shut. I tried to smooth down what I'm sure was a pretty severe case of bed hair, and then threw back the covers and padded into the other room.

"What is it?"

Ethan held out a cordless landline telephone. "It's Jeff for you. Apparently, it's urgent."

Frowning, I took the phone from him. "Jeff? What's up?"

"Sorry to interrupt you, but I was able to dig up some more information about Paulie Cermak and his criminal history."

I frowned. "You know Celina's already been arrested, right?"

"And that a warrant's been issued for Mr. Cermak after her little confession last night. Oh—and I hear Ethan's warrant was torn up, so congrats on that. But that's not the issue."

"So, what did you learn?"

"I found the original police report—and it listed the vic's name. Well, a last name and first initial, anyway. Guy or gal named 'P. Donaghey.' Also from Chicago—"

Shaking my head, I cut him off. "Jeff, I know that name." I squeezed my eyes closed but couldn't place it. "Can you Google it?"

"Oh, sure." I heard fingers flowing across the keys. "Oh, this is bad."

"Tell me."

"'P. Donaghey' stands for 'Porter Donaghey.' He was Seth Tate's opponent in his first mayoral election."

Now I remembered where I'd seen Paulie's photograph before. "Paulie Cermak punched Seth Tate's opponent in the face."

Ethan's eyes went as big as saucers.

"Wait, there's more. I've got pictures. Campaign events. Tate's on the podium, and you can see Paulie in the background."

"Send the images to Luc," I told him. "Same way you did before." Something else occurred to me. "Jeff, in that file you found, did it say anything about who represented Paulie? The attorney that got the file sealed, I mean?"

"Um, let me scan." He went quiet for a moment but for a little nervous whistling.

"Oh, crap," he finally said.

Only one lawyer made sense. "It was Tate, wasn't it?"

"It was Tate," Jeff confirmed. "Cermak punched Tate's opponent, and Tate got him off. Paulie Cermak and Tate know each other."

The phone still pressed to my ear, I looked at Ethan. "I don't think that's the end of it, Jeff. If Paulie's involved with drugs, raves, and Celina, and Paulie and Tate know each other, then how much is Tate involved with drugs, raves, and Celina?"

"What's the theory?" Ethan quietly mouthed.

"Tate's under pressure to reassure Chicagoans about vampires. He decides to be proactive—he helps create a problem; he helps solve the problem. Wham, bam, thank you, ma'am, and his poll numbers are up by twenty percent."

"Oh, I gotta tell Chuck about this," Jeff said.

"Can you get an arrest warrant for Tate?"

"On this little evidence? No. You don't have anything that ties Tate to, as you said, drugs, raves, or Celina. It's not enough that Paulie knows him."

"Not enough? What more do you want?"

"You're the Sentinel. Find something."

I hung up the phone and looked at Ethan, apology in my expression.

"I knew it wasn't over," he said. "I knew just as well as you did yesterday. I just wanted to momentarily bask in the possibility that we could find a few hours of peace."

"We had a few hours," I pointed out with a smile. "Otherwise I wouldn't be standing in your apartment in a T-shirt and with some serious bed hair."

"That is true. Your bed hair is rather serious."

"You're funny at dusk, Sullivan."

"And you're adorable. I assume it's time for you to wreak havoc again?"

"My file's already annotated. Better more demerits in my file than more pressure on the House." I moved up on tiptoes and pressed my lips to his cheek. "Call Luc and Malik and get them ready for the fallout. I'm going back to Paulie's house."

"One moment," he said, and before I could ask him why, he was tugging my T-shirt to pull me closer. He kissed me brutally, and then pulled back so abruptly I nearly stumbled backward.

"What was that?" I asked, my voice suddenly hoarse.

He winked. "That was the kiss you owed me. Now go get your man, Sentinel."

Twenty minutes later I was dressed, katanaed, and on my way to Garfield Park. Ethan, Luc, and Malik were in the Ops Room, ready to send out troops, but hoping to save the House any more involvement than necessary. They'd also conferenced in Jeff in the event I needed computer assistance.

Unfortunately, I knew something was wrong when I pulled into Cermak's driveway. The garage door was open and the Mustang was gone. The house was dark and empty, even the cheap lace curtains stripped from the windows.

I pulled my car to the curb just past the house.

"I was this freakin' close," I cursed, pulling out my cell phone and dialing up the crew.

"He's gone," I told him as soon as Luc answered. "The Mustang's gone, and the house is empty."

But then, my luck changed.

"Hold on," I said, turning off the car and slinking down in the seat, my eyes on the rearview mirror. The Mustang pulled up to the curve. Paulie hopped out of the car and hustled toward the garage.

"What's going on, Sentinel?" Ethan asked.

"He's back. He's running into the garage. Maybe he forgot something."

Sure enough, not ten seconds later, Paulie hustled out of the garage with . . . a steering wheel in hand.

"He forgot a steering wheel," I dryly informed the crew, wondering if Paulie had any idea he'd soon be brought down by a car accessory. Ah, well. His loss, my gain.

After a moment, he pulled the Mustang back into the street. I waited until he'd passed me, then turned on the car and pulled out behind him.

"He's leaving again, and I'm on his trail," I told them. "I'm about two blocks back, so hopefully he can't see me."

"Which direction?"

"Um, east for now. Maybe toward the Loop?"

I heard Malik's voice. "Maybe he's trying to bust out Celina?"

"If he and Tate are friends, he wouldn't need to do any busting. In any event, I'll keep you posted."

I hung up and put the phone down again, and then concentrated on tailing Paulie through the city. He was the kind of driver that irritated the crap out of me: he had a fine car with undoubtedly a solid engine, but he drove like his license was on the line.

Too slowly. Too carefully. Of course, there was a warrant out for his arrest, so it made sense for him to avoid giving the cops any reason to pull him over.

It took twenty minutes for him to reach the Loop, but he didn't stop there. He kept moving south, and that was when I got nervous again.

I dialed up the crew.

"We're here," Luc said.

"Send out some backup," I said. "He's heading for Creeley Creek."

I didn't bother entering Creeley Creek through the front gate; I didn't want to give the mayor and his apparent crony that much warning. Instead, I parked a few blocks up, buckled on my katana, jumped the fence, and snuck across the grounds. I'm sure there must have been security somewhere, but I didn't see any, so I moved around the house, peeking through the low, horizontal windows until I saw them—Tate behind his desk while Paulie chatted animatedly from the other side of it.

But they weren't alone. Who was perched on the edge of Tate's desk?

Celina Desaulniers.

I closed my eyes, ruing my naïveté. Why would Celina have confessed to horrible acts in front of humans? Because she had a relationship with the mayor that ensured she'd get off scot-free.

This must have been part of her big plan. Seduce the mayor, make friends with a drug distributor, and create a drug intended to remind vampires of their predatory roots. When the shit hit the fan, she could take credit for giving vamps the time of their lives, and invite humans to join the party. And she could do it all with impunity.

It wouldn't surprise me to learn that she'd glamoured Tate into doing it. He was a politician, sure, but he had seemed to genuinely care about the city. Had Celina created the entire ruse and wooed him with polling data?

I really, really hated her.

Irritation pushing aside my fear, I moved back to a nearby patio, crossed it as surreptitiously as possible, and tried the door. My luck held—it was unlocked. I padded quietly down the hallway to the room where I'd seen them, then pushed my way inside.

They all glanced at the door.

Paulie was the first to move. He backed up a few feet, moving closer to the corner of the room—and farther from the angry vampire.

I stepped inside and shut the door behind me. "This looks like a cozy meeting."

Tate smiled lazily. "These young vampires have no manners these days. Didn't even wait for an invitation, did you?"

The faux cheer worried me—and made me wonder if he was still under the influence of Celina's glamour. I flipped the thumb guard on my sword, unsheathed it, and moved closer. No point in pretending we were here for fun.

I pointed the katana at Celina. "You set us up."

Celina picked at a fingernail. "I did the right thing, as the GP has made clear to you time and time again. Why are you even here?" She rolled her shoulders, as if irritated.

I squinted at her in the mood lighting. "Lift your head, Celina, and look at me."

Remarkably, she did as she was told. I could finally see her eyes—which were wide, her irises almost completely silver. She wasn't running the show—she'd been drugged.

I'd had it wrong. Again.

I looked up at Tate. "You're controlling her with V?"

"Only partially. I assumed you'd come calling when you figured out the connection between Mr. Cermak and me. When the police report was accessed, I received an alert. In the meantime, I thought we might amp up the drama a bit. I understand Ms. Desaulniers was quite a warrior; I decided to test V's effects on a woman already known to be skilled. Does it make her a better fighter? A worse one? As a former researcher, you must appreciate my approach."

"You're crazy."

Tate frowned. "Not even a little, unfortunately."

Celina hopped off the corner of the desk and walked along its length, trailing a fingertip across the desktop. I kept my sword trained on her, and one eye on Tate.

"You said you were only partially controlling her with V. How else are you controlling her?"

He just sat there and smiled at me—and in that moment I felt the telltale prickle of magic in the air. But not the mildly irritating stuff Mallory and Catcher threw off. This was heavier—oilier, almost, in the way it suffused the room.

I swallowed back a burst of fear, but solved another bit of the puzzle. "You added the magical binder to the V."

"Very good. I wondered if you and yours would discover that. Call it a signature, of sorts."

"What *are* you?" I asked, although I knew part of the answer: he wasn't human. I don't know why I had never been able to feel it before, but now I knew it was true. The leaden magic he was throwing off was nothing like Mallory's or Catcher's.

Frowning, he sat forward and linked his hands on the desktop. "At the risk of sounding incredibly egotistical, I am the best thing that's happened to this city in a long time."

Was there no end to this guy's ego? "Really? By creating chaos? By drugging vampires and putting humans at risk?" I pointed at Celina. "By releasing a felon?"

Tate sat back again and rolled his eyes. "Don't be melodramatic. And you'll recall Celina took the fall for the drugs. Very tidy how that wrapped up. The least I could do was reward her a bit—here in the privacy of my own home, anyway."

I guess he'd been in on the plan to fake Celina into a meeting at Street Fest—and to make a confession. She confessed because she knew Tate would let her off the hook; the confession served Tate by "solving" the V problem. I glanced over at her. She seemed to be completely unaware Tate was talking about her. She'd stopped moving at the side of Tate's desk and begun drumming her fingers nervously across the top. It looked like the V was beginning to kick in, to give her that irritating buzz.

"Frankly, Merit, I'm surprised you don't appreciate the tremendous boon that V offers to vampires."

"It makes you feel like a vampire," Celina intoned.

"She has a point," Tate said, drawing my gaze back to him. "V lowers inhibitions. You may think me callous, but I believed V would help weed out the less agreeable portion of the vampire population. Those willing to use V deserve to be incarcerated."

"So now you're entrapping vampires."

"It's not entrapment. It's good urban planning. It's self-selection for population control. I understand you aren't susceptible to glamour. Doesn't that make you different? Better? You don't have the same weaknesses. You're stronger, with better control."

I swung the katana in Celina's direction. "Make your point, Tate."

"Do you know what kind of team we could make? You are the poster girl for good vampires. You save humans, even when the GP would seek to bring you down, to punish you for your deeds. They love you for it. You help keep the city in balance. And that's what we need, if there's any hope for vampires and humans to survive together."

"There is no way in hell that I'd work with you. You think you're going to walk away from this? After setting up vampires and contributing to the deaths—to the endangerment—of humans?"

His stare went cold. "Don't be naïve."

"No," I said. "Don't justify your evildoing with some bogus, trite 'this is just the way the world works' lip service. This is not the way the world works, and my grandfather is proof of it. You're egotistical and completely crazy."

Celina's finger drumming increased in pace, but whatever magical control Tate had on her was effective. She wouldn't act without his permission. "Can I kill her now, please?"

Tate held up a silencing hand. "Wait your turn, darling. And what about your father?" he asked me. "He isn't crazy, is he?"

I shook my head, confused by the non sequitur. "This isn't about my father."

His eyes wide with surprise, Tate let out a belly-raucous, mirthless laugh. "Not about your father? Merit, everything in your life since you became fanged has been about your father."

"What is that supposed to mean?"

He gave me a look best saved for a naïve child. "Why do you think that you, of all people in Chicago, were made a vampire?"

"Not because of my father. Celina tried to kill me. Ethan saved my life." But even as I spoke the words aloud, my stomach knotted with fear. Confused, I dropped the sword back to my side.

"Yes, you've told me that before. Repeating the lies doesn't make them truth, Merit. Awfully coincidental, wasn't it, that Ethan happened to be on campus when you were?"

"It was a coincidence."

Tate clucked his tongue. "You're smarter than that. I mean, truly—what are the odds? Don't you think it would have been beneficial for your father to have a vampire in his pocket—his daughter—when the riots ended? When humans became used to the concept of the fanged living among them?"

Tate smiled tightly. And then the words slipped from his mouth like poison.

"What if I told you, Merit, that Ethan and your father had a certain, shall we say, business arrangement?"

Blood roared in my ears, my knuckles whitening around the handle of the katana. "Shut up."

"Oh, come now, darling. If the cat's out of the bag, don't you want the details? Don't you want to know how much your father paid him? How much Ethan, your father's partner in crime, took from your father to make you immortal?"

My vision dimmed to blackness, memories overwhelming me: the fact that Ethan and Malik were on the U of C quad at the precise moment I'd been attacked. The fact that Ethan had known my father before we met him together. The fact that Ethan had given me drugs to ease the biological transition to vampire.

I thought he'd drugged me because he felt guilty I hadn't been able to consent to the Change.

Had he actually felt guilty because he'd changed me at my father's bidding?

No. That couldn't be right.

Like I'd imagined him into being, Ethan suddenly burst into the room, fury in his eyes. He'd come to back me up.

Tate was still in the room, but he all but disappeared from view. My gaze fell on Ethan, the fear powerful, blinding, deafening as blood roared through my veins.

Ethan moved to me, and scanned my eyes, but I still couldn't find words to speak the question. "Are you all right?" he asked. "Your eyes are silvered." He looked back to Tate, probably suspected my hunger had been tripped. "What did you do to her?"

I gripped the handle of my sword tighter, the cording biting into the skin of my palm, and forced myself to say the words.

"Tate said you met with my father. That he paid you to make me a vampire."

I wanted him to tell me that it was a lie, just more falsehoods thrown out by a politician grasping at straws.

But the words he said broke my heart into a million pieces.

"Merit, I can explain."

Tears began to slide down my cheeks as I screamed out my pain. "I trusted you."

He stuttered out, "That's not how it went—"

But before he could finish his excuse, his eyes flashed to the side.

Celina was moving again, a sharpened stake in hand. "I need to move," she plaintively said. "I need to finish this *now*."

"Down, Celina," Tate warned. "The fight isn't yet yours."

But she wouldn't be dissuaded. "She has ruined enough for me," Celina said. "She won't ruin this." Before I could counter the argument, she'd cocked back her arm and the stake was in the air—and headed right for me.

Without a pause, and with the speed of a centuries-old vampire, Ethan threw himself forward, his torso in front of mine, blocking the stake from hitting my body.

He took the hit full on, the stake bursting through his chest.

And through his heart.

For a moment, time stopped, and Ethan looked back at me, his green eyes tight with pain. And then he was gone, the stake clattering to the ground in front of me. Ethan replaced by—transformed to—nothing more than a pile of ash on the floor.

I didn't have time to stop or think.

Celina, now fully feeling the effects of the V, was moving again, a second stake in hand. I grabbed the stake she'd thrown, and praying for aim, I propelled it.

My aim was true.

It struck her heart, and before a long second had passed, she was gone, as well. Just as Ethan had fallen, there was nothing left of her but a pile of ash on the carpet. My instinct for preservation replaced by shock, I glanced down.

Two tidy cones of ash lay on the carpet.

All that was left of them.

She was dead.

He was dead.

The realization hit me. Even as others rushed into the room, I covered my mouth to hold back the scream and fell to my knees, strength gone.

Because he was gone.

Malik, Catcher, my grandfather, and two uniformed officers burst into the room. Luc must have called them. I looked back at Tate, still behind his desk, a peppery bite of magic in the air but no other sign that he was even vaguely worried by what had gone down in his home.

No way was I letting this go unpunished. "Tate was distributing V," I said, still on the floor. "He drugged Celina, let her out of jail. She's gone." I looked down at the ash again. "She killed Ethan—he jumped in front of me. And then I killed her."

The room went silent.

"Merit's grieving," Tate said. "She's confused the facts." He pointed at Paulie, who was now rushing toward a window on the other side of the room. "As I believe you already know, that man was responsible for distributing V. He just confessed as much."

Paulie sputtered as the officers pulled him away from the window. "You son of a bitch. You think you can get away with this? You think you can use me like this?" He pulled away from the uniforms, who just managed to wrestle him to the floor before he jumped on Tate.

"This is *his* fault," Paulie said, chest-down on the floor, lifting his head just enough to glare at Tate. "All of this was his doing. He arranged the entire thing—found some abandoned city property for the warehouse, found someone to mix the chemicals, and set up the distribution network."

Tate sighed haggardly. "Don't embarrass yourself, Mr. Cermak." He looked over at my grandfather, sympathy in his expression. "He must have been sampling his own wares."

"You think I'm dumb?" Cermak asked, eyes wild. "I have tapes, you asshole. I recorded every conversation we've ever had because I knew—I just *knew*—that if worse came to worst, you'd throw me to the wolves."

Tate blanched, and everyone in the room froze, not quite sure what to do.

"You have tapes, Mr. Cermak?" my grandfather said.

"Dozens," he said smugly. "All in a safe-deposit box. The key's around my neck."

One of the uniforms fished inside Cermak's shirt, then pulled out a small flat key on a chain. "Found it," he said, holding it up.

And there was the evidence we needed.

All eyes turned to Tate. He adjusted his collar. "I'm sure we can clear this up."

My grandfather nodded at Catcher, and they both stepped toward Tate. "Why don't we discuss this downtown?"

Four more officers appeared at the office door. Tate took them in and nodded at my grandfather.

"Why don't we?" he said politely, eyes forward as he strode from the room, a sorcerer, an ombudsman, and four CPD officers behind him.

The first two uniforms led Paulie away.

Silence descended.

Probably only minutes had passed since I'd thrown the stake. But the minutes felt like hours, which felt like days. Time became a blur that moved around me, while I—finally—had become still.

I stayed on my knees on the lush carpet, hands loose in my lap, completely helpless before the remains of two vampires. I was vaguely aware of the grief and hatred that rolled in alternating waves beneath my skin, but none could penetrate the thick shell of shock that kept me upright.

"Merit." This voice was stronger. Harsher. The words— the base, flat, hopeless sound of Malik's words—drew up my eyes. His were glassy, overlaid with an obvious sheen of grief, of hopelessness.

"He's gone," I said, inconsolable. "He's gone."

Malik held me as the ashes of my enemy and my lover were collected in black urns, as they were sealed and carefully escorted from Tate's office.

He held me until the room was empty again.

"Merit. We need to go. There's nothing more you can do here."

It took me a moment to realize why he was there. Why Malik was on the floor beside me, waiting to escort me home.

He'd been Second to Ethan.

But he was Second no longer.

Because Ethan was gone.

Grief and rage overpowered shock. I'd have hit the floor if Malik hadn't put his arms around me, holding me upright.

"*Ethan.*"

I struggled, tears beginning to stream down my face, and pushed against them to get away.

"Let me go! Let me go! Let me go!" I whimpered, cried, made sounds better suited to the predator than the girl, and thrashed against him, skin burning where his hands clamped my arms. "Let me go!"

"Merit, stop. Be still," he said, this new Master, but all I could hear was Ethan's voice.

CHAPTER TWENTY-FIVE

That night we mourned publicly: eight enormous Japa‐
nese *taiko* drums lined the sidewalk outside the House
their players beating a percussive dirge as Ethan's ashe
were moved into the House.

I watched the progression from the foyer. Out of respect, and
to guard Ethan's progression into the afterlife, Scott and Morgan
took the lead, Malik behind them, a new Master engaged in hi
first official act—transporting the remains of his predecessor into
secured vault in the Cadogan basement.

When the urns were placed inside and the vault was closed and
locked again, the rhythm of the drums changed from fast and an
gry, to slow and mournful, covering the range of emotions I slippe
through as the night wore on.

The grief was heavy and exhausting, but it was equally matched
by anger and fear. As much as I grieved Ethan's loss, I was afraid
that he'd communed with my father, sold me into a life of vampir
ism to ease some financial concern.

I wanted to rail at him. Scream at him. Cry and yell and bang my fists against his chest and demand that he exonerate himself, take it back, prove his innocence to me.

I couldn't, because he was gone.

Life—and mourning—went on without him.

The House was draped in long sheets of black silk like a Christo sculpture. It stood in Hyde Park like a monument to grief, to Ethan, to loss.

We also mourned privately, in a House-only ceremony by the shores of Lake Michigan.

There were circles of stones along the trail beside the lake. We gathered at one of them, all wearing the black of mourning. Lindsey and I stood beside each other, holding hands as we stared out at the glassy water. Luc stood at her other side, his fingers and hers intertwined, grief breaking down the walls Lindsey had built between them.

A man I didn't know spoke of the joys of immortality and the long life Ethan had been fortunate enough to live. Regardless of its length, life never quite seemed long enough. Especially when the end was selected—perpetrated—by someone else.

Malik, wearing a mantle of grief, carried bloodred amaranth to the lakeshore. He dropped the flowers into the water, then looked back at us. "Milton tells us in *Paradise Lost* that amaranth bloomed by the tree of life. But when man made his mortal mistake, it was removed to heaven, where it continued to grow for eternity. Ethan ruled his House wisely, and with love. We can only hope that Ethan lives now where amaranth blossoms eternally."

The words spoken, he returned to his wife, who clutched his hand in hers.

Lindsey sobbed, releasing my hand and moving into Luc's embrace. His eyes closed in relief, and he wrapped his arms around her.

I stood alone, glad of their affection. Love bloomed like amaranth, I thought, finding a new place to seed even as others were taken away.

A week passed, and the House and its vampires still grieved. But even in grief, life went on.

Malik took up residence in Ethan's office. He didn't change the decor, but he did station himself behind Ethan's desk. I heard rumblings in the halls about the choice, but I didn't begrudge him the office. After all, the House was a business that he needed to run, at least until the receiver arrived.

Luc was promoted from Guard Captain to Second. He seemed more suited for security and safety than executive officer or would-be vice president, but he handled the promotion with dignity.

Tate's deputy mayor took over for the city's fallen playboy, who was facing indictment for his involvement with drugs, raves, and Celina.

Navarre House mourned her loss. The death of Celina, as a former Master and the namesake of the House, was treated with similar pomp and circumstance.

I got no specific rebuke from the GP for being the tool of her demise, but I assumed the receiver would have thoughts on that, as well.

The drama had no apparent end.

Through all of it, I stayed in my room. The House was virtually silent; I hadn't heard laughter in a week. We were a family without a father. Malik was undoubtedly competent and capable, but Ethan, as Master, had turned most of us. We were biologically tied to him.

Bound to him.

Exhausted by him.

I spent my nights doing little more than bobbing in the sea of conflicting emotions. No appetite for blood or friendship, no appetite for politics or strategy, no interest in anything that went on in the House beyond my own emotions and the memories that stoked them.

My days were even worse.

As the sun rose, my mind ached for oblivion and my body ached for rest. But I couldn't stop the thoughts that circled, over and over, in my mind. I couldn't stop thinking about him. And because I grieved, because I mourned, I didn't want to. Events and moments replayed in my mind—from my first sight of him on the first floor of Cadogan House to the first time he beat me in a fight; from the expressions on his face when I'd taken blood from him to the fury in his expression when he'd nearly fought a shifter to keep me from presumed harm.

The moments replayed like a filmstrip. A filmstrip I couldn't, however exhausted, turn off.

I couldn't face Malik. I don't know what he'd known before following Ethan onto campus that night, but I couldn't imagine he didn't wonder about the strangeness of the task—or its origin. I wouldn't deny him the right to run the House as he saw fit, but I wasn't ready to make declarations of his authority over me. Not without more information. Not without some assurance that he hadn't been part of the team who'd sold me to the highest bidder. My anger became a comfort, because at least it wasn't grief.

For seven nights, Mallory slept on the floor of my room, loath to leave my side. I was hardly capable of acknowledging her existence, much less anything else. But on the eighth night, she'd apparently had enough.

When the sun slipped below the horizon, she flipped on the lights and ripped the blanket off the bed.

I sat up, blinking back spots. "What the hell?"

"You've had your week of lying around. It's time to get back to your life."

I lay down again and faced the wall. "I'm not ready."

The bed dipped beside me, and she put a hand on my shoulder. "You're ready. You're grieving, and you're angry, but you're ready. Lindsey said the House is down another guard since Luc took over as Second. You should be down there helping out."

"I'm not ready," I protested, ignoring her logic. "And I'm not angry."

She made a sound of incredulity. "You're not? You should be. You should be pissed right now. Pissed that Ethan was in cahoots with your father."

"You don't know that." I said the words by habit. By now, I was too numb and exhausted with grief and rage to care.

"And you do? You were human, Merit. And you gave up that life for what? So some vampire could put a little extra cash into his coffers?"

I looked up as she popped off the bed, holding up her arms. "Does it look like he's hurting for money?"

"Stop it."

"No. You stop mourning for the guy who took your humanity. Who worked with your father—your *father*, Merit—to kill you and remake you in his image."

Anger began to itch beneath my skin, warming my body from the inside out. I knew what she was doing—trying to bring me back to life—but that didn't make me any more happy about it.

"He didn't do it."

"If you believed that, you'd be out there, not in this musty room stuck in some kind of stasis. If you believed he was innocent, you'd be mourning like a normal person with the rest of you

Housemates instead of in here afraid of the possible truth—that your father paid Ethan to make you a vampire."

I stilled. "I don't want to know. I don't want to know because it might be true."

"I know, honey. But you can't live like this forever. This isn't a life. And Ethan would be pissed if he thought you were spending your life in this room, afraid of something you're not even sure he did."

I sighed and scratched at a paint mark on the wall. "So what do I do?"

Mallory sat beside me again. "You find your father, and you ask him."

The tears began anew. "And if it's true?"

She shrugged. "Then at least you'll know."

It was barely after dusk, so I called ahead to ensure my father was home before I left . . . and then I drove like a bat out of hell to get there.

I didn't bother to knock, but burst through the front door with the same level of energy I'd applied to my week of denial. I even beat Pennebaker, my father's butler, to the sliding door of my father's office.

"He's occupied," Pennebaker said, staring dourly down from his skeletal height when I put a hand on the door.

I glanced over at him. "He'll see me," I assured him, and pushed the door open.

My mother sat on a leather club chair; my father sat behind his desk. They both stood up when I walked in.

"Merit, darling, is everything okay?"

"I'm fine, Mom. Give us a minute."

She looked at my father, and after a moment of gauging

my anger, he nodded. "Why don't you arrange for some tea, Meredith?"

My mother nodded, then walked to me, put a hand on my arm, and pressed a kiss to my cheek. "We were sorry to hear about Ethan, darling."

I offered up as much gratitude as I could. At this point, there wasn't much.

When the sliding door closed, my father looked at me. "You managed to get a mayor arrested."

His voice was petulant. He'd been supporting Tate for years; now he had to build up a relationship with the new deputy mayor. I imagine he wasn't pleased by that.

I walked closer to his desk. "The mayor managed to get himself arrested," I clarified. "I just caught him in the act."

My father humphed, clearly not mollified by the explanation.

"In any event," I said, "that's not why I'm here."

"Then what brings you by?"

I swallowed down a lump of fear, finally lifting my gaze to him. "Tate told me you offered Ethan money to make me a vampire. That Ethan accepted, and that's why I was changed."

My father froze. Fear rushed me, and I had to grip the back of the chair in front of me to stay upright.

"So you did?" I hoarsely asked. "You paid him to make me a vampire?"

My father wet his lips. "I offered him money."

I crumpled, falling to my knees as grief overwhelmed me.

My father made no move to comfort me, but he continued. "Ethan said no. He wouldn't do it."

I closed my eyes, tears of relief sliding down my cheeks, and said a silent prayer.

"You and I don't get along," my father said. "I haven't always made the best decisions when you were concerned. I'm not apologizing for it—I had high expectations for you and your brother and sisters.…" He cleared his throat.

"When your sister died, I was struck, Merit. Deadened by grief. Everything I've done for you, I wasn't able to do for her." He lifted his gaze, his eyes so very like mine. "I wasn't able to save Caroline. So I gave you her name, and I tried to save you."

I understood grief firsthand, but not his willingness to play God. "By making me a vampire without my consent? By paying someone to assault me?"

"I never made a payment," he clarified, as if the intent weren't enough on its own. "And I was trying to give you immortality."

"You were trying to force immortality upon me. You said you didn't pay anyone—but it was Celina's vamp who attacked me. Why me?"

He looked away.

Realization struck. "When Ethan said no, you talked to Celina. You offered to pay Celina to make me a vampire." She must have told Ethan about the offer, which is why he'd known me to be at U of C.

Ethan had been keeping an eye on me. He'd saved my life … twice. Grief pierced my heart again.

My father looked down at me. "I did not pay Celina. Although I understood later that she found out about my offer to Ethan. She was … displeased that I hadn't made the same offer to her."

My blood ran cold. "Celina sent the vampire to kill me, and she arranged for the death of other girls who looked just like me."

The puzzle pieces fell into place. Celina had been rebuked by a human, and she'd taken out her embarrassment on his daughter—and on those who looked like her. I shook my head ruefully. One man's arrogance, and so many lives ruined.

"I did the right thing by my family," my father said, as if reading my thoughts.

I wasn't sure whether to be angry at him, or to pity him, if that was what he believed of love. "I can appreciate unconditional love. Love that's based on partnership, not control. That's not love."

I turned on a heel and walked toward the door.

"We aren't done," he said, but his voice was weak, and there wasn't much push behind it.

I glanced back at him. "For tonight, we most definitely are."

Time would tell whether there was any other forgiveness to be had.

The sun was shining, so I knew it was a dream. I lay in the cool, thick grass in a tank top and jeans, a crystal blue sky overhead, the sun warm and golden above me. I closed my eyes, stretched, and basked in the warmth of the sun on my long-denied body. It had been months without sunlight, and the feel of it soaking through my skin, warming my bones, was as good as any languid orgasm.

"Is it that good?" asked a voice beside me, chuckling.

I turned my head to the side, found green eyes smiling back at me.

"Hello, Sentinel."

Even in the dream, my eyes welled at the sight of him. "Hello, Sullivan."

Ethan half sat up, propped his head on his elbow. He wore his usual suit, and I took a moment to enjoy the sight of the long, lean line of his body beside me. When I finally made my way back to his face, I smiled at him.

"Is this a dream?" I asked.

"As we've not been burned to ash, I would assume so."

I pushed a lock of blond hair from his face. "The House is lonely without you."

His smile faltered. "Is it?"

"The House is empty without you."

"Hmm." He nodded, laid his head back on the grass, one hand beneath it, and stared at the sky. "But you, of course, don't miss me at all?"

"Not especially," I quietly answered, but let him take my hand in his, entwine our fingers together.

"Well, I believe, if I were alive, I'd be hurt by that."

"I believe, if you were alive, that you'd manage, Sullivan."

He chuckled, and I grinned at the sound of his laughter. I closed my eyes again as we lay in the grass, hands linked between us, sun above us, baking in the warmth of the afternoon.

My eyes were still closed when he screamed my name.

Merit!

I woke gasping, thunder booming as rain pelted the window. I jumped out of bed and threw on the light, positive the voice I'd heard—*his* voice—had come from inside my room.

It had seemed so real. *He* had seemed so real.

But my room was empty.

Dusk had fallen again, and he was gone. I fell back in bed, my heart pounding against my chest, and stared at the ceiling, body aching with the remembrance of loss.

But even the ache of remembrance was far better than the empty vacuum of grief. He was gone. But I knew now that he'd been the man I'd come to believe in. I had the memories of him, and if dreams were the only way I could remember him, be with him, so be it.

After scrubbing my face clean and pulling my hair into a ponytail, I pulled on clean clothes and headed downstairs. The House was quiet, as it had been for two weeks. The mood was somber, the vampires still grieving for their lost captain.

But for the first time in two weeks, I walked through the House like a vampire warrior, not a zombie. I walked with purpose, my heart still rent by grief, but at least now the emotion was clean, without the confusing additions of anger and hatred.

The door to the office was closed.

Malik's office now.

For the first time, I lifted my hand and knocked.

It was time to get back to work.

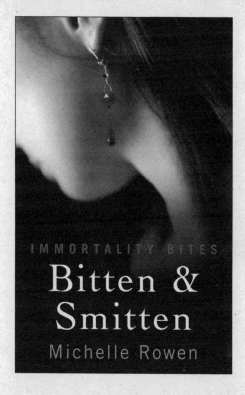

Chloe Neill was born and raised in the South, but now makes her home in the Midwest – just close enough to Cadogan House and St. Sophia's to keep an eye on things. When not transcribing Merit's and Lily's adventures, she bakes, works, and scours the Internet for good recipes and great graphic design. Chloe also maintains her sanity by spending time with her boys – her favorite landscape photographer and their dogs, Baxter and Scout (both she and the photographer understand the dogs are in charge).

Visit her on the web at www.chloeneill.com.